ALL I NEED

Jacquie Bamberg Moore

Reading Time Publishing
Brooklyn, New York

To Kimberly:
It was an honor meeting you
and a pleasure signing along iside
you. Best wishes in your writing
endeavors.
Be Blessed,
Jacquie B.Moore

Copyright © 2001 by Jacquie Bamberg Moore
Cover art by Kenly Dillard
Cover and text design by Jonathan Gullery

Reading Time Publishing
P.O. Box 973, FDR Station
New York, New York 10150
212-330-7213
www.reading-time.com

Library of Congress Catalog Card Number: 2001117983

ISBN: 0-9711924-0-5

10 9 8 7 6 5 4 3 2 1

First Edition

To my beautiful daughter, Irene,
whose will and determination have
been a source of inspiration to me

Love, Ackee

*

In loving memory of
Irene Williams
and
Cleveland Williams, Jr.

ACKNOWLEDGEMENTS

To God be the glory for the things He has done!

Working on this novel has given me the opportunity to pick up both new skills and new friends. And I want to thank every one of them for their love and support along the way. First, I have to say thank you to my best friend and number one fan: my husband, Dave, for his unwavering support and especially for all the nights I went to sleep while he sat up and did the worrying for me. I love you, Schmoo!

Thank God for old, dear, faithful and reliable friends as well as new, fresh and inviting ones. The following people are spectacular and have been especially supportive, believing in my ability to do this, even when I didn't believe it myself: Bernice L. McFadden, Nancy Flowers Wilson, Hunter Hayes, Vincent Alexandria, William Cooper, Deborah Maisonet, the women of Go On Girl! Book Club, especially my chapter members: Dorthea Thompson-Manning, Angelita Colon, Leona Deleston, Danielle Vilson, Lois Cooper and Donna Morgan. To my wonderful editor, Chandra Sparks Taylor, for all of her hard work and guidance. Her ability to help me see things from a different point of view is amazing! Fanchon Cornwall at Revelations Beauty Salon (a special note of appreciation for all those times you so willingly "squeezed me in" your appointment book at the last minute), Bishop Robert C. Jiggetts and my church family at Liberty Temple, Maureen Francis, AnnRose Lewis, Iris Russell, Gerald Cain and Bryna Rothenberg. To all of my Boys & Girls High School buddies: Arlene Edwards Sims, Hope Hall, Keadra Wilkes and Deanna Minto Worthey (keep those BBQs a-comin'). You guys have been like an extended family to me.

To my family: a million thanks! Especially for the countless votes of confidence and *super* support system: Mary Bamberg, Lisa Bamberg Phoenix, Iris Bamberg Mosley, Patricia Bamberg, Mary Hooks, LaToya Williams, Mary Williams, Michelle Williams, Melvin Gomes, Wendy Gomes, Angela Carter, Monique Carter, Michael Carter, Mother Lillie Lassiter, Maudlyn Loiseau, Joseph Loiseau, Larry Moore, Debbie Walters, Wanda McEachern, Delroy Llewellyn, Carolann Spence, Kirk Walker and Greg DeShields. We are an extension of one another, so I share this success with you.

Sometimes my mind forgets what my heart will always remember. So, if your name does not appear in these acknowledgements and it should, please take a minute to write it here, _____ then e-mail me and give me the "Oh, no you didn't" speech! LOL.

Jacquie Bamberg Moore
mymulay@aol.com

PART I

GOOD THINGS
COME IN THREES

CHAPTER 1

Umi slumped down on her sofa and kicked her shoes off. It felt good to finally be home after a long day of work. She slid out of her suit jacket, undid a few buttons on her blouse and loosened the clip that held her bun nice and tight at the nape of her neck. She raked her nails gently across her scalp and closed her eyes. Now that felt good—relaxing. That's a word that hadn't been in her vocabulary in quite some time. She eyed the goop (that mixture of sweat, dandruff and grease) under her nails. Yep, it was definitely time for a trip to the salon. She made a mental note to make an appointment first thing in the morning.

The long hours she was spending at the office were beginning to get to her. She stretched her arms above her head then reached for her remote control and saw the light on her answering machine blinking.

She hit the play button and smiled when she heard her best friend's voice. "Hey, girl, this is Michelle. I thought you would be home by now. It's seven-thirty. You must be working late again. Give me a call when you get in."

Maybe later, Umi thought, *I'm too tired right now. All I want to do is slip in to a hot bath and get some rest.*

She clicked the TV on and tuned in to CNN to see what the stock market was doing with her hard-earned money. Once she was satisfied with the day's report, she slid out of her pantyhose and turned to BET to see what John Salle was talking about. She turned up the volume and headed to the rear of her condo.

She dropped her clothing on the large rattan chair in her bedroom, which was already overflowing with two weeks' worth of clothing. She either had to invest in a housekeeper or carve out time to do some cleaning. Who was she fooling? She made a mental note to call a cleaning service right after she made her hair appointment.

In the large connecting bathroom, she was running her bath when the phone rang. *Oh no, not tonight. I promised my body I would give it some rest.* She planned on ignoring the call until she heard that sweet, husky voice leaving a message,

"Hi, Umi, this is Darren. When you get a chance, I'd love to hear from you—"

She made a mad dash for the cordless phone next to her bed. "Hello, Darren?" she answered, almost out of breath.

He chuckled lightly. "How are you, stranger? Haven't heard from you in quite a while."

Umi could sense he was surprised that she was home. "You know these long hours. What can I say? No real time for socializing." She went back into the bathroom, lit two scented candles and dropped a little bubble bath in the water.

"Oh, that's a shame because I miss you," Darren said in a sexy voice.

Umi started smiling. She knew where this was going: He wanted to come over. And she wanted to invite him, but she remembered her promise to herself.

Up until her workload had eclipsed her social life, Darren was occupying most of her waking—and sleeping—hours. Their dating was pretty intense and very sexual, but being in the rat race of corporate America himself, he was very understanding when she told him she needed to focus on her work.

She really needed to get some rest. "Darren, I would really like to see you, but tonight isn't a good time for me."

"Oh, I see." He said.

Umi believed Darren when told her he would be patient while she increased her clientele, and she appreciated his thoughtfulness. She knew he needed some serious TLC—time, laxation and communication—and she wanted to give it to him. But just when they were about to let the good times roll, Umi's priorities shifted and she had to step on the brakes and bring their love bug to a screeching halt.

"I hope you're not too disappointed. Maybe we can get together one day next week?" Her tone was almost apologetic.

"No, no problem. Next week is good. I'll give you a call."

The disappointment in his voice tugged at her heart. Umi

really liked Darren and was hoping to see him again soon. Not that
she was a stranger to heartbreak, if his patience should thin out
before her workload, but he was special to her and fit her ideal of
a "good man," so she was hoping for the best.

She promised Darren she would clear her schedule so that
they could spend some quality time together the following week,
and he agreed to adjust his schedule and meet with her when she
became available. After she hung up the phone and sank down in
the steaming-hot bath that was waiting for her, she closed her eyes
and went over her day in her mind.

Her board meeting had gone fairly well, besides the fact that
her secretary was extremely late and didn't have the proper charts
ready. She was going to have to do something about her—and
soon. She got promising leads and some inside information on two
prospective clients, which always made her a happy camper in the
wilderness of corporate America.

Umi's mind went back to the conversation she had with
Darren, and she laughed at the irony of her life. She worked hard
to be the best in her field, knowing that would attract a man of
quality with standards, now her workload left her with no time to
enjoy the quality man she'd attracted.

She smiled to herself at the thought of turning Darren down.
She wouldn't have been able to do that last year, when she first
met him at The Black Network, a meeting where successful black
people got together to either brag about their accomplishments or
kiss the butt of someone they would like to do business with. Umi
wasn't there to do either. She was there shamelessly trying to get
a man. Yeah, she mingled with a few people, took a few business
cards and handed out a few of her own. Business was always priority, but the night she met Darren, she had a hidden agenda, an
ulterior motive that would hopefully land her in the arms of a man
by the end of the following week.

When she first spotted Darren, he was talking to two other
gentlemen near the bar. He took of sip of his drink and caught her
staring in his direction. Dressed in an expensive dark-colored suit
and tie, well matched with his equally expensive leather shoes, he
looked like success—it was written all over his well-groomed face.
And that's just how she liked them. He acknowledged her with a tip
of his glass. She pinky-waved then turned and left the room.

She went to the ladies' room, fixed her hair and makeup, circled the room a couple of more times, spoke to a few familiar faces, made eye contact with her expensively dressed target, then headed for the coat check.

She was slipping into her sleek all-weather, when she first heard the sweet, husky voice that would bring her so much joy in the coming year.

"Leaving so soon?" He was standing behind her.

His cologne was already in her nostrils. He smelled good—expensive. She turned to face him and put on her award-winning smile. "Hi, Umi Grayson." She extended her hand.

He gave her a look that told her he liked what he saw. When he smiled, Umi almost dropped to her knees. He had the whitest, straightest teeth she had ever seen. They were framed by a set of dark, full lips that looked sweet and kissable. "Nice to meet you. Darren Alexander." He took her hand in his and held it way too long for it to be a business shake, which was quite all right since this exchange was anything but business.

"So you're leaving?" he asked.

"Yeah. I have an early day tomorrow."

"Do you mind if I walk you to your car?"

Gallant and debonair. Umi smiled a bit more warmly this time. She softened her voice. "I'd like that. Thank you."

He held the door open for her. "Umi. That's an interesting name."

By the time she got in her car, Umi had told him about the history of her name, they'd exchanged business cards and talked a little bit about their careers. They had sized each other up, made their own assumptions and reached their own conclusions, based on their limited information.

Umi knew the key to survival in the dating game was patience. It wasn't easy, but she managed to wait for his call, which came a few days later, and it had been fireworks since the very beginning. Not only was he good-looking, but Darren was charming, had the neatest home she'd ever seen a single man have and had skills in the bedroom that were off the scale! He was so good in bed, that on a couple of occasions when they met for lunch, Umi wound up having to take the rest of the day off because it would excite her, just being in his presence. Those were the days. Sipping expensive champagne in the afternoon in his duplex and making love so often that she lost count.

She sighed at the memory. At least she was becoming more disciplined and self-controlled. Her smile faded when she thought about the fact that she hadn't been with Darren, or any other man, since taking on two new accounts at the firm. Her job was swallowing up all of her time. Although she was glad about having the new accounts, when she took them, she promised herself she wouldn't let that happen.

*

"Hello?" Michelle answered the phone lazily. She was stretched out across her king-size bed, had been there since she finished cooking dinner three hours earlier.

"Hi, Michelle. What's up?"

Michelle recognized the voice right away. It was one of her best friends, Randi. "Same old things. Have you heard from Umi?" Michelle propped herself up on an elbow, cradling the phone between her ear and shoulder. With her free hand, she grabbed the remote and lowered the volume on her TV.

"No. She spoke to me briefly the other day. She said she had been planning to make time for us to get together, but I haven't heard from her since."

"Well, maybe no news is good news," Michelle reasoned.

Randi tsked. "No. No news is just that—no news. Umi is up to her neck in work. That girl is keeping her eye on the prize and her nose to the grindstone. I admire that, but I couldn't do it."

"Why not?" Michelle was already giggling, expecting Randi to deliver a punch line.

"It's just not in me. Too much work and not enough play makes Randi crazy as hell."

They laughed together.

Randi's giggles ceased as she asked, "How are Natalie and Greg?"

"All is well. Greg is swallowed up in a basketball game and Natalie is locked in her room. She says she's studying, but I'll bet anything she's on her phone."

"We were the same way when we were teenagers," Randi

admitted.

"Girl, who do you think you're kidding? You're still that way," Michelle joked.

"And what about yourself? What have you been up to?"

The question immediately soured Michelle's mood and brought the brightness in her eyes to a dim flicker, like the sun setting on a beautiful summer day. She wanted to say "absolutely nothing." Not one thing had she been doing with herself outside of being a wife and a mother. Not because she didn't want to, but because she didn't know what to do.

One day after watching an inspiring episode of *Oprah*, Michelle made a list of things she wanted to do to take charge of her inner self and to remember her spiritual being and to renew and strengthen her joy, but somewhere between planning the work and actually working the plan, she lost her enthusiasm. Maybe she needed more than one dose of *Oprah*. Perhaps after watching three or four episodes, she'd be more inspired.

"Well, you know," she started lightly, "making sure Greg and Nat are doing what they're supposed to be doing is enough to keep me on my toes. And this big house doesn't clean itself." She forced a laugh.

Randi didn't know where Michelle was headed, but her instincts—and experience—told her not to go there, so she changed the subject. "Girl, I miss hanging out with my two best friends. We have to arrange some kind of way to fit ourselves into Umi's busy schedule. Maybe we can catch lunch one day next week at the South Street Seaport. What do you think?"

"I'm all for it. Just give me a date and a time, and I'll be there," Michelle said. *It's not like I have a damn thing else going on in my life to keep me from being there,* she thought.

"Good."

Michelle rubbed her hand across her forehead in an effort to wipe away her negative thoughts. For the sake of keeping her sanity, she really needed to try to stay more positive.

She listened to Randi ramble off tentative plans of how they could spend their day if Umi should be able to clear her calendar. Michelle threw in a few "Sounds good me to me's" and a couple of "I'd bet that'd be fun's" before trying to wrap up the conversation.

Michelle enjoyed talking to her best friends, but sometimes she became so depressed after catching up with the goings-on of their lives and having nothing of her own to report. Outside of her usual updates: "Natalie is doing well in school" or "Greg is representing his engineering company at an overseas summit" or "I racked up on new towels and bedding at the white sale at Nordstrom's," it was all beginning to get on her nerves. But she kept her thoughts a secret and rolled with the conversation. "So, you'll work out the details with Umi and call me back?"

"No problem. I'll speak to you then, okay?"

"Okay, bye." Michelle hung up the phone feeling a little low in spirit, but the idea of getting together with her two best friends made her smile. Randi was right, it had been a while since the three of them went out and did something together.

Umi and Randi had such busy lives with their careers and their boyfriends—just the opposite of hers. They spent their days at board meetings and business lunches. She spent her days being a full-time wife and mother. She had to admit, being at home during the day had its perks, but it dulled in comparison to the fast-paced lives her two best friends were living.

"Hey, honey." Greg stepped into the bedroom. "Natalie and I are about to get into a game of Scrabble. Want to join us?"

"First things first." Michelle sat up and returned the phone to the nightstand. "Is Natalie's homework done?"

"Yep." He sat next to her on the bed and started playing with her feet.

She pulled away, tucking her legs underneath her. He knew she was ticklish and hated for her feet to be touched. She wagged a stern finger at him and raised her eyebrows. "And has the kitchen been cleaned?"

"You know it." He leaned in and placed soft kisses on her neck.

She fell back on the bed, laughing. "Okay, okay, but didn't I beat you two bad enough last time? You mean to tell me you want some more?" Michelle teased.

"I'm always up for a challenge," Greg said as he leaned over and covered her mouth with his.

Michelle could feel herself melting more and more with each kiss. After twelve years of marriage, Greg still knew what to do to turn her on. She loved that about him. She especially loved the way he looked at her when she was wearing something special for him and the fire and passion in his lovemaking that was always waiting to please her. She knew he was the perfect man for her the minute she laid eyes on him.

Shortly after she was born, Natalie's father declared he couldn't handle the responsibility of being a parent. Of course he didn't deliver the news to Michelle using those words. He said something more along the lines of needing space and wanting to find himself, whatever that meant. After two years of dating, a miserable pregnancy and more shouting matches than she cared to remember, part of her was glad to see him go, but then there's the other part that hated the day he walked out of her life, leaving her with a broken heart and a bunch of broken promises.

But it wasn't long after his departure that Greg walked in and replaced her doubts and insecurities with renewed joy, and a sense of self-worth and helped restore her dignity.

Greg willingly played the role of Daddy to a little girl he immediately fell in love with and felt deserved the privilege of having a father in her life. Natalie was only two years old then. Greg had always treated her as though she were his very own daughter and even insisted on legally adopting her after he and Michelle were married.

Michelle broke their kiss and eased from underneath him. "I thought you wanted to play Scrabble, not House."

Greg flashed her a wicked grin, "Yeah, let's play House. I'll be the husband and you'll be the Swedish housekeeper."

Although she knew he was joking, she became instantly angry. "Do I look Swedish to you?" She nudged him hard enough to show she wasn't playing anymore.

He backed up, confused and watched her move across the room to the door.

She turned back and eyed him with an attitude. "And I'm nobody's housekeeper."

She watched him slowly shake his head in bewilderment. Michelle knew she was being emotional and overly sensitive again, but she just couldn't help herself.

She went into the living room and began helping Natalie set up the game on the floor. When Greg entered the room, their eyes met. She smiled warmly and patted the spot next to her on the floor. His brow wrinkled in confusion, and he touched the spot where she'd nudge him. She turned her attention back to the game and pretended not to see him rub his wound.

"Come on, Daddy. I want to pick my letters." Natalie held up the bag for him to see.

Greg smiled at Natalie and took a seat next to Michelle on the floor.

Now sixteen, with a birthday coming in three weeks, Natalie was a teenager who would make any parent proud—a beautiful chocolate girl, tall and thin, with almond-shaped eyes and high cheekbones, just like her mother's. Puberty had visited her, leaving a shapely body and womanly charm. Not only was she blessed with beauty, but brains as well. She was an excellent student and very popular in school. All of her teachers deemed her one of the brightest in her classes and on the road to definite success.

Natalie put her hand in the bag, pulled out a handful of tiles and passed the bag to her mother. "Dad and I are ready for you this time, Mom."

"Oh yeah?" Michelle reached in the bag. She watched Natalie arrange her tiles, watched her brain tick as it went to work formulating words. She looked so much like her *real* father when she was concentrating. Her forehead and brows wrinkled just like his. As far as Michelle knew, Natalie had no recollection of her biological father. No scars or psychological issues of abandonment to mention. Greg was the only dad she had ever known.

In their two years of dating and twelve years of marriage, Michelle couldn't remember one single time when Greg had not been supportive of her or Natalie or hadn't encouraged their decisions or respected their opinions and ideas. She and Greg were very much in love, and she was proud of the life they'd built together.

*

After Randi got off the phone with Michelle, she turned up her radio, blasting 98.7 Kiss FM and danced to her favorite song. "Tomorrow is Friday, and I cannot wait to see Brian, with his sexy self!"

She snapped her fingers and boogy-oogy-oogied her way over to her closet to search for her best business suit, which could easily be converted into an after-work outfit. She was meeting Brain at After Five, a club for professional men and women, and she definitely wanted to look the part.

She pulled out three of her nicest outfits and settled on a sleeveless navy blue Liz Claiborne dress and matching blazer. She could easily take off her blazer if she got too warm after getting her party on. She certainly had plans for her and Brian to tear up the dance floor at After Five and later on they'd tear up the sheets back at his condo. She stood in front of her full-length mirror and held the dress up to her. Perfect. The dress stopped just above her knees, showing off her muscular calves. She smiled at her reflection. This was going to be the bomb with the navy blue sling backs she picked up at Nine West. She hung the suit on the inside of her closet door.

It was almost nine o'clock. She was ready to start winding down for the night. She turned down the radio and switched the station to CD 101.9, New York's favorite cool jazz station. The sound of Bony James filled her tiny co-op apartment and began relaxing her. To enhance the mood, she dimmed the track lighting in her living room and lit an aromatherapy candle.

Randi never really liked candles—until recently, when Umi brought her one from a business trip in San Francisco and forced her to light it. She told Umi she'd wasted her money, that she would never dream of burning any kind of candle in her house. Her mother raised her to believe that candle burning was ritualistic and demonic. The only time her mother ever lit a candle in their house was during the blackout of '76. But Umi insisted and Randi conceded, opening herself up to a new way to relax and unwind.

Speaking of Umi, Randi decided now would be a good time to catch her, since it was getting late. She went back into the bedroom and pushed one of the programmed buttons on her phone. Randi hung up when she heard Umi's recorded voice answer.

"Shit," she said under her breath. She was tired of leaving messages.

Randi took a shower and stretched across her bed to go over some press clippings for work the next day. Lately, she'd been unsatisfied with her position as a researcher at *The New York*

Times. She felt stagnate, like the job had become too small for her. She made the mistake of voicing her complaints to Umi, who immediately insisted that she go back to school so that she could take charge of her career and assume a higher position. Umi's words exactly. So, with constant encouragement from Umi, she finally made it through grad school at NYU and was ready to kiss her job as a researcher for *The Times* good-bye and was even more ready to sink her heels into a position in the editing department. But that hadn't happened yet. It would happen soon though. She had faith in her abilities.

What she didn't have faith in was men. In the past year alone, she had been with three different breeds of them. She was tired of dating men who were dating everybody and didn't have a clue about commitment. Aggravated with men altogether, she took a sabbatical from her pound puppies. Yep, swore them off limits for a whole month before she bumped into Brian at a barbecue at a mutual friend's house.

Brian was good-looking, well dressed and could dance his butt off. By the end of the night she was sipping on wine coolers and having multiple orgasms in a room at the Motel 6. So now she was dating Brian, seemingly as loyal as a St. Bernard. Although, they'd only been dating a couple of months, and it was too soon to tell, but so far she had no reason to put on her Sherlock Holmes routine. Brian pretty much did what he said he was going to do and was timely with returning her pages. That would always earn him extra points in her book.

Randi pushed her work aside, rubbed her eyes and reached for the phone to call her canine friend. He was away on an overnight business trip in D.C., so she decided to call and leave a sexy message on his voice mail at home. *He'll be pleased to get this message,* she thought as she waited for the machine to come on.

"Hello?"

Randi's heart skipped a beat when she heard a woman's voice on the line. "I'm sorry," she faltered. "I must have the wrong number."

"Are you looking for Brian?" the woman asked.

Randi couldn't find her breath. She wanted to ask the woman who she was and what she was doing in Brian's apartment, but before she could say a word, the woman interrupted her thoughts. "He's not here right now. Would you like to leave a message for him?"

"Yes," Randi finally found her voice. "May I ask who you are?" she asked with an attitude.

"No, you may not, but you may leave a message if you'd like," the woman said, matching her tone.

Oh no she didn't! Randi slammed down the phone and picked it back up to dial Brian's pager number. *Forget it.* She put the phone back on the base. She'd have to settle this matter face-to-face when he came home.

Damn. Okay. Don't get upset. She should have expected this anyway—sooner or later. Same old routine. "Every time I think I've found a decent man, he always proves me wrong. A dog will be a dog."

Randi ended her aromatherapy session, settled under the covers and tried to convince herself that there had to be a reasonable explanation.

CHAPTER 2

"Good morning, Mom." Natalie entered the kitchen fully dressed in tight jeans and a fitted shirt that left her navel exposed.

Michelle had to get used to these new styles. She started to say something, but didn't feel like getting into a word-for-word this early in the day.

"Good morning, honey." Michelle looked at her watch. Nine-thirty. "What's gotten you up so early this morning?"

"Don't you remember? Tonight is the athletic banquet at school." Natalie smiled proudly at her mother. "Oh, Mom, I forgot to tell you, I have some errands to run this morning. I need the car." She was at the counter pouring juice.

Here we go again. Michelle glanced up at her teenaged daughter with raised eyebrows and shook her head. "Not my car."

Natalie shrugged her bony shoulders. "Then I'll use Dad's." She finished her juice and took a seat at the table.

Michelle had been going over some calculations in her checkbook. She was on her way out to pay some bills and do a little shopping. She put her pen down and looked up at her daughter. "Natalie, you'd better ask him about that because he said he was going out this morning."

Natalie sighed heavily before leaving the kitchen. Michelle felt her frustration. Since Natalie had gotten her driver's license, the three of them had been sharing two cars, and it was aggravating to all of them. It always seemed like everyone needed the cars at the same time, and no one was ever willing to compromise, which meant Natalie always got the short end of the stick.

Michelle was back to crunching numbers when she heard Greg's baritone voice nearing the kitchen. "If you can wait until later, Nat, you can have the car, but right now I have to take it to the mechanic to get the brakes repaired."

"But I have an appointment, Daddy." Natalie was right on his heels and whining.

Michelle hated when she did that.

Greg opened the refrigerator, looked around for a minute, but came out empty-handed. "Then take your mother's car."

"Greg." Michelle gave him a hard look.

"What?" He knitted his eyebrows together in confusion.

She wanted to tell him to stop volunteering her car without asking her every time they reached this crossroad. She sucked her teeth in frustration.

Greg was lovable and a good man by most women's standards, but he had a streak of inconsideration in him that boiled her blood. It was the small stuff—and she tried not to sweat it. But all those small things were joining together and forming one big mass that was upsetting her more and more every day. For instance, would it kill him to drop his own shirts off at the cleaners every once in a while, instead of letting them pile up to the ceiling and waiting for her to haul them down there? And how many times did he have to watch her drag the garbage cans out to the curb on Mondays and Thursdays in her slippers and robe before offering to do it? And had it ever occurred to him that he could pick up a mop and broom sometimes too? He was taking her for granted. That's what it was. And she didn't like it one bit.

Michelle suppressed her thoughts and brought her attention back to the matter at hand. "I have things to do this morning. I've already told Natalie that."

"Oh, well, Nat. I guess you have to take the bus," Greg concluded nonchalantly and walked away.

"I have too much to do to take the bus. Pleeeaaassseee, Daddy." Natalie was begging now and following Greg into the living room.

"What do you have to do?" Greg was putting on his leather jacket.

"I have to pick up Rachael and be at the beauty parlor in about an hour." She looked at her watch. "Then we have to go to Hempstead to get our nails done and pick up our dresses for tonight. We're going to the athletic banquet tonight with Perry and Steve."

"I forgot that was tonight," Michelle told Greg as she entered the living room and began putting her coat on too.

Natalie was sitting on the arm of the sofa, arms folded tightly across her chest and pouting. Michelle's heart went out to her. For a change, she quickly thought of a plan to accommodate everyone.

"Greg, how long are you going to be at the mechanic?"

"I don't know. An hour maybe."

"Mom, I can't wait an hour," Natalie complained.

"Hush, girl," Michelle snapped and turned her attention back to Greg. "I'll ride with you, Greg, if you don't mind coming with me afterward to pay some bills and run a few quick errands."

Greg shrugged. "I don't mind."

Of course he didn't mind, she thought angrily.

Natalie's face lit up. The twinkle had returned to her eye and her smile had been restored.

"Natalie, next time you need the car, you have to tell us in advance, so some kind of arrangement can be made," Michelle lectured. "No more of this last-minute business."

"Thank you, Mommy." Natalie could hardly contain her joy as she kissed her mother's cheek and grabbed her jacket from the closet. She turned to face her parents. "You know, we wouldn't have to do so much planning and organizing if I had my own car. Things would be a whole lot easier that way."

Michelle looked at Greg with a frown. "Is this girl insane?"

He kept silent.

Michelle picked up her pocketbook. "Things would be a whole lot easier if you had your own money to buy it." She dug out her car keys and handed them to Natalie.

"Oh, Mom. It was just a suggestion, not a plan." Her head was tilted in that cocky way that drove Michelle crazy.

I swear this girl has gotten too grown for her own good lately. "You better get out of here," Michelle warned sternly.

Natalie was out the door before her mother could say another word.

"Drive carefully," Michelle called after her, momentarily forgetting she was annoyed as she let her motherly instincts take charge.

"Come on, honey. We better get going. You know how Allen is:

if you're one minute late, he'll take another customer ahead of you."
Oh, God, not Allen. She grabbed her Coach bag and followed
Greg outside. "Allen is fixing your car?"

Greg opened the car door for Michelle to get in. Everyone
knew Michelle didn't like Allen—including Allen. But she hadn't
always despised his best friend. In fact, at one time she adored
him. Greg and Allen met a little more than ten years ago when
they were assigned to play on the same basketball team at the community center in Hempstead. The four of them: Allen; his wife
Joy; Greg and Michelle used to hang out together on occasion.

About five years ago, Michelle and Joy returned from a shopping spree and walked right in on Allen having sex on his living
room floor with this hot, young tenderoni from Hofstra University
who was supposed to be baby-sitting Allen and Joy's two children.

That was the beginning of the end. Although Michelle and
Joy weren't what one would call tight friends, it seemed like they
were, the way Michelle was all involved and carrying on over the
situation. She was ready and willing to form an allegiance with
Joy's sisters, cousins and friends—women she didn't even know—
against Allen because he had done his wife wrong. She would have
been on the front lines, ready to lock arms and sway to the words
of "We Shall Overcome" in an effort to help Joy triumph over
heartbreak brought on by her man.

After Allen's divorce, it wasn't easy for Greg and Allen to
maintain their close friendship, but they somehow managed in
spite of Michelle's feelings about him. She bickered from time to
time, but mostly just kept her distance.

"Yeah, Allen's fixing the car," Greg answered as he slid into
the driver's seat and pulled out of the driveway.

Michelle bit her tongue. She didn't want to start rehashing
bad memories about Allen. And she knew Greg didn't want to
spend the morning defending him. She was glad he changed the
subject.

"That's not a bad idea Natalie had."

"Natalie's idea about what?"

"About buying her a car."

"Now who's insane?" Michelle shook her head. "No, Greg.
She's only sixteen and too young to have her own car."

"She has a birthday coming up, and I think a car would be

an ideal gift." He could see that Michelle wasn't buying it. "It doesn't have to be brand new, just reliable."

Michelle sat quietly thinking it over. She kind of got the feeling that her husband and her daughter had already discussed this issue.

"So what do you think?" Greg asked, interrupting her thoughts.

Michelle shifted in her seat to look at Greg. "I think Natalie's too young. A car is a big responsibility—there's maintenance, repairs and insurance. Who's going to pay for those things? Natalie doesn't have a job. Besides, I don't like the idea of her having so much freedom. With her using our cars, we can keep track of when she's coming and going."

"You're being overprotective." Greg kept his eyes on the road.

She didn't appreciate his comment. "I'm being a mother." She huffed. "Nat is mature, but she's still a teenager and needs monitoring." Michelle was straining to keep an even tone. She could feel an argument developing, but didn't care. She wanted Greg to understand that she didn't like the idea.

Greg patted Michelle's thigh and gave it a gentle squeeze as he pulled in front of Allen's garage. He shut off the engine and faced her. "How about you, me and Nat discussing this later? We can set the rules and she can pay for half of the insurance out of her allowance."

Michelle sighed heavily. "What is there to discuss? I don't like—"

Greg leaned over and kissed her softly on the lips. "Don't worry. Everything will be fine."

*

"Okay. So everyone understands that we're going to work in groups of three to evenly divide the workload on each account?" Umi stood at the head of the table in the conference room. She stared back at the twelve hardworking and reliable people who made up her unit. Together, they single-handedly worked their way to being the most talked-about advertising team, having obtained the most accounts in a year. They were also featured in *Crain's*

Magazine and in *The New York Times* Business Section, with a little help from Randi. Umi was very proud of herself, her team and their accomplishments.

"If there are no questions, I'll post a memo informing you of our next meeting. This meeting is officially over." Umi picked up her files from the table and started toward her office.

She hated Monday morning meetings. Her team members were still in weekend mode, which meant she had to work harder to motivate them.

"Good morning, Ms. Grayson, I forwarded three calls to your voice mail, and this came for you." Valerie handed Umi a large brown envelope.

Umi read the return address before responding. The envelope was from Mr. Davis. Probably a response to her proposal for his company—in other words, good news. She waited long enough for this account.

Umi eyed her secretary. "Good morning, Valerie. I'm glad you decided to come to work on time today."

Ignoring her boss' remark, she continued, "You have a package in the mail room, would you like me to get it for you?"

"Yes, please. Also, I would like to speak to you a little later in my office. We need to go over some things." Umi turned and walked to her office. She could feel Valerie's evil stare on her back. *If looks could kill...* Umi thought. *But since they can't, she'll get over it.*

Once inside her office, Umi took a seat behind her large oak desk and took notes as she listened to her messages. A smile came across her face when she heard Randi's invitation to have lunch with her and Michelle on Sunday at two o'clock at the South Street Seaport. She immediately reached for her calendar. Damn. She was meeting Mr. Davis at two, but she could easily reschedule him for a couple of hours. He made her wait. And what's good for the goose, was good for the gander.

"Valerie?" Umi spoke into the intercom.

"Yes, Ms. Grayson?"

"Please reschedule my two o'clock appointment on Sunday."

"When would be a better time?" Valerie asked.

Umi could hear papers rustling and waited a moment before continuing. "Two hours later would be fine. Thank you. Oh, and

Valerie, I need to see you in my office in about ten minutes."

Umi picked up the phone to call Randi and confirm.

"New York Times."

"Randi Young, please." Umi was put on hold. She examined her nails as she waited. Maybe she could squeeze in a manicure during lunch.

"Research. Ms. Young speaking."

"Hey, girl, it's me, Umi."

"Oh, Lord, it must be snowing outside."

They laughed together.

"Umi, I am so glad to finally hear from you. So you got my message about lunch on Sunday?"

"Yes, and I'll be there. Child, we have so much to catch up on. I miss you guys so much."

"We miss you too. Michelle is going to be so glad to know you can make it. You know how she is. She's been worried about you."

"Yeah, I know. Last week she left me a message telling me to take vitamins and eat a lot of vegetables since I'm not getting proper rest."

They laughed again.

"Maybe we can even do something after lunch," Randi offered.

"That sounds good, but my time is kind of limited. I have to see a client around four."

A silence fell between them. Randi was a little disappointed that Umi's clients were so important she had to schedule her friends around them. "Oh, well, I'm glad you can at least make lunch."

"At least lunch," Umi repeated cheerfully.

"I'm glad you called me back, and I'm extra glad you can make it on Sunday. I'll see you then, okay? I have to go. Bye." Randi abruptly ended the conversation.

Umi could hear the disappointment in her friend's voice. She hung up the phone just as Valerie tapped on the door.

"Come in."

Valerie stepped inside looking like a trapped mouse. "You wanted to see me?"

"Have a seat." Umi nodded toward one of the two leather

chairs in front of her desk. She shifted the same papers around on her desk, as she thought of a way to start in on Valerie. She hated this part of her job, scolding and correcting the people who worked for her, but it had to be done.

Umi began slowly, "Valerie, I am very unhappy with your work performance lately."

"I know, but—"

Umi put her hand up to stop Valerie. She had already heard every excuse in the book from her. "Let me finish." Umi began again. "I've spoken to you before about being prompt, limiting you personal calls and doing your work timely and efficiently. Valerie, you don't seem to be focused during the day."

"I have a lot on my mind."

"We all do, Valerie." Umi kept her voice smooth and even. "But while you're here I need you to be conscious of your duties and to perform them. You've been with me now for a little more than a year. I'm sure you've accrued some time. Why don't you take a couple of days off and pull yourself together?"

"I already used all of my days for the year," Valerie admitted softly.

"How about a short leave without pay?"

Umi watched Valerie's eyebrows shoot up into her hairline. Did she say something outlandish? Maybe she had. After all, Valerie was a single mother trying to support three or four children on her meager salary.

Valerie's eyebrows relaxed for a brief moment, before forming a V in the middle of her forehead. Her eyes went to the wall behind Umi. "I can't afford that."

Contrary to what Valerie might think, Umi understood her situation and her heart went out to her. She knew what it was like to want things and not be able to afford them or not be able to go places because your bank account was on empty. What Valerie saw—her expensive clothes, degrees on her office walls and lavish vacations—were all the result of her hard work and dedication.

Umi knew early on when she first hired Valerie that she saw them as being from two different worlds, the Haves and the Have Nots. Us versus Them. And no matter how Umi tried to lessen the distance between their two worlds, Valerie was resistant, even insisting on calling her Ms. Grayson, although Umi assured her that she didn't have to be so formal.

Regardless of all of that, Umi had to do what was required of her to keep her team on top. This was about business. "Okay, Valerie, listen. This is your final warning. I need you to be on point while you're in the office. Okay?"

"Okay."

"That's all. I'll see you after lunch."

Valerie left and Umi tried to bring order to the rest of her day.

*

Randi hung up on Umi, then called Michelle and got her machine. "Hi, Michelle. This is Randi. I just wanted to let you know that Umi called me and confirmed Sunday, two o'clock at the South Street Seaport. Give me a call when you get a chance. Bye."

She was genuinely happy that Umi was now heading her own advertising team, but she hated the fact that she just deserted her and Michelle. *I'm sure she has time for power lunches with other big advertising executives,* Randi thought angrily. Randi's mother always told her never to burn the bridge that brought you over. *Umi needed to remember who sat up with her all night and helped her study so that she could get the degrees that got her her job. And she better not forget the two women who helped her pay her bills while she used all of her money for tuition and books, when she couldn't get a student loan,* Randi thought.

She sighed. Umi was breaking her concentration. She had more important things to think about—like setting up a seek-and-destroy mission for Brian.

She should have just cursed him out when he called her and canceled their date Friday at After Five. But, no, she held her peace and even gave him another chance to meet her there that evening. Even though she hated going out on Monday nights, she bent her rule this time. Then, after canceling, Brian didn't even have enough decency to call her over the weekend. Probably because he was busy entertaining his houseguest.

That's all right. Every dog has his day, she thought. She had left a message on Brian's voice mail earlier, but didn't mention what was on her mind. She wanted to tell him about that when she saw him, so that she could see the look on his lying face.

At the club that night, she planned to just play it smooth and enjoy herself. Afterward, when she got his two-timing butt back to her apartment and made him think he was going to taste some of her sweet fruit, she'd drop the bomb on him and send his sorry ass home with blue balls. Now that was a plan.

"Hey, Randi. What's up?"

She looked up from her desk to see who interrupted her thoughts and saw her coworker Franklin walking by. "Hey, Frank."

"I'm on my way to Gino's to get a sandwich. You want to join me?"

She was kind of hungry. "Okay, let me get my coat." Randi took out her compact and checked her hair and makeup. Her short hair was curled to perfection and framed her small oval face, giving her a youthful look. She quickly closed the compact and slid into her coat, and ran out to meet Franklin by the elevators.

Franklin Whittaker—tall, dark and handsome with a pair of light eyes that could wet any woman's panties—worked in research with her and was the only other African-American researcher on staff. Randi used to have a little crush on him until she found out he was married and had a daughter.

"Are you working on any major projects now, Randi?"

Randi saw him eyeing her slim waist and beige-toned skin. She wondered if he could smell her perfume. As hard as he was staring at her, she also wondered if he could see her dark, lacy bra and panties.

"I just completed one. Why?"

He smiled sweetly at her. "Well, I was just given a little project, and I may need some help with it." The elevator arrived and they stepped on with a few other people. "So, I was wondering if you wouldn't mind helping a brother out."

Yeah, right. Randi sensed she was being set up, but she went along with the game anyway. She got her mental dog leash ready and let Franklin lead the way.

When they got to Gino's, the place was packed as usual with the regular lunch-hour crowd coming in from all of the corporate buildings that filled Midtown Manhattan.

They ordered their food and luckily spotted two women leaving a table in the rear of the deli. One of the women shamelessly eyed Franklin like a hungry piranha as they approached the table, not even caring that Randi was standing right next to him. She ignored the jealous stare the woman gave her. She wasn't about to get into a catfight over someone else's man.

Franklin was a gentleman about the situation. He gave the woman a slight nod, acknowledging her then turned his attention to Randi and finished filling her in on the details of his project. "So, does this sound like something you might be interested in?"

She shrugged. "I don't see a problem with it. But I want to see what you've done so far." *Franklin ain't nothing but a dog,* Randi thought as she ate her sandwich and smiled in his face. *A very handsome dog—still a dog by any other name is just the same.*

Lunch with Franklin went rather nicely. He certainly was a suave smooth talker. Even though their conversation stayed on business, his deep tenor sent chills down her spine and into her panties. She enjoyed his company, his conversation and all the jealous stares she got from other women. Now those were a real ego booster. Randi could see how a woman would easily fall in love with him. *But not me. Love don't live here anymore,* Randi thought.

She used to think that women like Franklin's wife were very lucky to have found someone so thoughtful and kind—and not to mention good-looking, but how lucky was she if she had someone like that and couldn't have him all to herself?

Michelle, on the other hand, was one black woman who hit the jackpot when it came to love and romance. She and Greg had something together that would put the Huxtables to shame. Randi would never know what it was like to be in a secure relationship at the rate she was going.

When they got back to their office, Franklin went to his desk to get the project information for her, and Randi went to the ladies' room to freshen up.

When she got back to her desk, she went through her messages and came across one from Brian canceling their date at After Five that evening. She moaned and grumbled as she snatched the phone off the hook. She called his office to see what his reason was for canceling their date this time.

"May I speak with Brian Mosley, please?" She had an attitude. "I'm sorry, he's gone for the day. Would you like to leave a message?" the receptionist asked pleasantly.

White people got on her nerves being pleasant all the damn time. "No, thank you." She slammed the phone down. Now she was mad. Brian was a waste of time, and time waited for no man—neither does Randi Young.

She thought she had figured out the male species, maybe not to an exact science, but she at least had a strong premise for their behavior. One thing she couldn't quite grasp was why in the hell did they lie so much? And about every little thing? If Brian didn't want to kick it with her anymore or something new and improved had come along, he could have told her instead of playing these sick, childish games with her.

She took a deep breath and tried to relax. *Think, Randi. Think. Now what?* "I'm all dressed up and nowhere to go," Randi mumbled under her breath. This was downright pathetic. She considered going to After Five by herself, then decided against it. So she did what she always did when in doubt: Randi dialed the familiar number and waited as the phone rang. "Hi, Mom, want some company tonight?" She tried her best to sound cheery.

"Hi, baby. I'd love some. I could use some help finishing up this old jigsaw puzzle."

Randi rolled her eyes.

"What time are you going to get here?"

"I'm coming straight after work. Want me to pick up some butter-pecan ice cream?"

"That sounds good. It'll go great with the marble cake I baked this morning. Are you all right? You don't sound like yourself."

"I'm fine, Mama," she lied.

Randi was sure her mother wasn't convinced. She knew her little girl too well, but thank goodness she left it alone.

"Okay. I'll see you when you get here," her mother said.

"Bye, Mama."

Randi wanted to make it seem like Brian wasn't a big deal. She tried to fool herself by painting the picture that he was just another passing phase and in a few months he would be nothing more to her than a memory. And maybe that was true, but secretly she really liked Brian and hoped he would be around for while. She was starting to care for him a little, and that was probably the reason for her being so angry about his shady behavior. Well, whatever the reason, she was sure to get over it. She always did.

Franklin came over to her desk and handed her a manila folder and a disk. Her mood lightened a little. She forced a smile and asked, "What's this?"

He returned the smile. His was more natural. "The disk has the beginning of the report on it. It's only a few paragraphs, but I thought you might want to see it. And in the folder are photocopies of articles I plan on using when I get—I mean when *we* get to the final stages."

He's a trip, Randi thought. "I didn't actually commit to helping you yet." She sucked in one side of her cheek in an effort to stifle a smile.

"I know. I'm exercising my right to assume." His smile broadened.

If she looked into his beautiful eyes a second longer, she was going to melt. She turned her attention to the items in the folder.

Franklin waited patiently for her to finish reading. When she closed the folder he asked, "So what do you think?"

"I think you're off to a good start." She couldn't contain her smile any longer.

"Has anyone ever told you, you have a beautiful smile?" he asked coyly.

Her smile disappeared and her relaxed vibe became instantly rigid. "Look, Franklin, I'll let you know tomorrow if I can help you out."

He was caught off guard and started to apologize, but she cut him off, told him she had a few phone calls to make and politely dismissed him.

By quitting time, Randi was physically and emotionally drained. But she was still looking forward to seeing her mother and felt good about her decision to spend the evening with her. She had vowed to spend more time with her mom since her father's death. His sudden heart attack a year ago was a shock to their family. Mostly because for his age he appeared to be in good health.

Randi would never forget the phone call she received from the emergency room at Kings County Hospital, or the story her mother told, between sobs, of how she had come out of the shower that morning and found her father on the bedroom floor.

Her parents had been married for forty years and they had had Randi and her younger brother, Hugh Jr. immediately. The Young clan was a small, tight-knitted group who believed in the importance of family. In fact, everyone gathered during the holidays and could fit in one person's house with room for guests. It was this closeness that made her father's absence painfully obvious and more difficult. Her mother had been strong the entire time. Even if she had some breakdowns, no one ever knew it.

The afternoon went by without a word from Brian. When Randi got downstairs in the lobby, she spotted Franklin, who immediately started in her direction.

Now what? She wasn't in the mood for games at this moment.

"Randi, I just wanted to apologize again for—"

She waved her hand. "Don't worry about it. No harm, no foul."

"You sure?"

She nodded.

Franklin looked over his shoulder at two of his coworkers who were waiting for him. "I have to get out of here, but I wanted to talk to you some more about the project. I can give you a call tonight, if you don't mind." He was wearing the most innocent look he could muster.

He's actually asking for my phone number. Randi managed to keep her smile to herself and without giving it a second thought, she scribbled her home number on the back of one of her business cards and handed it to him.

Yeah, he was married, but she had to admit, the attention was flattering.

CHAPTER 3

Michelle waited in line at the registration desk. What was taking so long? How many people could be joining a gym in the middle of the day? Michelle began to glance around at all the different people in the gym and wondered what brought them there. She wasn't totally sure why she was there herself.

"Next." A young white girl who looked just a couple of years older than Natalie was standing on the other side of the desk wearing big earrings and way too much black lipstick.

Michelle stepped up to the counter. "I would like the full package for six months please."

After signing up, Michelle made her way to her assigned locker and began changing her clothes. She was right on time for an aerobics class. She really didn't need to shape up, but she needed something to occupy her days, and joining a gym was a healthy way to do it.

She wished she had someone to join with her, but everyone had something to do or somewhere to go during the day. Everyone had a life except her.

Michelle stepped into the aerobics class and took a seat on the floor to begin her warm-up stretches. The women looked friendly enough, she thought, so she got up and walked over to a petite brown-skinned woman to introduce herself. As she got closer, she realized that the woman had a beautiful face, perfectly shaped eyes and mouth and beautiful bone structure. *Maybe she's a model or an actress,* Michelle thought. *They can sometimes be cold.* She had almost lost her nerve and started to go in another direction when the woman looked up and caught her eye.

"Hello," Michelle said in her nicest tone and smiled. She extended her hand and hoped she didn't sound nervous or look desperate—or both.

"Hello." The woman shook her hand. "First time here?"

"Yeah. My name is Michelle."

"Hi, Michelle. Gail. This class is pretty fun. I'm sure you'll enjoy it."

"Okay, class, let's line up!" the instructor shouted. "New victims to the rear!"

Michelle left Gail and made her way to the back of the room. *Victim? Whatever.* She was in great shape. She was only there because she wanted to stay that way. She was very happy and very comfortable with her size-six body. And for a woman over thirty, her breasts were still firm and her hips and waist were still slender and sexy. That was a lot more than she could say for some of the sloppy-looking, twenty-somethings in the class.

When the last routine ended, Michelle sat on the floor for a moment to catch her breath. She was covered in sweat and panting like she'd just been running from the police. She looked up and Gail was standing over her smiling. Michelle quickly dried her face with her towel.

"Was it really that bad?" Gail asked, smiling. She extended her hand and helped Michelle to her feet.

"No, not really," Michelle answered as they headed to the locker room to change. "The routines were kind of hard to catch on to, but it actually felt pretty good to get the old blood pumping again."

"Humph, you won't be saying that in the morning," Gail teased.

"I don't know what I'll feel like in the morning, but right now I'm starving."

"If you have time for lunch, there's a great health-food restaurant on the main floor," Gail invited. "I eat there all the time."

Michelle was a little hesitant. Gail seemed nice and all, but one never knew these days. She thought for a moment. *Oh, what the hell, it's not like the girl is inviting me into a dark alley.*

"Sure." She gladly accepted the invitation. Gail seemed nice enough and the Lord knew she needed the company right now. With Umi and Randi being so busy, Michelle had been spending a lot of time by herself. She hated to admit that sometimes she was downright lonely.

"Great, I'll meet you outside the locker room." Gail left to go to her locker.

Michelle took a hot shower and changed into her regular clothes. If she had known she was going to meet a new friend, she would have dressed better. She didn't want the woman to think she was tacky. She applied a little makeup—not enough to look made up, but enough to keep her from looking plain. She brushed her hair back and went out to meet Gail.

When she got out in the hallway, she spotted Gail in a corner on her cell phone, so she stayed by the locker room door and planned to go over when she finished her call, but Gail spotted her and waved for her to come over.

" . . . Is that all he said?" Gail said into the phone. "Okay. We can talk about that when I get back." Silence. "Any more messages? Then, I'll see you soon. Bye." She put her phone away and turned to Michelle. "Ready?"

"Yep."

After they got their food, Gail suggested they sit near a window so that they could get some sun. They began talking about themselves and some of the things they enjoyed and discovered they had a lot of things in common and shared similar thoughts on a lot of issues. This made both of them feel more at ease and the conversation kept rolling along effortlessly.

"So what brings you to the gym in the middle of a business day?" Michelle secretly wondered if Gail was as lonely and desperate as she was.

"I pretty much make my own schedule. I'm a florist, and I own a shop in Roosevelt Field mall. So sometimes I can afford to sneak away and leave my manager in charge." Gail took a bite of what looked like pasta and spinach. "What about you?"

Michelle's mouth went dry, but she knew the question was coming, so she had an answer already rehearsed. She took a sip of water and hoped she wouldn't sound pitiful. "Well, my husband is an engineering analyst, so I decided to stay home and raise our daughter. Now that she's almost grown, I have a lot of free time on my hands." Hearing the words out loud almost made her feel sorry for herself. She definitely wasn't prepared for Gail's response.

"I envy you, girl," Gail said.

"You do?"

"A husband and free time." She jokingly waved her hand at Michelle. "The two things I've always wanted."

"Really?" She couldn't believer her ears.

"Michelle, let me tell you, girl. You have something that's not available to a lot of women these days."

"It's not all it's cracked up to be." Michelle shook her head.

"You're rested and relaxed. That alone will help you outlive other women your age, especially those who are running the rat race in corporate America." Gail took another bite of her food and pointed the fork at Michelle. "Consider yourself lucky."

"Oh yeah?" Michelle thought about Umi for a second.

"Think about what a working mother does in a day: Having to drop the children off in the morning and rushing to work. Then having to pick up the children and rushing home, only to start her second job. Cooking dinner, bathing children, combing hair, helping with homework, washing dishes—"

"Okay, okay." Michelle laughed. "I'm getting tired just listening."

"I think about my mother. She raised three girls all by herself. I watched her work herself into an early grave. Besides that, she made sure we had everything we needed and sometimes things we wanted, but she never got the chance to do anything for herself."

"I'm sorry about your mother."

"It's okay. She's been dead for almost ten years now. I think about her sometimes and when I do, I make sure I take time out for myself, by making my mental health, my spiritual health and my physical health priorities."

On her way home, Michelle kept going over her conversation with Gail. Gail had a good point: She was truly blessed with all that she had. So why did she feel so unsatisfied? Was she ungrateful? Had she become one of those women who would never be satisfied, no matter what they had? By the time she pulled into the driveway, Michelle figured all she needed was a hobby. Maybe she would take a knitting or an embroidery class. Those were things she always wanted to learn. Or maybe she would sign up to volunteer at the senior citizen center. If she really gave it some thought, she would find something to do with her time.

Michelle walked in the house and was welcomed by the smell of fresh-baked cookies. She glanced at her watch. It was already 4:30. "Natalie!"

"I'm in the kitchen, Mom!"

Natalie and her best friend, Rachael, were at the table eating cookies and doing their homework.

"Hey, honey." She leaned over and kissed her daughter's cheek. "Hi, Rachael. What's up?"

"Hi, Mrs. Vaughn. My mom asked me to remind you about the PTA meeting next week. She wants you to give her a call."

"Okay."

"Mom, can I spend the night at Rachael's house? Her mom said it would be alright, and she'll drop us at school in the morning on her way to the library."

"The library?"

"Yeah. She volunteers there three days a week now," Rachael said.

"When did she start doing this?" Michelle felt a little jealous.

"I don't know." Rachael shrugged. "About two weeks ago."

"Oh," was all Michelle could say. She was right: Everybody had a life except her.

"So can I spend the night?" Natalie asked again.

"I don't see a problem with it. Don't give Mrs. Parker a hard time."

"I won't."

"Rachael, are you going to look at cars with Natalie and her dad this weekend?" Natalie was so excited about the idea of getting a car, she was already planning her first road trip.

Michelle was surprised that Natalie agreed to all of the strict stipulations that she and Greg had set for her in order to get the car: She had to pay half of the insurance from her allowance, be in by ten o'clock on weeknights, keep her grades up and let them know where she was going and when to expect her back at all times. But Natalie gave her word that she would abide by the rules. Michelle still wasn't settled with the idea, but Greg insisted that everything would be okay and that they were only going to look—

not buy.

"I wouldn't dream of missing it," Rachael answered dramatically.

"You better not," Natalie teased.

"Rachael, did you enjoy the athletic banquet on Saturday?"

"It was the bomb."

"You girls looked beautiful. I made duplicates of the pictures you took here. I'll give you a set when I get them back."

"Thanks. At my house, my mom broke out the video camera. I don't know if it was the angle she was shooting from or the lighting, but Perry's head looked so big." Rachael laughed.

"Oh yeah?" Natalie shot back. "What about those moon boots Steve was wearing with his tuxedo? He said they were Timberlands. Yeah, right."

"I didn't see any moon boots. Which one was Steve?" Michelle asked.

"The ugly one," Natalie answered.

"And Perry is cute, with that big water head?" Rachael was laughing.

Natalie laughed too. "That's because he has a big brain."

"Oh, please." Rachael waved her hand at Natalie.

"Mom, I'm going upstairs to pack my overnight bag. See you."

"Bye, Mrs. Vaughn."

As the girls headed upstairs, Michelle heard Natalie say, "Girl, you're silly."

"You too."

More laughter.

As soon as Natalie's room door closed, the loud music came on.

"How can they stand being locked in a room with all that noise?" Michelle asked out loud. But there was no one to answer. She was alone again. She began cleaning the kitchen to prepare dinner.

*

Umi slid her shiny Mercedes into a parking space, checked her makeup and hair in the rearview mirror and headed toward the

Italian restaurant where her two best friends were waiting for her.

This had been their official celebratory meeting place ever since their high school graduation day. Of course it had been under new management twice and had three grand openings, but mostly everything was the same as it was the first time they were there. Every occasion called for a visit: when they graduated from college; when one of them started a new job; of course, when Michelle had Natalie and especially when one of them got a raise or a promotion. Even when there was no occasion to be celebrated, they found themselves back there just to be together and enjoy one another.

Umi entered the restaurant and spotted Michelle and Randi right away. She was so excited about seeing them, she almost ran to the table. "Hey, ladies!" She flashed them a huge grin.

She realized she hadn't seen Randi and Michelle in such a long time, when she noticed how different they looked. Randi, who usually wore her hair long, was sporting a nice short Halle Berry-ish cut and Michelle was a couple of shades darker, thanks to her recent trip to Bermuda.

"Hey, lady!" they sang out as Umi took her seat.

They hugged and kissed and carried on until the waiter arrived to take their order.

"How have you been?" Randi asked Umi.

"I'm okay—"

"Just okay?" Michelle interrupted. "You look better than okay. In fact you look great in that suit."

"You look great yourself." Umi blushed. "And you, Randi. I love what you did with your hair, girl."

"Thanks." Randi ran her fingers through her mane. "I'd look a whole lot better if I had your money," she teased.

"Money has nothing to do with it. All this is God-given." Umi raised her hands in a pose and laughed.

"Don't blame that mess on God," Randi responded with a chuckle. The silver hoops in her ears dangled wildly when she moved her head.

Umi could never understand why Randi enjoyed dancing on her nerves. "You're starting already?"

The waiter came and brought their salads.

"Umi, you look good, girl, but how do you feel?" Michelle started on her salad. "How are you holding up under these long hours you've been pulling?" Randi and Umi always accused Michelle of being the motherly one, and statements like that made her guilty as charged.

"I'm surviving." Umi shrugged. The last thing she wanted to do was get Michelle's motherly side revved up.

"I'm sure between all those long hours, you've found some time to play. It just hasn't been with us." Randi's eyebrows were arched high.

"For your information, I haven't had a lot of time for myself or anyone else," Umi said defensively. She knew Randi was going to start, but she wasn't expecting it so soon. Damn, she just sat down.

"Not even Darren?" Randi baited.

"Not even."

Michelle and Randi exchanged a glance that Umi picked up on.

"What?" Umi put her fork down.

"Nothing," Michelle said and filled her mouth with salad.

"Y'all talking about me behind my back, now?" Umi was beginning to get a little angry.

"No. Michelle just thinks that you have free time, but you're spending it with another class of friends."

"Wait a minute, Randi." Michelle put her fork down too. "I never said that."

"Then who said it?" Umi wanted to know.

Silence.

"I know you did, Randi," Umi concluded and picked her fork back up. She reminded herself not to trip. She already knew how Randi could be when she wasn't the center of someone's world.

By the time the main course arrived, Umi was off the defensive, Randi was satisfied that she got on Umi's nerves, and Michelle was enjoying the company.

"How are Greg and Nat?" Umi asked.

"They're fine. Greg wants to buy Natalie a car for her birthday," Michelle announced without a trace of excitement.

"Oh, good thing you reminded me." Umi reached in her bag and handed Michelle a sealed envelope. "This is for Natalie. A car, huh?"

"Go, Nat," Randi said.

"I don't like the idea, so this is only a trial run. We'll see how she handles the responsibility, then decide if she can keep it."

"And if she isn't responsible enough?"

"Then it'll be parked in the driveway until she learns to be."

"It sounds like a lot of freedom," Umi said.

"Yep," Randi said as she cut into her food. "Speaking of freedom, how have you been letting your freedom ring?" she asked Umi with a smile.

"What?"

"You said you haven't seen Darren or anyone else, so I'm interested in knowing how are you getting your groove on." Randi laughed.

"You are so nasty. Mind your business," Michelle scolded, but laughed too.

Umi could always rely on Randi to be a troublemaker. This time she would surprise her and take the bait. "You know, ladies," Umi lowered her voice and leaned in closer. "I can ring my own freedom bell."

"Umi, don't tell me you've resorted to that." Randi giggled. "I could never really get in to that."

Michelle kept quiet.

Umi was surprised to hear that remark coming from Randi. Of the three of them, she was the one with the insatiable sexual appetite. As for Michelle, she always kept her love life under lock and key. That was probably rule number one in the wives' handbook: Never discuss your sex life. Randi thought it was because there was nothing to tell. In her opinion, married people didn't have sex with each other, they had it with other people.

"What?" Umi raised her voice. "I don't need a man to do anything for me when I can do it better myself. Besides, I don't have time to waste a whole evening on dinner and conversation before I get to what I really want anyway. This way I can just cut out all that other stuff, get right to it and be in bed in time enough to catch my *Matlock* reruns."

Randi thought that was funny.

"Why should you care how she spends her time alone? Just because you don't enjoy it, doesn't mean she can't," Michelle told Randi.

"I know. I was just saying." Randi backed down.

"Umi, don't let Randi make you feel bad. Before I married Greg, I had a lot of lonely nights too. I understand where you're coming from." Michelle patted Umi's shoulder.

"But I'm not lonely. This is what I choose."

"Over a man?" Michelle asked. Even she couldn't understand that.

"Now, that's one I've never heard," Randi said, and they broke out in a hearty laugh.

When she caught her breath, Randi said, "I tell you, this is just like the good old days."

Michelle raised her glass in a toast. "To the good old days."

"The good old days," they toasted.

Randi took a sip of her wine and gave Umi a look. "We have to do this more often."

Umi glanced at her watch. "Oh, shoot. I'm going to be late for my four o'clock. Excuse me, y'all." She took out her cell phone and called Mr. Davis. She left a voice mail apologizing for her lateness and left instructions for him to call her.

"Ladies, I was enjoying myself so much, I lost track of time."

"Umi, we understand you have business to take care of. We're just glad you could make it," Michelle said.

"When are we going to see you again?" Randi asked.

"Call me, and I'll make time. I promise." Umi was already standing with her bag in her hand. "I'll speak to you later," she called over her shoulder and was gone.

"I'm worried about that girl," Michelle said softly.

"Mm hmm," Randi agreed and finished her drink.

Umi made it to the Olympic Towers in Midtown in about thirty minutes, but there was no sign of her client. She decided to wait a few minutes, then call to reschedule. Just as she was ordering herself a drink at the bar in the lobby, her cell phone rang.

"Ms. Grayson speaking."

"Hello, Ms. Grayson, this is Mr. Davis. I just received your message, and I'm a little confused. I got a call from your secretary saying you wanted to change the meeting to Tuesday, two days later."

Umi could feel herself beginning to boil. She had told Valerie two hours later, not two days later. "I apologize for the misunderstanding, Mr. Davis. It seems my assistant and I got our wires crossed, but Tuesday at any time is good for me."

How could Valerie do this? She knows how important Mr. Davis' account is. Calm down, Umi. Just do whatever you have to do to salvage it. She took a deep breath and dabbed her forehead with a napkin from the bar.

"Actually, Ms. Grayson, I had a little time to think your proposal over and decided to have another firm handle my account."

Umi couldn't believe her ears. "Oh, I see."

"I'll keep your card on file for future reference."

Umi wanted to tell him to shove the card up his ass. Instead she gracefully ended the conversation.

On her way home, she kept going over the whole scenario in her head. Rewinding it over and over to see where she went wrong. First she blamed herself: *I should have never rescheduled to have lunch with the girls. I should have said something to convince Mr. Davis to reconsider while I had him on the phone.* Then she laid the blame where it really belonged—on Valerie. Umi felt like calling her at home and firing her right then.

"Stupid! Stupid!" Umi hit the steering wheel with her fist and wished it were Valerie's head. She could feel the tears stinging her eyes. She blinked them back as she pulled into Carvel's and picked up a pint of pistachio ice cream to drown her troubles in.

*

Michelle neatly hung her suit on the back of the chair in her bedroom. She'd let it get some air before putting it back in the closet. Lunch with Randi and Umi made her nostalgic for the old times when hanging out together was a regular occurrence.

She remembered the first time they met back in Brooklyn at Boys and Girls High School in Bedford Stuyvesant. She and Umi were juniors, and Randi was a sophomore. That was when the most important things in life were passing classes and attending all the sporting activities since they were on the cheerleading squad. It was at cheerleading practice that they deemed one another best friends, and it had been that way ever since.

It was their different personalities, views and opinions that wove the very fabric of their friendship and kept them balanced. Randi was loud and rambunctious—you could count on her to be laughing loud in the hallways or saying something rude to a boy. Umi was constantly striving for perfection, needing to make the honor roll and wanting to maintain excellent attendance. She allowed herself to have fun along the way, but not too much. And Michelle was just plain old Michelle, middle of the road, average student and friends with practically everyone.

Umi, coming from her modest middle-class home on East Forty-eighth Street in East Flatbush, would take the Number 46 bus to Utica Avenue and Fulton Street, Randi would walk to school from her apartment building on St. John's Place in Crown Heights, and Michelle would take the J train from her two-family home on Woodbine Street in Bushwick, then transfer to the A train to get to Utica Avenue. And every day, without fail, they would meet in front of the school on the Fulton Street side, near Utica Avenue.

They would sit out by the tennis courts, laughing and talking until the bell rang for homeroom class. They usually saw one another during the day in the halls, and Umi and Michelle had economics together. But at the end of eighth period, they would always meet in the locker room to change for cheerleading practice together.

After practice, Randi and Umi would walk with Michelle to the A train. Then the two of them would walk up Utica Avenue together to St. John's Place where Umi would get the Number 46 bus back to East Flatbush and Randi would walk a few doors down to her apartment building. They had a routine and rarely deviated from it.

"Boy, that was a long time ago," Michelle said aloud, bringing her thoughts back to the present. Nothing much had changed. Randi was still a little on the wild side and loved a good argument. Umi, in all of her achievements, was still searching for perfection. And Michelle was still just plain old Michelle.

She examined her body in the three-way mirror inside the walk-in closet she shared with Greg. She was in pretty good shape for her age, a little thick in the middle, but her weight was perfect for her five-foot-six-inch frame. And the light-brown highlights she'd recently added to her hair blended well and complimented her walnut complexion.

Michelle heard Greg's car pulling into the driveway, so she slipped into a pair of leggings and a T-shirt and headed downstairs.

Natalie burst through the door, stopping her in her tracks. "Mom! Mom!"

"I'm right here. What are you screaming about?" Michelle was standing at the bottom of the stairs.

"Come out and see my new car!" Natalie was jumping up and down with a wide smile.

"You got the car?" Michelle hoped she sounded excited and not as worried as she felt.

"Yes!"

"Let me put my sneakers on. I'll be right there."

When Michelle got outside, Greg was bent under the hood of a light blue Honda Accord. Natalie and Rachael were sitting inside the car with the music blasting.

Michelle walked up behind Greg and patted him on his backside. "This is nice." Her voice was flat. Her fear and anger had her insides doing flip-flops.

"Thank you." He turned around with a smile on his face. "We got a good deal on it too."

"I thought you were only going to look." She raised an eyebrow.

Greg didn't answer, but gave her a look that told her not to start.

No problem. She decided to go along with the program for the moment and give him an earful later. "What year is it?"

"1990."

"That's ten years old. Is it going to be reliable?"

"The car is in pretty good shape," he assured her. "If you want we can take it by the garage and let Allen have a look at it."

Michelle huffed. "I hope you know what you're doing." She was excited for Natalie, but still didn't like the idea of her having her own car. She walked around to the driver's side. "This is nice, Nat."

"Mommy, can me and Rachael go to Manhattan for my birthday?"

Michelle ignored her. "Hi, Rachael."

"Hi, Mrs. Vaughn."

"Can we?"

"I'll think about it." Michelle didn't want to spoil Natalie's day by telling her no.

"Mommy, get in. Let's go for a spin."

"Where are we spinning to?"

"Let's go to Roosevelt Field," Rachael suggested excitedly.

Greg closed the hood. "Purring like a kitten."

"Daddy, we're going for a ride."

"Greg, you want to take a ride with us to Roosevelt Field, maybe treat the ladies to some ice cream?"

"Let's go."

"I better get my pocketbook." Michelle started toward the house.

"While you're in there, get my helmet. Natalie's driving." Greg laughed.

Greg was sitting in the passenger seat when she came back out, so Michelle sat in the back with Rachael.

Natalie adjusted her mirrors, buckled her seat belt and slowly backed out of the driveway. Before they even hit the highway, Michelle felt comfortable enough to close her eyes and snap her fingers to an R&B tune that was playing on the radio.

Rachael sat quietly and listened while Greg gave Natalie "helpful tips" the entire ride.

Natalie got them to the mall safely and pulled into a tight spot with skill and ease. Michelle was impressed, and Greg was so proud, he was beaming.

In the mall, Greg treated them to an early dinner as well as ice cream, then afterward insisted on going to Footlocker to look for something they never found, so they walked around in the store for a while and finally came out with sweatshirts and biking shorts for Natalie and Rachael. Michelle wanted to go to Nordstrom's and pick up a few Mac items, but they didn't have the colors she needed, so she ended up buying perfume for Natalie.

Nordstrom's wore Greg out, so they decided to head back to the car for his sake. Greg and Michelle walked hand-in-hand and the girls walked ahead eyeing every cute boy in the place. It reminded Michelle of the afternoons she spent in Kings Plaza Shopping Mall with Randi and Umi when they were teenagers.

"Michelle? I thought that was you."

Michelle turned and stood face-to-face with her new friend. "Gail, how are you?"

"Fine. Doing some shopping." She held up a Nordstrom's bag. "That's one of the benefits of working in the mall. My shop is not far from here."

"Gail, this is my husband, Greg; my daughter, Natalie; and her friend Rachael."

Everyone said a polite hello. Michelle and Gail chatted for a few minutes and made a date to meet at the gym the following week.

"I'll see you then."

"Okay, bye."

"Who was that?" Natalie asked when they were back in the car.

"I met her at the gym. She's in my aerobics class."

Twenty minutes later, Natalie was pulling up in front of Rachael's house.

"Good night, Mr. and Mrs. Vaughn. Nat, call me when you get home," she said as she got out of the car.

They've been together all day, what more could they have to talk about? Michelle wondered. She smiled and said, "Tell your mother I said hello."

CHAPTER 4

"Hello?" Randi answered the phone.

"Hey, baby," Brian answered. "How's my girl doing?"

His girl? He had some nerve. It had been two weeks since she last spoke to Brian. He didn't even have enough decency to respond to the messages she left for him, now he had the nerve to call like nothing had happened.

Randi started to hang up on him, but changed her mind. He was going to hear it from her, and he was going to hear it now.

"How do you think I'm doing?" She was enraged.

"You sound angry."

His innocent tone made her even madder. *Don't let it get to you,* she told herself in an effort to keep her cool. "Brian, there are some things we need to talk about." *Like you coming over here and getting your shit then getting the hell out of my life.*

"I'm glad you said that because I really need to talk to you too. Besides, I miss you, Randi." He slurred his words in the sexy way she loved so much.

Then why didn't you call? Drop a sister an e-mail? Put a message in a bottle? Damn. Something? She thought angrily.

She knew it was just a matter of time before she got this phone call full of bullshit and lame-ass excuses. She could hear Brian's mind racing like a computer, trying to come up with a valid reason for his disappearing act. She waited patiently for him to begin.

"Look," he started slowly, "I know you're upset that I didn't call sooner, but I just needed a little time to sort out a few personal things."

"Personal things, huh?"

"Yeah, I had a lot going on." He paused. "You don't want to

hear about all of that."

You were hoping I wouldn't want to hear it. "Yes I do."

He sighed heavily before speaking. Randi sat up on her bed, expecting to hear an old lie with a new twist, but she wasn't prepared for what came out of his mouth. True or not, she believed Brian when he said he had become comfortable with her and was willing to give what they had a chance to grow. That he needed the past two weeks to rid himself of the other women in his life, and to ensure that the process of detachment went smoothly.

Randi had already forgiven him by the time he explained that his sister told him she had called when he was out of town a few weeks ago, but he was afraid to call her back before he had a chance to prepare answers to the questions he knew she'd ask.

She was silent on line. Her mixed emotions had smothered her voice.

"You still there?"

"Yeah," she barely managed.

He continued, "Randi, the past few weeks were just a temporary inconvenience for a permanent improvement. I'm ready to step up and be the man you said you never had the pleasure of having. You probably don't even remember telling me that." His voice was deep and gentle.

She could have said that. She was so full of wine coolers the first time they hooked up she was talking nonstop. He didn't wait for her to answer. Randi guessed it wasn't really a question.

"I want you to know I was listening to you and I got the message loud and clear when you said you were tired of tired brothers and their tired games."

Like the game you're trying to run on me now? Randi had been in this situation before and knew better. The part of her that was still hurt and unwilling to forgive was coming to life. She found her voice. "Brian, you think I'm stupid?"

"Why do you say that?" His tone didn't change.

"First, you cancel two dates without an explanation, then you disappear altogether. Now you want to resurface and think we can just pick up where we left off. Don't disrespect me and don't insult my intelligence. Brian—"

"Randi."

"And don't cut me off. You, you—" She couldn't finish. Her

words were stuck in her throat, and tears were threatening to come forth. She wanted to believe that her eyes were filled with tears of anger, but again she knew better. She had broken one of her most important rules—never get emotionally involved.

Brian was silent on the other end.

"You hurt me," she said softly.

"I never meant to do that. I'm sorry." Randi had a tough exterior that he liked, but he wanted to see more of the soft side he was seeing now. "When can I see you? I want to hold you in my arms and make it up to you," he said sweetly.

Randi dried her face on her sleeve and let out a jagged breath. Even though she was still angry with him and he wasn't quite off the hook, she missed him and wanted to see him. So she told him that he could come over. Besides, they still had a lot to talk about, had some boundaries and rules to set if they were going to be spending time together.

Randi had to act fast. Brian lived nearby in a co-op on Willoughby Street and Myrtle Avenue, it would only take him about twenty minutes to get to her co-op on Carroll Street and Eighth Avenue. She jumped into a hot shower, slipped into a silky, hot-pink nightgown with matching panties and before she could completely pin her hair up and apply some makeup to her beige-toned face, her doorbell was ringing. The doormen in her building knew Brian, so his visits were never announced.

She opened the door with a big smile. "Hi." She posed sexily and eyed him seductively. He looked good.

He stepped into the apartment, closed the door behind him and without a word, he pulled Randi into his arms and kissed her deeply. His lips were soft and persistent, his tongue was playing around in her mouth, and his hands were all over her.

He broke their embrace, stepped away from her and looked at her from head to toe. "You are beautiful," he said softly.

Still smiling, Randi offered him a drink and slid her Anita Baker CD in the changer before taking a seat next to him on the sofa.

"So, what have you been up to?" Brian asked.

"Not much. Last weekend I had lunch with my girlfriends at the Seaport."

He smiled at her. "I missed you."

Randi recognized the hungry look in his eyes. She knew exactly what he missed.

Brian set his drink down and moved closer to her. He lifted her feet onto his lap and gently massaged them, then he lifted them to his mouth and gently kissed each toe on her left foot.

Randi giggled a little and relaxed. He felt so good that she forgot she was mad at him. She stood and removed her panties before straddling his legs. She was face-to-face with him. She let her tongue dance with his as she unbuttoned his shirt.

Brian returned her kisses with ones just as passionate, then picked her up and laid her on the sofa. He licked her stomach and thighs playfully, before reaching her sweet spot and letting his skills go to work.

Randi closed her eyes, sucked in her breath and released a long moan. Without interrupting her pleasure, Brian slid out of his pants and boxers and held himself tightly to ease his throbbing. Randi grabbed his ears, pulled him closer and thanked God before jerking away from him. Her chest was heaving up and down and her body was twitching from sheer delight. She welcomed the feel of Brian's body on hers as he slowly lowered himself on top of her.

His slow groove felt good, but Randi wanted more. She dug her fingernails in his butt, raised her hips up off the sofa to meet his and gave him a few jumbled instructions. Brian obeyed, moving faster and deeper with each thrust, until she let out a scream and they both went limp.

They were lying in each other's arms on the living room floor, had been there almost twenty minutes listening to the each other breath before Brian finally spoke. "Mmm, you were so good, baby." He gave her a little squeeze.

Randi snuggled closer to him. She was hoping they could go for round two after he rested a little. "Brian?"

"Hmm?"

"Don't go to sleep. You know how you are," Randi teased.

Brian laughed out loud and started stroking her hair.

She ran her fingers through the hair on his chest, then slid her hand down and massaged until she got a response. She lowered her head and began giving him an oral treat.

"Ohhh yes, Randi," Brian moaned and moved with her rhythm. He watched her closely and guided her head with his hand. Randi knew he wasn't going to last much longer and didn't want the fun to end without her, so she climbed on top of him, steadied herself and moved on him until her head felt light and she lost her balance.

She wanted to stop, but Brian wouldn't let her. He held her in place by her waist and thrusted deeply until he met up with her at that place.

When she finally stood, the room was spinning and her legs felt weak. She used the wall to help keep her balanced as she went to the bathroom and wet a hand towel. On her way back to the living room she snatched the comforter off her bed.

"Here." She handed him the towel and dropped the comforter on the floor.

"Thanks."

The clock on the VCR read 10:30. Tomorrow was Monday. She hated Monday mornings. Although she was a little tired, she didn't want to miss the opportunity to talk to Brian about what was on her mind. She returned to the comfortable spot next to him and immediately began dozing off. She stirred a little to keep herself awake.

"Brian?" She shook him a little, but there was no response. Randi pushed herself up on one elbow to look at him. He was sleeping like a baby. She kissed him on his cheek, then got up and went to bed.

The next morning, Randi jumped out of bed and headed straight for the living room. "Brian, would you like some juice before you go?" she called.

She noticed that he was gone and had left a note. She smiled as she read out loud:

SORRY I HAD TO LEAVE YOU, BUT I HAD TO RUN HOME AND
CALL MY MOMMY. SHE ASKED ME TO TELL HER THE
MINUTE I FELL IN LOVE.

LOVE, BRIAN

Love? Randi rushed to get dressed and leave for work. She was in such a good mood, she was actually humming on a Monday morning. What a wonderful way to start the week.

*

"Oh, my God, Greg, did you see that?" Michelle squealed and moved closer to her husband.

"I know you're not scared. It's just a movie."

"Look at all that blood!" Michelle pointed at the TV and shivered.

Greg laughed. "It's just a movie, Michelle."

"I can't watch this anymore." She buried her face in Greg's chest.

"Come on, it's almost over. This is the best part."

Michelle shook her head while it was still in his chest. "What time is it?"

Greg looked at his watch. "It's ten-thirty." A half hour after Natalie's curfew and she still wasn't home.

Michelle lifted her head to say something, but didn't get the chance because Natalie walked through the front door.

"Hi, Mom. Hi, Dad." She headed straight for the stairs.

"You're late," Michelle called out.

"I know." Natalie didn't stop.

"Come here, Natalie."

Natalie turned and came to sit on the arm of the loveseat facing her mother.

"Where were you?"

"At Rachael's house." Natalie's eyes went to the floor.

Michelle had a feeling she was lying. "You were late the first time because you were taking Rachael home and got stuck in traffic. Is that right?"

"Yeah."

"The second time you were late, you said you lost track of time at Rachael's house. Is that also right?"

Natalie nodded.

"Again, you're late because you were at Rachael's house. Did Rachael move? Because the last time I checked she only lived ten minutes from here."

"Fifteen."

"Ten, fifteen, whatever. It's a weeknight. You know the rules, Natalie. You've had that car two weeks, and you've already broken your curfew three times."

Natalie sighed loudly.

Michelle stood in front of her. "You want to get stink with me? I'll show you stink. This is your third strike, and you're out. From now on, I want you to come straight home from school and put that car in the driveway and don't move it until I say so."

"What?"

"You heard me. No car, no Rachael's house and nothing else."

"Dad." Natalie's eyes were pleading with him for help. He kept his eyes focused on the television.

Michelle continued, "I want you to clean that basement. You had friends over last weekend to celebrate your birthday and you haven't been back down there yet to clean it up. I want it done this weekend."

Natalie stormed up to her room mumbling under her breath.

Michelle went to the bottom of the stairs. "And clean that room up. Shoes and clothes are everywhere. You should be ashamed of yourself." Then she turned to Greg, "This is your doing, you know that."

"What?" Greg clicked off the TV and followed Michelle upstairs to their bedroom. "Don't get so bent out of shape. When the newness wears off, she'll be back to normal."

She picked up on the uncertainty in his voice. "She'll be back to normal now or that car will be parked in the driveway forever." Michelle's words were forceful. She got out her nightgown and started getting ready for bed. "She's lying to me."

"How do you know that?"

Michelle raised her voice. "I know something is not right. All this time at Rachael's house? I'm going to give Kate a call tomorrow and see if Natalie's really over there all the time."

"Now you're going to spy on the girl?" Greg kept his tone level.

"She could be hanging out with some boy. What if she's having sex?"

"Calm down." Greg leaned against the dresser and watched

Michelle as she changed clothes.

Michelle caught him staring at her and sucked her teeth. "What are you looking at?"

"You're beautiful when you're angry," he answered sweetly.

"Greg, be serious, please."

"I'm being very serious."

Why did he always do this? She bit her bottom lip to keep from completely melting under his stare.

He walked over and slipped his arms around her waist and kissed her neck and shoulder.

"Greg, I'm worried about her."

"Shhh, let me take your mind off that for a little while. They fell back on the bed in a heated kiss.

Maybe he's right, she thought and closed her eyes, giving in to his kisses.

After making love, Michelle snuggled against Greg under the covers. The coarse hair on his legs rubbed harshly against her clean-shaven legs and sensitive thighs. The sharp smell of his cologne, mixed with the sweet smell of her hair grease gave a familiar odor to the air in the room. She shifted her legs away from his.

"I love you," he whispered softly.

"I love you too." Michelle lowered her head from Greg's shoulder to his chest. "I had such a wonderful time with Randi and Umi last Sunday, but I haven't heard from either of them since," Michelle began.

"Yeah? I was surprised when you told me Umi was there."

"Randi finally got her to slow down long enough to eat with us. It's good to see her doing so well." Michelle sighed.

"You don't sound too happy."

"I'm a little worried about her working so hard. And I'm really concerned about the fact that we don't spend time together like we used to. I don't want us to drift apart from one another after all these years."

"I wouldn't worry too much about that." Greg tried to encourage her. "What about your new friend in your aerobics class?"

"Oh, Gail. We eat together after our workout, but other than that, I really don't speak to her."

Greg kissed the top of her head and hugged her a little tighter. Michelle felt safe in his arms and soon her eyelids became heavy and her breathing grew even.

Michelle sat straight up in the bed. The telephone ringing had scared her. The clock on the nightstand read 2:15. Who would be calling at this hour? She shoved Greg. "Answer the phone," she said sleepily and lay back down.

"Hello?" Greg said in his husky sleep voice.

"Yes," Greg answered and listened for a moment. "There must be a mistake. My daughter is here in bed."

Michelle heard this and sat up. "What is it?"

"Go check on Nat." He had worry in his voice.

Michelle ran down the hall to Natalie's room, but when she looked inside, Natalie wasn't in her bed. Fear shot through her so intense that it nearly knocked her off balance. She ran downstairs and called Natalie's name in the dark. No answer.

She ran back to her room. "Oh, my God, Greg. Nat's not here."

He was already up and putting his clothes on. "Natalie was in an accident with the car."

Michelle clung to the side of the dresser to steady herself as she registered his words. She wanted to say something, but couldn't make her mouth move.

"Put your clothes on!" Greg barked. "And meet me in the car," he yelled over his shoulder as he whizzed past her.

They were silent all the way to the hospital. Greg drove with a stern worried look on his face. Michelle prayed all the way that Natalie wasn't hurt too badly. *Lord, let it be a fender bender,* she begged silently. She glanced over at Greg from time to time and wondered what was going through his head. His eyes were glued to the road.

When they arrived at the emergency room, Michelle spotted Rachael's parents. "Oh, God, Rachael was with her."

She ran over and sat with them while Greg spoke to the doctors. The expressions on their faces told her they hadn't heard any good news, but she had to ask anyway.

"How are they?"

"They were hurt pretty badly," Larry Parker answered slowly.

He was bent forward with his elbows resting on his knees. He had a baseball cap in his hand, which he kept turning around and around.

Michelle felt herself going numb. In the car, she had prayed for strength and promised herself that she would try to hold up. She saw a tear escape from Kate Parker's eye.

"Did the doctors say what happened?"

"From the looks of it, they lost control of the car and it turned over a few times on Peninsula Boulevard." Larry stopped twirling his hat long enough to put his arm around his wife and comfort her.

Michelle couldn't understand how that could happen. Natalie was a good driver. Natalie was home in bed. She went over the story again in her head, but started getting a headache when all the pieces wouldn't fit. She started to recall the conversation she had with Greg, telling him that Natalie was too young to have her own car, and it had only been two weeks and already an accident had occurred. She shook the thought from her head. Now was not the time to place blame.

"Natalie was already home. Where was she going so important that she had to sneak out of the house and on Peninsula Boulevard of all places?" Michelle wondered out loud.

She thought she saw Kate roll her eyes, but wasn't sure.

Greg and the doctor came over to join them. "Hi, my name is Dr. Fitzpatrick. We are running some tests to make sure the girls are okay," the doctor started and glanced down at his chart for a moment. "It seems that Natalie Vaughn's injuries are more severe than Rachael Parker's, although both girls are hurt pretty bad."

"When will we know something more concrete?" Kate finally spoke up.

"I will be able to tell you more by morning, that's when I'll have the results from the blood work, the x-rays, and the cat scans. The—"

"Cat scans?" Michelle interrupted.

"Yes. That's just to ensure that the girls haven't sustained any head injuries."

"And if they have?"

"If they have, we have specialists here who can work on them immediately."

The doctor spoke in a gentle tone that seemed flat and rehearsed. To Michelle, he sounded like he was giving a serious lecture instead of speaking to distraught parents. She sized him up quickly and decided he couldn't be more than thirty and probably fresh out of medical school. She sat silently and listened.

"The girls will be out of surgery in a few hours. Let's see how they recover and then go from there. Right now all we can do is wait and hope for the best. I'll be back shortly." He started down the hall.

"What are they operating on?" Michelle asked Greg.

He looked away. Michelle followed his eyes, trying to meet his gaze. Greg stammered before coming up with, "a broken arm, a broken leg. Those kinds of things."

Michelle felt a little relieved. She knew it had to be more serious than that, but for right now that answer was enough for her.

After sitting in the hospital's coffee shop all night, around ten-thirty the next morning, Dr. Fitzpatrick finally told them that Rachael had been in a coma, but had awakened sometime that morning. She had two broken ribs and her left side had been severely damaged and some corrective surgery would be needed.

"I want to see her," Kate wailed through her tears.

"You'll be able to see her shortly," the doctor assured her, then turned to Greg and Michelle. "Natalie has suffered some head injuries and has not come out of her coma."

Michelle held Greg's hand tightly as the doctor delivered the news.

"Her injuries are a little more extensive."

"Like what?" Greg asked.

"During surgery, we discovered some broken ribs, a lacerated liver and her stomach had been pierced. These are not serious injuries by themselves, but when coupled with other things they can be pretty serious."

Michelle's heart was racing and she felt hot. She wiped her forehead with her free hand, but never took her eyes off the doctor. "How serious?"

"Possibly fatal. But we don't want to get ahead of ourselves. She did well in surgery and she responded well to the blood transfusion, which seemed to help a bit."

"Can we see her?"

"She's being moved from recovery to the intensive care unit. As soon as they get her settled, you can go in. It's on the fourth floor."

An Asian doctor approached them and waited for an introduction.

"Dr. Chow, I want you to meet Mr. and Mrs. Vaughn and Mr. and Mrs. Parker."

The gentlemen shook hands.

"Hello. I looked at your daughters' charts this morning. I saw them in recovery and they are both looking pretty good." His words seemed a bit more sincere and Michelle was surprised that he didn't have even the slightest accent.

"I'm going to be leaving now," Dr. Fitzpatrick announced. "Dr. Chow is wonderful, and he will be keeping you updated for now."

"Thank you, Doctor." Greg shook his hand and Larry followed.

Dr. Chow led the way to the third floor and down a corridor to Rachael's room.

They stood outside for a moment, then Larry turned to Greg and Michelle. "If you don't mind, we would like to see her alone."

"No problem, man. We understand." Greg patted his shoulder.

It wasn't until then that Michelle realized Kate hadn't said one word to her since they'd been at the hospital. Michelle couldn't recall Kate even looking at her. The thought quickly left her when the doctor told her and Greg to follow him to see Natalie.

When they reached the nurses' station and signed in, Michelle began to realize the seriousness of it all. The still quietness, the hushed voices, the humming of machines all made her feel disconnected from reality. But this was very real. The accident was real, the doctors were real and the possibility of Natalie not living was real.

Natalie's door was closed when they got there. Suddenly the door opened and a young black woman stepped out. She couldn't have been much older than Natalie.

She smiled warmly at Michelle and Greg. "I adjusted her IV

and got her more comfortable." She spoke only to the doctor then continued down the hall.

"I'll leave you two. If you have any questions, just ask one of the nurses at the station to page me."

Greg nodded and opened the door.

Michelle gasped when she saw all the machines and wires hooked up to her baby's body, and a small noise escaped from her throat. The bandage on Natalie's head came down and covered half of her left eye, which was puffy and discolored. Michelle felt Greg's hand shaking in hers.

"Oh, my God," was all he said. He leaned over her and kissed the fresh bandages on her forehead. Then he touched her hand softly.

Michelle wiped at her tears, but they kept coming. Soon she was completely blinded by them as she tried to keep her sobs hidden in her throat.

Greg hugged her tightly and let his own tears fall freely in his wife's hair.

*

It had been almost two weeks since she fired Valerie, and Umi was tired of answering phones and getting her own mail and coffee. She was especially tired of Valerie's threatening phone calls. First she was calling to beg for another chance, and when Umi didn't give in to her sobs, Valerie was stupid enough to think that threats would work. She really had nerve thinking she could keep a job with such poor work habits.

Umi was constantly bothering the other secretaries to type her letters and take a few messages for her, and when they refused, she had to do them herself. She tried to bait them by ordering lunch for the entire secretarial pool the previous Friday, and it worked for a short while, but they were busy facilitating work from their own executives, so it didn't last very long. In addition to all of this, Umi was interviewing people to fill Valerie's position.

Umi looked up when she heard a knock at the door. "Come in."

One of the secretaries stepped in. "Hi, Ms. Grayson, these are for you." She handed her a long white box tied with a big red ribbon. Umi knew right away what was inside.

"Thank you." Umi waited for the secretary to leave before reading the card. She smiled. Darren. She hadn't seen or spoken to him in weeks. She was surprised he was still interested in her.

Umi picked up the phone, dialed his office and waited for him to answer the phone.

"Thank you. They're lovely."

"So I have to send you flowers to get you to call me?" Darren teased, smiling.

"I'm sorry, I know I haven't been doing a good job at keeping in touch. Don't be mad at me," she said seductively.

"As a matter of fact, I am mad at you."

Umi loved playing little games like this. "Well, I'm going to have to do something about that." She knew he was turned on and that was exciting her. Umi started running her hands along her inner thighs and was about to get into a little phone sex when there was a knock at the door and a gentleman stuck his head in.

Umi jumped a little and tried to regain her composure, "Hold on a minute, please," she said in a professional tone before turning her attention to the young man in the doorway. "How may I help you?" she asked.

"Sorry I startled you," he said and stepped inside the office. He extended his hand. "My name is LaVelle King, and Executive Staffing sent me here regarding a secretarial position. I asked for Ms. Grayson and someone pointed me in this direction," he explained.

"Darren, I'm going to have to call you back." She put the phone down.

Umi stood and shook his hand. "I'm Umi Grayson." She gave him a warm smile. He was attractive, probably in his mid-thirties. She had never thought about a male secretary before, but she kind of liked the idea.

"So, Mr. King, do you have a résumé?"

He handed Umi a folder.

"Have a seat." She scanned his résumé briefly. It was nicely done, but wasn't very impressive. He had huge gaps in his employment history and had no work experience in the advertising field.

"I see it's been quite a while since your last job."

"Yes. I was in the army."

"Oh, where were you stationed?" Umi lowered the paper and made eye contact. He was very attractive—nice eyes and a beautiful smile.

"I was in Virginia for four years."

"I'm sure the agency has tested you extensively, but do you mind if I ask you to show me some things on the computer?"

"Not a problem."

He stood and followed Umi out to Valerie's old desk, where she got him set up at the computer.

The balance of the interview went fairly well. LaVelle had done excellent on the tasks Umi had given him. He was the best person she had interviewed so far. She liked him and thought he would make a fine addition to her team. *And he has been in the army, at least he'll be on time,* Umi thought.

"Thank you for coming in, Mr. King. I'll give the agency a call next week." She shook his hand and walked him to the elevators.

When Umi returned to her office, she entertained the thought of calling Darren back, but decided against it when she looked at all the work piled on her desk. She busied herself with the most important things first and worked straight through the day.

Her stomach was grumbling so loud, she wasn't sure if she heard a knock on the door, but when she heard it again, she glanced at her watch. It was 6:30 on a Friday evening. She thought she was alone.

She got up to open the door and was both surprised and delighted. "Darren, what are you doing here?"

"I know the workaholic you are, so I figured you'd still be here and would like something to eat." He held up a picnic basket. "Since I can never take you to dinner, I thought I would bring dinner to you." He smiled.

Umi stepped over to him and kissed him deeply. She had missed him so much that she wanted to swallow him whole. They stood awkwardly staring at each other. She broke the silence. "Where did you get all this stuff? A picnic basket this time of year?"

There's a nice deli near my office, and they had the basket with bread in it on display. I asked if I could have it and filled it with all of your favorite things."

"You are so sweet. Why are you so good to me?"

"Because you're special, and you deserve it." He kissed her lips.

"How did you get all this stuff here from the World Trade Center?" Umi spread out the blanket he'd brought with him and took a seat on one corner. She was impressed by his thoughtfulness.

"I grabbed the first taxi and told him to get me to the Empire State Building as fast as he could." Darren joined her on the blanket and started spreading out the goodies.

"He was going to drive as fast as he could, whether you asked him to or not," Umi joked.

They ate and talked about business, updated each other on mutual acquaintances and discussed their friendship in length. Darren wanted to know if it was going to go any farther. Umi wondered the same thing.

"It's been a year, Umi, and the more you play hard to get, the more I want you."

"It's not an act. I am very hard to get—not because I don't want you to have me, but my career is very important to me, and I don't want you to take that lightly." She took a sip of her wine.

"I know, baby. I can stand by you while you work your career."

"No, you can't." Umi swatted at him playfully.

"Why not?" He was serious.

"You say that now, but in a few months, you'll be singing a new tune."

"Do I have to remind you that it's been a year? I have given you plenty of space and opportunity. Now I'm laying my cards on the table." He took Umi's hand and stared into her beautiful eyes. "You are the woman I want to spend my days and nights thinking about and loving. I want to commit to you and your career." He smiled.

Umi laughed and gave him a big hug.

"Is that a yes?"

"Yes." She was filled with joy. "But let's take things slowly and let them happen naturally."

"Then let's naturally seal it with a kiss."

Umi allowed Darren to make sweet love to her on the picnic blanket on her office floor. She let herself go for a while and let Darren take control of her body, and it felt wonderful. His touch was tender and his moves magnificent as he took her to the height of passion over and over with his skill and creativity.

They relaxed for a while, enjoying the silence that surrounded them after a busy week. Umi didn't know what Darren had on his mind, but she was thinking about the major personal decision she just made to enter into a relationship that she knew she didn't have time for. But she wasn't going to worry about that right now. She'd just have to wait and see how long this relationship was going to last.

Darren paid for a taxi to take her home to Brooklyn and made her promise to call once she got there.

CHAPTER 5

Michelle sat on the edge of Natalie's canopy bed with her head buried in her hands. She had been in that same position for hours. She had gone in there to look through some of Natalie's things to try and figure out what she and Rachael were doing on Peninsula Boulevard Friday night, but her nerves were so shaken and she was so afraid of what she might find, she couldn't move.

It had been four days since the accident and neither of the girls was getting any better. Natalie still hadn't come out of her coma and Rachael was awake, but her jaw had been wired shut and she had to be fed through a tube. The poor girl looked so miserable when Michelle went to see her. She tried to stay awhile and cheer her up, but Rachael's tears flowed constantly, and Michelle had to leave before she broke down herself.

Greg was taking care of all the business. He arranged to have the tangled remains of Natalie's car removed and stored in case there was an investigation later. He had also been handling all of the transactions with the insurance company, and he stayed on top of what the doctors were doing at the hospital. He was aware of every move that was made and as usual, he was in control. Michelle was glad for that because she certainly couldn't focus on these things.

The accident was so horrific, that it was the top story on the news the entire weekend. A reporter from every radio and television news station was calling for an interview. Some were even persistent enough to come to the house and others took it a step further by showing up at the hospital, but she and Greg, as well as the Parkers, maintained their silence.

She overheard several stories about the accident on the news: one reporter said that it seemed the girls had been run off the road intentionally, another thought that foul play was involved. One reporter had the nerve to imply that her child was a wild teen driving recklessly. The reporters' speculations sparked a constant flow of phone calls, letters, fruit baskets, flowers, greeting cards and unwanted and uninvited guests wanting to express their compassion and asking about what *really* happened. So Michelle kept all of the televisions and radios off and told the postman to leave whatever he had on the doorstep.

Whatever the truth was, it had to be somewhere in Natalie's room and Michelle was going to find it. Just as she willed herself to stand and open the first drawer, the doorbell rang. Michelle closed her eyes and waited to see if the person would go away. When the bell rang a third time, she went downstairs to answer it.

She opened the door and was surprised to see Kate Parker. "Hello, Kate. Come in."

Kate's eyes were dark and swollen, and she was wearing an all-weather coat over a jogging suit and sneakers. She didn't have on any makeup and her hair was pulled back in a messy ponytail. She looked tired and worn down, pretty much the way Michelle felt.

"Hello, Michelle." She didn't make eye contact when she spoke. She stepped into the living room, and the two women stood awkwardly in silence.

"Have a seat," Michelle offered.

"I didn't come to stay." She adjusted her pocketbook on her shoulder and continued, "I just wanted to know if you were completely satisfied that you have destroyed my life."

"Excuse me?" Michelle's eyes narrowed.

"I didn't want to say this to you. I feel bad about what happened to our girls, but your daughter is not the angel you have made her out to be."

"What?" Michelle was starting to heat up. *Where was this coming from?*

"In fact, I should have said something sooner. Your daughter has been a bad influence on Rachael for the past year, if not longer. Rachael has been coming home late, and every time it's because she's somewhere with Natalie. She's been studying with Natalie, but her grades have been getting worse and worse. I—"

Michelle held up her hand, cutting her off. "Kate, let me tell

you something. Natalie couldn't make Rachael do anything she
didn't want to do. Natalie has been coming home on time and *her*
grades haven't been dropping," Michelle lied. The lie was more
for her than it was for Kate. Why hadn't she done something when
she saw the changes in Natalie's behavior?

"You can save that lie for yourself. Natalie is a sneak. She
pulled the wool over your eyes, but I saw right through her. One
day last week I went in Rachael's room to drop off some laundry,
and in the middle of the day, Natalie was asleep in my daughter's
bed. I bet you didn't know that."

Michelle was shocked, but tried not to show it. "What was
she doing there and why didn't you say something to me about
it?"

"She begged me not to tell on her and said she was there
because when she came to pick up Rachael for school, she suddenly felt too sick to go herself."

"Then where was Rachael?"

"My daughter took Natalie's car and was in school, where
she should have been."

Michelle couldn't believe her ears. Who did Kate think she
was? Lying—and right to her face in her own house.

Kate wasn't finished. "You spoiled that girl. You gave her
everything except a good dose of common sense. I blame myself
for not speaking up sooner, for not separating those two when I
saw Natalie leading Rachael down the wrong road."

"Kate, don't make Natalie out to be a villain and Rachael a
victim. No matter what you say or where you place the blame to
make yourself feel better, Rachael is just as wrong as Natalie.
Whatever they were doing that night, they were doing it together.
Believe it."

Kate pointed her finger in Michelle's face. "Hide from the
truth if you want to, Michelle. You've created a monster, one that
has changed our lives forever."

Michelle had had enough. "Get out, Kate." She opened the
door and waited. "And the next time you feel bold enough to step
in my house and call yourself putting me in my place, I advise you
to think about it first."

Kate moved toward the door and spoke softly, "Michelle, I
love you like a sister. We have been friends for a very long time,

and I would never say anything to intentionally hurt you. The truth will come out sooner or later and when it does, I'll be waiting for your apology."

Michelle rolled her eyes and slammed the door. "Bitch!"

Now she was really scared and confused. Michelle took a seat on the sofa and wondered if Kate was right. She told Greg the night of the accident that she thought Natalie had been lying to them. If only she had followed up on her suspicions.

Physically exhausted and emotionally spent, Michelle took a couple of aspirin and lay down on the couch with an ice pack on her head and tried to let her mind go blank for a while. She was spending a lot of time at the hospital and when she came home to rest, she couldn't.

Michelle sat up when the door opened. "Greg?"

"Yeah?" Greg walked in the room and dropped in the chair as if his body weighed a ton. He was in his gym clothes and reeked of sweat and beer.

He was at the gym? Inconsiderate. She put her feelings on hold in order to tell him about Kate's visit. "Kate was here today."

"What did she want?"

"She had the nerve to blame the accident on Natalie."

"What?" Greg's forehead wrinkled, the way it always did when he was about to get mad.

She replayed the conversation and stopped from time to time to let Greg vent.

After telling Greg the story, she felt a little better. Greg comforted her and helped ease her worry a bit by pointing out that Natalie wasn't reckless, and anyone who knew her would say the same. He also reminded her that no one knew what happened the night of the accident and whatever Kate said was purely speculation.

"I have to get a shower." He stood.

"Where were you?" she asked, even though she already knew.

"I was at the hospital with Nat, then around one o'clock I met Allen at the court to shoot some hoops."

"To shoot hoops?" Michelle had an edge in her voice.

"Yeah. It helps me blow off steam, relax."

"While you were off playing ball with Allen, did it ever occur to you that I might need you here or that Natalie might need you at the hospital?"

"Don't start, Michelle. I don't feel like doing this."

"Doing what, Greg?" Michelle stood in front of him. "Why didn't you tell me you were going to play ball before you went? You know why? Because you know you shouldn't have been there." She answered her own question.

"No. Because I don't have to check with you every time I make a move." He walked past her and headed upstairs to their bedroom.

Michelle followed close behind. "No, you don't have to check with me, Greg. You wouldn't listen to me anyway, just like buying Natalie that car."

"If it hadn't occurred to you, this same accident could have happened even if she was driving one of our cars."

"How could she have gotten the keys in the middle of the night if we had them? You don't listen to me! You never listen to me! This whole thing could have been avoided if you didn't always have to play Big-Shot Dad and give Nat everything she asked for!"

Michelle was breathing hard. She met her husband's stare and held it. Greg was at least two shades darker than her, but right now he was beet red.

"Are you saying what happened to Nat and Rachael is my fault?" Now he was standing in her face.

He stood an entire foot over her and was a hundred pounds heavier. Up close, she had to hold her head back in order to look in his face. Michelle stepped away from him. For a split second, she actually thought Greg was going to hit her. She had to think before she answered. *Was that what she was saying?* She felt tears on her cheeks.

"All I'm saying is that you wanted her to have the damn car. I said it wasn't a good idea."

"So it's my fault," he repeated and stormed out of the room.

She went behind him and stopped at the top of the stairs when she heard the front door slam. She knew he was gone and sank to the floor in tears. This was the second time a man had walked out on her when she needed him the most.

*

Randi was weaving in and out of evening rush-hour traffic on the Southern State Parkway trying to get to Michelle's house. She had been so busy over the weekend that she didn't know anything about Natalie's accident until Umi called her at the office that morning. She was shocked and concerned for Michelle. She wanted to leave work that very minute, but she was on deadline with an assignment and couldn't, so she told Umi to meet her at Michelle's at seven.

Her week had been so packed with adventure she could hardly stand it. For starters, Brian called her every day at work to tell her how much he missed her and couldn't wait to see her. On Wednesday he stopped by and surprised her with food from her favorite Japanese restaurant. And to top it all off, he surprised her Friday night, by sweeping her off to enjoy a weekend in the Pocono Mountains.

The entire weekend was filled with romance and adventure. They rented a chateau in the mountains, complete with a private pool, Jacuzzi, Swedish sauna and a heart-shaped bed. Saturday evening they saw a stage performance of *Romeo and Juliet* in a nearby theater and enjoyed a romantic candlelit dinner for two. The evening was so special, she thought she might bust wide open and tell Brian she loved him and would have his babies.

Sunday morning they had breakfast in the chateau. Brian wanted to get an early start back to the city, so they checked out a little after eleven to head back to New York. On their way, Brian spotted an apple orchard and wanted to stop for a few minutes. Yeah, right, a few minutes? He had her climbing trees and picking apples in the cold for almost three hours. When they finally got home, Randi was so sore she needed a full-body massage.

Brian stayed at her apartment for a while after he dropped her off, and then went home to prepare for work the next day. Once he was gone, Randi ran a tub of hot water, poured in some Epsom salt and stayed there until the water became cool. When she finally got in the bed, she was asleep before her head even hit the pillow.

Now she was on her way to comfort Michelle. Randi pulled in behind Umi's Mercedes and practically ran to the front door. After she rang the bell, she bent down to pick up some of the mail and sale circulars that had accumulated.

Umi opened the door. "Hey."

"Hey, lady. What's up?"

"Nothing." Umi helped her bring in the mail.

"How long have you been here?"

"A few minutes."

"I was stuck on the Southern State." The smell of fruit and flowers filled her nostrils before she was fully in the house. "Smells good in here. Where's Michelle?"

"She was asleep when I got here, so she went to take a shower and put some clothes on."

"How is she?" Randi followed Umi into the kitchen.

"I can't tell yet. I'm making some peppermint tea. Want a cup?" Umi offered.

Randi took a whiff of the rising steam. "Heck, yeah. That smells good."

"And it tastes even better. I bought it with me because I read that it's a relaxant."

Randi got the mugs, spoons and sugar bowl and arranged them on the table. Umi brought over the teakettle and set it on a trivet and took a seat.

"How have you been?" Umi asked.

Randi wanted to jump at the opportunity to tell Umi about her weekend with Brian, but thought it might be a little selfish to start bragging right then. "I'm okay. I've been spending a lot of time with Brian." She smiled big and moved her eyebrows up and down.

"Well, well." Umi smiled.

"Hey, ladies," Michelle said softly as she entered the kitchen and took a seat at the table. She looked tired.

"Hey, lady." Umi hugged her across the table and Randi followed.

"How are you feeling?" Randi asked.

"I don't know. I haven't felt anything for the last few days."

"Poor thing," Randi said.

Umi filled Michelle's mug with tea. "Try this. It might help you feel a little better."

"How did y'all find out about the accident?"

"I heard it on the news last night and called Randi immediately to tell her about it."

"What happened?" Randi asked.

"You don't have to talk about it if you don't feel like it, sweetie." Umi rubbed Michelle's forearm and flashed Randi an annoyed glance for being so thoughtless.

"There's nothing to talk about. I don't know what happened either. The car was wrecked, the girls were hurt."

Randi couldn't resist, even with Umi's warning. "How?"

"Randi, I wish I knew. Natalie came home after curfew, I yelled at her about it, she went to her room and slammed the door. The next thing I know the phone was ringing and someone was telling me my child was in the hospital."

"Oh, my God." Umi put a hand to her mouth.

"Not Natalie. Sneaking out?" Randi said in disbelief.

"That's what I thought," Michelle said, "but Kate thinks otherwise."

"Who's Kate?"

"Rachael Parker's mother."

"Oh, Lord, don't tell me Rachael was with her." Umi prayed out loud.

Michelle nodded. "Kate was over here earlier and blamed the whole accident on Natalie."

"The nerve," Umi declared angrily as she sipped her tea.

"That's not all. She said that Nat was a sneak and a bad influence on Rachael."

Randi sucked her teeth. "We should go over there and beat her smart ass."

Umi gave Randi a don't-be-stupid look. "Michelle, don't listen to Kate. That was just hurt and anger talking. She's just as confused as you are, and she's looking to place the blame on something or someone. I'm sure she didn't mean it."

Randi rolled her eyes at Umi and wondered when she got her social worker's degree.

"I'm not so sure, Umi." Michelle shook her head sorrowfully.

"About what?"

"I told Greg before the accident, that I thought Natalie might be lying to us or hiding things from us."

"She's a teenager. Teenagers don't tell their parents everything," Randi reasoned.

"No. I mean her behavior was changing. She was coming in late, her grades were slipping and she had a huffy attitude when I scolded her. Things like that."

"That doesn't sound like the Natalie I know," Umi said softly.

"What do you think it is, Michelle?" Randi asked.

"I thought she might be having sex, but I really don't know."

"What does Greg think?"

"Who knows? He's not saying much. Anyway, we had an argument earlier, and he's been gone ever since."

"He probably just went to cool his head. Y'all really don't need to be arguing. This is the time to stick together," Umi said.

"I know," Michelle agreed.

"So you've been here all by yourself?" Randi asked.

"Yeah, but my mother will be arriving some time tomorrow."

"That's good," Umi said as she finished her tea.

"Did you check Nat's room?" Randi asked.

Michelle shook her head.

"Then what are you waiting for?" Randi stood. "We'll help you."

"You don't have to if you're not ready." Umi gave Randi another warning with her eyes.

"The answers she's looking for are right upstairs," Randi said, answering Umi's glance.

After a long silence, Michelle agreed, and they headed upstairs.

Natalie's room was kind of small, but she had so much stuff in it, for the first few minutes they just stood around looking.

Finally Umi spoke up. "Okay. This is going to be a big job. I'll take the dresser; Michelle, you do the closet; and Randi, start on the chest of drawers."

After doing a dual job of searching and cleaning, the women came up with nothing out of the ordinary. Randi found a phone book and thought that Michelle should call some of the numbers in it and see what she can come up with. Michelle hit the jackpot when she found a shoe box in the rear of the closet with lacey panties and condoms inside. That only confirmed that Natalie was having safe sex, which was what Michelle thought anyway. Umi came up empty-handed.

They were exhausted and sat down for a rest. Michelle sat Indian-style at the foot of Natalie's canopy bed, Umi was at the head of the bed with her feet hanging off the side and Randi had stretched out on the floor.

"What time is it?" Randi asked.

Umi glanced at the alarm clock on Natalie's nightstand. "Almost eleven o'clock."

"No wonder I'm so tired. It's past my bedtime." Randi yawned. "I think I'll take a personal day tomorrow."

"You should spend the night," Michelle offered.

"I'm glad you said that, because I can't hack that ride back to Brooklyn tonight."

"What about you?" Michelle asked Umi.

"Girl, I can't take any time off. My new assistant is starting on Wednesday, and I need to prepare some things for him."

"Tomorrow is Tuesday. And what new assistant?" Randi asked.

"I fired that silly girl Valerie. An agency sent someone over to interview for her position. His name is LaVelle."

"LaVelle?" Randi and Michelle said in surprise.

"Yes, girl, and he is a fox." Umi started kicking her feet with excitement.

"That name reminds me of LaVelle Drew from Boys and Girls. Remember him, with those thick glasses?" Randi started laughing on the floor.

"And that stink coat he used to wear in the winter?" Umi said.

"Oh, God, all four winters we were there." Michelle laughed too. Her first real laugh in days.

"Umi?" Randi called from the floor.

"Huh?"

"Your feet stink."

They started laughing again. "Shut up, you liar."

"Girl, you're a mess," Michelle added.

"Damn, Natalie has more shoes than me." Randi was looking under the bed.

"Pull them out from under there and put them in the closet with the other ones."

"I can't reach those boxes. You have to pull the bed out,

they're against the wall."

"Shoes or shoeboxes?" Umi asked suspiciously.

Randi didn't answer, she sat up and they looked at one another.

Michelle was the first one on her feet. "Help me move this bed."

They pulled the bed out and set the shoeboxes in the middle of it.

Michelle was taking her time, so Randi snatched the lid off the smaller box and they sat in amazement. There was a 45-revolver and wads of money neatly stacked and held together with rubberbands.

Umi whispered, "Oh, my God."

Michelle had already figured drugs had to be in the other shoe box, so she wasn't quite as shocked when she removed the lid and saw small Ziploc bags filled with marijuana.

"My baby? A drug dealer?" Michelle shook her head. Guilt so strong came over her she started crying. "Why?"

"Oh, Michelle, don't do this to yourself." Umi wrapped her arms around her.

Randi moved back to her spot on the floor. She didn't want to get emotional. "Michelle, you couldn't have known."

"Why couldn't I? If I had been paying more attention to her, I would have seen this happening. Right in my own house, right underneath my nose, and I didn't have a clue." She sniffled.

Umi rocked her softly. "Don't beat yourself up about it, Michelle. You are a wonderful mother, and you and Greg have done a great job raising Nat. Now, I know there is a reasonable explanation for this, and when Natalie recovers and gets home, she's going to sit her butt down and explain it."

"Umi, this is self-explanatory. My child is a drug dealer and possibly a user." Michelle moved out of Umi's embrace and went to the window. Her next-door neighbor's children were raking leaves together in their backyard. They were playing around and scattering more leaves than they gathered. When their playful laughter reached her ears, it sent a pain so sharp to her heart she had to squeeze her eyes shut to keep from doubling over. Michelle turned from the window, and tuned in to the conversation in the room.

"Maybe she was holding this stuff for somebody, and it does-n't even belong to her," Randi said from the floor. "You know, guys get their girlfriends to hide things for them all the time."

"That's true," Umi agreed.

It did make sense. Michelle thought for a minute. "You're right. That could be it. She was probably just holding it for some-body." But that didn't make her feel any better. At this point, noth-ing would. She was having trouble believing that her daughter would be involved with drugs or drug dealers. She had taught Natalie better than that or at least she thought she had.

"Let's put this stuff away." Umi covered the shoeboxes.

"Don't say a word of this to anybody, until we get a chance to talk to Natalie about it," Michelle said wearily.

The ladies agreed to keep silent and put the shoeboxes back under the bed.

*

It had been a month since they found the drugs in Natalie's bedroom, and it had been eating away at them.

Umi finally agreed to spend the night that Monday and had returned to Michelle's house at least twice a week since then. She was worried about Michelle and wanted to stay near her while so much was going on. She also enjoyed all the good food Michelle's mother was cooking up every night.

Meanwhile, Brian wouldn't give Randi a break. She had dropped by Michelle's three times since that Monday night and the last time, Brian came with her. Umi thought that was inap-propriate and said something to her when they were alone.

Michelle wanted to know what Natalie was hiding, and now that she knew, she seemed to be in a worse state of mind. She couldn't eat or sleep, was very withdrawn and even stopped going to the hospital.

To make matters worse, Greg had not been home since their argument. This made Umi mad enough to bite nails, but when Michelle mentioned his absence, Umi made excuses for him, by telling her friend that men handled emotional situations differently and encouraged her to be patient and strong. As far as they knew, Greg was staying with Allen, but found ways to come home to pick up clothes, stay at the hospital with Natalie and handle all of their business, while craftily avoiding Michelle.

Grace, Michelle's mother, had seen him at the hospital once and tried to convince him to come home, but was unsuccessful. She told Umi and Randi that he was so angry he was on the verge of tears. And to top it all off, there was no change in Natalie's condition. Although Rachael seemed to be coming around a little, she still had a feeding tube and was very weak.

The only thing that seemed to be going right was LaVelle King. He was perfect from the start—always punctual and polite, and he did everything Umi asked without a word of complaint. He was beginning to stir up a little fan club among the other secretaries, but he acted as though he didn't notice them falling all over one another trying to talk to him or show him where things were in the office. One day, Umi stood by amused while she watched three women show him how to remove a simple paper jam from the copier.

"Come in," Umi called in response to taps on her office door.

LaVelle stuck his head in Umi's office. "Good morning, Umi."

"Good morning." Her desk clock read 8:45. Early as usual. The thought delighted her.

"Can I get you something?"

"No, thank you. I've already helped myself." She nodded toward her coffee mug.

"Okay." And he disappeared leaving the door slightly ajar.

Umi could see LaVelle at his desk, having his breakfast and attending to a few light tasks. He clicked away at his keyboard for a few minutes, and then opened his memo pad—the one he used for his shorthand notes during dictation. He began typing again, when the phone rang and interrupted him.

"Good morning, Ms. Grayson's office. Hello? Hello?" He quietly returned the phone to the base and continued working. During the month he had been working for Umi, the hang-up and crank calls from her old secretary Valerie were a frequent occurrence.

"Hi, LaVelle. Are you working on anything now?" Umi flashed him a grin as she approached his desk. She couldn't help but notice how attractive and masculine he looked sitting behind his desk. Him being her secretary had made her team the talk of the office again.

"I'm finishing up the minutes from last week's team meeting."

"Oh, good. When you're through, I'd like to send a fax to Mr. Dagwood, and please send his secretary a fruit basket or something thanking her for her help last week."

"Okay."

Umi retreated to her office, where she was finally relaxing. After Valerie caused her to lose one of the most impressive accounts she'd ever worked on, she was spinning her wheels playing catch-up. Finally, this account with The Dagwood Corporation was coming through for her, and she needed it to regain her footing in the advertising industry. She practically worked Mr. Dagwood's secretary to death the week before having her find and e-mail inside information to her about Mr. Dagwood and his corporation. Having pertinent information was essential when trying to win someone's account, and who could help her out better than his secretary, who just happened to be a sister who had worked for him for ten years.

Umi stepped out to have lunch and when she returned, LaVelle was already back and working at his desk. That alone made her smile. "Hi, LaVelle."

"Hi, Umi. This envelope came from The Dagwood Corporation." He handed it to her and watched her face light up.

Umi wanted to jump up and down. The big thick envelope from Dagwood was a good sign, but she kept her excitement contained and her voice even. "Thank you, LaVelle. Things are finally looking up with this account."

She started toward her office, then turned suddenly. "Uh, LaVelle,"

It took a moment for his eyes to travel upward and meet her stare.

So, he's checking out my ass, huh? Umi was almost flattered.

LaVelle finally closed his gaping mouth and innocently tucked his lips inward and waited for her to continue speaking, but she couldn't remember what it was she wanted to say. The silence between them lingered for a moment, before the phone rang.

LaVelle reached for the receiver, "Good afternoon, Ms. Grayson's office."

Silence.

"Certainly, hold one moment, please." LaVelle put the call on hold. "Mr. Dagwood is on the line." His eyes barely met hers. "Thank you." Umi rushed to her office to take the call. Afterward, she read through her mail, saving the Dagwood envelope for last. She was disappointed when she opened it and only found hard copies of the things his secretary had e-mailed her.

*

At his desk, LaVelle was trying to get over his embarrassment. He couldn't believe she busted him. The phone rang again. He answered, repeating the standard greeting.

"Ms. Grayson, please."

"May I ask who's calling?"

"Valerie."

"I'm sorry, Ms. Grayson is unavailable," LaVelle lied. "Would you like to leave a message?" He was trying to be as professional as possible, but Valerie's constant calling was getting on his nerves.

"This shit is beginning to irk me. Why won't she take my calls?" Valerie said. "You're lying. I know she just came back from lunch."

"What?" LaVelle was shocked.

"That's right. I'm watching her and I'm watching you too." Valerie slammed the phone down in his ear.

LaVelle placed the receiver back in the cradle. Umi warned him about how crazy Valerie might get. He considered telling Umi, but decided he could handle Valerie's idle threats. Besides, he didn't want Umi worrying about Valerie, when she really needed to be focusing on her accounts.

RRRIIINNNGGG.

LaVelle glanced at his watch, the day was only half over, and he already felt a headache coming on. He answered the phone repeating the standard greeting for the hundredth time.

"Good afternoon, Ms. Grayson, please."

LaVelle recognized the voice, but decided to ask anyway.

"May I ask who's calling?"

"Darren Alexander."

"Hold on, please." LaVelle didn't particularly like Darren. Although they only met once, it was enough for LaVelle to deem him superficial and conclude that Umi could have done better. He didn't know whose call annoyed him more, Valerie's or Darren's.

CHAPTER 6

Michelle was in bed with the covers pulled up to her chin, flipping through television channels. She had no energy and simple things were getting harder and harder for her as the days went by. Getting out of bed in the morning was a chore all by itself, and eating and keeping the food settled in her stomach was another battle. She had already stopped taking daily showers—every two or three days was the most she could handle. Leaving her bedroom for long periods of time was also out of the question. She hadn't been downstairs in more than a week, and she hadn't been out of the house even longer than that. Her mother arrived and took charge of the house in addition to taking care of her and visiting Natalie every day.

Grace stuck her head in the door. "Baby, I see you're awake."

"I'm up, Mama." Michelle didn't move her eyes from the television.

Grace stepped inside with a tray of food. "I brought you some Cream of Wheat and sliced pears." She set the tray on the side of the bed and took a seat as she steadied it.

"I'm not hungry."

"I know you don't feel hungry, but I want you to try just a little bit of this for me."

This was their morning ritual. Grace tried to get Michelle to eat. Michelle refused. Grace persisted. Michelle finally gave in.

Michelle sat upright in the bed and Grace helped her position the tray in front of her and she took in some of the creamy hot cereal. It felt warm in her mouth, but she couldn't taste the cereal itself or any of its ingredients.

Grace was sitting on the empty side of the bed. Michelle knew she was being monitored and continued eating slowly. She was glad her mother had rushed to her side as soon as Michelle told her what had happened to Natalie. Her mother didn't hesitate to leave her home in Jacksonville, Florida, where she lived in a beautiful retirement community, when Michelle called crying. Grace told her she'd set her lights on an automatic timer, ask her neighbor Edna to look after her flower gardens and be on the first thing flying to New York.

"I can't eat any more of this, Mama." Michelle moved the bed tray away from her.

She had eaten most of the hot cereal. "Well, you did pretty good, sweetie. That should hold you over until this afternoon when I fill you up with my chicken soup." Grace's voice was light and cheery as she removed the tray.

"Thank you, Mama." Michelle patted her mother's hand. "Thank you for taking care of me."

Tears almost escaped from Grace's eyes, but she blinked them back. "Let's try to get you in the shower and open a couple of windows in here."

"I don't have the energy to take a shower."

"A shower will revive you. Besides, if you don't get a shower soon, you'll be smelling a bad as your uncle Freddie that time he got drunk and messed on himself at your aunt Hazel's house."

"Oh, Lord, that bad, Mama?" Michelle let out a small giggle.

"If not worse." Grace had already raised the Venetian blinds and cracked two windows facing the houses across the street.

Michelle made it through the shower and slipped on some fresh leggings and a T-shirt. She was heading back to bed, but her mother stopped her and made her go downstairs and sit with her in the kitchen.

Grace had the back door open and CD 101.9 was sending smooth jazz over the airwaves. The sun was shining brightly and a cool breeze was blowing through the kitchen. "I'm in the mood to play some cards."

The deck was sitting on the table next to Grace. If Michelle knew her mother, she was probably downstairs playing Solitaire or Hearts every chance she got.

"How about a good game of Gin?"

Michelle shrugged her shoulders. "I'm not in the mood for

cards."

"Well, playing Gin with you is not exactly what I would call a good game anyway."

Michelle knew she was being set up, but just couldn't resist. "What is that supposed to mean?"

Grace grinned slyly.

"Get the cards," Michelle said flatly. "Gonna tell me I can't play Gin. If I remember correctly, it was me and Daddy who taught you how to play."

"And I've been beating you ever since." Grace smiled.

"Deal, please."

Grace and Michelle played Gin all afternoon. First, they played just for sportsmanship, but when Grace kept up a good game and a lot of trash talking, Michelle wanted to gamble. So Grace convinced her to play for Ritz crackers. Before they knew it, Michelle was eating almost as much as she was winning.

"I need some juice." Michelle put her hand to her throat.

"Don't change the subject because you're losing. Just deal. I'll get the juice." Grace stood. "And I'm watching you." She playfully wagged a finger at her daughter.

"You're only ahead by three crackers, and I don't need to cheat, I'm going to beat you fair and square." Michelle shuffled the cards and dealt them.

Grace turned a low fire on under her pot of chicken soup before she sat back down. "Let me see what I have here." She picked up her cards and arranged them in her hand.

Playing cards with her mother somehow removed Michelle from the present and swept her back to their old house in Brooklyn, where she grew up and card playing was a regular weekend activity for her and her parents.

Her mother was a middle-school math teacher and used playing cards instead of flash cards to teach Michelle simple arithmetic. That was because Michelle's father was a gambling man. He wasn't a reckless gambler, but one of the few who knew how to make a healthy sport of it. He knew his limitations—knew when to step away from the table and quit.

Her father was a kind man, with soft eyes and an easy smile. He was murdered during a card game in a small gambling hall when Michelle was only ten years old. He wasn't actually playing in that particular game. He already had his winnings in his pockets from earlier games, but was hanging around when a heated argument erupted between two of the players. One man pulled out his gun and fired, hitting her father in the chest and killing him.

Her mother kept his memory alive in their house by always keeping a good game of cards going. Michelle figured it was her mother's way of staying close to him—it was her way as well.

For almost a whole day, she didn't think about death, drugs, missing husbands, sick daughters or car accidents. Instead, she felt comforted by the memories of her childhood and the safety of her mother's care. It was ironic, the relationship she had with her mother, how her mother knew just what she needed and when she needed it and as a mother herself, she could let so much go unseen with her own daughter.

The next morning Michelle was up early. She showered and put on her favorite old blue jeans and sweatshirt and headed downstairs to have breakfast with her mother.

"Good morning, Mama."

Grace smiled at her daughter. "Good morning, honey. I'm glad to see you up and around." They greeted with a kiss. "I hope you have an appetite because we can't let these grits, eggs and sausage go to waste."

Michelle closed her eyes at the wonderful thought of a solid breakfast. "Mmm, that sounds good." She poured two glasses of juice and set the table for her and her mother.

"I put some of those biscuits from last night in the oven. They should be ready. Get them out and butter them for me."

Michelle did as she was told and by the time she sat down at the table, Grace had already filled their plates and was waiting to bless the food.

In the middle of breakfast, Grace said what had been on her mind for the past few days. "Michelle, I was thinking that maybe you would like to go with me to see Natalie today," she started.

Silence.

Grace finally looked up when she didn't get a response.

"Where have I gone wrong?" Michelle choked out through

her sobs.

"Oh no, sweetie. You haven't done anything wrong." Grace stood and brought Michelle over to the sofa. Grace held her daughter in her arms just as she had years ago. "You haven't done anything wrong. You're a wonderful mother and wife."

"Then why is my happy home being torn apart? My good husband is never home anymore. My beautiful daughter is lying on what could be her deathbed and pitiful old me, I need my mother to take care of me like I'm a two-year-old." Michelle stopped to catch her breath and wipe at her tears. "It's just not fair. What have I done to deserve this?"

It broke Grace's heart to see her daughter like this. Struggling to hold back her own tears, she managed a calm and gentle tone as she spoke, "I want you to listen to me. This is not your fault. Right now it's important for you to keep positive thoughts and a prayerful spirit. I'm not going to let you have a pity party and walk around here feeling sorry for yourself."

"Nobody knows how I feel." Michelle spoke into her mother's soft chest.

Grace gently rubbed her daughter's back as she spoke. "God knows, and He's going to guide you through all of these situations you're facing now."

"Mama, I know everything you're saying is right, but I still feel guilty."

"Why? Guilty for what?"

Michelle wanted desperately to tell her mother about the drugs and the gun, but she couldn't bring herself to do it. "I feel guilty because I failed Natalie as a mother. I didn't even know my daughter was in the streets in the middle of the night." At least that was part of the truth.

"Oh, Michelle." Grace let out a little chuckle. "There have been times when I didn't know where you were or your father either for that matter."

"When? I was always where I was supposed to be." She sat up and dried her wet face.

"Oh, is that so? I remember a time when you were so in love with Natalie's father, the two of you snuck off together for an entire weekend and you told me you were staying at Randi's house."

"Did I do that?" Michelle was embarrassed.

"Yep, you did."

"How did you find out?"

"Never mind. My point is: It's impossible for you to track Natalie's every move, and it's only natural for her to hide things from you at this age. Both of you are doing exactly what you should be doing at these stages of your lives. You haven't done anything to cause this situation. Accidents happen. Now we just have to pray for the best."

"You really think so, Mama?"

"Oh, I know so. You put your mind at rest and focus on keeping yourself healthy because Natalie needs you to be strong for her now."

Michelle smiled at her mother's encouragement. "You're right, Mama. Natalie needs me to be strong right now. I think I'm ready to go to the hospital with you today."

Grace wanted to shout with joy. She gave her daughter a long hug. "Well, let's get going. I should call Ms. Dean and see if she can squeeze us in for relaxers while we're out." Grace stood.

"Mama, Ms. Dean isn't working out of her basement anymore. She has a shop in Roosevelt Field."

"Then I think we should pay her a visit."

Michelle ran her hand over her thick hair. "I think so too."

Grace and Michelle stayed at the hospital for a couple of hours. As promised, Michelle stayed strong and spoke cheerfully to her comatose daughter. She softly brushed Natalie's hair and put it in a neat ponytail. Meanwhile, Grace watered Natalie's flowers and threw out some old fruit. Then she pulled out a bottle of lotion and massaged Natalie's dry skin until it was shining. Michelle watched silently. Those were the kinds of things she never thought to do, things that seemed to come so naturally to her mother. Before they left, Michelle straightened up some of the teddy bears that visitors brought by and lined them up on the windowsill.

As they were signing out of the intensive care unit, Natalie's doctor spotted them and came over.

"Hello, Dr. Chow."

"Hello, Mrs. Frazier. Mrs. Vaughn, nice to see you again." He gently touched Michelle's shoulder.

"Have there been any changes in Natalie's condition?" Grace asked.

"She's pretty stable. Her heartbeat and blood pressure are steady. She seems to be in a relaxed state, which is good because she's healing quickly. The longer she stays still, the better the fracture to her head will heal, as well as her other injuries."

"Well that's good to hear."

"You'll be contacted immediately if there's any change at all in her condition."

"Thank you, Dr. Chow." Grace shook his hand.

"My pleasure." He waved good-bye and was gone.

After they left the beauty salon, Michelle seemed to automatically come alive. There was something about having a fresh hairdo that was reviving. She was full of energy and practically dragging poor Grace in and out of every store in the mall. When Michelle decided she had spent enough money for the day, they ate an early dinner at Sbarro's and stopped by Gail's flower shop on the way to the car.

When they entered the shop, Gail was behind the front counter sifting through some papers.

"Hey, stranger."

Gail looked up into Michelle's face and smiled. "Well, I've been wondering about you. Where have you been?"

"I've been going through a family crisis."

Her smiled faded. "I'm sorry to hear that. Are you okay?"

Michelle shrugged. "Kind of. I want you to meet my mother, Mrs. Frazier. Mama, this is Gail. We usually hang out at the gym together."

"Nice to meet you." Grace shook Gail's hand.

"I have to say, you don't look like you could be Michelle's mother—her sister, maybe, but definitely not her mother." Gail admired Grace's youthful face and build.

"Oh, hush, child." Grace blushed.

Michelle thought her mother would be used to those kinds of remarks by now. Having aged so gracefully, she was complimented whenever she revealed how old she was.

"So, how have you been?" Michelle asked.

"Not so good. I've been going through a crisis of my own."

Gail paused to remove her glasses. Michelle didn't even know she wore glasses. "I recently caught my manager stealing money from me and altering receipts. Now, I'm spending every waking minute trying to retrace receipts for the last three years she's been here.

"Get out of here." Michelle covered her gapping mouth.

"Yes, girl. My accountant is going over my taxes with a fine-toothed comb. I hope this doesn't become more of a headache than it already has. Now, I'm managing the shop in addition to everything else." She made a sweeping gesture with her hand.

"That's a shame. If you need any help, let me know," Michelle offered politely.

"I hope you really mean that because I just might take you up on the offer." Gail scratched her head with her pencil.

"You have your hands full, so we're going to let you get back to work," Grace said.

"Gail, do you still have my number?"

"Give it to me again, just in case."

Michelle scribbled her name and number down on a piece of paper, then left Gail to her work.

*

Randi saw Franklin coming toward her desk looking fine as ever. When he could get a clear view of her, she put her head down and pretended to be reading. He walked in front of her desk, made a sharp left and headed toward the elevator bank without stopping.

"You better not pass me without speaking," Randi said, her head still down.

"Ah-ha. I knew you were watching me."

"Ah-ha. How could I miss you, parading around here like a peacock?" Randi shot back sarcastically.

He lowered his voice a little. "A parade is only interesting to those who are watching."

Randi smiled a little. "Is there a reason you stopped by here?" She put down the papers she was reading, giving him her full attention.

"Actually, yes." He gently tapped her shoulder. "I found some new information on our project."

"Oh yeah? Me too. I've been meaning to e-mail you, but I've

been kind of busy."

She noticed Franklin taking in her long legs as they flowed sexily out of her hunter-green miniskirt. She was going to continue to play hard-to-get and drive him crazy for a while.

"Uh, Randi, if you're not doing anything later, why don't we get together and go over some of that new information." He unconsciously licked his lips.

"Are you asking me out? I don't think so." Randi playfully rolled her eyes.

"I don't think so either." Franklin's voice was serious. "Not a date. Just two friends having dinner and going over work."

"Just dinner?" Randi eyed him suspiciously.

"And work." Franklin maintained his serious tone.

Randi knew he was full of shit, but followed his lead anyway. "Well, I don't usually work on Friday nights, but I can make an exception this time."

"How nice of you." Franklin's tone was a little snotty.

That made Randi smile. She always enjoyed a good game of cat and mouse.

"Where should we meet?" He returned to his serious tone.

"Oh, you're letting me pick?" She thought for a moment. "Be at my place by eight."

"I'll bring Chinese food," Franklin said as he walked away.

Randi watched his butt move in his slacks. Entertaining. It could be a slim possibility that Franklin was devoted to his wife and was only stopping by her apartment on a Friday night to go over work, but her experience told her otherwise.

Randi rushed home after work to straighten up her living room and tidy up her bedroom—just in case. She ran into the bathroom to freshen up and on her way out, the doorbell rang. She glanced at her watch. "Timely. I like that."

Randi spoke into the intercom and told the doorman to let Franklin in.

"Hello, Franklin," Randi said when she opened her apartment door.

His hands were full of greasy Chinese food bags and overstuffed office folders. "Hey, Randi." He handed her the bags.

"I'll put these in the kitchen. You can have a seat in there."

She pointed toward the living room with her chin.

"I hope you like lo mein," Franklin called out.

"My favorite," she called back as she rested the bags on the counter. Randi turned and Franklin was standing in the doorway of the kitchen. She stopped for a minute and eyed him. Fitted blue jeans, a silk sweater, black Clarks. Nice.

He felt her staring. "What?"

"Nothing." She hunched her shoulders. "I just never saw you casually dressed. You look different." She wiped her hands on a dishtowel and dropped it on the counter.

"Different good or different bad?" He raised one eyebrow.

"Different, different. That's all." She got a knife and started slicing a tomato for a salad to have with dinner.

He watched her make a mess. "You're doing that all wrong. Let me show you." He came over and took the knife from her and sliced the tomato in smooth, even strokes.

"Impressive. Where did you learn to do that?"

"I took some cooking classes in school." He gave her a boy-ish grin that made her insides do flip-flops.

"Oh." She picked up the other tomato.

"Here, let me help you with that." He stood behind her and placed his hands over hers. "Steady now." Together they sliced the tomato in seconds. "Wasn't that simple?" he asked with that same grin.

Randi wanted to answer him, but couldn't. Even after he released her and moved away, she still felt his body on hers. She simply nodded and reminded herself that she was trying to have a relationship with Brian and that Franklin was a married man.

"We can eat in the living room." Randi lifted the bowls of salad and turned to face him. He was watching her with a twisted smile on his face. "What?" She couldn't hold back her own smile.

He ignored her question, kept smiling and took the bowls from her. "I'll carry this." He quickly headed to the living room.

Randi was expecting him to make a move on her, and she secretly wished he'd hurry up.

"Okay." Franklin was sitting on the sofa. He opened a folder and began explaining his research and the progress he had made.

She was only half listening as she toyed with her salad and wondered if Franklin's tongue was playful like pink Bubblicious

gum or spicy like Big Red. She was concentrating more on his lus-
cious lips than the words that were coming out of them. They
looked so soft and sweet.

". . . If that's okay with you?" Franklin asked.

"Huh?" Randi was embarrassed. She hadn't heard a word he
was saying.

"You're not even listening to me. What are you thinking
about?" He put his papers down and turned to face her. He was
wearing that smile again.

"Thinking?" she asked, trying to wipe the stupid look off her
face.

"I can tell. Your body is here, but your mind is light-years
away."

"Oh." She was trying to think of something intelligent to say
to excuse her behavior. "Not light-years, just in the kitchen. I'm
starving. Do you mind if we eat now?" She stood.

"Sure." Franklin took the salad bowls and led the way to the
kitchen.

Randi could feel Franklin's eyes all over her body as she
piled their plates with lo mein and got silverware and drinks. "I'm
all out of ice. I hope you don't mind. The soda is cold, it was in
the refrigerator."

He took a deep breath. "No, I don't mind, but I do mind you
keeping those lips from me."

"What?" She spun around to face him. Was she hearing right?
Before she could respond, Franklin had her backed into the counter
in a lip lock. His tongue was strong and skilled as it danced with
hers, she could hardly catch her breath. Nothing playful about this,
it was definitely Big Red.

She tried to resist at first, but he felt so good to her, she was-
n't able to put up a fight. This was different from what she was
used to. She immediately began to wonder about the rest of his
skills.

Franklin lifted her and eased her buttocks on the counter. She
wrapped her legs around his waist and tried to smother a moan as
he planted soft kisses on her neck and ear.

She laid her head back on the cabinets, letting him have full
access to her body. He took advantage of every inch of it, kissing
her breasts and stomach through her shirt. That alone was enough

to make her scream, but she contained herself.

"Franklin." Randi pushed his head away from her.

"Hmm?" He looked at her, confused.

"Let me down."

His face was balled up in confusion.

She repeated herself. "Let me down."

He lifted her and lowered her to her feet.

She steadied herself, straightened her clothes, then reared back and slapped him with all of her might.

He jumped away from her and touched his face where she hit him. "Randi, what's wrong with you?" he yelled.

"I knew you came over here just to fuck me! Well, if you want to fuck me, you're going to have to do it on my say-so!" Her hands were on her hips and her neck snaked in rhythm with her words.

Franklin had such a confused look on his face she almost laughed, but managed to hold it in as she ordered, "In the bedroom."

"What?"

"Go!" Randi commanded and pointed to the rear of the apartment.

Franklin went silently, moving slowly toward the rear of her apartment, with Randi following closely behind him. It took every fiber of her being to keep from laughing. *I bet his ass is scared. He probably thinks I'm crazy.*

When they got in the bedroom, Randi slammed the door behind them and leaned against it. "Now, take your clothes off," she ordered sharply.

His heart was racing, and the thought of manhandling her entered his head, just as he caught a glimpse of mischievousness in her eyes.

He was on to her freaky game now, and it instantly turned him on. He did as he was told until he was completely naked and on his knees in front of her. Randi lifted her skirt and rested one foot on the bed. No panties. She guided Franklin's face to her soft center and let out a deep moan on contact. That was only the beginning. For the next ninety minutes, she gave him order after order until the two of them were so exhausted they could hardly move.

Randi was in her afterglow when the phone rang. She purposely answered with her sleepy voice. "Hello."

"Hey, baby, you're asleep?" Brian asked.

"Yeah. I wasn't feeling well." She shifted away from Franklin as she lied, giving him a cue to be quiet.

He put his index finger to his lips like a small child playing a game and began dressing.

"I'm going to be back earlier than I thought, and Pops can't meet me at the airport. My flight arrives tomorrow morning, and I'm going to need you to meet me at LaGuardia Airport at ten-fifteen. I'm arriving on Delta."

"No problem. Delta."

"Do you think you'll be feeling well enough to meet me?" Brian sounded so sweet being concerned about her. It almost made her feel guilty.

"I'm sure I will. I'm going to lay back down and get some rest. Have a safe flight, and I'll see you tomorrow. Love you too. Bye." Randi put the phone in the cradle and stared at Franklin's back as he bent down to tie his shoes.

He stood and faced her. "I'm going to get out of here and let you get some rest for real."

"Franklin, you came over here to work on your research project, and we haven't even started yet." Randi gave him a big grin.

He returned the smile and sat on the bed near her. "We'll have a lot more opportunities to work on that project. Let's not try to do it all in one night." He gently bit at the part of her breast that was uncovered.

"Whenever you have time." She grabbed her robe from the rocking chair and walked Franklin out to the living room, where he gathered his files and jacket.

"So, I'll see you at the office," Franklin said awkwardly.

"Yep. At the office." Randi felt even more uncomfortable than she sounded as she closed the door. She hadn't given a second thought to what it was going to be like working with Franklin at the office. Oh, God, what if somebody at the office found out about them? She took a deep breath to help calm herself. She would just have to do everything in her power to keep those nosy white folks at her office out of her business.

Randi hated meeting people at the airport. She had already

driven around Delta's terminal three times, and there was no sign of Brian. She couldn't sit outside the arrival gate because she would be towed or ticketed, so she had to keep moving and hope that Brian would spot her car.

She jumped when her cell phone rang. "Brian?" she asked sweetly.

"The one and only."

"Where are you? I've been driving around—"

He cut her off with a laugh. "Calm down. I'm standing at the arrival gate watching you. Come back around. I'll be standing at the curb."

Randi circled the terminal once more and pulled up to the curb in front of Brian. She popped the trunk for him to put his bags in.

Brian got in and kissed her softly as she pulled off. "Curbside service. I like this kind of treatment."

"If you like my curbside service, you'll love my bedside manner."

"Oh yeah? I've been thinking about that bedside manner all morning." He gave her breast a soft squeeze.

When they got back to Brooklyn, they stopped at a deli and picked up breakfast because Brian wasn't sure what he had in his refrigerator. At his apartment, they sat up in his king-size bed and watched Saturday morning cartoons as they ate bagels and drank orange juice. After breakfast Brian showed Randi, in several different ways, how much he missed her.

Randi was positioned comfortably in his arms and smiling as she thought about how lucky she was to have two great lovers who were willing to go the distance to satisfy her. She really cared for Brian and should be bothered by her cheating, but she wasn't bothered at all, in fact she was living the old cliché that two is better than one.

*

Umi glanced at her watch as she got off the elevator. It was already eight-thirty—a little late for her. She usually arrived at her office around seven-thirty and stayed as late as eight o'clock on most nights. She really didn't mind working the long hours though.

She knew it was her perseverance that brought her this far, and she wasn't about to stop now. Anyway, LaVelle was there now, and he didn't mind working those long hours with her, and he was pretty good company too.

Umi said good morning as she passed a few familiar faces on the way to her office. "Good morning, LaVelle." She flashed him a smile as she went into her office. She was hanging up her blazer when LaVelle poked his head in.

"Can I come in?"

"Sure."

He stepped in and handed Umi her mail and a cup of hot coffee. Umi had already gotten used to Lavelle's efficiency and how thoughtful he could be at times.

"Thank you." She rested her butt on the edge of her desk, facing him. She set the coffee mug on a coaster and briefly flipped through the envelopes then tossed them on her desk.

"Are you ready for some good news?" LaVelle started when he had her attention.

"Lay it on me." She smiled.

"I spoke with Georgia, Mr. Dagwood's secretary, this morning. She said that Mr. Dagwood is going to be in a meeting today at eleven o'clock with some of his executives to decide which firm will be handling his advertising."

"Who are the candidates?" Umi asked, trying to size up the competition before getting excited.

"She's not sure, but she said that it's between us and two other firms."

"Well, LaVelle, that is good news. At least we're in the pickings."

"At least we're in the pickings," he repeated happily.

"Uh, LaVelle, listen." Umi softened her tone a little and looked into his eyes. "I really want to thank you for being so diligent and working all of these hours with me. I can't tell you how much I appreciate it."

"No problem, Umi." He matched her sincere tone. "I hope these hours aren't too much for you. You were running a little behind today," he teased.

"Keeping tabs on me?" Umi returned the tease with a warm glance that made her a little nervous and excited. Was she losing her mind? She was in her office flirting with her assistant. A red flag went up in her mind.

"Just want you to know that I notice everything." LaVelle swept his eyes over her body from head to toe.

Umi kept silent as she tried to pull herself together and find her way out of this danger zone and back on safe ground. Although LaVelle was very charming and alluring, he was also her assistant. She had to reconstruct the wall of professionalism between them— and quick. Besides, she was happy in her committed relationship with Darren, and LaVelle was well aware of that.

In fact, she was late that morning because she and Darren had made love all night long and she slept at his condo and could barely pull herself away from him in order to leave for work. She couldn't do this to Darren and most importantly, she didn't want to mess up her working relationship with LaVelle. Office love affairs could become messy.

She cleared her throat. "LaVelle."

"Umi." He stepped closer to her and reached for her hand. But before they could make contact, a loud bang made them both jump. Valerie stood at the door with her hands on her hips and fire in her eyes.

The swinging door hit Valerie a couple of times before she stepped in and slammed it shut. "Can't return any of my calls?" she sneered in Umi's direction.

Umi was in such shock, she couldn't respond at first. Finally, she willed herself to speak. "Get out of here before I call security!" Her voice trembled with fear.

"I left messages with your faggot secretary." She rolled her eyes at LaVelle and headed straight for Umi.

"Who do you think you are? Playing with people's lives! You're not God! I have children at home to feed, bitch!" Valerie yelled in Umi's face.

LaVelle stepped between them and pushed Valerie back toward the door. "You have to leave," he said forcefully.

"Not without a fight!" She cleverly reached around LaVelle and landed a blow right on Umi's face.

In a quick response, LaVelle slapped Valerie, grabbed her hands and twisted them behind her back, forcing her to lay face down over Umi's desk. "Call security," he yelled out to Umi.

She was already dialing. Her hands were shaking, and her face felt like it was on fire where she had been hit.

Valerie wiggled, cursed and screamed for LaVelle to release her, but he held her tightly until building security arrived with a policeman. When Umi opened the door for them, a small crowd had gathered near her office. She was so embarrassed she closed the door immediately after the two men entered. She couldn't believe this was happening to her.

The officer took statements from both women and asked Umi if she wanted to press charges against Valerie.

"Yes." Her voice was still a little shaky.

"I want to press charges against that bitch too!" Valerie yelled in the officer's face as he approached her with his handcuffs. "For endangering the welfare of a minor! How am I supposed to feed my children? She doesn't give a damn about children 'cause she ain't got none."

Was that supposed to offend her? Umi was not embarrassed because she put her career first. She shot back angrily, "And you've got too many." She was tired of Valerie's bullshit. She had to step out of herself and go back to the old school. She stepped toward Valerie, put her hand on her hip and cocked her head to the side, "Do you think you're scaring me, Valerie?" Umi could tell that Valerie was shocked, but not for long.

"You better be scared because I don't threaten, I promise. And that goes for you, too, faggot boy." She hissed at LaVelle, but he was unmoved by the threat.

Umi was heated now. "Then you need to promise yourself you'll get some help, because you need it." She was feeling braver by the minute and started craning her neck. "Instead of hunting people down and blaming them for you losing a job you damn well didn't deserve, you should be figuring out how you're going to feed your own children because they belong to you, not me." Umi wasn't going to raise her voice and be indignant. She knew she eventually had to face the crowd of people listening on the other side of her office door, but her words were steady, forceful and laced with plenty of home-girl attitude.

The officer finished filling out his report and handed both women papers to take to the local precinct to follow up on the charges and obtain a court date.

"Are you going to be alright?" the security guard asked Umi before leaving. She had known him ever since she started working at the firm several years ago.

"I'll be fine. Thanks for all of your help." Umi shook his hand. She stood away from the door so she wouldn't have to the see the crowd as Valerie was being taken out in handcuffs and cursing at the top of her lungs like a maniac.

LaVelle closed the door and watched her as she inspected her eye in her compact mirror. Over at the small bar she kept for entertaining, he found a linen napkin and some ice and made her an ice pack. "If it means anything, I think you did the right thing by standing up to Valerie."

Umi didn't respond.

"Are you okay?" he asked as he handed her the ice pack.

Umi nodded, but kept her hands folded in her lap. She looked pitiful. He had never seen her like this.

"Let me help you." He knelt in front of her and carefully placed the ice pack on her eye.

"Ouch." She winced.

"Sorry. It's going to hurt a little."

"It hurts a lot," she grumbled. Actually her pride was hurt more than her eye. She was so embarrassed that it was beginning to make her angry. How did this happen? She had let her guard down when she knew better.

She replayed the scene in her head, remembering some of the things Valerie said. "LaVelle, how come you didn't tell me Valerie was still making threatening phone calls?"

She could tell that her tone had surprised him, but he regrouped quickly. "I didn't want to bother you with Valerie's mess. You had your hands full with the Dagwood account—"

"Mess?" Umi cut him off and raised her voice a notch. She pulled away from his hand, which was holding the ice pack to her eye. "Do you think Valerie was joking when she threatened me? We could have both been seriously hurt here today."

LaVelle stood. "I knew she was angry, but I didn't know she would follow through—" He started to offer up his defense, but Umi cut right through him.

"Do what I hired you to do!" She was angrier now than she

was before, just knowing that this whole thing could have been avoided. She stood and faced him. "I didn't hire you to think for me or protect me. Nor did I hire you to decide which calls I should receive. You are my assistant, not my bodyguard! You were way out of line, LaVelle, and I won't stand for it again. Consider yourself warned." Umi turned her back to him and started pouring herself a drink at the small bar. She was done talking.

"You're the boss," LaVelle responded quietly.

"And don't you forget it," she said after she heard her office door open and softly close.

Umi sat at her desk and nursed her drink for thirty minutes, as she thought of her next move. She would have to live down the glares of her coworkers. That shouldn't be too much of a problem, since she knew no one would be bold enough to confront her on the issue. She would have to follow through with the police report and court dates. The thought made her headache more intense. She glanced at her eye in the compact mirror again and sighed. She looked like she had just gone twelve rounds with Evander Holyfield. She would definitely have to explain this episode to Darren.

The intercom interrupted her thoughts. "Ms. Grayson, I have Georgia from the Dagwood Corporation holding."

Umi forcefully snapped the compact shut, causing it to fall and bounce around on her desk. She massaged her temples with her fingertips. "Dagwood," she repeated softly. Her desk clock read 1:30. They were probably out of their meeting. She couldn't focus. What if it were bad news? Could she handle it right now? What if it were good news? Was she okay enough to proceed with business as usual? She hated this out-of-control feeling, especially when business was on the line.

Finally she spoke into the intercom. "LaVelle, take a detailed message and forward the rest of my calls to my voice mail. I'm going to be leaving early today." There. She had made her decision. Be it good or bad.

"Certainly, Umi."

Well, at least LaVelle sounded like himself. She hoped she was doing as good a job at pretending as he was.

She picked up the phone and started dialing. She felt instantly better when she heard Darren's deep silky voice on the other line.

"Darren Alexander."

"Hi."

"Hi, baby. How's your day going?" Darren asked.

"Not good." Umi felt a lump growing in her throat as she fought back her tears.

"You don't sound like yourself. Are you okay? What happened?" He asked, concerned.

"I don't want to talk about it here. I was calling to see if you could meet me at my place in about an hour. I'm leaving the office now." She sniffled.

Now, he was alarmed. "Sure. I'll be there in an hour."

When Umi hung up the phone, she felt a little better, but she was nervous about having to face the nosy people in her office. She encouraged herself by reciting a short affirmation from one of Iyanla Vanzant's books, then she wiped her face, threw on her blazer and shades and stepped out of her office with her head held high.

She stopped at LaVelle's desk. "I'll see you in the morning," she said and headed straight for the elevator without stopping. She knew people were watching and whispering, but so what, it wouldn't be the first time.

When she pulled into her driveway, Darren was standing on her front steps waiting for her. He looked handsome and worried as he waited for her to get out of the car. As soon as she got to the bottom of the stairs, the questions started. "Are you okay?"

She didn't say a word. She took off her shades and let him see for himself.

"What happened to you?"

"Valerie," she said flatly.

She opened the door and headed straight for her bedroom and started undressing. Darren was right on her heels.

"Who?" He took a seat in the large rattan chair.

"My last assistant. The one I fired." Umi was in her bra and panties and searching in a drawer for a T-shirt. "Well, she burst into my office today in a fit of revenge and landed a blow right on my eye. The police were there, and it was big mess." She found a T-shirt and pulled it on along with a pair of biking shorts. She left her suit discarded across the bed.

"Where was your assistant? Why didn't he stop her?"

The question aggravated Umi. "He was in the office with me, we were going over the Dagwood account. Anyway, Darren, that doesn't matter. LaVelle is my assistant, not my bodyguard." Her tone was edgy. She went into the bathroom for a jar of cold cream. She caught a glimpse of her reflection in the mirror and wanted to cry.

"I know, but he should be able to stop anybody from entering your office at their own free will."

She quickly turned the bathroom light off and returned to the bedroom and shoved the cold cream at Darren. "Would you have asked that question if my assistant were a woman?"

"Her job description would still be the same, wouldn't it?" He dabbed a little of the cream on her bruised and swollen face.

"Don't answer my question with a question."

Ignoring her attempt to argue, he closed the jar of cold cream. "This isn't going to help you. What you need is a cold compress." He stood.

Silent tears escaped Umi's eyes and slid down her cheeks.

Darren hugged her tightly in an effort to comfort her. "Shhh, the most important thing is that you're okay." He kissed the top of her head.

"I'm not okay. I'm upset about the whole thing. I hate feeling this way—so out of control."

"Umi, some things are just beyond your control." His voice was soft and reassuring.

A couple of hours later she was relaxed enough to get dressed and have an early dinner with Darren at a neighborhood Chinese restaurant. He spent the night at her house, and the comforting and reassuring went on until almost midnight, when they both passed out. Umi had never let her guard down with a man before. She kind of liked the idea of him rushing to her side in the time of trouble. She'd never had that happen before, mostly because she never shared her problems with anyone other than Randi and Michelle. It was a strange new feeling that she could definitely get used to.

CHAPTER 7

Randi finally managed to pull herself away from Brian long enough to meet Umi over at Michelle's house. She loved all the attention he was showering her with, but sometimes it was a little overbearing. All things considered, it was a lot better than the way he was treating her a few months ago. Besides, whenever she needed a breather, she would simply call Franklin, and he was certainly a breath of fresh air.

Randi pulled in front of Michelle's house and parked her Nissan Sentra behind Umi's Benz. She rang the bell and Grace answered the door.

"Hey, Ms. Grace." Randi stepped inside and hugged and kissed Grace.

"Hey, Randi." Grace closed the door behind her.

"How are you?" she asked as she threw her jacket over the arm of a chair.

"I'm okay. Michelle and Umi are in the kitchen eating." Grace led the way.

"I smell the food. Y'all eating early. It's only two-thirty." Randi glanced at her watch. "Hey, ladies!" she called out as she entered the kitchen.

"Hey!" they responded.

"Y'all starting the festivities without me, huh?"

"Well, grab a plate and catch up, girl," Michelle said.

"These greens are the best I've ever had. I love well-seasoned greens, Ms. Grace." Umi's head was buried in her plate.

"How are you feeling?" Randi patted Michelle's hand as she began serving herself.

"Sometimes up, sometimes down." She shrugged slightly.

"And Nat?"

"As best as can be expected." Michelle lifted her glass to her mouth.

"And what about you, Greasy?" Randi joked about Umi's mouth.

"I'm good," Umi said between bites. "Y'all have to forgive me. I haven't eaten so many good meals in a long time. Ms. Grace you should visit more often."

"Well, eat up, girl. Put some meat on your bones," Grace said.

"Mama, don't you know thin is in?"

Grace rolled her eyes.

"When I'm at those business luncheons, there are tables filled with expensive food that no one can identify, yet they're all raving about how wonderful everything tastes. Some of it is good, but girl, ain't nothing like a plate of baked chicken and greens."

"I know that's right," Randi agreed. Her plate was piled high with a baked chicken leg, macaroni and cheese, collard greens and a biscuit.

"You know this kind of Southern cooking tastes good, but it'll send you to an early grave," Umi said, without missing a bite of food.

"Oh, please, the south is full of old people. People who've been eating this kind of cooking all their lives." Grace dismissed Umi with a wave if her hand.

"Mama, it's a proven fact that foods heavily saturated in fat aren't good for you. They'll clog your arteries, and they can lead to all kinds of sicknesses."

"Michelle, ain't a thing wrong with me."

Randi licked her fingers and intervened. "It's difficult to say why some people get sick and some don't."

"I guess some people are just genetically predisposed," Umi figured.

Grace was bored with the entire conversation. "Who cares? Help me load this dishwasher," she said to no one in particular and stood.

Umi was so full, she didn't want to move but she got up and followed Grace's orders as they cleaned up the kitchen. She wanted to tell them about the episode with Valerie, but didn't get the chance. As soon as she came through the door, Michelle started talking about her situation with Greg and giving her an update on Natalie's condition. Then Grace fixed her a plate of food that kept her occupied until Randi showed up and now they were all moving to the living room where Michelle had a card table set up and prepared them for a game of Spades. Maybe she'd get a chance to tell them later.

"Ooh, I'm full. I'm going to have to go to the bathroom in a minute." Randi rubbed her stomach as she took a seat at the card table.

"Thank you for sharing that," Michelle responded as she took a seat on Randi's right.

Umi frowned as she decided which seat to take. "I don't want to be Randi's partner."

"Then you don't want to win," Randi said smartly.

"You cheat too much," Umi said and took the seat across from Michelle.

"I don't cheat!" Randi said defensively.

The women flashed one another knowing glances.

"I get caught stealing money from the Monopoly bank one time, and I'm labeled for life. Really that happened when we were in college, can we please get passed it?"

"Once?" Michelle asked slyly.

"Once," Randi declared and rolled her eyes. "Have a seat, Ms. Grace, and let's win this game. I hope y'all are ready to lose," she said to her opponents.

Halfway through the game, Umi and Michelle were trailing by almost a hundred points and Randi was talking enough junk to keep everybody laughing. Michelle led the next hand with the king of hearts. Grace followed with the five of hearts. Umi threw out the ace.

"Umi, watch the board," Michelle said, annoyed.

"You threw out the king?"

"No talking across the board," Grace warned.

Randi ended the hand with the three of hearts and laughed.

Umi took the book and led with the five of clubs. Everyone followed and Randi won the book with the king of clubs.

"My black king has done it for me again," Randi gloated.

"Oh, please," Umi said.

"What do you know about black kings?" As usual, Randi loved putting Umi on the defensive.

"Not much, except they're limited." She chuckled.

"Humph. Don't get me started," Grace said, eyeing her cards.

"It's me you don't want to get started," Michelle added.

"Michelle, you need to stop. If anybody in here knows what it's like to have a black king in her hand, it's you," Randi said.

Michelle shook her head. "It looks like my king has jumped right out of my hand and right into another woman's arms."

This statement brought the card game to a screeching halt.

"You don't know that," Grace warned.

"Mama, it's been more than four months since I've seen King Greg." She shook her head sadly. "Don't get me started."

"Well, it's been the same amount of time since Greg has seen you. Are you in someone else's arms?"

"Good point, Ms. Grace," Randi said.

"Randi, you and Umi are different from me. Y'all both have promising careers. My family *is* my career."

Randi thought for a moment. Was she hearing Michelle say she was jealous? Not the Michelle who had everything any woman could want? "It doesn't have to be. You could easily enter the workforce. You always have your bachelor's degree to fall back on."

"And who said that family wasn't a priority?" Umi started. "Michelle, you were fortunate to have found someone like Greg who was already established in his career and supportive of your decision to be an at-home mom. That doesn't come along very often. Shoot, I would like to be married, I don't want to settle for less than I deserve."

"Umi, you're already married—to your work," Randi responded.

Why did Randi always have to go there? She was never satisfied until she had someone completely pissed off. Umi didn't want to seem sensitive, so she let it go.

Grace responded in Umi's defense. "I'm sure that's not by choice. Every woman wants someone to love and someone to love her back." She gave Umi a knowing nod. "Nowadays you have to be self-sufficient. When I was young, it was alright to have your husband support you, but times have changed." She waved her hand at the thought.

"There are women who have it all," Randi reasoned. "I don't believe that a choice has to be made between a prosperous career and a happy marriage."

"I didn't say that women on the whole have to choose, but the women at this table have chosen," Michelle said flatly.

"Then the choice was mine to make and I'm happy." Randi laid her cards on the table, literally.

"Me too," Umi lied. She desperately wanted a family, but did she want it with Darren? How much of her career would she have to give up? "Besides, a career is guaranteed success if you work hard at it. On the other hand, you can work hard at a marriage and still have it fail."

"If a marriage is hard work, then it's not a healthy marriage," Grace lectured. "Marriage is a work-in-progress, but you should always enjoy it and be comfortable in it."

"Umi, I have to disagree with you on one thing." Randi leaned back in her chair. "There are glass ceilings in every career, and they are especially built for African-American women like you and me, so success isn't guaranteed in the workplace or any other place." She wanted to set that record straight because of her own struggles at the *New York Times*.

"I never said that I wasn't happy, just not fulfilled," Michelle said to get the conversation back on track.

"Michelle, if it'll make you feel better, you should look for something to occupy your time," Umi suggested.

Michelle shrugged. "It's a thought."

"Okay, my time is up." Randi got up from the table.

"Where are you going?"

"Nature is calling, and I have to answer." She was already heading upstairs.

"You're so nasty." Michelle frowned.

"Enjoy yourself!" Umi called out.

In the bathroom, Randi kicked the conversation around in her head while she let nature take its course. It just goes to show, the grass always looks greener on the other side. Michelle had the nerve to be jealous of her career—a career that was going nowhere. Being jealous of Umi's prosperity was more realistic, there weren't

many young black women in her position. But even with all of
Umi's fanfare, Randi knew for a fact that Umi was longing for a
family and also knew, firsthand, that it wasn't easy coming home
to an empty house every night. Umi was talking a lot of junk at
the table, but her denial was as transparent as Saran Wrap. Now,
Grace was the only one making sense, as far as Randi was concerned. Times had definitely changed.

Randi wondered what it would be like to be married to Brian.
As she let her imagination carry her off to a place far from
Michelle's luxurious bathroom, the large sunken Jacuzzi became
a home in the suburbs, the mint-green marble became acres of the
greenest grass and trees, the large sink and counter area was now
a two-car garage where their luxury cars would be parked.

She pictured Brian and her pulling into the driveway at almost
the same time, as they would every night after a day at work. Brian
would step out of his car, and his expensive suit would fall perfectly on his frame. He would be beautifully groomed, looking like
he stepped out of the pages of *Ebony*. Then she'd step out of her
car dressed to kill and looking like the power woman she was.

Inside, they would be greeted by a wonderful aroma coming
from the kitchen, where their housekeeper, Marguerite, would have
prepared an exquisite dinner for them and the children, Brian Jr.
and Gabrielle.

Randi could picture the house of her dreams vividly in her
mind. The entrance would be a large foyer with hardwood floors
throughout, including a long staircase that led to the second story.
To the left of the foyer would be the grand room filled with expensive furniture and a baby grand piano. To the right of the foyer
would be her very modern kitchen, fully equipped with all the latest hi-tech appliances and a traditional dining room.

At the top of the long staircase there'd be three bedrooms, a
large bathroom and the master suite. This room would be lavished
in the finest woods, silks and leathers. Cool pastels and lace would
adorn the bed and windows during the summer and the most comfortable flannels would take their places in the winter. The walk-in
closet would be filled with expensive clothes and shoes. The attached
private bath would have the two things no rich woman's private
bathroom should be without: a large Jacuzzi and a wine rack.

"Randi, did you fall in or what?"

Michelle's banging startled her and brought her back to the present. "Occupied," Randi sang out in a high soprano.

"Goodness, girl, what are you doing in there?"

"Trust me, you don't want to know." Randi laughed. "Go away! I'll be out in a minute."

She heard Michelle's footsteps walking away from the door and could faintly hear her downstairs reporting to Umi and Grace. Randi examined her face closely in the mirror and was saddened with the thought that she wasn't Brian's wife and they didn't have any children. Hell, they didn't even have Marguerite. She ran her hands over her hair, straightened her blouse and gave herself a big, reassuring smile. No, she didn't have a husband, house or children now, but she would have them one day and that day had to be soon. "'Cause, girl, you ain't getting any younger," Randi told her reflection and started piecing together her plans to make her dream come true.

*

Michelle turned up the radio in her car and let the soothing sounds of Sadé engulf her as she merged into the flow of traffic on the highway. She'd just left her mother behind in the hospital with Natalie, who was still in a coma. Her body cast had been removed, and she was no longer hooked up to any machines, except the I.V. fluid and the tube that fed her. Now Michelle was hoping and waiting for her to regain consciousness, and the doctor assured them that after that happened, she would almost be her normal self again.

It was likely Natalie would need some therapy to help her with the use of her arms and legs again, but Michelle figured therapy wouldn't be so hard to get through since Natalie was young and in good condition. She just wanted to get her baby back home so that she could talk to her and get to know the daughter she felt had become a stranger. It would be just like old times, she thought. No, it would be better than old times because now she would be a more attentive mother and friend.

As she exited the highway and headed toward Roosevelt Field mall, Michelle knew it wouldn't be exactly the same because Greg wouldn't be there. She was sure that whatever differences were between them, they would never be worked out. She had not

seen or heard from him since their argument, and she missed him
dearly. The only reason she knew he was still alive was because
the bills were being paid. Also, every time she went to the hospital one of the nurses would say, "You just missed your husband."
Or "Your husband was here earlier." They had no clue how her
heart would break every time she heard those words.

She wasn't as angry with Greg as she was with herself for not
putting her foot down when he insisted on buying the car for
Natalie. During the argument she was pretty heated and said things
she shouldn't have, but she didn't want to lose her husband. In fact,
now more than ever before she wanted to talk to him, tell him what
was on her mind. Reconcile even. But how was she supposed to
do that? Send up smoke signals? She had no way of contacting him.
Besides, Greg could be stubborn as a mule when it came to certain
things, and she knew that it wouldn't be easy to bridge the gap that
had come between them. Her mother advised her to give Greg time
and that was advice she would follow.

Michelle cleared her mind as she slid into a parking spot in
front of Nordstrom's. She wasn't really one to follow other people's advice—not even her mother's. She considered herself an
independent thinker and liked making decisions that fit her life,
instead of trying to fit into someone else's reasoning.

Although some of the things that were said in her living room
the weekend before were stuck in her head. Umi's defense to her
right to make it to the top of corporate America was impressive;
and Randi's stand that a family would be nice to have but a career
was just as good, was equally convincing. Both women were passionate about the roads they'd chosen and seemed satisfied,
whether they were lying or not.

Anyway, for a change, Michelle took Randi's advice to make
use of her degree and get out into the workforce, which was what
sent her sailing to the mall on a Tuesday morning. She wanted to
take advantage of a sale that had been running since Sunday, and
pick up a navy-blue suit just in case she landed an interview.

Just being in Nordstrom's made her feel like spending money.
She didn't know if it was the smell of new things, the arrangement
of items or the saleswomen waiting to spray her with something
foreign and expensive, but whatever it was, it sent Michelle racing to the Jones New York section. She browsed the aisles for

almost an hour before deciding to try on a navy-blue power suit. She couldn't decide on the matching skirt or pants and after exhausting the saleswoman, she finally chose both.

"Will that be cash or charge?"

Michelle handed the woman her gold card without answering as she eyed a rack of silk scarves.

"Those are thirty percent off," the saleswoman offered. "Would you like to take a look?"

"I think I will." Michelle headed toward the rack and searched for something to compliment her new ensemble.

"Excuse me, miss. Are these on sale?"

Michelle turned toward the voice. "I don't work—"

"Michelle!" Gail sang out. "I didn't even recognize you."

Michelle was surprised to see her as well. It had been more than a month since her last trip to the gym. "How are you?"

"Do you really want to know?" Gail rolled her eyes.

"Do you really want to tell me?" Michelle teased.

"So much has happened since I last saw you."

"I haven't been to the gym in a while."

"Me either." Gail sighed. "I just haven't had the time."

Michelle remembered her dilemma with her manager. "Is everything okay at the shop?" She was almost embarrassed for asking, but somehow sensed that Gail wanted to talk.

Gail shook her head slowly, and her eyes went straight to the floor.

Michelle's heart went out to her friend. "If you have some time, maybe we can get something to eat. Do you have to get back to the shop right away?"

"The shop is closed," Gail answered so softly Michelle had to strain to hear her.

Now it was Michelle's turn to eyeball the floor. "I'm sorry, Gail."

They stood in awkward silence. Gail put on a smile, letting Michelle know that she was handling her situation. "Thank you. Can I still take you up on that invitation to get something to eat?"

"Sure." Michelle returned the smile and looked at her watch. "It's too early for lunch and too late for breakfast." They stood thinking for a minute. "First, let's get out of here, then we'll decide."

"Okay."

They decided to go to a small coffee shop on Old Country
Road and took a window booth in the back that gave them a view
of the parking lot and garbage Dumpsters. They ordered salads
and began catching up.

Gail led the conversation, explaining that a friend of hers was
an artist and some of his work was being displayed later at an art
gallery in New York City, and she had an extra ticket to offer, if
Michelle was interested.

She continued, "Well, as you can guess, my money is kind
of tight but I wanted to wear something nice this evening, so I
went into Nordstrom's to pick up something simple—"she hesitated for a moment"—but nice."

"But nice." Michelle nodded in agreement as she thought
about the new four-hundred-dollar suit in her trunk.

"So do you think you'll be interested in coming to New York
City with me later? I could really use the company." Gail laughed
nervously.

"I don't mind. I didn't have anything planned. What time?"

"The showing is from four to ten, but I didn't want to be in
New York City too late." She raised an eyebrow.

"I know what you mean. What if we leave around four, then
we would get there between five and six, not too early or late."

"That sounds good. It would give me time to get ready," Gail
agreed.

After they finished their salads, the waitress kept giving them
an annoyed glare, so they ordered herbal teas and kept the conversation rolling.

"How are your husband and daughter?"

Michelle didn't want to even start on that subject. "They're
fine, thanks. But I'm more concerned about you. How are you
doing?"

"I'll be okay." She sipped her tea slowly.

Michelle could tell she was deciding where to start and how
much to reveal. She waited patiently for her to begin her story.

"I have learned so much in these past few months about the
IRS and the court system. More than I've ever cared to know."
She giggled sadly. "Trying to prosecute Veronica, my manager,

for falsifying receipts, tampering with legal documents and stealing my hard-earned money has not been easy. And at the same time, trying to avoid being prosecuted for tax evasion and other things." She took a deep breath. "Finally, my attorney thought it wasn't such a bad idea when I decided to close up shop. Just for a little while, not permanently. I'm still leasing my space at the mall, but too many things are happening for me to totally concentrate on running it."

"I'm sure," Michelle agreed. "It sounds like your plate is full."

"Full and running over, girl." She laughed. "Some days I don't know if I'm coming or going."

"I know that feeling well." Michelle laughed too.

She was suddenly serious again. "During the day, I've been trying to sort out my receipts for the last three years, but to tell the truth, I can't make much sense out of them. One time I add them up and get a figure, but when I double-check them, I get a different figure. Forget the tax tables." She waved her napkin, as though it were a white flag. "I stopped trying to figure those out."

"What about an accountant?" Michelle asked.

"I had to let him go. Too expensive. I would like to hire another one, but I'm too scared to part with the money. I don't have any money coming in, and I don't want to exhaust my savings."

The light in Michelle's head went off instantly. As Gail rambled on, Michelle was putting together something that would help both of them.

"I'm sorry, Michelle. I'm talking your head off about my problems."

"No, it's okay. I think I know someone who can help you."

Gail's eyebrows went up.

"Just hear me out. What if I told you I know someone who has an accounting degree? She's not a CPA, but could help you just the same." Michelle was smiling warmly as she sold herself to Gail.

"I have a lot of work to be done and not a lot of money to pay. Your friend may not be interested in helping me once he knows that."

"*She's* not interested in making a lot of money, and I know she wouldn't mind helping someone in a jam." Michelle's smile grew.

It didn't take Gail long to pick up on Michelle's hints. "Michelle, I can't ask you to do that for me." She shook her head.

"You didn't ask. I offered. And I would love to help you." She patted Gail's arm.

"You heard me say I can't pay you much."

Michelle sipped her tea as she waited for Gail to reconsider.

Gail let out a long sigh, "Can we talk about it when I see you later?"

She put her cup down and smiled. "We can do that."

Before leaving, Michelle insisted on doing two things: picking up the bill and complaining to the manager about their waitress' attitude. They laughed easily together as they walked out to the parking lot to their separate cars.

"I'll pick you up at four," Gail called from her car.

Michelle beeped her horn in response and headed home.

True to her word, Michelle's doorbell rang at exactly four o'clock. Michelle ran downstairs and quickly modeled for her mother, who was on the sofa doing a crossword puzzle.

Grace looked over the top of her glasses and eyed Michelle from head to toe and nodded her approval.

"Thank you, Mama." Michelle had a hard time deciding what to wear. She didn't want to look too flashy or too expensive for Gail's sake, but she did want to impress her since this was their first time going out together. She chose a chocolate-colored dress that flowed to her ankles and accented it with a black blazer, black leather riding boots and a black belt. She threw on a gold bangle and a wide gold herringbone necklace and gold hoops to compliment the outfit. She decided earth tones were best for her makeup and made sure her hair was just right.

Michelle took one more look in the mirror before opening the door for Gail.

"Hey, Michelle. Don't you look stunning?"

"Thank you. So do you. Come in and say hello to my mother."

Gail was stylishly dressed in a silk black pantsuit that had to cost more than anything Michelle could ever pull out of her own closet. She wore a simple diamond choker and matching bracelet that completed the outfit perfectly.

Gail stepped inside and her eyes swept over the living room area, "You have a lovely home." She waved to Grace on the sofa. "Hello."

"How are you, sweetheart?"

"Fine, thank you."

"Mama, you remember Gail? We stopped at her flower shop in the mall."

"Yes." Grace nodded sweetly.

"Well, Mama, we're gonna get going. I'll be home early." Michelle kissed her mother and was out the door.

The ride to New York City was pretty smooth. Michelle was usually uneasy when riding with someone for the first time, but Gail was sliding her new Lexus through traffic with such skill that she became immediately relaxed with her driving. Gail led the conversation mostly and kept it light. They talked about music in the seventies and high school and college days, but never once was business or family brought up.

When they got to the art show, Michelle felt as though she had been transformed to another world, one she never knew existed. There were rich black people from all walks of life examining paintings and enjoying expensive wines and cheeses. Michelle thought Umi would fit in perfectly if she were there, although Umi wasn't interested in art and wouldn't know a Crayola from a Van Gogh.

Gail went off to find her friend, leaving Michelle alone and a nervous wreck. She helped herself to a glass of champagne, chose a secluded corner and stayed there. When Gail didn't return right away, she occupied her mind by dividing the people in the room into categories. Most fit into the typical expensively dressed married bourgeois couples. There were a lot of free-style, dreadlock wearers floating around, and of course there were the back-to-Africa-hold-tight-to-your-roots people present at every black function. A few people fell into the Artist category. These were the ones who had a starving artistic slash musician look about them, but who were really holding it down at the bank, and finally a few white people who felt comfortable enough to openly admire the work of black artists were sprinkled in.

Michelle finished her drink and casually circled the room to eavesdrop on a few conversations, just to get the flavor of the people. She passed a group of dreadlock wearers and listened as they spoke with articulate foreign accents about their recent return from an art show in the South of France. She kept moving passed two women and overheard one telling the other how excited she was about having secured an original painting for fifteen thousand dollars. Michelle was completely awed. She could never part with that kind of money and not have a piece of property or at least a tan from a lavish vacation to show for it.

"Enjoying yourself?"

The deep voice startled Michelle, and she turned to look in the face of one of the most gorgeous black men she had ever seen. His white teeth peeking out between his full lips were enough to send her emotions spiraling. His dark, slim face was framed by perfectly groomed dreadlocks that danced on his shoulders. He was wearing a simple black turtleneck sweater and black slacks that hung so well on him, she could tell right away they were tailor-made.

"Uh, Michelle," she stammered and extended her hand.

The confused look on his face made her want to hide hers.

He smiled nicely. "Hi, Michelle. Are you enjoying yourself?"

She closed her eyes for a minute to regain her composure before saying something else stupid. "I am. Yes. Uh, enjoying myself."

"So you found Michelle?" Gail magically appeared out of nowhere and draped her arm around Michelle's shoulders.

"It was easy to find the most beautiful woman in the room." His words were drowned in an elegant English accent.

Michelle was embarrassed by the compliment. "Thank you."

"Michelle, this flirt here is my friend Trent. Has he been harassing you?"

Michelle found her voice and thought she would show Trent that she was capable of holding a conversation. "No, he's actually been making me feel quite welcome." Her eyes were locked with Trent's as she spoke.

"Can I freshen your drink for you?"

"Thank you." She handed him her glass, and he disappeared into the crowd. "Girl, he is too much," Michelle quietly squealed.

"And you are too married." Gail jokingly slapped her left hand.

"I know, but a little flirting never hurt anybody."

"Not until it turns into an affair, it doesn't."

Okay? Where did that come from? Did she miss something? Were Trent and Gail an item? That had to be it. Damn, she'd over-stepped her boundaries already. She had to make sure that didn't happen again. She didn't want to run the risk of embarrassing or upsetting Gail.

Michelle considered herself warned and when Trent returned, she was back to being herself—a decent married woman. She politely thanked Trent for the drink and followed him as he took them on a tour of the gallery showing them his work and sharing a little history behind each painting. He also pointed out what he thought was outstanding talent and what was not.

By the end of the evening, Michelle felt so comfortable with Gail and Trent she didn't want to leave. She even convinced Gail to stay much later than they'd originally planned, although the time went by quickly as Trent dazzled them and kept them laugh-ing with his stories. He had Michelle's undivided attention up to the moment he walked them to the parking garage and made her promise not to be a stranger.

"Where did you meet Trent?" Michelle asked as they headed back to Long Island.

"I used to date a friend of his." Gail was fiddling with the radio stations. She finally slid a CD into the changer.

Yeah, right, Michelle thought. Maybe Gail didn't want to talk about it, so she changed the subject. "Oh, I had such a good time tonight. I didn't know an art show could be so stimulating."

"It wasn't the art, it was the people. Do you really think you would have had so much fun if you were trapped in a roomful of white people of the same caliber?"

Michelle shrugged. She hoped Gail wasn't one of those peo-ple who saw everything from a black-and-white viewpoint. "I guess most black people can still be fun after reaching the top of the heap."

"That's because they know how hard it was trying to get to the top of that heap. I'm sure every person in that room had a war story or two."

"I know that's right." Michelle closed her eyes and relaxed a bit. She thought this would be a good segue. "I'm also sure that every person in that room has needed someone's help along the way."

Michelle slowly opened one eye and saw Gail smiling at her. "Keep your eyes on the road before you kill us, girl."

"I'm gonna throw you out of my car," Gail joked.

"Did you think about it?"

"I did." She kept her eyes on the road.

Michelle examined the side of Gail's face and tried to read her mind. She wondered if Gail felt like she did, like she was losing something she wanted so much and worked so hard to have.

They were silent the rest of the way to Michelle's house. Gail pulled to the curb, turned off the engine and shifted in her seat to face Michelle. "I have to start by saying that I'm glad you offered to help me, but—"

"I knew there was a but," Michelle interrupted with a sigh.

"Okay, Michelle, I honestly feel funny about accepting a handout. I barely know you except for a couple of lunches and trips to the gym." Her words were rushed and flat.

"Do you feel funny about going to jail?" Michelle watched her face carefully as the streetlights cast funny shadows across it. "Because without my help that's where you might end up."

Gail's face was hard to read, but Michelle knew she was considering her words. "Michelle, I would feel better if you'd let me pay you."

"You can't afford to pay me, but I'll take an IOU." She smiled at her idea.

"An IOU?" Gail repeated, unsure.

"I'll work for you now and when your shop reopens, you can pay me a little at a time."

Gail fiddled with the radio again before responding. "Michelle, I have to know something."

"Okay?"

"Why are you doing this for me?"

Michelle honestly didn't know, but it felt right to her at the moment. She answered as best as she could, choosing her words carefully. "Gail, I think although we're from two totally different worlds, we have much more in common than you know."

"We do?"

"Yep." Michelle nodded.

"And that makes you want to help me?" Gail was skeptical.

"It does. So when do I start?"

"Okay then, you can come by my house tomorrow morning and we can get started." Gail smiled.

"I'll see you around ten?" Michelle started to get out of the car.

"Michelle, wait." Gail gently grabbed the hand of her new friend. "Thank you."

"Thank me later. Just have everything I'll need to get started waiting for me tomorrow." Michelle closed the door behind her and waved to Gail as she pulled off.

PART II

THREE THE
HARD WAY

CHAPTER 8

Umi was stretched out across her bed in an old sweat suit, armed with the remote control and aimlessly flipping through television stations. Five hundred channels and not one of them was showing anything interesting enough to hold her attention longer than a minute. It was Saturday night, and she had absolutely nothing to do. She tried to call Michelle and Randi, but they were both out, and Darren's job had sent him to Ohio for sensitivity training. Usually she would jump on her computer and do a little work, but there was no work to do. Her load had decreased tremendously since she finally landed the Dagwood account. It wasn't easy, but when a picture of her and her team appeared in the company's newsletter and in the business section of the *New York Times*, she knew it was well worth the effort. The big fat bonus in her paycheck wasn't so bad either.

With nothing else in mind, Umi finally decided she'd clean out her junky hall closet, which was something she vowed to do when she had some time. Cleaning was something she hated to do. No one could ever accuse her of being a domestic—cooking and tidying things up were just not her forte. She was far from a slob, but she could never touch Michelle when it came to doing things around the house.

Umi tied her hair up in an old scarf and started pulling everything out of the closet, making two piles: one of things to keep and another for the garbage. After everything had been pulled out and separated, she started going through the garbage pile just to make sure there was nothing in it she wanted or could possibly give to the Salvation Army.

She set aside her tennis rackets and decided to hold on to them in case she ever decided to restart her lessons, lessons she

had to quit several years ago because she didn't have time for them
any longer. Everything else in the pile was bagged up and set by
the door to go out later. Then Umi dusted the shelves, swept and
mopped the inside of the closet.

While she waited for the closet floor to dry, she sat on the
sofa and went through some of her photo albums. She laughed at
old pictures of herself, Michelle and Randi and remembered the
events like they happened only yesterday.

She was caught up in her memories when the doorbell rang.
Who could it be? She wasn't expecting anyone. When she opened
the door, she was surprised to see Greg standing on the other side.

Umi stared at him for a moment. His face was solemn and
his eyes were hollow and sad. She didn't know whether she should
hug him or strangle him. "Well, this is certainly a surprise," she
said in her straightforward, no-nonsense tone, before stepping back
to let him in.

"I want to talk to you." He shoved his hands in his jacket
pockets as he stood awkwardly in her foyer.

Umi let out a deep breath and softened her stance a little. She
decided to hear him out and then let him have it. "Come on in.
Watch your step, I'm doing some cleaning."

Greg made his way to the living room and sat on the loveseat.
He rested his elbows on his knees and rubbed his hands together.
"How's Michelle?" he asked slowly.

"Why don't you call her and ask her yourself?" Umi rested
her butt on the arm of the sofa facing him.

Greg sighed loudly. "It's not that simple, and you know it."

Umi waited patiently for him to tell her why he was there.
She had already decided that he wouldn't be staying long, so he'd
better get on with it. She folded her arms across her chest as a signal for him to get started.

Greg got the message and began slowly. "It's been a long
time since I've seen Michelle, and in that space of time a lot has
changed, including my feelings about some things. And I'm sure
Michelle doesn't want to have anything to do with me. She thinks
Natalie's accident was my fault."

"She does?" Umi raised her eyebrows innocently.

Greg gave her an I-know-you-know look.

"Okay, she may have believed that at first, but like you said, a lot has changed in the past few months, and Michelle may not feel that way anymore."

"How do you know? Has she said something about it to you?" Greg's tone was filled with hope.

"No, not directly, but I kind of get the feeling that Michelle would like to see you. I know for a fact that she misses you. Not because she said it, but because she shared her life with you for so long, it's only natural for her to miss you."

"I miss her, too, and I want to see her. You don't know how many times I've pulled up in front of that house and just couldn't get up the nerve to go in. I know that sounds silly, a man won't go into his own home, but when I think of the argument we had that day, it brings me to tears. She had so much conviction and blame in her voice that she almost had me believing the accident was my fault."

Umi could see the pain on his face and felt sorry for him. "But you know it wasn't your fault, right?"

"I know it wasn't. I only wanted to do something special for Natalie."

"That's right."

"I love Michelle, but I haven't gotten over that accusation, not even after all of this time and I probably never will." Greg shook his head sadly.

"Never is a long time, Greg." Umi moved to the sofa, a little closer to him. In a funny way, she felt like she was betraying Michelle by talking about such a delicate issue with Greg. This was definitely something he should be discussing with a neutral party, and she was anything but that. No matter what, she would always side with Michelle and support her.

"Some days are better than others. One day I feel like I can get past this and make amends, but other days that accusation strikes me at the core of my heart and I feel so hurt by the one person I thought could never hurt me."

Umi could identify with that feeling all too well. She had been blindsided by a few people as well and knew that it could be difficult to overcome. She sat quietly and listened.

"Honestly, I don't see a future for us."

"What do you mean?" Umi tried to mask her alarm.

"I mean I misjudged Michelle. I would have never thought

in my wildest dreams that she would turn on me. Or that she could ever blame me for Natalie's accident. I thought that we would always be on the same team and that we would get through this and everything else together. I was wrong. I don't know my wife as well as I thought I did."

"I guess that's because when she said those things to you, she wasn't herself. You and I both know the kind and sweet person Michelle is. All things considered, people have done and said a lot worse in a crisis."

Greg shrugged as he gave Umi's words consideration. "I want to believe that Michelle accused me because she didn't have her head on straight and I gave thought to the fact that she was definitely in emotional turmoil but I'm afraid to know if what she said is what she really feels. I can't live with that."

"How will you ever know if you don't speak to her? Communication is the key." Umi knew if Greg had one conversation with Michelle, it would set them back on track. Neither one of them could live without the other. Umi wanted to tell Greg how Michelle felt and the real reason behind Natalie's accident, but that would be out of line. It was Michelle's place to fill him in on the missing pieces. Umi just hoped Greg was smart enough to really listen to her and read between the lines.

Greg finally managed a smile at Umi's encouragement. "If I know anything about my wife, it's that she'll share her feelings with you. So do you think she'll talk to me? Do you really get a good feeling that we might be able to set this straight?"

"That depends."

"On?"

"If you can get over your hurt, if you can forgive her and if she can forgive you."

"Forgive me for what?" His handsome face wrinkled up as he sat upright.

Umi gave him a sharp look for asking such a stupid question. "You don't know?" She stared back at his blank face. Umi shouldn't have been surprised since men always seemed to forget when they'd played a role in disaster. "You walked out on your wife in the middle of a family crisis, a critical time when she needed your support and guidance." Her voice was harsh and condemning.

His shoulders slumped. "You're right, I can't argue with you there. I should have been there for her."

"You're damn right, you should have been there." Umi rolled her eyes and scooted closer to him, resting her hand on his arm. Her tone was calm when she spoke. "That brings me to my point. She accused you of something horrible and that's something Michelle would never do in her right mind. And you walked out on her at a time when she needed you and that's something you would never do in your right mind. So by now it's safe to assume that everyone's minds have been restored and amends can begin."

Greg looked at her sincerely. "Umi, you're truly a special woman. Michelle and I are lucky to have you for a friend." He gave her a long, tight hug.

"She's lucky to have you too." Umi spoke into his broad shoulder. She felt hopeful that she might have just rescued her best friend's marriage. They were silent for a moment, and Umi became immediately uncomfortable. "Let me get you something to drink." She broke their embrace, hopped up and headed for the kitchen. "Is soda okay?"

"Yeah." Greg shifted slightly.

When Umi returned with their sodas, Greg was sitting on the floor going through her photo albums.

"You know, I forgot about these old times. That's why I love old pictures: They remind you of yourself and all the things you used to do."

"I know." She sat on the floor next to him, keeping a comfortable distance.

"I remember this." He pointed to a picture of Michelle, Randi and Umi at Coney Island. They were standing on the boardwalk posing in their bathing suits. "If I recall, I took this picture. It was the first time I met Michelle and Randi."

"No. The first time you met Michelle and Randi was at my house. This was taken the next day," she reminded him and took a sip from her glass.

"You might be right, but I know it was during my first trip to New York. I had such a good time, I went back to Baltimore telling all my boys about y'all."

"I remember the horrible scene between Randi and that fool you hooked her up with." Umi chuckled lightly. "I can't remember his name, but I don't know what you were thinking trying to fix him up with Randi."

"That was Freddie. He saw one picture of Randi and was in love. I had to at least get the boy a phone number. I had no idea he would speak to her once and drive all the way to New York to meet her and then try to get her in the bed the same night." Greg shook his head. "I told him Randi was a little on the wild side, but I didn't mean that wild." He laughed at the memory. "I wonder whatever happened to him?"

"You don't keep in touch with your friends from Baltimore?"

"Some of them. I don't know if you've ever met Otis."

"Is he the one with the bald head that played basketball?"

"Nah, that's Charles. He's married and lives in Virginia. I speak to him occasionally. I keep in touch with Otis and another guy who lived next door to me named Will. Other than that everybody I keep ties with is from college or people from the job. And you don't want to get too close to them, know what I mean?" He laughed.

"Yeah." Umi laughed along with Greg.

It was ironic that Michelle and Greg met and fell in love through her, especially since she had intended on being with Greg herself. They met during her sophomore year at Delaware State University and Umi liked him immediately. They had a couple of classes together and teamed up as study partners.

One day they were cramming for finals when Greg mentioned that he had an aunt in New York and would be visiting with her during the summer, so Umi gave him her address and phone number with the hopes of getting a summer romance going. Greg had recently broken up with his high school sweetheart after learning the hard way that a long-distance romance was difficult to maintain, since she was attending Michigan State. Umi saw his breakup as her opportunity to get closer to him by being supportive and that meant talking him through a lot of lonely nights. They were never intimate—not even a passing kiss—but she thought all of that would change once she caught up with him in New York.

That never happened. Michelle and Greg hit it off right from the start. It didn't matter that Michelle had a baby and was struggling to get her degree. He was in love and so was she. Umi could have been jealous, but she wasn't. She figured that it wasn't meant to be. Instead she was happy to be the vehicle that brought two people that she cared about together.

Greg was flipping through the album, inspecting every picture, especially the ones that Michelle appeared in. "Ha, y'all did some silly stuff. I bet this was Randi's idea." He was pointing to a picture of the three of them dressed as Charlie's Angels, wearing wigs, hot pants and horrible makeup.

"You got that right. She always could influence us to do something crazy. I think that was at our high school's talent show." Umi scratched her head and remembered her scarf. Embarrassed, she slid it off and tucked it under her thigh.

"Oh yeah, Michelle told me about that. Who fell on the stage? Was it you or Randi?"

Umi laughed out loud. "She told you about that? I fell, but not during this skit. It was during an African dance number we did for Black History Month."

Umi was rattling on about some of the things they did in high school and how painful it was for them to part at the end of the summer when she and Michelle left for college, leaving Randi behind at Boys and Girls High School.

"Greg, are you listening to me?"

"Yeah." He was staring at pictures from his wedding. "I almost forgot how beautiful she looked on that day." He had a faraway look in his eyes.

"Yeah, she was a beautiful bride." Umi joined him in the memories. "It was a beautiful wedding, thanks to the coordinator, if I must say so myself." Umi playfully patted herself on the back.

"Umi, I need you to do something for me." Greg's voice was serious.

"What's that?"

He looked into her eyes and held her stare. "I want you to talk to Michelle for me."

She looked away and shook her head. "Greg, I would love to help you, but I don't think I should get in the middle of this."

"You don't have to get in the middle of anything, just talk to her and convince her to meet with me. Just kind of break the ice for me," he pleaded.

"If she wants to talk to you, she won't need any convincing from me." Umi stood. She didn't like where this was going.

"Umi, I love Michelle and I miss her. At this very moment, I have come to realize that I want to see her and make things right." He was standing too.

Umi felt sorry for him for a brief second. She wanted to help, but didn't want to get in the middle of their marriage and have her good intentions backfire. "Greg, I don't know if—"

"Umi, don't make me beg." He clasped his hands together in a prayer-like fashion.

Umi huffed, "Don't." She put her hands up to stop him, then turned her back to him. She swore she wouldn't get in the middle of this situation. She could hear Greg's anxious breathing behind her.

She closed her eyes and rubbed her temples before turning around to face him. "Look, I can't promise anything, but I'll mention something to her when I see her."

An instant smile spread across his face. "And when will that be?"

She gave him an annoyed look.

"Okay, okay. Thank you, that's all I'm asking is for you to casually mention something."

She returned the smile. "You realize that this means you owe me?"

"Oh yeah?"

"Yeah, and you can start repaying by helping me pack this stuff back in the closet, Begging Billy."

"It's a good thing you agreed to help me, because if you hadn't, I was going to take all my clothes off and run up and down your street screaming your name until you changed your mind." They laughed.

"Then I'm glad I decided when I did."

"Me, too. You saved us both an embarrassing moment."

After Greg helped Umi packed everything away and had left, she went over the evening and was glad he had stopped by and sought her help. She would keep her promise to assist him in making amends with Michelle and just hoped it didn't blow up in her face. She also thought about her past and present relationships with men and how they either ended or faded. Her thoughts immediately went to her working relationship with LaVelle. Things hadn't been the same between them since she pulled rank on him. She decided she would invite him out to a friendly lunch to ensure there were no hard feelings.

*

Be attentive. Those were the words Randi's mother uttered without hesitation when she told her that she was interested in spending her life with Brian. Good advice, but easier said than done. Brian was just as busy as Randi, if not busier. He was putting in a lot of extra time at work since his boss was scheduled to retire in a few months and Brian wanted to fill his position.

Meanwhile, Brian's preoccupation with work gave Randi the time she needed to see Franklin. And she certainly had her hands full with him. Their hit-and-run relationship had turned into a full-blown affair. He'd started sneaking out of his house in the middle of the night to see her for quickies, which she enjoyed, but they were way too risky in her opinion. He also started taking her for long lunches at the Marriott in Brooklyn, and he would plant sly little kisses on her neck and breasts when they were alone in the office or in the elevator.

It all had gotten a little out of hand, but Randi loved the attention. She knew she would eventually have to cut Franklin off before she married Brian, but she was going to enjoy every bit of him up until that point.

"When am I going to meet him?" Was her mother's first question following the advice. Randi promised her mother she would come over for lunch on Sunday and bring Brian with her. This way her mother could meet and inspect him, and Randi could show Brian that she wanted something more by bringing him home to meet her mother.

Randi set her oven timer for forty-five minutes and slid in the lasagna. Brian would be over in about an hour and she still hadn't showered or changed her bed sheets. She rushed around the living room picking up magazines and old newspapers left behind from Franklin's last visit. Surprisingly, they actually did some work on their research project. Their first joint project went so well they were asked to work together on another one. Her supervisor was so pleased with what they produced, she said at the next supervisors meeting she would mention having researchers work as partners. Franklin was happier than a pig in slop when he heard that.

Randi intentionally left work in the middle of the day to prepare for this evening, which was not easy to do on a Friday at the *New York Times.* She only made two stops: first to the supermarket to pick up the ingredients for her lasagna, then to the liquor store for something to compliment her dinner, and she was still running behind schedule.

She took a quick shower, put new silk sheets on her bed, gelled her short hair back, tied it down tight with a scarf and threw on her biking shorts and an old college T-shirt.

By the time the bell rang twenty minutes later, she slid her headscarf off and was ready and waiting.

"Hi." He took a minute to kiss her sweetly at the door. "Sorry I'm a little late. I stayed a few extra minutes to shoot the breeze with some of the guys and Mr. Gans."

"I figured as much." Randi took his leather bag and rested it by the sofa. "I hope you're hungry. I cooked."

"What?" He rushed to open the oven door and peeked in. "I know that's not lasagna."

"Oh, yes it is."

He eyed her suspiciously and smiled. "What's the deal?"

"No deal." She shrugged. "I just wanted to do something nice for you. Why don't you get comfortable while I set the table?" She tugged playfully at his tie.

"Okay, but I know something's up," he called as he headed toward her bedroom.

"Nothing's up," she answered him from the kitchen.

Brian returned wearing the only outfit he had at her apartment—an old sweat suit. He stood in the entranceway and watched her as she moved around the kitchen with grace and skill.

She looked over at him and smiled warmly.

He smiled back and then sat down at the table. "Girl, this smells good."

"And it tastes even better," she said, her smile still gleaming.

"You know what? One of the guys from the office loaned me his Chris Rock video. Why don't we eat this in the living room while we watch it?"

She started to protest. She had her heart set on a romantic

evening, but she didn't want to start an argument now. She shrugged and began setting up the TV tables in the living room.

They each had two helpings of lasagna and drank half the bottle of wine, while they watched Chris Rock deliver jokes that had them laughing until their eyes watered. Brian kept rewinding the video to hear the same punch lines over and over.

When the video ended, Brian hit the stop button and the evening news appeared on the screen. He stretched out on the love seat. "Boy, I'm stuffed." He patted his tight abs. "Chris Rock is funny as hell." He laughed again.

"He was alright. I could have done without all of the degrading jokes about women." Randi was lying on the sofa, looking up at the ceiling.

"They're just jokes. I don't think comedians really believe the things they say, its just part of the job. Something to get the crowd laughing."

"I hardly see anything funny about blind people needing dogs."

"But I saw you laughing." He was grinning and pointing accusingly at her.

"No you didn't." She threw a pillow at him.

They laughed together.

She sat up. "I'm going to go get ready for bed."

"Did you say *bed*?" His eyebrows did a dance on his forehead.

"I most certainly did." She sashayed past him and headed for her bedroom.

"Whoa." He grabbed her from behind and carried her the rest of the way.

"You are so silly. Put me down." She playfully fought him off.

"Now you want to fight me?" He put her down and put his hands up, skipping around in a boxing motion.

"Stop, Brian. I don't want to fight you."

He stopped and eyed her seductively. "What do you want then?"

"I want to win." She slapped his face, threw her hands up, mocking him. "Now, what you wanna do? What you wanna do?"

"Oh, I see, you want to sucker-slap a brother. Alright, then."
He lunged for her and they fell on the bed together laughing.

"Are we boxing or wrestling?" she managed to ask between
laughs.

"You're crazy, girl. Got me jumping around after all that
good food I just ate." He stretched out on his back, trying to catch
his breath.

Randi straddled him and slowly rubbed her pelvis against
him. She watched the smile on his face grow—along with another
part of him.

"You want me?" she asked in her little girl voice.

His eyes were closed. He nodded in response.

She stood. "I'll be right back." She grabbed her silk nightgown and went into the bathroom. When she returned, she quickly
modeled for him, twisting and turning so he could admire her tight
body from every angle, before kneeling in front of him and pulling
down his sweatpants. Just the sight of his large member straining
to stay hidden in his bikini briefs was enough to make her want
to jump all over him, but she exercised restraint and let her tongue
slow-dance with him first.

After their lovemaking, Randi was exhausted as she snuggled tightly in Brian's arms. Now she was ready to put phase two
of her plan in motion.

"I spoke to my mom today," she said slowly.

"Oh yeah? Is everything alright?"

Randi sighed heavily for effect. "Yeah, she's just lonely. She
wanted to know why I haven't been over more often."

"I thought you dropped in on her at least twice a week?"

"I usually do, but lately I've been so busy at the paper, I
haven't kept it up."

"You have been working hard." He was stroking her hair.

An image of Franklin popped into her head. She closed her
eyes tightly until it disappeared, then continued. "I promised her
I would stop by on Sunday and have lunch with her. I also promised her that you'd be with me."

"What? Why did you commit me before asking me? I have
plans on Sunday."

"Plans to do what?"

"I was going to go to the gym." His voice was a little strained.

"You can still go. Just go before or after lunch with Mama."

"Randi, you should have spoken to me first."

"What is the big deal?" Her voice was beginning to strain as well. "You don't want to meet my mother?"

She could tell by his silence that the accusation caught him off guard.

"This is not about lunch with your mama. This is about respecting my time. You should have asked me first."

There was a long silence between them.

Randi didn't know why he was tripping. She was just about to ask him, but he started speaking.

"I would love to have lunch with you and your mother on Sunday, but next time, I want you to ask me before you commit me to anything." His voice was soft again.

"Yes, Big Daddy." She spoke in her little girl voice as she played with the hair on his chest.

He covered her hand with his. "I'm serious, Randi. Don't do that to me again."

"Okay." She dragged the word out and nestled deeper in his big arms. She was expecting him to put up a fight about not being ready to meet her mother, or say something about it being too big a step for him. She was glad to have avoided such a conversation. Maybe he was interested in taking their relationship to another level as well. The thought brought a smile to her face. She relaxed as her head filled with plans for their wedding day until she drifted off to sleep.

As soon as her day started, Randi knew it was going to be a crazy one. Whenever her phone rang early on a Sunday morning, that was a sure sign that the day wouldn't be normal.

"Good morning." Her voice was full of sleep.

"Hey, baby, what's up?" Franklin's voice was full of life on the other end.

"Franklin, why are you calling me so early in the morning?"

He knew instantly by her tone, that she was alone. "I wanted to catch you before you started your day to see if you can fit me in somewhere."

"I'm sorry, boo. I already have plans. We can do something tomorrow after work though." Randi was rubbing the sleep from her eyes.

"Plans with Brian?"

Was that jealousy she was hearing? "Of course with Brian," she answered matter-of-factly.

"Oh, well it doesn't have to be long. Maybe we can just get breakfast and I'll have you back in time to do whatever you have to do."

The offer sounded tempting, but she had a schedule to keep. She started running down her day in her head. She wanted to do her laundry and get that out of the way first, then she was going to get dressed and go to Brian's apartment by one-thirty, so they could head over to her mother's house together. It would be kind of tight, and she wasn't sure if she should try to squeeze Franklin in.

"Well, I have a full day and—"

"I really need to see you," he said softly.

She couldn't help but smile, hearing him beg for some of her time, as fine as he was. Her ego was so big it was about to burst all over her bedroom. "Okay," she finally agreed. "But only breakfast."

"That's my girl."

She could picture him smiling on the other end of the phone. "When and where?"

"How about Junior's restaurant at ten?"

It was seven-thirty. She could get a little more sleep and still get to the restaurant on time. "Okay. I'll see you then."

"I can't wait."

She hung up the phone and rolled over on her side and was out like a light. By nine-thirty, Randi was showered, dressed and out the door heading for Junior's on Flatbush Avenue, which was just a short walk from her apartment. The spring breeze was blowing her hair all over her head and she looked like a wild chicken by the time she met up with Franklin, who was standing outside the restaurant waiting for her.

She kissed him quickly on the lips. "This wind is something else. I need to get to the ladies' room," she said as they entered the restaurant. They were escorted to their table. She set her bag and jacket on her chair. "I'll be right back."

In the bathroom, she raked her fingers through her wild hair, admired her reflection in the mirror and was back at the table in a flash.

Breakfast went smoothly. She enjoyed her French toast and eggs, and Franklin was wolfing down a plate of grits and ham. They laughed and talked as usual and everything was going fine until Franklin suggested having a quickie at the Marriott, which was just a few blocks away.

"Franklin, I already told you my time is limited. I have plans today."

"So what? Tell Brian something came up."

"Do I ask you to tell Jackie that when you can't get away to be with me?" Randi shot back angrily.

"No, you don't." His eyes were apologetic. "I just want to be with you."

"You are with me." Her voice was still annoyed.

He glanced at his watch. "Look, if we leave now, we can make this breakfast a more memorable one, and I can have you home in an hour."

"Yeah, right." Randi laughed at him softly. Seeing him beg always did something to her.

"We've done it before," he sweetly reminded her as he ran his fingers along her hand.

"Franklin, you are going to make me late," she whined.

"No, I'm not. I promise." He was smiling broadly.

He threw thirty-five dollars on the table and rushed her out of the restaurant and right into a room at the Marriott.

Experience speaking for itself, Randi should have known better than to let Franklin convince her that she'd be home in an hour. It was one-fifteen when she got home all sweaty and smelling like hot sex. She wanted to kick herself for not sticking to her schedule. Now her laundry wasn't done and she was going to be late for lunch.

She had four messages on her machine. The first was a hang-up, the second and third were Brian looking for her. Covering up shouldn't be a problem. She would simply tell him she was downstairs in the laundry room. The last one was her mother asking questions about what Brian liked to eat or was allergic to. She hit the erase button without listening to the entire message. Her mother was one of those people who could easily leave a five-minute message, and she didn't have that kind of time.

She was glad she'd ironed her clothes before leaving for breakfast. She was in and out of the shower and into her clothes in a flash. She was making good time, but was tripped up when she couldn't find her beige Kenneth Coles. She started searching through shoeboxes like a madwoman when it hit her that she loaned them to Michelle a few months ago.

"Damn." She thought about changing her clothes, but didn't have time for that, so she slipped into a pair of black patent leather Donna Karans, that completely threw off her mint-and-beige ensemble, but they would have to do. She grabbed her makeup bag to take with her and would do her face when she got to Brian's. Then she grabbed her wallet, threw it into her beige Coach bag and was out the door.

Brian only lived a few blocks away, so when she got in the car she called him from her cell phone to tell him to be downstairs. When she got his machine, she figured he was probably already in the lobby waiting and didn't bother leaving a message. When she pulled in front of his co-op, it was a little after two. She was more than thirty minutes late.

"Can you ring 16B, please?" she asked the doorman, who had seen her a million times, but could never remember her name.

"Mr. Mosley isn't home, Ms. uhh—"

"Ms. Randi."

"Ms. Randi," he repeated.

She was confused. "How long ago did he leave?"

"I'm guessing about an hour or so."

"Did he leave a message for me?"

"No, ma'am. He walked right out without a word."

Randi thought for a moment. *Where could he have gone? He knew I was coming.* "I'll have a seat and wait a minute. Maybe he'll show up."

He nodded. "Would you like a newspaper?" He pointed to a rack in the corner.

"Thank you." She took a paper and sat stiffly on the leather sofa across from the concierge station and opened the paper wide enough to shield her from the doorman's stare.

By 2:45, Randi couldn't stand waiting another minute. She
knew her mother was pacing back and forth by now wondering
what was keeping her and Brian.

She returned the newspaper to the doorman, jumped in her
Sentra and headed for her mother's house on the other side of
town. When she arrived her mother opened the door before she
could even ring the bell.

"I've been worried sick. What took you so long? You said
two o'clock." When she realized Randi was alone the final question came. "Where's Brian?"

"Can I get in the door, Mama?" Randi was aggravated with
the entire situation. She set her jacket and purse on the sofa and
flopped down next to them. "Something came up and Brian could-
n't make it at the last minute."

"Oh." Her mother sounded as disappointed as Randi felt.

"But there's no reason why we can't enjoy lunch together,
right?" She patted her mother's arm softly.

"You're absolutely right." Dollie threw on a fake smile and
pretended not to notice her daughter's disappointment. "Let's go
in the kitchen. Hugh called a while ago and said he'd be stopping
by later."

"Yeah?" Randi hadn't seen her littler brother in a while and
was a little excited about seeing him. "I haven't seen Hugh in about
two months."

"He's busy at the hospital all the time. They always have him
on call."

"He loves his work though." She followed her mother into
the kitchen.

Randi and her mother shared a pleasant and quiet afternoon
together. They ate lunch, followed by ice cream and pie and bat-
tled each other in what seemed like a never-ending game of
Connect Four. By six o'clock Hugh still hadn't shown up and
Randi couldn't get Brian off her mind, so she decided to head
home.

"I'll call you later, Mama," Randi said as she slid into her
jacket.

"You sure you don't want to wait a little longer for your
brother. I know he's coming. He has to drop off my pressure medication."

"No, I have to get ready for work tomorrow. Tell Hugh to give me a call when he has a minute." She kissed her mother's cheek.

Randi didn't think she could feel any lower than she already did. But when she got home and had no messages on her machine, she did the unthinkable and sank just a bit lower. It was only a little before seven o'clock, but she was exhausted. She took off her clothes and slung them over the chair in her bedroom and climbed into bed in her bra and panties.

She wanted so badly to call Brian, but she could hear Umi's voice in her head scolding her for wanting to and encouraging her not to. *Be strong, black woman. Be strong.* She rolled over, closed her eyes tightly and forced herself to go to sleep.

CHAPTER 9

Umi sipped her herbal tea patiently as she waited for LaVelle to return with her coat from the coat check. They were going to take a walk along Emmons Avenue in Sheepshead Bay and take in some of the fresh spring breeze that was blowing in off the water nearby.

It seemed silly now, after having had a wonderful lunch with him, but Monday morning when she got to her office she had been a little nervous about asking him out. She didn't want to give him the wrong impression, so her invitation had to be the perfect blend of business jargon and friendly intention. She smiled as the conversation replayed in her head.

"LaVelle, can you come in when you have a moment please?" Umi spoke into the intercom.

A few seconds later, there was a tap at the door and he entered, sharply dressed as always, with pen and pad in hand, ready to jot down anything she said as soon as it came out of her mouth.

"Have a seat." She looked through the files on her desk, pulled one out and skimmed through it. "I want a memo to go out to the team announcing a meeting next Wednesday, the twentieth at ten o'clock. This meeting will be in addition to our regularly scheduled monthly meeting. Here is a list of topics that will be covered." She handed him a piece of paper and waited as he looked it over.

Since the incident with Valerie and everything surrounding it, Umi's relationship with her assistant wasn't as relaxed as it was before. LaVelle was always polite and on task, but there was a difference. There were no more warm smiles greeting her in the mornings or any other extra pleasantries he'd showered her with before, especially when they were alone together like now. Before,

there'd be friendly chitchat about how he could jazz up any kind
of vegetable so that it was pleasing to eat or funny stories about
his army days. She wasn't trying to initiate anything other than
business, but she missed the friendliness they shared from time to
time.

"Okay. Is there anything else?" His voice was warm, but
laced with just enough bass to let her know he was all business.

"Actually, yes." Umi took a deep breath as she prepared to
ask him out to lunch, but lost her nerve. "I went over some of the
preliminary outlines you drew up for the Dagwood account. Is that
all of the feedback you got from the team?"

"That's all. I spoke to Greta as she was leaving last Friday,
and she told me she had something she was working on for the
Dagwood account, and it would be ready shortly."

"Maybe you should add that to the list of topics for
Wednesday's meeting. List it as Dagwood Account. We worked
our butts off to get this account, now we have to show Mr.
Dagwood that he's made a worthwhile decision."

"I agree," he said, still writing on his pad.

He looked up at her, deep into her eyes. They shared a silent
exchange, and then he stood to leave.

This was her chance, while she had him here. "Uh, LaVelle,
one more thing." Umi stood, too, and came around her desk to
face him. "I was wondering if you'd like to have lunch with me
next weekend." Her heart was pounding in her chest. She hadn't
considered what she'd do if he turned her down.

He didn't answer right away, as he recovered from shock.
But his eyes said it all, the warm look let her know immediately
that all was forgiven and the invitation was happily accepted.

"Lunch sounds wonderful. Let me know when." He gave her
that winning smile she loved so much.

"I'll do that." She was speaking to his back as he went
through the door.

"Ready to go?" LaVelle's husky voice brought her back to
the restaurant. He held her coat open for her.

"Yes, thank you."

They headed out and started on Emmons Avenue. Umi had-
n't been to this part of town in a while and had no idea that it had

become such an attraction. It had recently been built up and was filled with several upscale seafood restaurants and clothing stores. So many people were out along the stretch that she and LaVelle kept getting separated by the crowd. She finally grabbed his jacket sleeve and held on to him.

"Why don't we go over and take a look at the yachts?" LaVelle broke their silence.

"Good idea."

They walked along the pier and LaVelle's eyes filled with wonder and excitement as they approached the dock. "You know, when I was a little boy my uncle had a yacht. One summer he took my family sailing. My dad, who is his older brother, my mother and me and my sister. Ever since then, it's been my dream to own one."

They stopped and leaned on a post as he continued with his story.

"The funniest thing is, my sister can barely remember being there. It had such a profound effect on me and not the slightest effect on her."

"That is funny. Was she too young to remember?"

"I don't think so. She's four years older than me."

"Oh." Umi wanted to ask him how old he was, but didn't want to get too personal.

"Have you ever had that happen to you? An event that you remember so vividly, but someone else who was there with you may not remember it very well?"

"I'm not sure, but I do have a lot of memories from my youth that have stuck with me through the years." *Most of them involving lying, cheating, no-good men,* the voice in her head added as she smiled at him.

"Oh yeah? Anything you care to share?"

"No, not really." She grinned slyly.

"I bet." He smiled.

Umi took in his easy smile and flashed him one of her own.

"You strike me as the type of person who's always together, even as a kid," he teased her. "Never losing your cool. I can picture you as the little diplomat on the playground, but not the instigator." His white teeth were gleaming in the sunlight.

"Me?" She playfully pointed to herself.

"Yeah, you. I admire that characteristic. Were you like that with your sisters and brothers?"

"My sister and I never fought."

"Not even once?"

Umi shook her head.

"Okay, an argument?"

"Not even. She was three years younger than me and from the time she was born she was always very sick." Umi's voice softened a little as she remembered the sister who was in and out of her life quickly. "She was born with a rare kidney disease that kept her weak and bedridden. We didn't share the things that most siblings share as children. She died when she was seven. I was only ten, but it definitely had a life-changing effect on me."

"I'm so sorry to hear that. It must have been hard for you."

"It was at the time, but I'm glad for that experience because I learned something at a very young age that most people never learn throughout their entire lives: I learned the value of life and that it should be taken seriously. And everything we do eventually affects the quality of our lives, whether it's not finishing school, bad relationships, drugs, poor money management and on and on and on." They were standing closely together, leaning on the same post.

"Wow, that's deep. I've never looked at it from that standpoint, but you're absolutely right. It ties into my own theory that you never meet anyone by mistake."

"What?" Umi laughed at him.

"It sounds funny, but everyone you meet has been put into your life to serve a purpose. Think about it for a minute, your sister was in your life for a short time, but it was enough time for you to learn a lesson that has made you the accomplished woman you are."

"Wrong, Freud. I stand as the woman I am today because of hard work and dedication."

"Okay, then is it fair to say that it was a tragedy that motivated you?" He gave her a cocky, overconfident smile.

"Just to be fair, I'll say you're close, but not exact." She returned the smile.

"Touché."

"I'm glad that's settled. Now can we talk about something a

bit more pleasing?" she asked.

"Okay, but one more question."

Umi let out a loud sigh as a signal that he was pushing it.

"Were you lonely being an only child?"

"I was far from lonely. I had a lot of friends and my mother's sister didn't live far from us, so I went over to play with my cousins often. And when I got to high school I met two girls who have been my best friends until this very day."

"That's a long friendship." He playfully counted his fingers.

She swatted at him. "It hasn't been that long."

He was laughing and shielding himself. "You're right."

"Now it's my turn to ask some questions."

"Okay, shoot."

"Did you have a close relationship with your sister?"

He was nodding before she could even finish the question. "The best. Like most blacks in the sixties, we didn't have a lot of money. My dad was in the army. When he came home, he delivered mail until he retired. My mom worked as a secretary for this white guy who owned a small company. He would have her there twelve hours a day sometimes. A few times my dad went down to the office and made her come home. She would be so angry because we couldn't afford for her to lose her job. Well, in the meantime, my sister was raising me. She was my baby-sitter, my mother and my best friend."

They continued walking along Emmons Avenue as he told his story.

"We talk about the stages of our relationship and laugh at them. At first she was the ruler, then when I became a teenager and formed my own opinion, we sort of became partners, and as a man, she's my advisor, but always my friend."

"That's sweet." Umi listened as he talked about his sister. "What did she advise you on?"

"First girls, then women, and everything that came along with getting to know them and getting to know them better." He laughed at himself. "It's too bad she couldn't school me on how to handle my ex-wife, Sabrina. If she had a tenth of your common sense, we could have probably had a successful marriage"

So that's the fool's name that lost this gem. Umi appreciated the compliment, but wasn't comfortable getting so personal.

However, since the door had been opened, she decided to enter. "Gee, thanks, but your ex-wife couldn't have been all that bad, after all, you married her."

"You have a point, but I didn't marry her, I married the person I thought she was. She was a fake the entire time we dated. She filled my head with made-up stories about herself, I guess to impress me and then after we were married, she dropped all these bombs on me." He was shaking his head as though he still couldn't believe it himself.

Umi didn't want to pry, but couldn't resist. "Like what?"

"Big things, Umi. Not little white lies you tell to make yourself look good, but unnecessary things that only counseling can help. For instance, she shared an apartment with her sister and her sister's son, well once we were married she let me know that the little boy is not her nephew, but actually her son."

"What?" Umi stopped in her tracks. "You're kidding, right?"

"Nope, and it only gets worse. Once I got over that hurdle, I got hit with another blow. The people she had been introducing me to all that time as her parents are really her aunt and uncle. Her real parents were strung out on drugs and couldn't take care of her and her sister. She never told me this. I found this information out from one of her relatives at a wedding we went to."

"Well, she was probably just embarrassed about her real parents." Umi tried to reason, although the girl did sound like she needed professional help.

"I'm the man she chose to spend her life with, and she couldn't tell me that?" His hands went up in disgust. "I had to get out of that situation and quickly, but it wasn't easy. I tried to make it work for more than two years, but the longer I stayed married to her the worse it got. Finally, I packed my things and shipped out."

"I feel sorry for the child. It must not be easy for him," Umi said.

"He's a sweet kid too."

"It sounds to me like you did the right thing by getting out of that situation." Umi shivered against the steady breeze. "It's getting kind of nippy."

"You want to stop for some tea?"

She weighed her options carefully. On one hand she would have loved to spend more time with him, but on the other, she knew it wasn't such a good idea to get too close too quickly. She had to stay focused and remind herself that this lunch was just to ensure that there were no hard feelings, and not a date.

"I would like to, but it's already after four o'clock, and I have some things I need to do at home." *Like call Darren.* She had told him she would be with Randi this afternoon.

"Yeah, me too. I hadn't realized it had gotten so late. Time really flies when you're having fun."

They talked some more on the way to her car.

"Thanks for lunch, Umi. I really had a good time."

"Don't mention it. I enjoyed myself too." Then without giving it another thought, she gave him a quick kiss on his cheek. "I'll see you in the office tomorrow."

"Right. Tomorrow." He opened her door for her to get in and watched her pull off.

*

Michelle pulled the lid off another storage box, this one was labeled JULY - SEPTEMBER 1997. In the two weeks she'd been coming to Gail's house, she had managed to sort, organize and calculate only one year's receipts. Gail had the right idea about holding on to receipts, but she didn't organize a single one of them. She just threw them all in a storage box.

She probably would have gotten more done, but the first day she came over, Gail gave her a tour of her beautiful house, which had a sort of art-deco style to it and was decorated with expensive things. It was a fairly large house for one person, but Michelle didn't bother questioning her friend. One thing was certain: Gail sure could afford it. Between her shop and her investments, the girl was making money, and her money was making money.

In addition to not getting anything done on the first day, the following week, Michelle missed a day because she had to see her mother off. Grace was finally returning to Florida after spending almost six months with her. She hated to see her mother go, but it didn't make much sense for her to stay since Michelle would be over at Gail's most of the time.

Michelle managed to work out a system to help her through her day. She arrived at Gail's by nine o'clock, worked until noon, then took a break to go see Natalie and was usually back and working by two o'clock. Sometimes Gail would stay in and make lunch for them and other times Michelle wouldn't see her the entire day. Michelle worked out of Gail's home office, which was a room she had added onto the side of the house with a separate entrance. Some days she would hear Gail's car pulling in and out of the driveway, but wouldn't see her.

She set the box on the floor, took a seat next to it and was sorting receipts into piles labeled BUSINESS LUNCHES and SHOP SUPPLIES when Gail came in.

"Hey, Michelle. How's it going?"

"Pretty smoothly."

"Glad to hear that." She spoke in her usual upbeat tone, which always put Michelle in a lighter mood. "I stopped by the deli on the way in and picked up some lunch for you." She held up a bag.

"Thanks, but lunch this time of day? It's after three."

"I figured you would have eaten by now, but you can take it home and have it for dinner." She set the bag on the desk.

"What did you get?"

"Tuna on rye." She sat on the floor next to Michelle. "Can I help?"

"No. You're paying me to do this, remember?"

"I remember." Gail scooted away from the piles of receipts and rested her back against the wall. "I have to go back to court in about six weeks, and I thought that maybe if I took some of the sorted receipts with me, it would at least show the judge that I'm working on complying with his orders."

Michelle thought for a moment. "Gail, this is way more than six weeks worth of work."

"I know. It's probably more like six months." Her observation made Michelle laugh. "So let me help just a little and maybe we can get it done in five months instead."

"If you start interfering, it's going to take more like a year." Michelle started busying herself with the receipts again. "I work better by myself."

"Then I'll do something that doesn't have to be done around you."

Michelle put down the receipts she was holding. "Okay, since you insist. I've written down a list of categories that most of your receipts will fall into. If you come across a receipt that doesn't seem to fit into any of the categories, put it in a miscellaneous pile and I'll sort through it when you're done."

"Now that's something I can do." Gail stood. "Where's the list?"

"On the desk. The next box to be sorted is labeled OCTOBER - DECEMBER 1997."

"Girl, I don't even remember what I was doing in 1997. Oh, yes I do. I hired a hit man to kill someone who broke my heart. I wonder if I'll find that receipt in there."

"If you do, it goes in the miscellaneous pile." Michelle laughed at her own joke.

"It should go under medical expenses, since getting that jerk out of my life was just what the doctor ordered."

They laughed in unison.

"I know that's right. Having your heart broken is no joke."

Gail sighed and leaned back in the chair behind the desk. "You know what I hated most? Loving and hating the person all at the same time."

Michelle waved her hand in the air. "I'm a witness. Been there. Done that."

"What about wanting to call all the time?"

"Been there too," Michelle testified from the floor.

"Oh no, this is the real kicker." Gail was sitting up now and banging her hand on the desk for emphasis. "What about finally calling and the number has been changed?"

Michelle thought about her own situation. She couldn't even call Greg. Didn't even know where he lived. The thought made her sad. She didn't want to talk about this anymore. "What about focusing on the positive? We finally heal and move on with our lives."

"You're right. And most importantly: A valuable lesson was learned."

"That is most important because experience is the best teacher. That's what my mother always says." Michelle was back to sorting receipts.

Gail came and sat on the floor near her. "But you know what, Michelle? Even after all these years, when I think about it, I get that twinge in my heart that lets me know something is still there."

Michelle put her receipts down again. It didn't look like she was going to get much done with Gail around. "I think that happens because healing emotionally takes a long time. We have a few good days and think we're passed it, but not really. Only the top layer has healed. The hurt is still very raw underneath."

Silence had surrounded them. Just as Gail opened her mouth to ask a question, Michelle began speaking again.

"I know, Gail, because I'm living it right now." Her words were soft and full of emotion.

Gail reached over and held Michelle's hand. "I'm sorry. I was so caught up in my own bullshit, I just started rambling. You don't have to talk about this if you don't want to."

"I'm okay." Michelle smiled bravely and gave her hand a quick squeeze. "At least I can say that my top layer has healed."

"Honestly, Michelle, when I saw you with your family in the mall, you and your husband looked so in love. I would have never guessed."

"When you saw us that day, we were in love. The trouble didn't start until a couple of weeks later."

Michelle told Gail the story from start to finish, of course leaving out the part about the drugs she had discovered in Natalie's room and a few other minor details she wanted to keep to herself. She practically emptied a box of facial tissue as she went through the part about the girls being hooked up to machines and Kate's vicious words about Natalie.

Gail listened quietly and dabbed at her own tears as Michelle told her heartbreaking story. "Wow, I don't know what to say. I was prepared to give you a ton of advice on how to handle a cheating husband or his nagging ex-wife. I had no idea you were going through something like this." She moved closer to Michelle and put her arms around her shoulders.

Michelle relaxed in Gail's embrace and let her head fall on her chest. She dried her eyes with her already soggy tissue and cleared her throat. "I'm sorry, Gail. I didn't mean to come here and talk your head off about my problems."

"Shhh, don't worry about it. I'm here whenever you feel like talking." She was rubbing small circles on Michelle's back with the palm of her hand.

"Thank you." She sniffled as she welcomed Gail's massage. The feel of Gail's hand on her back was almost intoxicating. She let her eyes close and took in the feeling. She didn't mind the back massage, or even when Gail started massaging her scalp, but her eyes shot wide open when she felt Gail's other hand gently circle her thigh. She pulled away a bit.

"I'm sorry. Do you want me to stop?" Gail's voice was low and husky.

After a moment, Michelle shook her head and relaxed again, letting Gail's massage continue. It wasn't long before Gail's hand reached her center and was teasing her through her pants. The sensation was so inviting that Michelle didn't bother to stop her. Instead she shifted to give Gail's fingers a better aim. That's when she felt the warmth on her neck, then Gail's tender lips and soft, wet tongue.

Michelle's first instinct was to stop, but she couldn't fight the thrill her body was receiving. She even shocked herself when she realized she was moving in rhythm with Gail's hand. And that's all she realized, other than outside the sun was going down.

Michelle rolled over and pulled the sheet over her head to shield her eyes from the sunlight, when she suddenly remembered where she was and became paralyzed with fear. She didn't know why she had a strange feeling in her stomach and an awful taste in her mouth. Then it all came rushing back to her. The champagne and strawberries, the kissing, the *sex!* Michelle shut her eyes tightly, trying to calm her nerves and silently begged God to forgive her. She became stiff as a board when she heard the door open. She could hear a dresser drawer open and close and Gail's feet moving over the carpet.

"Gail?" she called softly from under the sheet.

"Well, good morning, sleepyhead." Gail sat next to Michelle and pulled the covers back.

Michelle's face must have told it all because Gail's eyes were immediately filled with concern. "Are you alright?"

Hell no, I'm not alright! She sat up in the bed, "Gail, we need to talk." Michelle was so confused she didn't know where to start.

"I think we should talk." She patted Michelle's hand. "Why don't you shower and get dressed, and if you feel like it we can

go out and get breakfast, or maybe I should say lunch." She gave
Michelle a broad smile to lighten the tense mood in the room.

"I laid out some things for you to wear. They're brand new,
the tags are still on them and there's a new toothbrush in the bathroom."

Michelle sat silently and kept her eyes focused on the trees
outside.

"I'll be downstairs." Gail left the room and Michelle came to
life. She jumped out of the bed in a panic. She had to get out of
there. What was she doing? How did she let this happen? She paced
around the room several times before she stopped herself and sat on
the foot of the bed until she pulled her thoughts together.

After her shower, Michelle put on the clothes Gail laid out
for her. A beautiful Calvin Klein set, a long skirt and matching
tunic and an Express bra-and-panty set. She had calmed down
enough to prepare something to say to Gail when she got downstairs. The first thing was she wouldn't be returning to her house.
She would explain that she would keep her promise and do the
work, but just not there; she would work from her own home
instead. That would be the best thing.

When Michelle got downstairs, Gail was in the kitchen flipping through a magazine.

"Hi." Gail put her magazine down. "Ready for some breakfast?"

Michelle sat across from her at the table. "I'm not going to
be able to make breakfast, Gail. And by the way, I'm not exactly
sure why last night happened, but I'm sure that it won't ever happen again. I want to let you know that I'll continue to help you,
but I'll do the work at home from now on." The words came out
of her mouth so fast, her bluntness surprised her, but she said it,
and it was easier than she thought.

Gail nodded as Michelle continued. "And in all fairness, I
think you should know that I don't appreciate one bit how you
took advantage of me last night."

"Took advantage of you? Now, you're out of line. Michelle,
I understand you're upset, but you know last night happened
because you wanted it to." Gail was trying her best to keep her
voice level.

"I wanted to make love to you? Oh, no, missy, you're mistaken. I'm not like you. I'm far from gay." Michelle's tone was harsh.

Gail inhaled deeply before responding. Michelle could tell she was struggling to keep her cool, but she didn't care. "In case you didn't know, you don't have to be gay to want physical attention."

"Oh, I know. You're gay when you want that attention from a person of the same sex—and that's not me." Michelle stood up to leave. "Where are my things?"

Gail took another deep breath and softened her tone. "Michelle, I don't want you to leave like this. If you're worried about it, last night didn't make you gay. It was just two lonely women sharing a moment together. And you're right, what happened last night wasn't fair to either of us or our friendship."

Michelle was surprised by Gail's softened attitude and wasn't sure how to respond. She shifted her weight to one foot and folded her arms across her chest. "My things?" she managed to whisper.

"In the living room." Gail looked away.

Michelle gathered her belongings and headed home. When she got there, she didn't know what to do with herself. Her mother was back in Florida, Umi and Randi were at work, and she was alone again.

She made herself busy around the house, straightening up here and there and tidying up this and that. After a couple of hours, she couldn't stand it anymore. She picked up the phone and called Gail. "We need to talk."

CHAPTER 10

Randi suffered through the first three days of the week alone and in silence. She turned off her phone at home and ignored the messages left by Brian and Franklin. At the office, she buried herself in work and gave Franklin the cold shoulder every chance she got. She was so disappointed over the turn of events the previous weekend and worst of all she found herself feeling a bit jealous and possessive because she didn't know where Brian was on Sunday when he promised to be with her.

Even though she knew the men in her life weren't completely at fault, she just couldn't accept total responsibility for what happened on Sunday. Franklin's greediness and Brian's forgetfulness were where she was happy placing the blame. Now she really had to play her cards right if she was going to follow through with her plans to marry Brian. She needed to show him that she was angry and force him to make up with her, but she couldn't get too angry and push him away. And as far as Franklin was concerned, she could care less what he decided to do. She was going to give him her ass to kiss until she felt better.

It was already after two, and the cafeteria would be emptying out, so Randi decided to get a snack from the vending machine. She was right. When she got there the cafeteria was completely empty. She took her time at the machine deciding between a Snickers and a Twix.

"Well, I thought I'd never get a chance to be alone with you again."

She pretended not to hear the smooth baritone voice she loved so much.

Franklin stepped closely behind her and kissed her neck.

"Don't touch me." Randi moved away from him.

"Randi, how many times do I have to apologize for last weekend? I just wanted to spend time with you." His voice was soft, but not soft enough to make her give in.

Randi faced him and kept her voice low in case someone was walking the halls outside. "That's just it. It's all about what you want. You didn't give a damn about me or the fact that I told you I already had plans."

"That's not true, and you know it. Maybe I let my desire rule my common sense, but that's only because I enjoy being with you."

"Franklin, save the fancy talk. You're just plain-old selfish, and I can't be bothered with someone who's selfish and senseless." Randi put her hand on her hip. "You messed up my entire day, and for what? A simple fuck that could have happened at anytime."

"You know you're anything but simple." He almost smiled. "I didn't mean to mess up your plans. Let me make it up to you." His voice was sincere.

She got her candy out of the machine and turned to leave.

"In Orlando."

Randi stopped dead in her tracks. "What?" She turned to face him.

"Let's go to Orlando. This weekend. Just you, me and Mickey." He hit her with his winning smile.

Randi entertained the invitation for a split second. "I don't think so."

He grabbed her hand and started swinging it from side to side. "You know you want to," he sang.

"I'm mad at you. Give me my space to be mad and get over it. Invite me in another week or two." She tried to pull her hand out of his, but he wouldn't let go.

"Hey, Frank, man. What's up?" One of the guys from the office entered the cafeteria.

Franklin dropped her hand like a hot potato. "Hey, Pete, nothing much. What's up with the softball team this year?"

Randi started heading for the door without a word.

"Uh, Ms. Young, think about it and get back to me," Franklin called out to her.

"Fuck you," she mumbled under her breath and went back to her desk.

Randi was emotionally and physically drained when she got home. After work she stopped at the supermarket for milk and cereal, and the Chinese restaurant to pick up dinner. When she entered the lobby of her building, the doorman stopped her.

"Ms. Young, a gentleman left this envelope for you." His Spanish accent was so heavy, she always had to listen closely to understand him.

"Thank you, Hector." She took the envelope and opened it in the elevator on her way up. Inside was a round-trip ticket to Orlando and a simple note from Franklin that read: *I'll see you there.*

Randi couldn't stop the smile from spreading across her face and shook her head. "You are too much." She spoke out loud as she entered her apartment, put her bag down and kicked off her shoes. She studied the ticket closely. The flight was scheduled to leave the next evening at 5:30 out of Kennedy airport and would be returning Sunday night.

"How did he manage to do this so quickly?" Her excitement restored her energy as she planned in her head what to pack. She put her groceries away, changed into her shorts and T-shirt and ate her Chinese food in the living room in front of the television.

When the phone rang, she answered it immediately. "Hello."

"Hey, girl. What's up?"

"Hey, Umi, you don't want me to answer that question."

"That much, huh?"

"You said it. Actually, I was going to give you call," Randi lied, but since she was already on the phone, she might as well run it pass Umi and see what she thought about her accepting Franklin's gift.

"If you were angry with a man, would you accept a gift from him?"

"Depends on the situation."

"Okay, I had an argument with a man—"

"Brian?" Umi interrupted.

"All parties shall remain nameless to protect the innocent and the guilty," Randi recited.

"Come on, who is it?"

"If you have to have a name, we'll call him, umm, Fred."

"Fred?" Umi laughed.

"Can I finish?"

"Okay, go ahead." She was still laughing.

"Okay, Fred and I had an argument, now he's trying to make up with me by giving me a lavish gift."

"Lavish? What is it?"

"A weekend in Orlando."

"Take it," Umi said flatly, without hesitation.

"Umi, I'm supposed to be angry."

"Be angry, not stupid."

She had a point there. "I don't want to give in too soon or he'll think that every time we argue, he can buy me with a gift."

"I wouldn't worry about that happening, unless you start to see a pattern forming when you argue."

"Well, this is our first argument."

"Then why are you worrying about it? Go and have yourself a good time."

"You're right. I am going to go and enjoy myself." Randi said it as though she had just decided, when all along she knew she wouldn't miss it for the world.

"When are you going?"

"Tomorrow," Randi squealed. She couldn't contain her excitement any longer.

"Tomorrow?" Umi asked, surprised. "Girl, you're a nut. I guess that answers my question then. I was calling to see if you wanted to get together this weekend."

"Oh, maybe next weekend."

"We can talk about it later. You'd better start packing."

And that's just what she intended to do. Randi hung up, tossed the remainder of her food in the garbage and hit her closet.

The next morning she called in sick, then went to Macy's and paid way too much for a bikini, a sundress and a pair of shades. By four o'clock, she was in a taxi and heading to Kennedy airport.

When Randi entered the terminal, she spotted Franklin imme-diately. As he headed toward her, she took in his handsome face and lean body and was more than glad she'd decided to come. He was casually dressed in a pair of Dockers and a white Polo shirt. He carried a leather carryall over his shoulder and when he approached her, his cologne smelled so good, it made her center tingle.

He hugged her tightly and gave her quick peck on the lips. "Hi."

She smiled seductively. "Hi."

He took her overnight bag from her and led the way to a row of empty seats. "You look terrific," he said as they sat at the end of the row.

"Thank you." She was tastefully dressed in a Jones New York dress and matching blazer. She looked at him over the top of her new shades. "So do you."

"Well, you know I have to try and keep up with you." He laughed and stroked his goatee. He looked at his watch. "We have a few minutes before we board, you want to get a drink or something?"

"That sounds good."

"You stay here, and I'll be right back." He stood. "Rum and Coke, right?"

"Yeah. With lots of ice and a lemon."

"No problem." Randi watched him from the back as he walked away. As far as she was concerned, he looked good coming and going. She picked up a discarded newspaper and started skimming its contents as she fantasized about her weekend. She could picture the two of them holding hands and running through Walt Disney World like children. She could also picture long nights of passionate lovemaking and early-morning walks on the beach. Randi snapped out of her daydream when a middle-aged white woman came and sat one seat over from her. *With all the empty seats in this terminal, she chooses to sit right up under me.* Randi rolled her eyes in the direction of the woman, who seemed to be unmoved by her.

What was taking Franklin so long to return with their drinks? She looked at her watch. They would have to board shortly. She looked around the terminal and spotted Franklin about fifteen feet away, with drinks in his hands, trying to get her attention.

He was mouthing something to her, but she couldn't make it out. She picked up their bags and went over to him. When she reached him, she dropped the bags at her feet and put her hands on her hips. "Franklin, what is wrong with you?" she demanded.

"Why don't you tell her what's wrong, Frank?" a woman's voice answered from behind her.

Randi turned around and was face-to-face with the white woman who was seated next to her. "Excuse you?" Randi gave her a look of death.

"Business, Frank? Now I see for myself what all of your business is about." She threw Randi a nasty look

That was her cue. Randi stepped from between them and stood on the sidelines. Franklin's wife kept her voice at a normal tone, but people who were standing within earshot began staring at them.

There was a momentary silence between Franklin and his wife as they spoke with their eyes, a language that excluded Randi and everyone else around them. Then Franklin found his voice. "Jackie, what are you doing here?"

A slap across Franklin's face was her response. The jolt sent the drinks in his hands sailing through the air.

"Fuck you!" She started toward the terminal exit, but turned back to finish what she started. "And Randi Young, your number better not show up on my Caller ID no more." Then she disappeared through the door.

Randi was in such shock, she was at a loss for words. She looked around at all of the strangers watching her and wanted the floor to open up and swallow her whole. She wanted to believe that all of this was a nightmare and any moment now she would wake up in her bed. But she knew it was real when she felt a trickle of sweat run down the middle of her back and heard a woman announcing boarding for the flight she was so eager to get on a short while ago.

Then Franklin picked up his bag and went after his wife, leaving Randi looking like a fool.

"Ma'am, would you like me to help you to a seat?" an airport security guard asked her gently.

Her head was spinning. "Uh, n-no thank you," she finally managed to stutter. "I'll be okay." She picked up her bag and forced herself to walk out of the terminal. The air outside was thick and hot compared to the air-conditioned terminal. Randi felt like she was moving in a fog.

"Taxi, miss?" a faceless man asked her.

Randi got in the taxi without answering. She gave the driver her address and tried to calm her nerves by taking deep breaths. When that didn't work, she closed her eyes tightly and kept them that way the entire trip. The scene with Franklin's wife kept replaying in her mind. It was unbelievable that Franklin, with his pro-black attitude, was married to a white woman—a white woman with a lot of attitude and spunk—but still a white woman. That made Randi see Franklin in a different light. She wasn't even trying to think about him leaving her there to look like a fool while he chased a woman he said he didn't love.

"Okay, miss, we're here," the driver announced, interrupting her thoughts.

Randi opened her eyes and was glad for the familiar surroundings. "How much?"

"Thirty dollars."

Randi looked through her Coach bag, but her wallet wasn't there. *That's strange. I must have put it in my overnight bag.* When she looked, it wasn't there either. She had been robbed! In the midst of all of the drama in the airport terminal, someone lifted her wallet.

"Oh, God." She started to panic when Hector came out of the building and opened the taxi door for her.

"Back so soon, Ms. Randi?"

She was so glad to see him. "Uh, my flight was canceled. Hector, please do me a favor. I seem to have lost my wallet. Can you pay the taxi fare for me, and I'll pay you back tomorrow?"

He was already digging in his pocket and peeling ten-dollar bills from a stack. "No problem, Ms. Randi."

He helped her with her bag to the elevator and asked, "Are you alright?"

"I had a long day, Hector." She fought back her tears as she got on the elevator and turned to face him. "Thank you for helping me."

He smiled and waved to her.

Inside her apartment, Randi made a mental list of things to do. She wanted to change her phone number, just in case Franklin's wife tried to call her. Then she needed to make a list of everything in her wallet, starting with her credit and bank cards. She would also have to replace her driver's license and job ID. The thought made her tired.

First things first: She checked her answering machine. Three hang-ups. Probably Franklin's wife. Then she jumped in the shower and ran the water as hot as she could stand it and stayed in there until she felt her muscles beginning to relax. Afterward she slid into her usual biking shorts and T-shirt and got her pad and pen and started on her lists.

She knew she wasn't completely relaxed when the phone ringing made her jump. She wasn't about to answer it. She listened to see if the caller would leave a message.

"Randi, this is Brian. I've been trying to reach you. Baby, I know you're mad at me, but I want you to call me so we can talk this out. I miss you."

Randi couldn't stop the tears from pouring down her cheeks. She was losing sight of her goal by wasting time with Franklin. Although, she didn't see that being a problem anymore after what just happened. She abruptly brought her pity party to an end, wiped her face with the bottom of her T-shirt and decided to give Brian a call the next day.

*

The alarm clock was blaring so loud, Umi wondered why she was the only one hearing it. She rolled over and nudged Darren with her elbow. "Hit the snooze." Her voice was hoarse and dry.

"Huh?" He hit the snooze button then turned over and put his arm around her. "Good morning, sunshine."

Umi loved the way she felt in his arms, and she definitely loved waking up in his bed, but what she didn't love was the all the running around she had to do so early in the morning. She would have to race home, shower and get dressed, do something with her hair—and after a night with Darren, that wasn't easy—and finally try to make it to the office by eight o'clock.

When she felt his hand traveling down her thigh, she stopped him. "Darren, I have to get up. I have a team meeting this morning." She started to pull away.

"Come on, we have time for a quickie." He playfully begged and held her tightly.

"No." She sang the word, but didn't move out of his embrace.

"I'll make it real quick. A quick quickie."

"Then I won't enjoy it, so what's the use?" She sat up on the edge of the bed and stretched big. "I have to get going if I want to get to the office on time."

She found a pair of Darren's sweatpants and threw them on under the big T-shirt she had slept in. She left her clothes from the previous night strewn over a chair, grabbed her pocketbook and jacket and headed for the door.

To help keep her alert during the thirty-minute drive to her condo, Umi put on the Will Downing CD LaVelle loaned her and got on the Belt Parkway.

Umi and LaVelle had been alone in the office, working late Friday night, setting up charts for the team meeting when she heard the jazzy tunes coming from his computer speakers.

Her office door was open, and she could see him moving about outside, so she called out to him. "LaVelle, who are you listening to?"

He came to the door bopping his head. "That's an old Will Downing CD my sister sent me."

"That is smooth. Turn it up." She joined him in the head bop.

He watched her closely before moving, then disappeared. A second later the music was coming in loud and clear and Umi started snapping her fingers too. She could hear LaVelle outside laughing at her.

When the song ended, she went to the door and bumped into LaVelle on his way in. "I was just coming to see these."

He was handing her the completed charts. She looked them over and pointed out a few changes she wanted to make. "I think these are great, but if the colors used in the pie chart are the same as the ones used on the bar graph, it would be less confusing." As she talked, a slow oldie-but-goodie started playing. "Oooh, I haven't heard this in years." She smiled and shook her head at old memories.

"Dance?" LaVelle opened his arms wide and put on his captivating smile.

Umi hesitated for a moment. She wasn't so sure it was a good idea, but just couldn't resist the invitation. She rested the charts on her credenza and slid into his arms. She closed her eyes and let him lead her in a slow two-step. Will Downing's sexy voice,

LaVelle's cologne and the pressure of his strong hands on the small of her back were a deadly combination that was making Umi feel very relaxed. When the song ended, they parted slowly and stared awkwardly at each other.

"Thank you for the dance." Umi's tone was telling more than she cared to reveal.

"No, thank you." LaVelle was reading her like an open book. He pulled her back into his arms and kissed her deeply.

Umi couldn't stop herself. She fell into the kiss headfirst and wrapped her arms tightly around his neck, allowing his hands to travel freely over her curves.

The memory made Umi wish she had stayed for that quickie Darren offered her.

After the kiss, everything went back to business-as-usual. Umi straightened her suit and LaVelle went back to his desk to complete the charts. She was uncomfortable not knowing if he could handle such a delicate situation. She'd just have to wait and see.

"Good morning." Umi gave LaVelle a smile as she approached his desk. She wanted to sound and act just as she did before the kiss.

"Good morning, Umi." LaVelle returned the smile.

"Is everything ready for the meeting?" Her eyes met his briefly and shifted away.

"Yes. I just finished setting up the boardroom, and if I'm not mistaken, I believe everyone is here."

Umi looked at her watch. "You can let them know I'll be ready to begin at ten o'clock." She went into her office and breathed a sigh of relief. Thank God there was no unusual behavior from him. She sat at her desk and started working on her notes for the meeting when LaVelle announced Randi's call.

"Hey, Randi. How was Florida?" Umi asked excitedly.

"I don't know. I never made it." Randi's voice was low.

"Don't tell me that fool stood you up."

"Oh no, he showed up, but so did an unexpected and uninvited guest."

Umi rolled her eyes. Randi always had a way of overdramatizing a situation. She knew she would be sorry for asking, but she had to anyway. It was obvious her best friend wanted to talk. She took a deep breath. "What happened?"

"To keep it simple, another woman showed up and the trip was canceled."

Umi only had an hour and thirty minutes before her meeting and that wasn't enough time to prepare her notes and console Randi too. "Do you want to tell me who showed up and who canceled your trip?"

Randi picked up on Umi's impatient tone. "Did I call you at a bad time?"

Umi knew the question was a setup. When Randi was in a bad mood, nobody was spared her bitterness. "Randi, I'm at the office, and I have a lot of things happening right now. Can I call you back later in the day or when I get home tonight? This way I can talk freely and give you my undivided attention."

"No problem, Umi, whenever it's convenient for you to be a friend."

"Randi, that's not fair," Umi started, but Randi hung up on her. Umi made a mental note to call her that evening and brought her attention back to her notes.

Umi entered the boardroom with her files under her arm, her notes in her hand and LaVelle on her heels. She looked around the room, taking a head count, and as usual was delighted to see that her entire team was there and ready to get down to business.

"Good morning," she said as she took her seat at the head of the table and arranged her papers. "I want to begin this meeting a little differently. Usually we review events and happenings that have occurred since the last meeting, but today I need to talk about the Dagwood account." Umi took a minute to glance at her notes.

"As usual, I have gotten good feedback from you guys, and I've gone over your materials thoroughly, but I'm not grasping your concepts and ideas. However, a good thought came to mind when I combined separate materials I received from two of you."

LaVelle was watching her closely as he took the meeting's minutes. His stares were making her uncomfortable, and she tried not to look at him directly.

After answering a few questions from her team members about Dagwood, she moved on to the charts and finally a round

of questions and answers. The meeting didn't last very long, and
Umi was more than ready to close. LaVelle's eyes on her were giving her a mixed sensation of uneasiness and thrill, making it hard
for her to concentrate. Besides that, her conversation with Randi
kept playing in her head.

"Before we close, I have good news and better news that I'd
like to share with you." She was beaming with pride. "First, the
good news: Our team will be honored this year at the annual advertisers banquet for closing the best deals of the year."

Applause and excited chitchat followed her announcement.

She held up her hands, signaling the group to quiet down.
"Now, for the better news. Someone on this team will be promoted
to the position of executive advertiser and will be heading his own
team of advertisers." Umi's hard work was paying off. One of her
team members being promoted would probably get her bumped
up to an executive board member of the firm or even higher.

The clapping and chattering started again. Finally someone
asked the question that was undoubtedly on everyone's mind.
"Who?"

Umi didn't actually have an answer to that question. Of
course she was a key component in the decision-making process,
but that process hadn't even begun yet. "I don't know, but we'll
all find out at the annual advertisers banquet. That's when the
announcement will be made."

"Who decides who will get the promotion?" a team member
asked.

"A selected board of executives," Umi lied and picked up
her files. She faced her team. "With all topics and points covered,
this meeting is officially over." She walked out of the boardroom
leaving her excited team to rehash the meeting and say all the
things they'd never say in her presence.

When Umi got to her office, she checked her messages, then
tried to call Randi, but got her machine. "Randi, I hope you're
alright. I'll give you a call tonight when I get home."

Umi could hear the meeting dispersing as a few people
passed her office. She began organizing her desk and realized her
calendar was missing. She had probably left it in the boardroom.
"LaVelle?" She spoke into the intercom and waited. No answer.
She would have to get it herself—and quick. She had personal

appointments in it and didn't want the wrong person to get his hands on it.

She entered the empty boardroom and began searching under the table and in the chairs around the area where she was seated. Nothing. She scratched her head and put her hands on her hips as she mentally retraced her steps. Just as panic began to set in, LaVelle spoke up.

"Looking for this?"

Umi jumped. In the back of the room, LaVelle was holding up her calendar. "You scared me." She put her hand over her heart. "What are you doing in here?" She started toward him.

"Waiting for you. I knew you would come back for this." He was waving her calendar with a devilish smile.

"Thank you." She reached for it, and he pulled it out of her reach.

"Not so fast. You owe me more than a thank-you." His voice was soft and playful. He grabbed her hand, pulling her to him and covered her mouth with his.

Umi pushed away from him. "LaVelle, are you crazy? We can't do this here. If we get caught—"

He grabbed her by her waist and kissed her again. This time Umi let the sensation of his lips linger and responded by opening her mouth to welcome the force of his tongue.

She didn't know how it happened, but somewhere during that kiss, she lost her sanity, because only an insane person would do what she did.

LaVelle lifted her onto the board table, then skillfully removed one of her shoes and one side of her undergarments and kissed and teased her center with his tongue.

Although she was afraid of being caught, she couldn't stop what was happening to her. It was as though she was enticed by the fear and the possibility of being caught. She steadied herself with her hands and tried to stay as quiet as possible as she moved with the rhythm of his tongue.

LaVelle stood and kissed her once again, allowing her to taste what he tasted, before giving her what he really wanted her to have.

Her head fell back and her eyes were closed tight with pleasure. Umi clamped her legs around his waist and enjoyed the sweet moves he was laying on her. When she couldn't take it anymore and her legs started to turn to jelly, she let out a small scream, then let her legs fall to his side. He kissed her sweaty forehead, and they shared a nervous laugh. She lay back on the table trying to regulate her breathing and watched LaVelle clean up with paper towel left over from the meeting.

He redressed and came over to her. "Let me help you." He took her hands and pulled her up to a sitting position and handed her the roll of paper towel.

"My legs feel weak," Umi moaned as she struggled to get up and pull herself together.

He was watching her as she dressed.

"What are you looking at?" she asked as she slid her foot into her shoe.

"Are you okay?" he asked sweetly and handed her the calendar. She nodded and gave him a half smile. But was she wasn't so sure she was.

*

Michelle rolled over and rubbed the sleep from her eyes. The clock by the bed read 6:35. She would have to get up shortly and get ready for Gail's court appearance in Mineola at nine o'clock. She and Gail stayed up all night preparing receipts and rehearsing what she would say to the judge if she were called to speak.

She could hear Gail snoring softly on the other side of the bed. She moved closer and put her arm around her waist and shook her a little. Gail stirred for a moment and was still again. Michelle started running her fingers over Gail's short stylish hair, hoping this would wake her.

Michelle thought about the past few weeks and how her relationship with Gail had taken a turn. After a few heart-to-heart talks that had lasted for hours on end, Michelle came to the realization that she was comfortable with who she was and her "friendship" with Gail. She started spending a lot of time with Gail doing the things she loved and the things she used to do with Randi and Umi. She pretty much considered Gail as much a friend as Randi and Umi, but with a special added feature.

The more time she spent with Gail, the harder it was to be

away from her. She was hardly home anymore because she was either staying over at Gail's, going shopping with Gail, going out to eat with Gail or just spending quiet time with her. She hadn't seen Umi or Randi in a long time and she missed them, but not seeing them was a perfect excuse not to tell them about Gail. She wasn't sure how they would handle the news, but she was considering telling them about her the next time they got together.

Gail shifted under the covers.

"Gail?" Michelle called softly.

"Huh?"

"Are you up? We have to get moving. Today is your big day."

Gail pulled the covers over her head and sighed. "Do I have to?" she whined.

"Yes, you do." Michelle pulled the covers back revealing her puffy-eyed friend. "Good morning." She smiled big.

"Morning." Gail rolled over and sat up and scratched her head.

"You'd better get a move on. You don't want to be late." Michelle was up and heading toward the bathroom connected to Gail's bedroom.

She started the shower and brushed her teeth at the sink. She heard the radio come on as it did every morning, and Gail singing along while she was getting ready. It was funny how quickly she had become familiar with Gail's routine.

Michelle undressed and jumped in the shower. Just as she was lathering up, Gail rushed in singing and popping her fingers to Diana Ross's version of "Why Do Fools Fall in Love?"

Michelle joined in from behind the curtain.

"Girl, take me back! They don't make them like that anymore," Gail said and playfully poked her head in the shower.

Michelle turned around and read the familiar look in Gail's eyes. "Oh no. If you start that, we'll never get out of here."

Gail ignored Michelle's warning and got in the shower with her nightgown on and kissed her softly. "You're beautiful."

"Stop." Michelle blushed. She could never get used to the compliments Gail was always showering her with. She never knew what to say in response.

Michelle was pinned against the shower wall and panting softly as Gail's kisses traveled south. The water falling over her

felt warm and delighting and so did Gail's tongue. She was enjoying herself and didn't want to stop, but they were pressed for time,
so she wiggled free from Gail's grasp.

Gail stood. "That was for good luck. And if it works, we'll
really celebrate later."

Michelle was still trying to catch her breath. Gail knew
exactly what to do to please her—and please her quickly. "Look
at you. You're all wet." She touched Gail's hair and helped her out
of her nightgown. Seeing Gail's wet body sent a sensation through
Michelle, but she forced herself to ignore it. "Let me get out so
you can get ready." Michelle stepped one foot out and Gail gently grabbed her hand, stopping her and planted one last kiss on her
lips.

"Hurry up." Michelle pulled away and got out of the shower
before the smile spread across her lips.

Michelle, Gail and Gail's attorney, a handsomely groomed
black man who looked to be in his mid-forties, waited patiently
on a hallway bench for Gail's name to be called. The narrow hallway was lined with benches on both sides, leaving a pathway for
the constant flow of people going back and forth and in and out
of doors. Michelle skimmed through an issue of *Essence,* while
Gail and her attorney rehearsed their defense.

"All I have to say is that I didn't know," Gail reasoned.

"I already told you, ignorance is not an excuse. The judge is
not going to accept that you just didn't know," the attorney advised
her. "Although you're the defendant, you're here because you've
been victimized. That's what we're going to stick to."

A female court officer came through one of the doors and
called Gail's name. Michelle stood with Gail and her attorney and
gave her a hug. "Good luck," she whispered in her ear.

Gail squeezed her hand before following her attorney through
a door, pulling the boxes of organized receipts behind her on a
handcart.

Michelle returned to her seat and started on her magazine in
an effort to keep her mind occupied while she waited, which was-
n't very long. She was in the middle of her second article when
Gail and her attorney came through the door. They spoke privately
for a few moments, shook hands, and he walked away. Gail came

over to Michelle and sat down next to her.

She closed her magazine. "So, what happened?"

Gail shrugged her thin shoulders. "Nothing. They took the receipts and gave us a date to come back."

"What did the judge say? Did he ask you anything?"

"He didn't ask me anything. My attorney spoke on my behalf about me being the victim in this situation and told the judge I couldn't pay taxes on money I didn't know I had."

Michelle couldn't believe her ears. "That's it?"

"That's it. Someone will review my receipts, and I'm guessing that based on your work, they'll see that they've been altered for the past three years." She nonchalantly shrugged her shoulders again.

Michelle didn't know how Gail could be so relaxed knowing she could possibly spend time in jail for tax evasion. It wasn't like the judge told her she was clear of all the charges, was off the hook and could continue with life as usual.

"Let's get something to eat. I'm starving." Gail stood and led the way to the parking lot. "I want seafood. Do you feel like going to Red Lobster?"

"That sounds good—" Michelle was interrupted by her cell phone ringing.

"Hello?" She listened for a moment, before turning white as a ghost—not an easy task for a brown-skinned person.

Gail touched her arm. "Are you alright?"

"I'll be there in twenty minutes. Thank you for calling me." She turned her phone off and faced Gail. "That was the hospital! We have to get to Natalie!"

"Oh, my God, is she okay?"

"I don't know. They want me to get there as soon as possible." Michelle's voice was shaking with fear. During the ride she silently prayed that the thing she feared the most had not happened. This was all her fault. God was punishing her for something she did. She closed her eyes in an effort to shut out her negative thoughts.

Gail pulled in front of the hospital and touched Michelle's hand. "Want me to come with you?"

Michelle nodded and jumped out of the car. She was glad to have Gail with her at a time like this. She headed straight for the nurses' station when she entered the intensive care unit.

A nurse recognized her immediately, "Oh, Mrs. Vaughn, come with me."

Michelle followed her to Natalie's room. Her stomach was in knots and her head felt light.

They stopped in front of the door. "Wait here a moment." The nurse opened the door just enough to slide her thin frame through.

Michelle wiped her damp hands on the sides of her slacks.

The nurse returned a few seconds later. "I just wanted to prepare her for you."

"Have you contacted Mr. Vaughn?" Michelle asked.

"Yes. He's on his way."

Michelle opened the door and almost passed out. She couldn't believe her eyes. She couldn't feel her legs underneath her and almost choked on her own breath at the sight. Natalie had been propped up, her eyes were wide open, and she was watching television.

Tears sprang into Michelle's eyes and before she could stop them they were rolling down her cheeks. "Natalie," she whispered and practically ran to hug her.

"Careful of the wires." The nurse was standing in the doorway watching the reunion.

Natalie's eyes filled with tears.

"Oh no, baby, don't cry. Everything is going to be alright." She smoothed her hair back and kissed her forehead. "Mommy's here now." Michelle tried hard to fight back her own tears. "How are you feeling?"

Natalie moved her head in a wobbly response.

"Her voice isn't back yet. It may take a day or two," the nurse said from the doorway.

Her prayers had been answered. *Thank you, Lord! Thank you, Lord!* Michelle was overwhelmed with emotion and couldn't stop herself from crying. This was what she wanted most out of life, for her baby to get better, for a second chance at being a good mother.

Natalie coughed a little, and Michelle turned helplessly to the nurse.

She came closer to the bed. "Would you like some water,

Natalie?"

Again the wobbly head movement.

"I'll get it." Michelle took the water pitcher and filled it at the fountain out in the main hallway. When she returned, the nurse was gone and Greg was standing by the bed speaking softly to Natalie. She stopped in the doorway for a moment and stared at his back. Her heart was pounding heavily in her chest. She took a deep breath and went over and stood beside him.

"Hi." She smiled warmly.

He hesitated, before greeting her with a warm hug. Michelle felt surprisingly awkward in his big arms.

"How are you doing?" He was still holding her.

"I'm okay." She put a little distance between them. "And you?"

"I'm okay now." He nodded toward Natalie with teary eyes.

Michelle poured a few drops of water into a paper cup and held it up to Natalie's lips. She drank some, but most dribbled down her chin.

"Mommy," Natalie choked out in a hoarse whisper.

Michelle's tears started again. "Yes, baby."

"I love you." She managed to get the words out before she started coughing.

Michelle was so shaken with sobs Greg had to hold her in his arms to keep her upright. He rang for the nurse, who instantly appeared in the doorway. "Did you ring?"

"Yes," Greg answered. "Natalie's coughing a lot. Is she okay?"

The nurse took a look at Natalie and helped her take a sip of water. "Don't try to talk too much, sugar. Your throat is not ready for that yet." She patted Natalie's hand and turned to Greg. "She'll be fine. Try not to encourage her to speak."

He nodded as she left. Michelle's wet face was buried in Greg's chest. "I'm going out in the hall to get some air. I'll be back in a minute." She stepped out of his embrace.

"Will you be alright?"

"I think so."

There were a few people sitting in the waiting area, among them were Gail, Randi and Umi. They rushed toward her as soon as she entered the room.

Umi was the first to speak, "Oh, Michelle, I'm so sorry, honey." She hugged her friend tightly. Randi was next to hug her as silent tears rolled down her cheeks.

Michelle wiped at her own teary eyes and motioned for Gail to come over and join them and hugged her too.

"You guys don't understand." Michelle choked out the words. "Natalie came out of her coma. She's doing just fine."

"Thank you, Lord!" Umi cried and hugged Michelle again.

Randi put her hand over her heart and let out a sigh of relief. "When can we see her?" She was drying her face.

"I don't know. I haven't gotten a chance to speak with the doctor yet."

"Come and sit down." Umi led the way to a row of seats in the corner.

"Oh, by the way, Gail, I want you to meet my two best friends, Randi and Umi."

They shook hands and exchanged greetings.

"How did you guys know we were here?"

"Greg called me trying to get in touch with you. He said something about getting to Natalie right away," Umi explained. "So, I called Randi and we met here."

"I am so glad Natalie is okay," Randi said and leaned back in her seat and closed her eyes.

"Me too. Did you speak to Greg?" Umi asked.

"We spoke briefly. He's inside with Nat," Michelle answered flatly. She didn't want to get on the subject of her and Greg while Gail was there.

"I've been trying to call you, you know. You're never home anymore," Randi said with her eyes still closed.

"I've been working," Michelle said proudly.

"You're working? Good for you, Michelle." Umi patted Michelle's knee.

"When were you going to tell us?" Randi asked, from her laxed position. Sarcasm ringing clear in her voice.

Umi rolled her eyes at Randi and her selfishness. As long as they'd been friends, she should be used to her ways, but sometimes they really got on her nerves. Besides, she still hadn't gotten around to putting Randi in her place about hanging up on her the other day. "Ignore her. Where?"

"I work for Gail." Michelle was still beaming.

Randi sat up. Her eyes shifted from Michelle to Gail, then back again. "Doing what?" Her eyebrows were wrinkled up.

Michelle picked up on Randi's sourness and found it to be totally inappropriate. But right now she was sitting on top of the world, and nothing was going to knock her off. "Accounting. Gail is a florist, and I'm handling the books for her shop."

"Oh, how wonderful." Umi tried to sound upbeat. She was wondering why Michelle didn't mention it to them sooner.

Randi went back into her relaxed position silently. She had enough personal drama going on, and she didn't want to add Michelle's drama to it.

"So how did you two meet?" Umi carried the conversation, despite feeling betrayed.

"At the gym." Gail finally spoke up. "Michelle happened to mention she was looking for work, and I happened to have a position available. She's a wonderful person. Great to be around." She smiled broadly at Umi.

"Well, that worked out perfectly."

Michelle was beginning to feel uncomfortable with all the questions Umi was asking. She knew Umi well enough to know that she didn't like the idea of being excluded from her newfound career, and Randi didn't even have enough decency to hide her disapproval.

"I have to get back inside." Michelle stood and Gail followed. "Gail, thank you so much for coming with me." They hugged briefly. Michelle could tell Gail was just as uncomfortable as she was.

"No problem. Call me if you need anything." She turned to Umi. "Nice meeting you." Then she left without speaking to Randi.

Umi stood. "Well, Michelle, she seems nice."

"She is."

"I'm happy for you."

"Thank you. And I'm glad you guys were here for me today."

Randi stood and joined them. "As always." She patted Michelle's arm. "Act like you can call somebody, please." She playfully rolled her eyes.

"I will." She smiled.

"Don't get carried away with your new career and forget us,

now," Umi teased.

"I doubt if that will happen." She hugged them both.

"You're one to talk," Randi sneered as they headed toward the elevator together.

"Oh, shut up. I still have a bone to pick with you about hanging up on me."

Randi sighed loudly.

Umi turned back one last time for a final wave.

Michelle could faintly hear them arguing in the distance. She shook her head and smiled. She had just been surrounded by the women who completed her life, and she loved them all. She was still smiling as she headed back in to check on Natalie and Greg.

CHAPTER 11

"I know it's been a while. A little more than two months, but who's counting?" Randi was lying on her back staring at the ceiling with the phone cradled between her ear and shoulder.

"So when are you going to let me see you? I have something for you, and I know you're going to like it."

"Is that all you think about—sex?"

He laughed. "See where your head is. I'm not talking about sex. I really have a gift for you, sort of a peace offering." His voice was sincere.

So, you want to make peace, do you? She had Brian right where she wanted him, trying to make peace with her. Her smile was beaming, but she kept her voice level. "You can't buy my pardon, Mr. Mosley."

"And I'm not trying to. I only want to take steps toward being your friend again. I don't want you being angry with me."

"Well, I'm going to continue to be angry until you tell me what was so important you had to stand me and my mother up."

"Like I said before, I want to tell you that when I see you."

And he wants to barter as well? Randi thought for a minute. "Okay, Brian, we have an interesting situation here. I don't want to see you until you give me your story. And you don't want to give me your story until I agree to see you. Well, just to show you that I can be the bigger person, I'm extending an invitation for you to come over."

He snickered at her synopsis. "Okay, bigger person, you say when, and I'll be there."

Sucker! The word was bouncing around in her head like a ping-pong ball. "Tomorrow night is good. How about six o'clock?"

"I'll bring a movie."

"Don't be silly."
"I mean a comedy."
"Oh, alright. I'll have the popcorn ready. See you then."

All night Randi thought about her plan to get her relationship with Brian to the next level. It shouldn't be hard to do now since she had him right where she wanted him—at her mercy.

By the time Brian was scheduled to arrive, she was all decked out and waiting with popcorn in hand. She had already decided to play it easy and make amends quickly. Then, depending on the size of his gift, she would adequately show her appreciation of their rekindled friendship.

When the doorbell rang, she opened the door and greeted him with a warm kiss on the lips.

"Mmm. Hello," he moaned and squeezed her tight body.

"Hi." She put on her most seductive smile.

"*Life* with Eddie Murphy and Martin Lawrence." He held up the videocassette for her to see.

"Good. I haven't seen that yet." She led the way to the couch. "Let me get the popcorn. Oh, and I only have water and soda."

"Soda." He was already messing with the VCR.

Randi came back with the popcorn and drinks and sat on the love seat, away from him.

"Why don't you come sit next to me?" He patted the sofa next to him.

She stood up.

"Before you do that, could you put a little more ice in my glass, please?"

She looked at him like he was crazy. She thought he was there to give out gifts, not orders. She almost put her hand on her hip, craned her neck and let him know the maid was off duty, but she didn't want to stir up anything, so she bit her bottom lip, took the glass and headed to the kitchen.

"Will there be anything else?" she asked with an attitude when she returned.

He was smiling up at her. "Come here, girl. I missed you." He aimed the remote and the movie started.

They were cuddled together on the sofa and laughing hysterically, just like old times. Their hands occasionally touched in the popcorn bowl, and they would glance at each other lovingly. She really did miss Brian, but then again she missed Franklin too. What she really missed was all that good sex. Just being next to Brian had her pulsating, but she was keeping her body in neutral until she saw his peace offering.

"I bet all that makeup and stuff is hot. Especially with the lights and cameras," Brian commented.

"Whoever does their makeup, does a good job. They really look like old men." Her mouth was full of popcorn.

Brian was drinking from his glass.

"I wonder how they keep the actors from sweating." Randi reached in the popcorn bowl and grabbed another handful, but this time she got more than she was expecting.

Brian watched her face as she discovered the surprise in her hand.

Randi jumped up off the sofa, knocking the popcorn bowl to the floor. Her back was to him as she inspected her new treasure.

Brian clicked the television off and went over to her. He gently massaged her shoulders. "Are you okay?"

She turned to face him. "Brian, it's beautiful." Her eyes were glistening with tears. She threw her arms around his neck and kissed him long and hard.

"Damn, girl." He was panting and holding his heart.

He took the diamond ring from her and got down on one knee. He held her hand in his and looked up into her beautiful wet eyes. "I have never seen you look as beautiful as you are at this very moment." His hand and voice were both shamelessly shaking.

He cleared his throat and continued. "Randi, before I do this, I want you to know that I have enjoyed every moment I've spent with you from the start. And my heart has ached every moment I've been away from you these past months. That's why I know that I never want to be separated from you again. I want us to spend the rest of our lives together, grow old together, experience new things together, make babies and enjoy the finest things life has to offer."

Her tears had gathered in a pool at her chin and dripped down on him. She didn't bother to wipe them away. This was what she wanted, and it was happening for her.

"Randi Marie Young, will you be my wife?"

She couldn't get the word out. She simply nodded. Brian slid the ring on her finger and was up on his feet holding her tightly and making promises about keeping her happy and satisfied.

Randi's mind was in such a fog, she could barely remember him carrying her to the bedroom or him even making love to her. Now she was lying in his arms, listening to him snore lightly. She did it! Hallelujah! She followed through and accomplished her goal. Everything was going to be easy sailing from here on. All she had to do now was plan a big wedding, be a beautiful bride and live happily ever after in her huge suburban dream house. The thought made her so excited, she wanted to get up and call Umi and Michelle, but she figured she could hold out until morning.

"I need to see you right away." Randi was scrambling eggs in her nightgown as she spoke on the phone.

"Are you okay?"

"I'm fine."

"So this is not an emergency, and it can wait until another day?" Umi asked jokingly.

"Be serious, Umi. This is important."

"Okay, okay, but I have a date with Darren tonight, and I haven't seen him in a while, so I don't want to cancel. So make it quick. Do you want me to come over there?"

"Yeah, but I need to find Michelle. I want her to be here too."

"What is going on?"

"I'll tell you when you get here." Randi was about to burst with excitement.

"Well, good luck finding Michelle. How's three o'clock?" Umi was counting the hours in her head. She wanted to be home in enough time to get ready for her date.

"Three is good. I'll see you then. Bye."

Randi hung up and called Michelle's house and waited for the beep as usual. *This girl is never home.* "Michelle, this is Randi. Call me as soon as you get this message. I need to see you today. It's very important." Randi stressed her words. She hung up and called Michelle's cell phone and left the same message. She hoped Michelle would get one of those messages soon.

After they ate breakfast, Brian headed home to get ready for his regular workout at the gym. But of course she wouldn't let her fiancé leave without making sweet love to him. Damn, he was good. But she was even better.

Once he was out the door, Randi threw on her sweats and went to pick up a sandwich platter from the deli for her friends. Afterward, she stopped by a newsstand and purchased two bridal magazines to browse through.

When she got home, she had a message from Michelle letting her know that she would be at her apartment around two o'clock and hoped everything was alright.

Randi straightened up her living room, cleaned her bathroom, then got dressed and waited for her girls to arrive.

Michelle arrived first. Before opening the door, Randi turned the ring around on her finger so that the diamond faced her palm. "Hi, Michelle." They hugged. "I'm glad you got my messages."

"Are you alright? You had me worried, leaving me messages like that." She playfully hit Randi.

"I'm fine. I have wonderful news, and I wanted to share it with you and Umi."

"Is she here?"

"Not yet, but she should be here soon." Randi led the way into the kitchen. "You want something to drink?"

"I'll have ice water." Michelle sat at the table.

"So, how's work?" Randi set Michelle's glass in front of her and took a seat.

"Pretty good." Michelle took a long swallow.

"And Natalie?"

A big smile came across Michelle's face. "She's doing much better. She can't really talk much, but enough to get her point across. She really is amazing. She'll be starting therapy soon to help her with the use of her arms and legs again. And she's in really good spirits."

"She's probably happy just to be alive. Poor girl, she's been through so much." Randi shook her head. She was tempted to ask about her relationship with Greg, but decided to leave it alone until Michelle mentioned him.

"Do you mind if I have one of those sandwiches? I'm starving." Michelle was up on her feet.

"Help yourself."

"I love what you did with the place, Randi. You bought new furniture since I was last here."

"This furniture is two years old, girl. That's how long it's been since you've last visited me. You don't love me." She pouted playfully.

"Oh, stop." Michelle sat down with her plate. "I wonder what's keeping Umi. I haven't spoken to her since we were all at the hospital together, you know."

"You haven't spoken to anyone lately. What's gotten your attention these days? I know it's not only work," Randi said slyly.

"Then you know right. But it's not a 'what' it's a 'who' that has my attention."

"Who?" Randi's eyes opened wide. "Oh no, not you, Michelle. You've been getting your groove on?" She put one hand to her mouth and fanned her friend with the other.

The doorbell rang interrupting them. Randi jumped up to get it. "That's Umi. Hold that thought because I'm dying to know all about 'who.' " She laughed as she opened the door.

"Hey, Randi," Umi said as she stepped inside. She was wearing a sweat suit and had her hair tied up in a scarf.

"What happened to you?" Randi eyed her from head to toe.

"Oh, please. You said this wouldn't take long. You better not make me late for my booty call tonight." She threw the jacket to her sweat suit on the sofa.

Randi ignored her. "Come on. Michelle is in the kitchen."

Umi hugged Michelle when they got in the kitchen. "Hey, girl. How are you feeling?"

"I'm fine."

"What's up with Nat?"

"Doing much better."

"I have to get up there and see her soon. You tell her I said hello. Did she get my teddy bear?"

Yes, thank you, sweetie. She loves it." She kissed Umi's cheek.

"You're welcome." Umi helped herself to a sandwich and joined them at the table. She turned her attention to Randi "Now tell me what is so important I had to drop everything I was doing to get over here?"

Randi discreetly turned the ring around on her finger, and

then stretched her hand across the table for them to get a good look at her engagement ring. She was smiling as big as she could.

Michelle was the first to speak. She grabbed her hand to get a closer look. "Oh, my God, Randi, this is beautiful. Congratulations to you and Brian both." She hugged her across the table.

"Thank you, Michelle."

Umi waited patiently for her turn to view the ring. She eyed it closely before speaking. "I'm happy for you, Randi. This is beautiful," she said calmly. "Brian must have broken the bank to buy it." She hugged her friend. She felt a tinge of jealousy creeping up on her. Umi wondered how Randi was getting married to Brian this week and a few weeks ago she was involved in some talk-show drama at the airport. She couldn't wait to get the details on who was taking her to Florida and who the woman was that stopped the show. Especially now, since she knew it couldn't have involved Brian.

Randi was rattling on and on about finding the ring in the popcorn, how Brian proposed to her and what she had in mind for the perfect wedding. Umi was only half listening when she heard her name called.

"Huh?" She looked at Michelle, who had a look on her face like she could read Umi's mind. So what if she could, she was entitled to her thoughts. Umi shifted her eyes to Randi. "Well, first things first, do you have a date?"

"No, but I want to do it soon, like in three months."

What's the rush? She's probably pregnant, knowing Randi. Umi could feel Michelle invading her thoughts again. She took a bite of her sandwich and kept her attention on Randi. "Well, you better get the ball rolling. You have a lot of planning to do and not a lot of time to do it."

"I know, so I picked up these books to help us out." Randi ran into the living room to get her bridal magazines.

"Did she say us?" Michelle asked quietly.

Umi raised her eyebrows and shrugged.

When Randi returned, Michelle asked, "What exactly do you mean when you say us?"

"I mean I want you guys to be my maid and matron of honor." She couldn't wipe the smile from her face.

"Well, in that case, I would love to." Michelle gladly accepted to play a part in Randi's wedding.

"All I have to say is I'm not wearing purple or taffeta." Umi put on her fake smile.

"Well you can't look better than me, so I was thinking I should put y'all in something with lots of frills." They laughed together.

After drafting up a guest list that exceeded Randi's limit by almost forty people and trying to put together a reasonable budget, they were exhausted. As a kind gesture, Umi offered to write Randi and Brian a substantial check to help with the expenses. And Michelle followed suit by volunteering to pick up a few expenses and asking Gail to handle the floral arrangements, which Randi was extremely grateful for.

"I have to stretch out." Umi stood and headed for the living room. "I'm so full of sandwiches." She sat on the sofa.

Who told her to try and eat them all, old greedy cow, Randi thought as she sat on the love seat. She didn't know how Umi stayed so thin with such a hefty appetite.

"Those chairs are murder on your back, though." Michelle bent down and touched her toes before stretching out on the floor. "So Umi, are you still pulling those long hours?"

"Not really. I've slowed down a little, but a lot of good things are happening at the office." She was about to tell them about her possible promotion when Randi interrupted as usual.

"I bet, with your male secretary."

"Oh yeah, how are things working out with him?" Michelle asked.

"He's working out pretty good. I was about to tell y'all—"

"Did you sleep with him yet?" Randi wanted to know.

"Everybody is not overly sexual like you," Umi snapped.

"Ain't nothing wrong with a woman having sexual urges. Society tries to condemn sexually independent women like myself, but I'm not having it," Randi said. "Now, answer my question."

Umi rolled her eyes. "He's my assistant, not my plaything. And yes, his sex happens to be very good." She was giggling before she could finish speaking.

Michelle sat up and listened as Umi gave them a blow-by-blow recap of her experience with LaVelle in the boardroom.

"Are you going to do it again?" Michelle asked.

"Probably, but it's hard to say because right now Darren and I are trying to be a couple." She was a little embarrassed.

Michelle nodded. She could understand that.

"Sounds risky to me. What if you had gotten caught?" Randi asked.

"Like you got caught at the airport?" Umi threw the words like daggers and watched Randi's mouth drop open in surprise. Satisfied, she sat back and waited for Randi's response.

"What were you doing at the airport?" Michelle wanted to know.

Randi eyed Umi angrily. She didn't have to go there. "Well, since that's all behind me now—"she examined her engagement ring"—I guess I shouldn't be ashamed to say I've lived before I became Mrs. Mosley."

Michelle and Umi looked at each other and waited for the story.

"For a brief time, I was seeing someone who was otherwise engaged."

"Married," Umi said flatly. From the moment Randi told her the airport story, she guessed a married man was involved.

"Yes, married." Randi continued with her story, explaining her rendezvous with Franklin, the grand finale at the airport with his wife and her stolen wallet.

When she was finished, Michelle spoke up. "So I'm guessing that you knew he was married."

"Duh!" Umi said.

Michelle shrugged. She never figured one of her friends to be the other woman. With all of the sneaking around and secret phone calls, it just seemed to be beneath them.

Umi shook her head. So this was the junk Randi called her at work to talk about? And had the nerve to get an attitude with her because she couldn't talk about it at that very moment. Why were her feelings hurt anyway? Randi could be trifling at times.

Randi nodded. "It's not as bad as it sounds. Like I said, we were working on a project together, and one thing led to another." She tried to keep her voice light.

"Well, being a married woman—I'm still married, you know." Michelle eyed her friends for a response, but didn't get one. "I can't condone sleeping with another woman's husband. After you marry Brian, you'll see what I mean."

"I respect your opinion, Michelle, but that's behind me now, and I'm about to begin an entirely new life."

"I know. I just wanted to say that." Michelle dropped the conversation and Umi picked it up.

"You're about to start a new life, but you better hope your old life doesn't come back to haunt you once the shoe is on the other foot. It's a big difference when you're the wife. Right, Michelle?"

"How would I know? I don't think Greg ever crept out on me. If he did, I certainly didn't know about it."

"Well, you're the one who's creeping now." Randi flashed Michelle a wicked grin.

"The other person has to care for it to be creeping. Greg doesn't care." She shook her head.

"Oh, Greg would care if he knew somebody else was getting a taste of his M&M," Randi said matter-of-factly.

"I know that's right." Umi hated to agree with Randi, but she just happened to be right. Greg would have a heart attack if he knew Michelle was with someone else.

"I've been seeing someone who's really special to me. They're very nice and very single." She flashed Randi a look.

Randi huffed. "Can we have some details please?"

Michelle debated if she should reveal her affair with Gail.

"You could start with his name," Umi urged.

Michelle took a deep breath. "I'm seeing Gail."

Randi sat back in her chair in disbelief.

Umi sat straight up in shock. "How did this happen?"

"What kind of question is that?" Michelle became defensive immediately.

"I can't believe this shit."

"What is it that you can't believe?" Michelle tried her best not to raise her voice. "That I can be in love with another woman?"

"Oh, Lord. In love with another woman?" Umi was shaking her head in disbelief. "This is not you, Michelle. You're a wife and a mother, not a lesbian." Umi's words were harsh.

Michelle cringed at the word *lesbian*. She wasn't a lesbian, not in the stereotypical sense of the word anyway. She shook her head. "I'm not a lesbian. And I haven't been a wife or a mother in almost a year, if you care to remember."

"Is that what this is all about? Now I see the whole picture. You're not in love with another woman, you're just lonely."

"Don't go there," Michelle warned. "Don't you dare take my personal pain and shove it in my face during a disagreement."

"Michelle, you always said your biggest fear was being alone," Randi butted in softly.

She felt trapped. "I'm not lonely." Michelle stressed each word. "Umi, I don't know what's wrong with you. You've been in a funky mood since you came through the door."

"We're talking about you. Not only are you lonely, but shocked, depressed and God knows what else. But nobody's blaming you. You've been through a lot in the past year." Umi was sincere. She only hoped she sounded that way.

"Thank you for analyzing me, Dr. Grayson," Michelle snapped. "I see you have all the answers."

"I don't have all the answers, I just happen to know that another woman is not the answer you're looking for," Umi responded angrily and sat back in her seat.

Michelle never quite knew how to argue with someone she loved. She didn't know why she was arguing at all, but since Umi started it, she might as well say what was on her mind. "A relationship with Gail isn't what I need, it's what I want. And let me tell you something else: For the first time in my life, I'm doing something I want to do, and I don't need your damn approval or anyone else's."

Umi sucked her teeth in disgust.

Michelle continued, "And Umi, you're just going to have to respect that whether you like it or not."

"Umi, I'm interested in knowing what you need." Randi spoke up in Michelle's defense. "If she's happy, who are you to come and piss on her parade?"

"Randi, this is not about me and what I need," Umi barked and turned back to Michelle. "You need your husband." This was her chance to keep her promise to Greg. "You need to talk to him, you need to see him and then you need to patch your marriage up. You're trippin'."

Randi rolled her eyes. "Umi, you're always telling people

what they need to be doing. You've been on some trips before, too, you know." She challenged Umi with her eyes.

"Michelle, I don't really understand your relationship with Gail, but I care about your happiness and if you've found it with Gail, then I'm glad for you."

"Thank you for your honesty, Randi. I appreciate it."

Umi sat with her arms folded across her chest. She couldn't believe that the two women she'd known almost her entire life were changing on her. Randi, a mistress-turned-wife and Michelle, a lesbian? She stood up to leave.

"Where are you going?" Randi asked with an attitude.

"Home."

"You need to stop trippin', Umi." Randi was mad now.

"Oh, I'm the one who's trippin'? Umi was putting on her jacket. "My so-called best friends, Lady and the Tramp."

"Fuck you, Umi!" Randi jumped up, ready for battle.

Michelle gasped and stood as well. She made her way between her two friends. "Umi, wait a minute, now. You may not agree with the things that Randi and I have done, but you don't have a right to speak to us like that." Her voice was shaky as she fought back tears. She hated confrontation, especially between friends.

Randi craned her neck as she spoke. "She thinks she has that right because Ms. Umi knows what everybody needs, but—"

Umi interrupted her, "Oh yeah, I know. I know you need to go back to your husband and you need to leave somebody else's husband alone." She was pointing an accusing finger at both of them for emphasis.

Randi moved around Michelle and was in Umi's face. "And you need to get off your high-ass horse. Don't forget, we knew you before you *arrived*." Randi made a dramatic hand movement." So you can play that large-and-in-charge role at work, but that shit ain't happening up in here. You know the way out!"

Michelle spoke up. "Randi, wait a minute before you just start throwing people out." Her eyes were brimming with tears. "Umi, don't leave." She tried to grab her hand.

"She will not talk shit to me in my house," Randi was mumbling loudly to herself as she took a seat on the sofa.

Umi snatched her hand away in disgust and opened the door.

"I don't need this shit!" She walked out and slammed the door behind her.

"Bitch!" Randi called after her.

Michelle sat on the sofa next to Randi, laid her head back and closed her eyes. She felt a headache coming on fast and hard. A loud and uneasy silence fell between them. Michelle was replaying the argument in her head and was upset that things weren't handled differently. Meanwhile, Randi was wondering whether her wedding should be traditional.

CHAPTER 12

Umi stepped into her own house and slammed the door behind her. "There's just no excuse for them." She was speaking to the invisible person who had to listen to her vent the entire drive home. She was so angry about her friends' choices, especially Michelle's. She expected off-the-wall junk from Randi, but never from Michelle.

She hit the play button on her answering machine and almost smiled when she heard Darren's sweet voice letting her know he'd be at her house around seven o'clock. That gave her an hour to pull herself together. She wasn't going to let Michelle and Randi's nonsense keep her from enjoying an evening she had been looking forward to.

She went to her room, undressed and hit the shower. She set the water as hot as she could stand it, got in and let it run on her face and mix with her salty tears. After a good cry, she dried off and put on a pair of jeans, a sleeveless turtleneck and her boots. She dabbed on a little makeup and was sitting in the living room reading an article in *Today's Business Woman,* her favorite magazine, when Darren arrived.

She put on her fake smile and opened the door. "Hi."

"How's my sweet thing?" He closed the door behind him and kissed her passionately.

Starting so soon? She kept her smile in place and asked, *"My* sweet thing? Are we claiming ownership?"

"I would like to." His voice was soft and seductive.

Umi looked away, embarrassed by his openness.

Darren took a deep breath, went over to the sofa and took a seat. He noticed the open magazine. "What are you reading?"

She sat across from him in a single chair. "An article about women handling corporate mergers. Many major corporations are being turned over into the hands of women. Did you know that?" she asked with a little too much enthusiasm.

"Very interesting. No, I didn't know."

Darren was staring at her strangely. She shifted uncomfortably in her seat.

He glanced at his watch and stood. "I made reservations for eight. We should get going."

Umi grabbed her jacket, and they headed out. Darren drove his BMW, which gave her a chance to close her eyes and try to relax. The argument was still replaying in her head despite her efforts to put it on pause.

When they reached the restaurant, Umi was impressed, as she usually was when he took her out.

"How did you find this place?" she asked as she took her seat at the table in the rear of the small Brazilian bistro on the Upper East Side.

"One of the guys from the office told me about it, and I thought you might like to try the food." He reached across the table and touched her hand.

She smiled sweetly.

As the evening went on, she tried her best to be attentive and add to the conversation Darren was trying to carry, but the day's events wouldn't let her. Michelle's news kept resounding in her head. And she kept picturing Randi jumping in her face.

Finally Darren couldn't stand Umi's odd behavior any longer. He was eating something that looked like tapioca, when he put his spoon down and looked into her eyes. "Do you want to talk about what's bothering you?"

The tears immediately began to form in the corners of her eyes. She shook her head and stared into her untouched dessert plate.

Darren signaled for the waiter. "Check please."

He escorted Umi to his car and headed back to her place. She was silent during the drive, trying to form the story in her head so that she wouldn't look like the bad guy.

Back at her condo, Umi sat on the sofa, crossed one knee over the other and bounced her foot steadily as she waited for the questions to begin.

Darren sat across from her on the end of the chaise and stared at her for a moment. "I know you like to handle things on your own, but I don't like seeing you like this," he said slowly.

"I'll be fine." She waved her hand as she fought back the tears that were threatening to spring forth.

He got up and knelt in front of her. "I'm here to listen, if you want to talk." He held her hand.

She lost the battle with her tears and they began sliding down her face. "I had an argument with Michelle and Randi earlier today, and it's kind of bugging me."

He chose his words carefully, in an effort to get her to open up. "I know how close you are with your girlfriends. I can see why this is bothering you. If you were arguing, then you must have felt strongly about the issue."

She wiped her face on the sleeve of her jacket. "Yeah, well, kind of. It's not a big deal. See, Michelle and Randi have done some things that I don't agree with and when they told me about them today, I flipped. Simple as that."

He sat next to her. "Actually, Umi, it's never simple when best friends fight." He kept his tone soothing.

Darren was right. This situation was anything but simple. It was going to take serious repair work to undo what happened earlier. But she didn't want to think about that now. She smiled and squeezed his hand. She loved Darren's ability to make her feel better and give fair advice. She decided to open up and tell him about the argument.

"I don't know where to start, but to keep it short, Randi was dating a married man, his wife found out and caused a scene, but she doesn't think that's important now because another guy she was dating proposed to her and she accepted.

"And what do you disagree with?"

She gave him a strange look. "All of it. I know Randi, and she is not ready to marry Brian. Clearly, anyone who doesn't think it's a big deal when she practically destroys a marriage is emotionally challenged."

"Maybe because that was in the past, she wants to move on with more positive things in her life. Sometimes you have to look at things from the other person's point of view."

"In the past? It was about a month ago." Umi raised her voice in annoyance.

He quickly changed the subject. "Oh, what about Michelle?"

Umi took a deep breath. "She's just sickening. She has a lot going on right now. I told you about my friend whose daughter had the car accident, right?"

"Yeah, you mentioned her a while back."

"That's Michelle. Her daughter is doing much better now, but she still hasn't patched things up with her husband. So in the meantime, she decided to get a job and start sleeping with her boss, who just happens to be a woman."

Darren couldn't hide the shock on his face, but he recovered quickly when Umi scowled at him. "Have you ever known her to be interested in women?"

Umi shook her head.

"Well maybe this is something she always wanted to do or recently discovered about herself."

Umi didn't respond verbally, but her distorted face told a silent story.

"Look, Umi, whatever decisions your girlfriends have made, whether you agree with them or not, it's wise to keep your position as a supportive best friend."

"But—"

"And it's just as important not to be critical or judgmental."

He did make sense, but he wasn't seeing the whole picture. "How can I be supportive of something I don't agree with?"

"By sharing your true feelings with them, without passing judgment on them."

Umi let out a frustrated moan.

"I know you're smart enough to do that. I've seen you galvanize intelligent people before." He tried to lighten her mood.

She folded her arms across her chest. "Darren, if I'm not mistaken, it sounds like you're telling me I was wrong."

"No, not wrong. I just think you could have handled the situation a little differently." He answered honestly.

"So that's what you think?"

"What I really think is that you should call your friends up and try to make amends."

"Humph."

"At least consider it. But if I were you, I wouldn't let too much time go by."

"I'll consider it, but your advice is not easy to follow."

"Hey, who said being a best friend was easy?" He smiled at her.

"You got that right," she agreed and dropped her arms. She was actually feeling a little better. "Darren, I'm glad I got that off my chest." She inhaled deeply then gave him a big smile.

He softened his tone. "I'm glad I could help." He ran his finger down the length of her arm and entwined his fingers with hers.

She knew what he was trying to start, and she had been looking forward to this part of the evening, but right now she just wasn't in the mood for romance.

Darren leaned in to kiss her, and she pulled away slightly. "I'm sorry, Darren, I'm just not myself tonight." She could see the disappointment on his face.

"No, no, it's okay." He stood up and she followed. "Look, why don't you get some rest tonight and give me a call when you're feeling a little better?" He kissed her forehead.

She put her arms around his waist and rested her head on his chest. "I'm glad you understand."

Although she could tell from the look on his face, the disappointment in his eyes and the hesitation in his voice, that he didn't understand. But that was beside the point now. He wasn't going to get anything he wanted from her that evening.

She walked him to the door, and they shared a kiss before he left. She closed the door and leaned against it in disbelief. She actually let Darren Alexander leave her house without having sex with him. She shook her head. Too many strange things were happening to her in one day.

Umi changed into her nightclothes and climbed into bed. Despite her efforts to relax, she still felt unsettled about the day's events. She got her magazine, but couldn't concentrate on the articles. She almost picked up the phone and called Michelle, but stopped herself and let sanity settle over her.

Finally she decided a good movie was what she needed. Umi got out of bed and threw on her leggings and a T-shirt, then grabbed her keys and wallet and jumped in her car and headed for Blockbuster. It was eleven-thirty. If she hurried she could get there before the store closed at midnight.

The store was practically deserted when she arrived. There were two couples browsing the aisles and a group of teenagers laughing and horsing around. When the clerk announced that the store would be closing momentarily, Umi picked up a copy of *Glory* starring Morgan Freeman and Denzel Washington, a box of Mike and Ike's and checked out.

She headed back to her car and just as she reached for the door handle, she felt a sharp jab in her left shoulder that sent her forward onto the car. Her wallet, keys and the Blockbuster bag left her hands. She turned around and got a second jab in her chest area, which sent her to the ground. She covered her face when she caught a glimpse of the shiny sharp object heading straight at her and screamed as it tore through her arm. She tried to get up, but was unsuccessful. Her mind went blank and her body felt hot as the object pierced her over and over until she could feel nothing at all.

*

Michelle left Randi's house in a ball of emotion. She headed back to Long Island, crying on the Belt Parkway and on the Southern State. She went over the argument in her head and couldn't quite put her finger on what exactly caused Umi to turn on her. She felt especially bad for Randi, who invited her best friends over to share exciting news and had it end in disaster. How dare Umi be so insensitive? By the time she reached her exit, she was more emotional than when she left Brooklyn. She headed straight for the hospital to visit Natalie, since spending time with her baby was what made her feel her best.

Natalie was talking more, so their visits were like bonding sessions, which they both enjoyed. Natalie was always in good spirits and that made Michelle's heart fill with joy. As usual, she stayed a couple of hours and was more relaxed when she left the hospital. She was on her way to Gail's house when she changed her mind and went home. She'd just call Gail and explain why she didn't show up.

She pulled into the driveway and took a deep breath before getting out of the car. She hadn't been home in more than a week.

The mailbox was full and several newspapers and sale circulars had accumulated on the front steps. She hesitantly opened the door and stepped inside of her own house. She was so overwhelmed by the familiar smell and the memories that came flooding back, she had to put down what was in her hands and take a seat. She was enveloped by a welcoming spirit and a supernatural calm that made her bones tingle. She was moved by the realization of how much she missed being in this house with Greg and Natalie. She lay on the sofa and let her teary eyes rest.

When she first awakened, Michelle was a little surprised to find herself at home, then she remembered the events that brought her there. The VCR clock read 11:30. She had cried herself to sleep on the sofa. She got up and stretched her body out. She went over to the mantel and picked up an old picture of them. She was standing behind Greg, who was seated with Natalie on his lap. Natalie must have been about five years old at the time. Michelle put the picture back in its place, right next to one of her, Randi and Umi posing on a beach in Jamaica three years ago. She quickly put the picture down before becoming emotional.

What she needed to help clear her head was a good shower. She got some fresh towels from the linen closet and took a long, hot shower. The combination of a good cry, a restful nap and a piping-hot shower seemed to do her mind, body and soul some good.

She put clean linen on the bed, tuned in to her favorite jazz station, lit a lavender aromatherapy candle Umi had given her and headed for the kitchen to see what she could find to eat. There wasn't much. She threw together some tuna and found a few Ritz crackers to tide her over until morning. She went into the living room to pick up the mail, went back to her bedroom and dumped it on the bed. She toyed with the idea of calling Gail, then decided not to since she knew Gail would want to come over. As odd as it seemed, she wanted to be alone. She sat on the bed and started sorting the mail into piles of bills, junk and catalogs. There were three get-well cards from Natalie's friends, which Michelle didn't bother to read, and a postcard from Trent inviting her to one of his upcoming art shows.

She couldn't concentrate. Too many things were occupying

her thoughts. How could her relationships with the people closest to her just fall apart? Just the thought of the argument that took place earlier made her heart ache with grief. And the idea of never reconciling with Greg sent a pain through her too deep to bear. She had to find a way to repair these relationships, and she was going to put every effort into making that happen so that when Natalie came home, she would be coming back to the same happy family she always knew. Michelle stretched across her bed, knocking the piles of mail to the floor.

By morning, Michelle had conjured up a plan and was ready to start on the road to what she liked to call Operation Relationship Repair. She felt uplifted and a little excited. She started her day with a short walk and a much-needed trip to the supermarket. When she returned, she busied herself around the kitchen mentally preparing herself before phoning Gail to let her know she was alright.

"Hello?"

"Hi, Gail." Michelle's voice was light.

"Hi."

Michelle could hear Gail's voice dripping with anger, so she decided to skip the pleasantries and get to her explanation. "I know I was supposed to come over last night, but I was kind of in a sour mood and needed to be alone. So I came home."

Silence.

"Hello?"

"I'm here," Gail said nonchalantly. "I knew you were home. When I didn't hear from you, I got worried and went over to your house. I saw your car in the driveway and figured you were safe."

"I guess you're angry."

"No, I'm just glad you're alright. But the next time you decide to change plans on me, give me a call and let me know."

The edge in Gail's voice was making Michelle angry, but she maintained her calm. "No, problem, Gail, the next time I'll call. By the way, I was thinking about staying here for a few days and kind of straightening things up."

"Oh, I see," Gail hissed. "One afternoon out with your friends and everything changes. First, you cancel our date and now you're moving back home. What's next? You are going to finish the receipts for the shop by my next court date, aren't you? Or should

I prepare myself for another surprise?"

Michelle knew this conversation wouldn't be easy. "Gail, the receipts will be completed by your next court date. I was hoping you'd understand that I just need some time alone. Don't take it personally, it has nothing to do with you—it's me."

"Michelle, don't try and make me feel better. I know you told your friends about us, they disagreed with our relationship and now you want to end things. I've traveled this road before." Her voice became soft.

Michelle was learning that guilt was a powerful emotion when it was applied right. She didn't want Gail to be hurt, but being alone was something she needed, for the sake of keeping her sanity. "Gail, that's not true. I have so much going on that I haven't taken the time to really sort through all that's been happening. I know you've been hurt before, and I don't want you to be hurt by me, but I need some space."

"Take all the space you need, Michelle, and if something else comes up and you can't complete the receipts, it's okay."

"That's not fair, Gail. You're not even trying to see my side of things."

"Michelle, I'll speak to you later. I have to go."

"Gail," she called, but Gail had already disconnection. Michelle put the phone back in its cradle and sat down at the kitchen table for a moment. "Okay, that went well. I lied to the girl then broke her heart."

By Monday morning, Michelle had the bottom half of her home straightened and dust-free, just the way she liked it. She also came up with a way to find out where Greg was and how to get in touch with him. She originally thought about getting his phone number from the nurses' station at the hospital, but didn't want them involved in her private life any more than necessary. Then she thought about going to the hospital at different times to try and accidentally run into him like they did before, but figured that would be too obvious and would probably take too long.

What she was about to do was something she hoped she wouldn't regret, but it was her last resort, and she knew it was one sure way to get to her husband. She stopped at a red light and checked her hair and makeup in the rearview mirror. When the light turned green, she made a right and pulled into Allen's garage. She could see Allen. He had his head under the hood of an old car and was pointing out something to the two young men standing with him. She prepared herself for an unpleasant meeting, but sternly reminded herself to keep her eyes on the prize. She got out of the car and walked up behind him.

It was no secret that she didn't like Allen, and now she felt awkward having to ask him a favor. She hadn't given one thought to what she would say to him. "Good morning, Allen," she said stiffly.

He lifted his head and turned to look at her. She watched his face as he registered the surprise.

"What can I do for you, Mrs. Vaughn?" His tone was professional.

Okay, so much for being nice, Michelle thought. "I was hoping I could have a word with you." She kept her voice pleasant for the sake of his mechanics, and again reminded herself that she needed him right now.

"You boys take another shot at this, and I'll be back in a minute." He started walking toward the inside of the garage without inviting her.

Michelle followed quietly as he led the way through a corridor and into his office. "Have a seat." He nodded toward one of the chairs opposite his large oak-finished desk.

She sat down and took a look around his office. It was rather nice for it to be inside of a greasy car garage. A fish tank set against one wall, and a huge bookcase jam-packed with books and pictures took up space on the opposite wall. Allen, who had made himself comfortable behind his large desk, in a high-back leather chair, was waiting for her to begin.

"Well, I'm sure you know why I'm here. I was just wondering if you would help me."

Allen rocked back in his chair and folded his hands underneath his chin. "I think you're here because you're looking for Greg."

Michelle nodded.

He rocked upright in the chair. "Look, Michelle, I know how to get in touch with Greg. But he's my friend and I don't want to get involved in his marriage. I would be out of line if I gave you any information."

"Did he ask you not to give me any information?"

"No."

"Then why not tell me?"

"It's not about me telling you, it's about me minding my business."

She didn't try to mask her disappointment.

"Look, have you tried calling his job?"

She was on the verge of anger. "You know Greg is out on leave." She got that bit of information earlier when she tried calling his office. Michelle wasn't going to reduce herself to begging, but this was important, so she tried to appeal to Allen's sense of compassion. "Allen, I'm sure you know the circumstances between Greg and me, but I need your help in order to patch up my marriage."

"Nobody understands more than me, but I don't want to get involved."

Michelle sighed heavily before standing. Why did she think that Allen would help her salvage her marriage? What did he know about a good marriage, when he cheated his way through his? It was senseless trying to talk to him. "Thank you, Allen, I won't waste any more of your time." She walked to the door and opened it.

"Michelle, I'll let Greg know you stopped by."

She slammed the door behind her and was in her car before Allen's words registered. A smile came to her lips. Now Greg would know she was looking for him. That gave her renewed hope. She turned the radio on just as Luther Vandross was explaining in his deep tenor, why a house was not a home.

When Michelle got back to her house, she had three messages on her machine. Her heart skipped a beat as she waited to hear who had called. The first caller was Gail, wanting to know where she was and the other two were hang-ups—probably Gail as well.

Disappointed, she took a seat on the sofa and turned on the television. She flipped through a few channels and landed on the news. She turned up the volume so that she could hear it in the kitchen, as she prepared lunch.

"And now for the latest. The young Brooklyn woman who

was brutally attacked in Bensonhurst this weekend is reported to be in stable condition at an area hospital, after sustaining approximately nine stab wounds. The police have ruled out robbery and rape. The woman was discovered with her wallet nearby untouched. Over to you, Doug, for the weather."

Michelle shook her head pitifully as she returned to the living room with her food. *It's a shame how vindictive some people can be,* she thought and switched the station.

By the time she got in the bed, Michelle had made a list of things to do for the week to keep her occupied. She also started a jigsaw puzzle, had dinner and spoke to her mother on the phone for an hour—and she did it all alone and wasn't bothered by it one bit.

*

"Brian, you're going to make us late for work!" Randi was already standing at the door with her briefcase in her hand.

Brian came rushing from the bedroom. "How does this tie look?"

"It's fine, Brian. Let's go."

He opened the door for her. "After you, madam."

In the car, Brian popped in a Grover Washington, Jr. CD and pulled out of his parking spot.

Randi closed her eyes and laid her head back and listened to the smooth sounds. The memory of the argument in her living room the weekend before tried to creep into her thoughts, but she forced it away with pleasant thoughts of having spent the past few days with Brian. Every morning she would wake up in his strong arms, and they would make love before leaving for work together. She enjoyed riding with him into the Manhattan. He would drop her off on the West Side, then continue across town to his office.

After the ugly scene with Umi, Randi packed a few things and went over to Brian's apartment, and had been there ever since. She went back to her place only once and that was to pick up more clothes and toiletries to take back with her to Brian's apartment. After giving it some thought, the argument boiled down to one thing: Umi was jealous. Randi even found herself being mad at Michelle for pleading with Umi to understand her relationship with

Gail. Randi opened her eyes and was surprised that they were already in Manhattan. "That was quick."

Brian rested his hand on top of hers and entwined their fingers. He smiled lovingly at her. "We should go away this weekend," he thought aloud.

"Have you forgotten we're having dinner with my family this weekend?"

"Oh yeah."

"And I told Mama we had big news, so she's looking forward to us being there. I spoke to my brother, and he's going to be there too."

Brian stopped in front of her office building, and they shared a long kiss before she got out. She could feel him watching her hips sway as she went into the building. She turned back to wave as he pulled into the flow of traffic.

Randi got on the elevator thinking about Franklin while she rode up to her floor. It was already Thursday, and she hadn't seen him yet. He was purposely avoiding her since the scene at the airport. Coward. She hated a coward. To make matters worse, the project they were working on together was due on Tuesday, and she had wound up completing it by herself. It didn't matter anyway. She didn't have any time for him and his games anymore. She was busy planning her new life. She looked at her engagement ring. Besides, she was confident Franklin would pop up sooner or later.

"Hi, Mama," Randi said when her mother opened the door. "Mama, this is Brian, Brian this is my mother, Mrs. Young."

"Hello, Mrs. Young."

"Well, Brian, it's nice to finally meet you. I've heard so much about you. Come on in and take your coat off. Hugh and a couple of his friends are already here and so is Randi's Aunt Dottie and Uncle Willie."

Randi read the surprised look on Brian's face and shrugged. She didn't know her mother had invited so many people.

They followed her mother into the living room. "Hey, Hugh!"

"Randi!" He stood and gave his big sister a hug. "What's up, man? Brian, right?" He shook his hand.

"Yeah, how you doing?"

"Is that Corey over there?" Randi asked.

Hugh's lifelong best friend was sitting on the sofa sandwiched between two women. He was very handsome, but a bit rugged-looking. Corey and his family used to live next door, and when they were kids, he and Hugh were inseparable. When they became teenagers and went to different high schools, they parted a little. Hugh made new friends at Bronx High School of Science and Corey made new friends in the streets, since he hardly went to school. He got mixed up with the wrong crowd, dropped out of high school altogether and had a few run-ins with the law. After being released from prison about three years ago, he seemed to have left that rough lifestyle alone, but his street demeanor hadn't changed.

"Yo, Randi. What's up?" He stood and hugged her. "That's C-Lo, now."

"C-Lo?" Randi raised her eyebrows. "I remember when your mother brought you home from the hospital, boy. She was calling you Corey then, and I'm calling you Corey now."

"Oh, you got jokes." He smiled and sat back down.

Randi eyed the two women sitting on the sofa. She knew just by looking at them, which one was dating Corey and which one had Hugh's attention. She extended her hand to a petite, well-dressed woman who looked like she jumped right off the pages of *Essence* magazine. Her stylish haircut complimented her face beautifully. "Hi, I'm Hugh's sister, Randi."

She stood and shook Randi's hand. "Nice to meet you. I'm Toni, a friend of Hugh's."

Randi knew Hugh's taste in women. His professional and *GQ* image always had to be complimented by a woman of like status. His position as chief resident of geriatrics at one of the best hospitals in New York City said a lot for a young black man. Randi was sure he had more than his fair share of women, but he liked to keep only the well-dressed and well-educated ones by his side.

"Yo, this is my lady," Corey spoke up, pointing to the young woman sitting on his left wearing long rope braids and earrings the size of her head. That wasn't as bad as her black cat suit and red leather riding boots, which almost made Randi frown.

"Hi, I'm Randi." She managed a smile.

She waved silently from her seat.

"Excuse me. I'm going to see what smells so good." On her way to the kitchen, Randi stopped and put her arms around Hugh's waist, interrupting his conversation with Brian. "I met Toni." She looked up into his handsome face. He stood an entire foot taller than her.

He grinned widely. "What do you think?"

"I think she's nice."

"I do too. She's a dentist at Brooklyn Hospital."

"A dentist, huh?" Randi smiled.

"Yeah." He was beaming.

"Nice." She turned to Brian. "I'm going to see what's happening in the kitchen. Want to come?"

Brian draped his arm over her shoulder. "Hugh, we can talk more about that later."

"Cool."

In the kitchen, Dollie was transferring collard greens from a pot into a serving dish.

"Mama, do you want me to help you with anything?"

"Everything is almost done. You can get the gravy out of that pot and put it in the boat, then set the table so we can eat, precious."

"I'll set the table," Brian offered. He picked up a stack of plates and linen napkins and headed to the dining room.

Randi busied herself with the gravy. Working side by side in the kitchen with her mother reminded her of the good old days when they would be in the kitchen cooking for "the men of the house," her father and Hugh. She could still hear her mother saying, "if you want a good man, you have to be a good woman." So from the age of nine, her mother had trained her to prepare meals, make beds, clean house and of course, take care of Hugh. Unfortunately, she didn't teach her that a good woman had to be honest, dedicated and faithful. Those were qualities she was definitely lacking when it came to her relationship with Brian.

"Is dinner ready?" Hugh came in the kitchen interrupting her thoughts.

"In a minute."

"Brian, you're gonna need two more plates. Hugh, go in the basement and get two more chairs," Dollie instructed.

"Randi, go up and tell your uncle Willie and aunt Dottie that dinner is ready."

Randi ran upstairs and poked her head in her old bedroom, which now served as the guest room. "Hello."

"Hey, honey," Aunt Dottie said when she saw her niece in the doorway. Her mother's twin sister was lying across the bed.

"Chicken Little, ain't so little no more." Uncle Willie laughed. He was relaxing his big robust body in an old La-Z-Boy chair.

Randi laughed with him. "Mama said to let you know dinner is ready."

"It should have been ready an hour ago. I was in that kitchen cooking half the day, 'til my feet gave out." She grunted as she got up off the bed. "Mama always said she should have named Dollie 'Molasses,' 'cause she sweet and slow."

Once everyone was seated at the table, Dollie blessed the food and the eating began. For the first twenty minutes all anybody said was, "Pass this, please." Or "Can you hand me that?" Except for the musical sounds of silverware scraping china, the room was silent.

"Y'all must be hungry, 'cause ain't nobody saying a word," Aunt Dottie finally spoke up.

"Sorry, Aunt Dottie. Everything tastes so good. You really outdid yourself this time." Hugh winked at her.

"Thank you, baby." She smiled at him.

"That's what I'm talking about. I love a woman who can cook." Hugh grinned in Toni's direction.

"So, Toni, can you cook?" Randi asked.

"Oh, sure, I can cook, but I have such a busy schedule, I rarely get a chance to."

"I know what you mean," Randi said.

"Baby, you gotta make time to cook for your man," Aunt Dottie joined in. "Uncle Willie here didn't get this big on love. I had to feed him."

"Takes notes, Toni. My aunt Dottie is a wise woman." Hugh grinned.

"Well, I want to have a home-cooked meal too. Why don't you make time to cook for me, Hugh?" She raised her eyebrows at him.

"I know that's right," Randi chimed between bites.

Hugh wiped his mouth with his napkin. "I'll cook for a sister. There's no shame in my game. I'll be an apron-wearing, biscuit-baking, rump-roasting, lovin'-from-the-oven type of brother."

Everyone laughed.

"If that's what it takes to make her happy, son," Uncle Willie advised. "But if you want some home-cooked meals, you better start cooking her some."

"I don't mind cooking," Brian said.

"That's true. Brian will cook," Randi agreed happily.

"Y'all kids are still young, but as time goes on, you'll realize that a relationship is give and take," Aunt Dottie said.

"I understand what you're saying, Ms. Dottie, but I'm in the beginning stages of my career, and I just don't have time for some things," Toni said.

"Besides, times have changed since you and Uncle Willie dated," Randi reasoned. "Women have careers now. We're not confined to making babies and cooking meals."

"I agree, Randi," her mother joined the conversation. "But the basic fundamentals for getting a man and keeping a man haven't changed at all."

"Well, Mama, some men just don't want to be kept. Let's face it, some men are scared of commitment."

"And responsibility," Toni added.

"Man bashing? Give a brother a break," Hugh said.

Aunt Dottie ignored Hugh's remark. "And not to mention a long list of other things, but you still want one, right?"

"You have to take the good with the bad. You just have to know your limit on how much bad you're willing to take," Dollie advised.

Corey put down his fork. "Listen, I know from experience, women love when you treat them bad. If you show up late, don't show up at all and break promises, they'll do whatever you ask them to do."

His date rolled her eyes in response, but continued eating in silence.

Corey continued, "Soon as you start treating her nice, taking her out, buying her things, bringing her flowers and cooking her meals, she'll be behind your back with another man—one who's dogging her out."

Randi sat silently. She didn't want to go near that topic.

"Aw, boy, you sound like a knucklehead." Uncle Willie dismissed Corey's theory.

"If I must stand in defense of all womanhood, Corey brings about an interesting point," Toni responded. "Some women don't know how to appreciate a good man, but it's because we get so little practice."

Randi liked Toni and where she was taking the conversation. "I know I'm a good woman, and I won't stand for anything less than a good man."

"I have to say that I'm not afraid of commitment," Brian started. "As the saying goes, 'behind every great man there stands a great woman.' I've found my great woman and that's why I've asked her to be my wife."

Everyone was silent. Dollie was the first to speak up. "Wife?"

"Yep, Mama, Brian and I are getting married." Randi was busting with joy as she passed her hand around the table for everyone to admire the diamond on her finger.

"Congratulations." Hugh came around the table to hug them and wish them well.

Her mother followed. "You take care of my baby, now," she warned Brian as she hugged him tightly.

"Don't worry, Mrs. Young, she's in good hands."

"Boy, please, call me Mama." She hugged him again.

PART III

THREE TIMES A LADY

CHAPTER 13

"How are you feeling, Ms. Grayson?" Umi's nurse entered her room.

What a stupid question to ask, Umi thought every time she heard it. But each time she responded the same. "A little better than yesterday."

"Open wide, dear." The nurse put a thermometer under her tongue and started taking her blood pressure. "When we're finished with your vitals, I'll change your bandages."

Umi watched her as she studied the thermometer for a moment. She looked to be in her late forties or early fifties and spoke with a charming Caribbean accent.

"Okay, everything is good. I'll be right back."

She returned a few minutes later with a basin, ointment and fresh bandages. Umi winced at the thought of the pain she was about to endure.

"Do you want to start with the bandages on your back?"

"It doesn't matter." Umi slowly rolled over onto her stomach and braced herself.

The nurse started tenderly removing tape and gauze from a wound on her shoulder. "You're healing nicely, Ms. Grayson. You may be able to go home in a day or two. I'm sure you're ready to get out of here by now."

Umi thought for a moment. She was ready to leave, but she wasn't ready to go home. In the hospital she felt safe because she wasn't alone. "I'm glad to be getting better," she said softly.

"There was a detective here this morning wanting to ask you questions, but the doctor was with you and he didn't want to wait. He said he would come back later."

"Oh."

"Ms. Grayson, God was certainly watching over you, nine stab wounds and none of your vital organs were touched. You have a lot to be thankful for." She continued undressing and redressing the wounds as she talked. "This one is bleeding a little. I'm going to put something on it to keep it from getting infected. It may burn a little, okay?"

A little? It felt like fire. "Oh, my God!" Tears were forming in her eyes.

"It's all over." She sang the words. "Let me dress it and you're all done."

After the nurse left, Umi called her office and waited for LaVelle to answer.

"Ms. Grayson's office."

Just hearing his voice made Umi want to be at the office. "LaVelle, this is Umi." She tried to lighten the tone in her voice.

"Umi, how are you feeling today?" His voice was soft and full of concern.

This question again. "A little better than yesterday. How's everything at the office?"

"Everything here is going pretty smoothly, don't you worry about a thing."

"Did you tell the team exactly what I told you?"

"Yeah, I told them you had a family emergency and would be out of town for a while. Nobody suspects a thing."

"Good." She was relieved to hear that.

"Umi, I was wondering if it was alright if I came to see you tonight after work."

She smiled for the first time in almost a week. "Sure. I would love to see you."

"I would love to see you too. I'll speak to you then."

"Okay, bye." Umi put the phone down just as her nurse entered the room.

"Ms. Grayson, the detective that was here earlier is back and would like to speak to you."

She sighed heavily. "Send him in."

She disappeared and a tall, lanky white man with blond hair and watery blue eyes stepped into the room and eyed her from the door before speaking.

"Ms. Grayson, I'm Detective Heglock." He came over and

shook her hand. "Do you mind if I have a seat?"

"No problem."

He turned the chair next to her bed, so that he faced her. "I wanted to get more information from you about last Saturday night. Do you want to start by telling me about your evening?"

"I went out on a date that ended kind of early, so I decided to rent a movie and that's why I was at Blockbuster."

He scribbled something down on his pad. "I see. So you're single?"

Umi nodded and oddly thought about Randi for a brief second.

"Who was the gentleman the police contacted on your cell phone?"

"His name is Darren. He was my date that evening, that's why his number was the last one dialed on my cell phone. I called him on my way home from a friend's house earlier that day."

He nodded. "Do you know why anyone would want to hurt you?"

She shook her head. "I have no idea."

"Maybe a jealous ex-boyfriend or an envious girlfriend?"

"Nobody."

"I pulled up some files on you and—"

"I don't have a criminal record," Umi interrupted.

"No you don't, but you filed an order of protection a few months ago against a woman you had an altercation with. Do you want to tell me about that?"

"Oh, her name is Valerie Washington, and she used to work for me. I fired her, and she became resentful."

"Do you think she could have been involved in your attack?"

She shrugged. "I thought my attacker was a man." A knot was forming in her stomach.

"Possibly, but I don't think so, Ms. Grayson. I hope you don't mind, but I took a statement from your doctor, and he said that from the depth of your wounds, whoever attacked you wasn't very strong and could have possibly been a woman."

Her palms were beginning to sweat. Valerie! After all this time, Valerie was still out to get her. Her mind instantly went to LaVelle. What if she went after him? She was ready to panic.

"Right now, Ms. Washington is a prime suspect since robbery and rape have been ruled out. The only other motive for your attack would be revenge."

"So you already had this whole thing figured out?"

"It's usually pretty cut-and-dry when you're dealing with a law-abiding citizen like yourself and an amateur criminal, like Valerie Washington."

"So what's going to happen now?" She tried to mask her fear.

"Well, for starters, we're going to pick her up for questioning. We'll hear her alibi and move on from there."

"But if you know she's guilty, then why not just throw her in jail?"

He smiled briefly. "We have to go through certain procedures to protect the innocent and the guilty. Although we have reasonable doubt that she's your attacker, she's still innocent until we prove it." He stood and handed Umi a card. "Here, call me if you have any questions. I'll keep in touch." Then he was gone.

Umi picked over the dinner in front of her. Her mind was on a thousand different things, but food wasn't one of them. She looked up when the nurse came in with her thermometer and blood pressure machine.

"Not now. Can we do it later?"

"You know we have to do it now." She noticed Umi's untouched tray. "Not feeling hungry today?"

"Not really."

"You didn't eat your lunch either. If you want to continue healing, you're

going to have to get some nutrients in your body." She busied herself with the blood pressure machine and stuck the thermometer under Umi's tongue.

"I hope the detective that was here earlier didn't upset you."

Umi shook her head.

"Because if he did, the next time he comes around, I'm not going to let him in." She smiled as she read the thermometer. "I'm leaving for the evening. Tomorrow I want to remove your bandages and let those stitches get a little air. That'll help them heal. I'll see you in the morning."

"Good night," Umi said as she left.

She picked up her newspaper and was working on the crossword puzzle when LaVelle arrived.

"Umi?" He opened the door and called softly.

The sound of his voice made her smile. She put her paper down.

"Hi." He came into the room with a large bouquet of flowers and the latest issue of her favorite magazine. "These are for you." He kissed her cheek and handed her the magazine. He unwrapped the vase and set it on the windowsill.

"LaVelle, they're beautiful. Thank you."

He pulled the chair closer to her bed and sat down. "You're looking wonderful."

"Be for real." She rolled her eyes. "I look a mess." She touched her hair.

"Not to me."

"Well the doctor said I'm healing quickly and may be able to go home soon." She was so glad to see him she couldn't stop smiling.

"That's good news." He smiled back. He wasn't sure if he should ask, but did anyway. "What about the police? What are they saying?"

"Well, at first they thought it was a random attack and I just happened to be in the wrong place at the wrong time, but now, according to the detective who was here earlier, they don't think so anymore."

"What do they think?"

She knew she had to tell him, so he could be on the lookout just in case Valerie tried to come after him too. "They're pretty sure it was Valerie."

He sat back in his chair and shook his head slowly. "When I got your call, I immediately thought of her, but I pushed the idea from my head."

"I know this is going to sound naive, but I had forgotten all about Valerie. She was the farthest from my mind, even up until this morning when the detective mentioned her."

He stood and went to the window. He didn't want her to see the sadness on face. "So, are they feeding you good in here?" He changed the subject.

"It's hospital food, what can I say?" She sensed the change in his mood. "LaVelle, are you okay?"

He turned to face her, wearing his prized smile. "Yeah, I'm okay just knowing that you're okay." He sat on the side of her bed and touched her face.

She scooted over to make room for him. "LaVelle, you say the sweetest things to me. I should probably tell you how happy I am that you're here." She shifted her eyes away from him and stared at the sheet covering her.

He lifted her chin with his hand, looked into her beautiful dark eyes before gently covering her mouth with his. "And I should probably tell you something I've been wanting to say for quite some time—"

"Umi?" Darren magically appeared at the foot of her bed.

LaVelle quickly stood.

She wasn't sure what to say. Darren's face was so blank, she didn't know if she had been caught. "Darren? You remember LaVelle from the office, right?"

"Oh yeah. How are you doing, man?" Darren shook his hand.

LaVelle forced a smile. Umi could read the relief on his face. "Pretty good. Just checking on this lady of yours. Making sure she's in good enough shape to handle all of that work we're saving for her at the office."

Darren smiled too. "Oh yeah?"

There was a moment of awkward silence. "I'll leave you two alone. Umi, don't worry about things at the office. I have everything under control." LaVelle turned to Darren. "Nice seeing you again."

She wasn't ready for their visit to end and her heart felt heavy the minute LaVelle was gone.

Darren took a seat in the chair. Umi could see his mind racing a mile a minute. "How are you feeling today?" He asked.

"I'm okay. Are you okay?"

"I'm okay, just confused."

"About?" She knew what was coming.

"You told me that you didn't want the office knowing what happened to you?"

"Yes, I told you that, but there's a reason why I asked LaVelle to come here today." She had already mixed part truth and part lie to serve up as an answer. "I spoke with a detective today who thinks that Valerie was my attacker. He said that I should advise

LaVelle that he may be in danger."

"Valerie?"

Umi nodded.

"How?"

She shrugged.

"What are they doing about her?"

"The detective said they'd question her and move on from there." Satisfied that her lie went over smoothly, she felt more at ease.

"Are you sure you don't want me to call Michelle and Randi?" he asked worriedly.

She could really use her friends' reassurances right now, but shook her head anyway.

"I think they'd be concerned if they knew what happened to you."

"They're busy leading their new lives."

"Umi—"

"Darren, let's drop this, please." She sighed.

"Okay. I'll drop it for now, but I don't know how long you intend to keep up this Solo Superhero act, before you call your friends."

*

A lot was happening to Randi, and it was happening quickly. She and Hugh's girlfriend Toni had become bosom buddies and were working together on her wedding plans. Although Toni was busy balancing her career and Hugh, she somehow managed to carve out time to help Randi with whatever she needed.

Randi's first step was changing and reorganizing. She could no longer depend on Umi and Michelle's financial support, so she downsized the wedding to what she liked to call an "intimate party" of approximately fifty people. Since the wedding was no longer going to be quite as big, she changed the date so that it was only eight weeks away. The rest of the changes practically took care of themselves: instead of having a tailor-made wedding dress, she bought a very nice one from Neiman Marcus; Hugh volunteered to pick up a few expenses; and Toni readily agreed to be her one-and-only bridesmaid after Randi told her the heart-breaking tale about her original bridesmaids backing out on her after a terrible argument.

Monday evening, after work, she and Toni put together the invitations asking people to RSVP via telephone or e-mail since their time was limited. On Tuesday she dropped the invitations off at the post office. Tuesday and Wednesday evenings she and Toni shopped for Toni's bridesmaid's dress and shoes, which went pretty smoothly since they had similar taste.

It was finally Thursday, and Randi was beat. She made an appointment to meet with the florist that night, but she just couldn't do it. Her body was beginning to give out on her. The phone rang, interrupting her thoughts.

"Research."

"Hey, Randi, how's my girl doing?"

She smiled at the sound of her husband-to-be's voice. "I'm fine, just tired. I'm considering rescheduling the appointment with the florist tonight."

"You and Toni have been going practically nonstop. I think it's a good idea for you to try and rest. Baby, hold on a minute, the reception area is paging me."

Randi inspected her nails while she waited. They looked horrible—like she'd been walking on her hands. She needed a fill-in and her acrylic was lifting. She hadn't had time to get to the nail salon that week.

Brian returned to the line. "Randi, let me get back to you, I have to take an important call."

"No problem. I'll speak to you later." She hung up. She still had an hour before quitting time and was getting kind of restless. Most of the people in her department were already gone, but she had so much work to catch up on she didn't dare think about leaving early. What she needed was a sugar boost. She stretched, stood up and headed to the cafeteria to get something sweet.

She was standing at the vending machine when she heard voices coming toward the cafeteria. She was half surprised and somewhat delighted to see Franklin and Peter.

Randi quickly selected a soda and planned on walking out without speaking, but she stopped when Franklin called her name.

"Ms. Young." He approached her. "I want to talk to you." His business tone was sharp.

Randi saw his eyes dart toward Peter. "About what?" she
asked with annoyance. She could care less about Peter.

"About what happened the last time I saw you. I owe you an
apology." He looked over his shoulder at Peter. "Hey, Peter, let
me catch up with you later, man. I need to talk to Ms. Young."

"No problem. I'm getting out of here. I'll speak to you tomorrow." He nodded in Randi's direction and left.

She set her soda on the table and folded her arms across her
chest. "I'm listening."

"I was stuck. I didn't know what to do. Seeing Jackie there
caught me off guard."

She picked up her soda. "Don't waste my time, Franklin.
Nothing you say can make up for that scene at the airport." She
was pointing her finger at him as she spoke. "I saw a different side
of you that day. I saw the *real* side of you. A tired brother, who
thinks a sister is not good enough to marry, but definitely good
enough to fuck."

"Randi, that's not true. I'm used to defending my marriage
to a white woman, so your feelings don't come as a shock to me.
I happened to have dated a lot of black women before my wife—
"

"Just like the leader of the KKK just happens to have a lot
of black friends. Oh, please."

"Randi, let me put it like this. I don't love my wife—I
haven't for a long time, but at the same time I don't want to see
her hurt. She's a nice person and doesn't deserve that. That day at
the airport, I had to make a choice. I had to attend to one of you."

Randi rolled her eyes. "And you chose her." She was hurt.

"I chose the weaker of the two." He touched her arm. "My
wife is fragile and delicate. A scene like the one at the airport can
easily crush her spirits. On the other hand, you're the kind of
woman who will be able to rebound. You're strong and level-
headed, and sometimes I think my marriage would have lasted if
my wife had more of your qualities. But it has nothing to do with
her race—weak women come in all colors."

She had never thought of it that way. He *had* to run after her
weak, feeble-minded ass. She was the stronger woman, the one
who didn't *need* a man to come to her rescue.

"So you should be thanking me." She softened.

He raised his eyebrows.

"For being strong."

He smiled at her warmly. "Thank you."

She smiled back. "You're welcome. But Franklin, I don't want to see you anymore."

"Come on now, that's anger speaking."

"I'm not angry with you. You did what you had to do. But after what happened at the airport, it's too risky."

He stepped closer to her and slid his arms around her waist. "But I miss you and I know you miss me too."

"How do you know this?" She was smiling.

He kissed her forehead, her nose and finally her lips while massaging her back.

"Franklin, not here," Randi managed to say when she felt him fumbling with the zipper on her skirt.

"Yes, right here," he answered while planting kisses on her neck. He kicked the chair that was holding the cafeteria door open, and it slammed shut with a loud bang.

The noise worried her. "Somebody is going to come in here and catch us." His kisses were making her feel drunk, and her words were slurred.

"So?"

"So we could lose our jobs."

"So?" He was still kissing every inch of her face and neck.

Randi couldn't resist any longer, she kicked off her shoes and wiggled her way out of her pantyhose and panties. Franklin opened his pants, revealing himself to her and lifted her off the floor. She wrapped her arms tightly around his neck and her legs around his waist and moaned with delight as he entered her.

Beads of sweat formed on his brow and mixed with her sweaty passion as he pleased her. She panted out his name as she released all the anger she held for him.

Afterward they looked a mess. Franklin's shirt was stuck to his sweaty chest and back, and her hair was in disarray and her clothes wrinkled.

He walked her back to her desk. "How about lunch tomorrow?"

She shook her head. "I don't think so. I meant what I said." Randi was through with him. She had what she wanted, and she wasn't about to mess it up fooling with him.

He shrugged nonchalantly. "Alright, maybe another time. I'll see you around."

She knew this game. It was one she played herself. He wanted her to chase after him, but she wasn't going to do it. She watched him walk away and started getting her things to leave. As she put her jacket on, the phone rang. "Research."

"I have to know if was it as good as you remember."

Randi laughed. "Franklin, where are you?"

"In my car."

"Yes, it was very good, if you must know." She hung up on him, grabbed her bag and headed home.

When she got to Brian's apartment, she was greeted by a wonderful smell. "Brian, I'm home."

She went into the kitchen. Brian was setting the table wearing nothing but boxers and his "Kiss the Cook" apron.

"Hey, when I got here and you weren't home, I figured either the wedding held you up or something at work, so I thought I would surprise you with dinner." He kissed her.

Guilt flooded through her. "It smells wonderful. Thank you." She smiled and tried to swallow the lump in her throat.

"Everything will be ready in a few minutes." He took her hand and led her to the sofa. "Until then I want you to sit right here and relax."

When Brian disappeared into the kitchen, she picked up the phone and started dialing Umi's number to help her sort out the mess she was making of her life, but remembered they weren't speaking. She slammed the phone down and let her tears flow freely.

Randi somehow made it through dinner that night and the two weeks that followed without letting her guilt get the best of her. Although she promised herself she would never have anything else to do with Franklin, she had something to do with him two more times after their episode in the cafeteria. She loved Brian, but there was something about Franklin that drew her. She didn't want to believe that there was any truth to Corey's theory, but she seemed to be living proof. She told Franklin that she was in love with Brian and was going to be marrying him soon, but seemed to forget about that every time he propositioned her.

"Hello, Ms. Young?" The young man returned to the line, interrupting her thought.

"I'm still here, but please don't having me holding so long next time."

"I'm sorry about that. I spoke with the chef who is in charge of your reception, and he apologizes for the mix-up on the menu."

"That's not a problem as long as we're clear that I wanted crab cakes for the appetizers."

"Yes, we have it all straightened out now."

Relieved she'd gotten that settled, Randi moved down her list of things to do. She needed to call the limousine service and go over the pick-up and drop-off specifics. Although she wasn't ready to admit it, she knew things would be much easier if she had Umi and Michelle in her corner. Before she could make her call the phone rang.

"Hello?"

"Hi, honey. I'm glad I caught you."

"Hi, Mama." She wasn't in the mood for her mother right now. Her mother had become very involved with the wedding plans and at times had been downright demanding when Randi didn't agree with her ideas. Randi understood her mother was excited and meant well, but she was getting on her nerves.

"I wanted to tell you this, so you could write it down in your wedding planner. Sister Flora Mills from the church is willing to do a solo, just give her the song of your choice. She said if she didn't know the song, she has a lovely niece about your age who would probably know it and help her with it."

"Mama, that sounds good, but I'm going to have to call you back."

"Have you picked a song yet?"

"No, but it's on my list of things to do." Randi closed her eyes and said a brief prayer, asking God for strength.

"The song is an important part of the wedding, Randi, and if you want Sister Mills to sound good, you're going to have to give her plenty of time to practice. Especially if she's not familiar with—"

"Okay, Mama, you pick the song."

"Randi, I can't do that. This is your day, you should chose

the song."

"No, no, Mama. I completely trust your judgment. You give Sister Mills the song, and we'll talk more about it later."

"If you insist."

The excitement in her mother's voice aggravated her. "I'll speak to you later, Mama. Bye."

She needed a break. She relaxed on the sofa and rested her eyes. She could hear Brian coming into the living room.

"Hey, are you okay?"

"No. I feel a headache coming on."

He put his gym bag down and sat on the sofa. "I want you to slow down a little, baby. You're beginning to worry me with these late nights and early mornings." He gently rubbed her hand.

She kept her eyes closed. "I just want a perfect wedding, and it's not easy with only Toni and Mama helping me."

"I told you before, you should call Umi and Michelle."

"Please, they're not even invited."

"I think you're being unreasonable," he admitted honestly.

"You weren't there, Brian, to see the malice on Umi's face. I don't want her near me on my day. Jealous witch."

He changed the subject before Randi had the chance to get riled. "Why don't you take a day to rest? No more phone calls today. In fact turn the phone off. Whatever needs to be done can wait a day."

She opened her eyes and stared at him for a minute, then opened her mouth to protest.

He held up his hand and wagged a finger at her sternly. "Rest. I'm going to the gym and should be back around five o'clock. I'll pick up dinner. How does Chinese sound?"

"Fine." She gave him a weak smile. Knowing he was concerned about her made her feel good. And she really did need the rest.

He gave her a quick peck on the lips and stood. "You're my baby?"

"I'm your baby."

"Sure you're my baby?"

"I'm sure."

"Then I'll see you later, hopefully rested and wearing something silky." He was at the door smiling.

"Maybe."

"I love you. Get some rest."

"Love you too."

With Brian out of the house, Randi put her wedding planner away, turned on the television and stretched out on the sofa. She was watching the news on BET and dozing off when she heard a faint ringing. It took her a minute to recognize the sound of her beeper going off in the bedroom. She started to ignore it, but thought it might be Brian trying to reach her since she'd turned the phone off.

Reluctantly she got the beeper, but didn't recognize the number. Thinking it might be an emergency she picked up the phone to dial.

"Hello?" a man answered.

She could tell from the background noise, the person was on an outside pay phone. "Someone paged me from this number."

"Oh yeah, hold on a minute."

Randi could faintly hear him speaking to someone and was growing more anxious by the second.

"Hey, Randi, what's up. Can you talk?"

"Franklin, what is wrong with you? I told you not to page me. What if Brian were here?"

He smiled. "So you're alone?"

"Right now I am, but you can't page me anymore."

"I don't want to cause any trouble for you. I just want to know if I can spend a few minutes with you today."

Randi thought about it while they talked some more and decided it wouldn't hurt to see him for a few minutes. She would just have to make it home before Brian, and he would never even know she had gone out. She told Franklin to meet her at her apartment in forty-five minutes. Then she jumped in the shower, got dressed and went to meet her irresistible booty call.

He was standing in the lobby when she got there and as soon as they got into her apartment, they hit the bed, making wild passionate love like they were losing their minds. After such a vigorous workout and not having a full night's sleep in weeks, Randi was out like a light.

"Randi, Randi," Franklin called softly in her ear.

"Hmm?"

"Wake up, sleepyhead."

She rolled over to face him and was surprised to see him in his underclothes. "What time is it?"

"A quarter to seven."

"Seven!" She jumped up and rushed around in a panic before pulling her clothes together. "I had to be back by five. Oh, God. Oh, God," she said as she stepped into her panties.

Her thoughts were jumbled. She dropped the rest of her clothes on the bed and ran into the bathroom to quickly running a comb through her hair when she heard the jingling of keys in her apartment door. Her heart skipped a beat and her mind became cluttered with a hundred and one excuses. She ran back into the bedroom, where Franklin was pulling on his pants in a hurry. She searched his face for suggestions, but it was blank and wide-eyed.

By the time she blinked, Brian was standing in the doorway looking at them.

"I thought I'd find you here. What's up with this, Randi?" He motioned toward Franklin.

"Brian, I can explain. See I was—"

"Save it, Randi, I don't want to hear it. I'm just glad I found out before it was too late."

"Wait! Please, Brian, give me a chance to explain." She was desperately trying not to cry. She looked at Franklin and pleaded with her eyes for him to help.

Picking up the cue, he finally spoke up. "Excuse me. I'll get out of the way so you two can talk." He grabbed the rest of his things and walked past them both and left.

The hurt on Brian's face was too much to bear.

There were no words spoken. The same silence Franklin had shared with Jackie at the airport had come over them. The loud silence that develops when people are too hurt to speak and too guilty to offer an excuse.

Brian finally managed to speak. "Come pick your things up tomorrow. I'll have them packed." He turned to walk out.

"Brian, I—"

"Tomorrow, Randi, and I'm not joking." Then he left, softly closing the door behind him.

CHAPTER 14

Michelle was in the kitchen whipping up a hearty breakfast for Greg, who was still asleep upstairs—in *his* bed, in *his* house. Michelle was so excited to have him home she could hardly contain herself. She only slept a couple of hours the night before and was up bright and early to prepare her husband a home-cooked meal.

The previous afternoon when the doorbell rang, Michelle had no idea Greg would be standing on the other side of the door. In fact, she was expecting it to be Gail, because of the conversation they had earlier in the day:

"That's my whole point. You don't understand me." Michelle balanced the receiver between her ear and shoulder as she finished washing her breakfast dishes.

"I want to understand you, but you won't give me a chance," Gail whined.

Michelle dried her hands on a dish towel and sat at the table. She was tired of listening to Gail go on about how miserable she'd been for the past two weeks without her. But Michelle already made her mind up to salvage her marriage, and she wasn't going to give in to Gail's whiny demands.

She continued, "It was you who pushed me away. You decided to end our friendship for no reason."

Michelle sighed heavily. "Gail, I didn't end our friendship. You know exactly why I decided to come home. You're acting like I kept you in the dark."

"And you're acting like you don't care about me. If you don't want to be involved with me intimately, that's one thing, but you don't even want to see me."

Michelle knew it was coming. No matter how their conversation started, it always ended with how they felt about each other and if they'd ever be "close" friends again.

"You know I care about you, so don't start that. You also know I want to repair my relationship with Greg."

"You say you care about me, but you won't let me come over, I haven't seen you in weeks, and the only time we speak is when I call you." She was on the verge of tears.

Michelle was getting fed up. She massaged her forehead, "Oh, Gail, cut the desperation act. You've been a good friend to me. When I needed a shoulder to cry on, you were there, and I'm glad for the unique experience we've shared. I have no regrets, but now I want something else, and if you really want to be a good friend, you would give me some space."

"Is that what you want, space?" Gail asked with an attitude.

"Yep, simple as that."

"From the time I met you, Michelle, it's always been about what you wanted. You offered to help me because you wanted something to do with your time, not because you were concerned about me. And now you want your husband back, but has it ever dawned on you that he may not want to come back?" Her cruel words were fueled by her anger, and she couldn't stop. "Face reality, things are not always going to be the way you want them to be."

"Oh, *I* need the reality check?" Michelle huffed. "Let me tell you something: I may have let my anger drive Greg away, but I'm not going to let my stupidity keep him away. I broke up my marriage, and now I'm going to do whatever it takes to put it back together, regardless of what you think, 'cause I love my husband!"

Gail raised her voice to match Michelle's. "What's love got to do with it?"

"And another thing." Michelle wasn't finished. "You think I'm selfish and inconsiderate? You're the selfish one. You don't want me to work things out with Greg, so that *we* can be together. Oh no, honey, you won't ever get the chance to lay with me again, whether Greg comes back or not." She slammed the phone down.

"I don't know why I even entertain her," she mumbled as she left the kitchen and went upstairs. But she did know why—she didn't want to hurt Gail. This whole scenario was probably pretty confusing for her, but Michelle was too angry to be rational right now. She flipped the television on and got on the bed. She could feel soreness beginning to creep up her neck. Tension.

Michelle sat up when the phone rang. "This girl is getting on my damn nerves." She picked up the phone. "What is it, Gail?"

"I'm sorry," Gail said softly.

Silence.

"Can you forgive me for what I said?"

"You're forgiven." Michelle's tone was still huffy.

"Thank you. I had a minute to think about what you said, and I sincerely hope things work out for you and Greg."

"Oh, really?"

"Really. You're a good person, and you deserve to have what you want."

"That's a nice thing to say, Gail, but I have to go now." Michelle knew this trick well. Gail was lonely and wanted to talk.

"Okay, but before you go, I wanted to ask if I could stop by."

"No."

"Just for a minute. I want to give you something."

"Give me what?"

"Something in memory of our relationship."

Michelle rolled her eyes. This girl was relentless. "No, Gail, you're just trying to make an excuse to get over here."

"Maybe I am, but if I could see you one last time, it would make me feel better about losing you."

She actually sounded sincere, but Michelle knew if she let Gail come over, it would be hell trying to get her to leave. "Not tonight. Maybe we can say good-bye over lunch one day next week."

"When?"

"How about Saturday? We could eat at the mall?"

"Okay, I'll be there," she said, smiling. "So, you're sure you don't want me to come over?"

"I'm sure."

"What if I ignored you and showed up in fifteen minutes?"

"I'll be mad."

"I could live with that." Gail laughed and hung up.

Michelle put the phone down thinking how angry she would be if Gail showed up. She went into the bathroom and rubbed a little Ben-Gay on her neck, then returned to her spot on the bed.

Michelle groaned loudly when the doorbell rang almost an hour later. She slipped on her robe and stopped in the bathroom to throw some water on her face and brush over her hair before going to the door.

On her way downstairs, the bell rang again.

"I'm coming, I'm coming! I shouldn't even let your butt in."

Michelle snatched the door open and stood completely still. Her heart started racing and her mouth went completely dry.

"Hello, Michelle. Can I come in?"

Michelle backed up and closed the door behind him.

She finally managed to speak just above a whisper. "Greg?"

"Good morning." Greg gave her a big hug when he entered the kitchen.

"Good morning to you." She smiled as she let herself be enclosed in his strong arms. She inhaled deeply, taking in the familiar scent she had loved so much over the years.

He kissed the top of her head. "Did I tell you how much I've missed you?"

"All night." She grinned.

"I don't think that was enough. Why don't I tell you some more?" He kissed her neck passionately.

"That's sounds good," she said, moaning. "But how about telling me on a full stomach. I know you're hungry."

"Yeah, but not for food." He started on her neck again.

"Greg!" She laughed and pulled away from him. "Behave yourself and sit like a good boy." She pointed to the chair.

After breakfast, they went to the hospital and spent the day with Natalie. Michelle could tell that the nurses were surprised to see them there together, and so was Natalie. They sat with her through her physical therapy session and encouraged her from the sidelines. They were all excited when the therapist told them Natalie was doing very well and might be walking on her own sooner than expected.

Natalie didn't want them to leave, so they stayed as long as they could and promised to come back in the morning with the Scrabble game. They picked up dinner from a nearby Italian restaurant and headed home.

Michelle had plans to catch up on the past nine months they'd been separated and wanted to talk. So to make the evening exciting and the atmosphere comfortable, she filled the tub with hot water, lit her favorite lavender candles and grabbed a bottle of wine and two goblets from the bar in the basement.

She pinned her hair up in a neat bun and went downstairs wearing nothing but a silk kimono. Greg was on the sofa watching the news.

"Greg," she called to him softly.

He looked up from the television and smiled at her.

She took him by the hand and led him upstairs. In the bedroom, Michelle stood in front of him and seductively loosened her kimono and let it fall to the floor.

"Meet me in the bathroom in two minutes." Her voice was low and husky. She held up two fingers and went into the bathroom. She could feel his eyes on her and that made her smile.

Greg was undressed and in the bathroom as ordered. The look on his face let her know that he was pleased with what he saw.

"Are you going to join me? The water is nice and warm." She took a handful of bubbles and blew them in his direction. She sat up and made room for Greg to sit behind her. He eased down into the water and she nestled her behind between his thighs.

After a moment of silence, Greg spoke up. "It's quiet, I should turn on the radio."

"No. I wanted some quiet time with you, so that we can talk." She was massaging his knees under the water.

"Okay." He waited for her to begin.

"I want to catch up on things, you know, like, how did you keep busy while we were separated?"

"Well, I played a lot of ball with Allen in the beginning. I went home to Baltimore for a couple of weeks. The family was glad to see me."

"What did you say when they asked about Natalie and me?"

"They already knew what happened to Nat, so I told them you wanted to stay here with her."

She nodded. She liked Greg's family, but they could be pretty nosy sometimes, and she didn't want them knowing about their problems.

"The rest of the time, I was at the hospital with Natalie, thinking about you and working long hours, before going out on leave."

That all sounded good to her, but what she really wanted to know about was other women. "Was I the only woman you were thinking about?" she asked.

"The one and only." Greg grabbed her louver and gently ran it over her arms and legs as the lie rolled out of his mouth. It was just a brief romance with an old girlfriend while he was in Baltimore. No sense in getting her riled up over something that was purely physical and had no lasting meaning.

"You weren't with anybody the entire time we've been separated? You really want me to believe that?"

"So you don't believe me?"

"No."

"Is that because you were with someone else?"

"Gregory Vaughn, I am surprised at you." She shifted a little to get a look at his face. "Women are better keepers of themselves than men, you know that."

"Were you involved with someone else? Yes or no?" he asked again.

"I'm not answering you because you already know the answer." She turned back around.

"Okay, okay. So tell me what you've been up to for the past nine months." Curiosity was in his voice.

"I got a job and spent a lot of time with Gail from the gym."

"A job?"

"Yep. A J-O-B." Michelle told him all about Gail's dilemma and how she helped her out. Then she told him at length about the big fight with Randi and Umi, leaving out the part about her being romantically involved with Gail.

The water started getting cold before they got a chance to enjoy the wine. So they put on their pajamas and moved the party downstairs to the living room, where they ate their Chinese food and toasted to a new beginning.

*

Umi went to the front door again to make sure it was locked. This time she added the chain, just in case. She checked and double-checked the windows to make sure they were all closed and locked as well. Convinced that she was safe, she went to the kitchen and made herself a cup of peppermint tea to calm her nerves. She sat down at the kitchen table, opened one of the several bottles of medication she had and swallowed one of the pills down with a sip of tea.

She seemed to need a pill for everything these days: one to help calm her nerves, one to help her sleep, yet another for the pain, another to fight off infections and a multi-vitamin to help build her appetite and strength. At the rate she was going, she would either get better or become a pill popper.

Darren had stayed over three of the five nights she'd been home. She could tell that he was getting tired of taking care of her. He had no patience, and twice even raised his voice at her. She was tired of him being there anyway, but she felt much safer with him in the house.

The phone rang, causing her to jump out of her seat. She went over to the counter to answer it. Her hand was shaking like a leaf as she picked it up. "Hello?" Her voice was full of fear.

"Umi, this is Darren, I'm about a block away. I'll be at the door in a few minutes okay?"

"Okay." She hung up the phone and waited in the living room until she heard the bell.

Darren came in with McDonald's in one hand and an overnight bag in the other, both of which she was glad to see. "Hi, baby. How was your day?"

"Pretty quiet." She locked the door and followed him into the kitchen.

"Are you hungry?"

"Not really. I was just having some tea." She sat back down at the table and watched him move around the kitchen.

"But I picked up your favorite. Are you sure you don't want to try just a little?"

She shook her head sadly. It bothered her just as much as it bothered him that she couldn't do the simple things she used to, including eating a decent meal.

He opened the refrigerator. "Umi, I thought you said you were going to go to the supermarket today." His voice was edgy.

"I thought I would be ready to go out today, but I wasn't. I'll try to go tomorrow."

He sat across from her at the table. "Umi, listen to me. You
have to pull yourself together. No more babying you. Tomorrow
you are going to get your butt out of here and go to the supermarket."

His sternness took her by surprise. Before she could respond,
her emotions took over. "Damn you, Darren, I said I'm not ready!
Who cares if I don't have food in the house, is that more important than my safety!" She was shouting over her sobs. "Valerie
could be out there hunting me down like an animal, waiting for
me just like before!"

She stood up to leave, but he grabbed her before she could.

"Umi, listen." He had her by her shoulders and was looking
her in the eye. "Nobody is hunting you. Do you hear me?"

"She's out there, Darren, and she's going to try to kill me
next time." She was crying uncontrollably. She managed to pull
away and went into the living room.

After a few moments, Darren went into the living room and
sat next to her on the sofa. He was calmer when he spoke, "I'm
sorry, Umi. I guess tough love isn't the answer—I don't have the
answer. I just can't stand seeing you like this." He massaged her
hand. "I really want you to consider seeing a therapist."

"You think I'm crazy? I have a right to feel threatened. I've
been violated!" She was still crying.

"You're not crazy. I never said that you were, but you jump
at every little noise. Umi, you're afraid to watch the news or leave
the house. Honey, locking yourself in here is not going to help
you."

She blew her nose.

"This burden is too big for you to carry by yourself. How
about giving Randi and Michelle a call? I'm sure they would be
concerned about you if they knew what you were going through."

"You're full of shit, Darren. Why don't you just say what's
on your mind. I'm too much for you to handle. First you want to
dump me off on a therapist, now on old girlfriends. I don't need
a baby-sitter."

"Umi, I'm not dumping you off on anybody. I'm concerned
about you." He tried to keep his voice level.

"You know what, Darren, thank you very much for your concern, but I would like to be alone tonight."

"You know that's not what you want."

She stared him down before answering. "Clearly, you don't know what I want, that's why I'm asking you to leave."

He hesitantly got his overnight bag and headed for the door. "Umi, just remember that I love you, and I'm here to help anytime you need me."

Silence.

Once she heard the door open and shut, she ran to lock it and went to get in her bed. She was reading an article in a business magazine when she thought about LaVelle and wondered if he was safe. She pushed the thought from her mind, took a sleeping pill and let it carry her into a deep sleep.

The next morning, the ringing phone awakened her.

"Hello?"

Click.

She went into a panic. She jumped out of the bed and went to check the front door. It was still locked. She ran back to the bedroom, got Detective Heglock's card and dialed. She was disappointed when a machine came on asking her to leave a message.

"This message is for Detective Heglock. My name is Umi Grayson, and I wanted to let him know that I've been receiving hang-up calls that I'm concerned about. Please return my call as soon as possible."

As soon as she put the phone down, it rang again. She was afraid to answer, so she let the answering machine do its job.

"Umi, this is Darren, I'm sorry about upsetting you last night. I hope you're alright. Call me at the office. Bye."

She ignored the call, got up and forced herself to eat a piece of dry toast before swallowing three pills, two of which were sleeping pills. Although it was only 7:30 in the morning, she hoped they would help her sleep the day away. She turned on the television and flipped through the channels, waiting for the medication to kick in.

This time the rumbling of her stomach awakened her. Umi tossed and turned for a few minutes before getting up and going to the kitchen. She didn't have much to choose from, so she put together a few crackers with cheese and a glass of water. On her way back to the bedroom, she couldn't resist the urge to check the locks on the front door. When she got back to her room the news was on. She quickly turned the channel to a sitcom and began eating.

She was both surprised and relieved that she had slept the entire day. The clock on her nightstand read 6:30, and she thought about LaVelle. She hadn't spoken to him in a few days and wondered how he was. She had called to let him know she was home the day she arrived, and she hadn't heard from him since. She picked up the phone and dialed.

"Hello?"

"Hi, LaVelle, this is Umi."

"Hey, Umi, how are you feeling?"

"I'm a little better," she lied. "Uh, did I catch you at a bad time?"

"No, I just walked in the door."

"Do you want me to call you back later?"

"If you hang up this phone, it would break my heart."

This was Umi's first real smile since she'd been home. "I don't want to do that."

"I'm sure you're glad to be home."

"Actually, LaVelle, not really." She could feel the tears stinging her eyes.

"Umi, are you alright?"

She sniffled, trying to control her emotions. "I just wanted to make sure you were safe."

"Safe from what?"

"From Valerie."

"Don't worry about me. I eat Super Wheaties every morning, and they give me super powers to fight off the bad guys." He laughed.

She laughed too. "I'm serious, LaVelle. She could be out there trying to get you."

"No she's not. Valerie is going to lay low for a while because she knows she's in serious trouble. Trust me on this one, she's in way over her head."

"You think so?"

"I know so. I don't want you driving yourself crazy worrying about Valerie. She should be the one worrying. I hear women's prison is worse than the men's." He chuckled a little.

They talked for almost two hours about everything. He encouraged her not to fret over Valerie, filled her in on the current office gossip and made her laugh more than she had in months. Finally before getting off the phone, he agreed to come by after work the next day and keep her company. He promised that he would say a prayer for her and made her promise that she would eat a big bowl of super cereal to keep her strong.

The next day, Umi was so preoccupied with seeing LaVelle, that she hardly had time to be scared. She took a long shower, something she was afraid to do before because with the water running she wouldn't be able to hear someone breaking in the house. Then she washed and styled her hair and even put on a little makeup. She toyed with the idea of going out to the supermarket, but decided she wasn't quite ready for that.

By the time LaVelle called saying he was leaving the office and was on his way, Umi was ready and waiting.

When the doorbell rang this time, her heart skipped a beat— not out of fear, but excitement. She opened the door and went straight into his arms.

LaVelle let the bags in his hands fall to the floor and hugged her tightly. He could feel her body shaking with sobs and massaged her back in an effort to calm her. He closed the door with his foot, then picked her up and carried her over to the sofa.

"Hey, hey, come on now." He put her on the sofa and sat next to her. He wiped at her tears.

"I'm sorry, LaVelle. I'm messing up your shirt." She ran her hand over the wet spot and tried to stifle her tears.

"It's okay, I'll send you the cleaning bill." He smiled at her.

She smiled back, her face still wet. "I'm still a little emotional about the whole thing."

"Do you want to talk about it?"

She shook her head. Then shrugged.

He wasn't going to force her to talk. He changed the subject. "I picked up something to eat. Maybe we should get it off the floor."

She followed him into the kitchen with the bags.

"Are you hungry?"

"A little." She started setting the table. "I have to warn you, I haven't been out to the store since I've been home."

"No?"

"That's one of things I seem to be having trouble with. I'm afraid to go outside because I think Valerie is somewhere lurking around a corner, waiting for me."

He was fixing their plates. "It's good to talk about it. Expressing your fears will help resolve most of what you're feeling."

After dinner, they listened to the radio while they played a game of Scrabble on the floor in her bedroom and talked some more. Umi was so relaxed with LaVelle, she almost felt like her old self again.

"LaVelle, if you take one second longer, you're going to forfeit your turn."

"I'm thinking." He was studying his last two tiles. After a moment, he sighed. "I give up."

"Are you sure? You know, quitters never win and winners never quit." She was beaming, happy to be winning.

He opened his hand, showing her his tiles. "What am I going to do with an *X* and a *K*? Which letter are you holding?"

She opened her hand, revealing a *G*. "I was trying to get rid of this letter for the longest."

He looked at his watch. It was almost midnight. "Whoa, I didn't know it was so late. I should be going." He stood up and she followed.

"Uh, LaVelle," She touched his arm. "Normally, I wouldn't ask you to do this, but do you mind staying here with me tonight?" She was embarrassed and kept her eyes on the floor.

"I would love to stay, Umi, but are you sure that's what you want?" He asked with caution.

She nodded.

"Come here." He pulled her back down on the floor with him and wrapped his arms around her.

She felt safe and wanted to share her feelings with him. "LaVelle, ever since I've come home I've been taking an enormous amount of pills, even when I really don't need them. I'm worried that I might be addicted to them."

"You know you don't have to take them," he said gently.

"I have to. I can't even sleep without them."

"Well, if I stay here tonight, you're going to have to promise me that you'll try things my way."

"What way is that?"

"Stay here." He got up and went into the bathroom. Umi could hear water running in the tub. He came back into the bedroom. "There's a bath waiting for you, Madame." He smiled at her and helped her to her feet. "Why don't you jump in and I'll be right back."

"Where are you going?"

"To the kitchen to whip up some of my Super Sleep Potion." He laughed at himself.

She shook her head. "I hope it works."

In the bathroom, she disrobed and slowly sank down in the hot water and sweet-scented bubbles. She laid her head back, feeling more relaxed now than she ever had with the medication. She waited for LaVelle to return with his potion and wondered what it was.

"Umi, are you decent?" he called from outside the door.

She sank lower in the tub, so that the bubbles covered her breasts. "You can come in."

He entered carrying two cups of tea. Seeing her emerged in bubbles made his body come alive. He knelt by the side of the tub. "This is called Bubble Therapy. Is it working?"

"I think so?" She was smiling big.

He spotted one of the wounds on her shoulder. "Do your wounds still hurt?"

She was a little embarrassed but didn't mind talking about them. "Not really. They itch because they're healing though."

"And it's okay to get them wet?"

"Yeah. The thread will dissolve as I heal. So they don't really need any special treatment. I usually put cocoa butter on the ones I can reach, so the scars won't look so bad later."

"Oh." He nodded slightly.

His face was hard to read, and Umi wondered what LaVelle thought about her now after seeing her like this.

"What's in the cups?"

"It's Peppermint Potion Number Ten, known to the world as herbal tea."

When the Bubble Therapy ended, LaVelle waited in the living room while Umi dressed. Then he made her lie down on her stomach and massaged her back, neck and shoulders until she drifted into one of the soundest, non-medicated sleeps she had ever had.

In the middle of the night, Umi rolled over looking for LaVelle. He was gone. Afraid that he may have left while she was asleep, she went to check the locks on the front door. On her way, she spotted him fast asleep on the sofa in his undershirt and briefs.

His respect for her was a relief and, in a strange way, a turn-on. She watched him for a moment before going over to him and covering his mouth with hers. She watched his eyelids flutter as he came out of his sleep, then felt him respond by sticking his tongue in her mouth.

LaVelle sat up, and Umi straddled him, moving her hips over his half-erect penis.

"Umi, baby, I'm not prepared for this."

She put her fingers to his lips and stood to remove her panties. She watched his body respond as she came out of her silky underwear.

This time when she straddled him, she released a small cry as she felt him deep inside of her. She moved her hips back and forth until she couldn't take it anymore. LaVelle then lifted her and gently laid her on the floor, kissing her passionately as he took his time and made love to her, slow and sweet, like he wanted to do ever since he first laid eyes on her.

"Tell me it feels good to you," he whispered in her ear.

"Mmm, it feels good," she obeyed.

"Tell me again," he demanded passionately.

She held on to him tightly and repeated herself.

Those were the last words spoken between them. As the sun rose over Brooklyn, Umi and LaVelle climbed into her bed entwined in each other's arms and fell fast asleep. Unlike LaVelle, she had no idea that this was the start of something that would last forever.

CHAPTER 15

Greg was on the sofa, holding his head in his hands. Michelle had just dropped the bomb on him about finding the gun, drugs and money in Natalie's room.

"This just doesn't add up, Michelle, I'm telling you. There's a piece missing to this puzzle."

She listened to him explore the possibilities of how their daughter might be an innocent party in what looked otherwise. Michelle knew the heartache and disappointment he was feeling.

"Greg, the only way we'll know for sure is to ask Natalie. I plan on doing that once she's home."

He shook his head. "I can't believe it—not our Natalie." He looked up at her. "Are you sure nobody else knows about this?"

"Only Randi and Umi. I didn't even tell Mama."

"What about the Parkers? Have you spoken to them or Rachael?"

"I haven't seen Kate since the day she waltzed in here bad-mouthing Natalie." Michelle went into the kitchen and came back with a glass of water. She felt bad for him. She remembered how she felt the day she and her friends had discovered Natalie's secret. She tried to change the subject. "Why don't we go out and get some fresh air."

Reluctantly he agreed and insisted that she drive. In the car, Greg kept silent as she chatted idly. "You know I was thinking we should probably take a vacation when Natalie gets home. After being cooped up in that hospital so long, I'm sure she'd enjoy the Bahamas or Jamaica."

"I can't help but think that we've somehow failed her. Somewhere along the way, we lost track of her."

His words were familiar to her, because she used to think the same thing. "You're wrong, Greg. We haven't failed as parents. What happened to Natalie is not our fault—it took a long time for me to acknowledge that. More importantly, I don't want us wasting time by focusing on the shouldas and couldas. We have to be prepared to hear whatever she tells us when she gets home, which is not going to be long now." Michelle was pulling into a Dairy Queen. "Do you want something?"

He shook his head.

"I'll be right back."

She was sipping a milk shake when she got back in the car. "This is good. Want a taste?"

"Do you have your cell phone with you?" He asked, ignoring her offer.

"I left it at the house. Why?"

"I have to use the pay phone." He was digging in his pockets for coins.

"Who are you calling?"

"The hospital just paged me, and I left my cell at the house too."

"Why? Do they usually beep you?" She was trying not to become alarmed.

"Sometimes it's the nurses' station calling to say Natalie is looking for me. And once accounting beeped me with a question about our insurance. It could be anything."

"Oh, then see what they want." She was a little relieved.

Greg went to the pay phone and she tried to read his expression as he talked.

"We have to get to the hospital," he said when he got back in the car.

"What happened? Is Natalie alright?" She set her milk shake in the cup holder.

"I'm not sure. I spoke with Doreen. She said—"

"Who?"

"Doreen. She's one of the nurses."

He knew them by name? Michelle was surprised, not to mention jealous.

"She said Natalie had some trouble in physical therapy today, and we should come see about her."

Michelle was already on the road and heading to the hospital. "When we went with her to therapy the other day, I thought he was pushing her a little too hard, but I didn't want to say anything. She seemed so proud of herself."

"Don't get all bent out of shape. Wait until we hear what the doctor says," Greg said nervously.

At the hospital, they were heading straight for Natalie's room, when a nurse stopped them. "She's not in her room."

"Where is she?" Michelle was scared now. She knew something was wrong.

"They moved her to another one."

"Why?" Greg was almost shouting.

"I think you should speak with the doctor. He'll be back in a minute."

Greg led the way to the nurses' station, where he spotted Doreen. "Where is Natalie? Why did they move her?"

She took them to a small waiting area and closed the door. Michelle was on pins and needles.

Doreen began in a soothing tone. "While Natalie was in therapy today, she went into cardiac arrest. They rushed her into the cardio ward, where she experienced congestive heart failure."

Michelle was confused by the medical terms, but she knew enough to sense that this was serious.

"I have to assure you that they are doing everything they can to stabilize her."

Their conversation was stopped by voices outside the room. Michelle could hear a woman reporting that Natalie Vaughn's parents were here. Just then the door swung open.

"Oh, doctor, this is Mr. and Mrs. Vaughn." Doreen made the introduction.

"Is she okay?" Greg asked. Michelle picked up on the fear in his voice, and it made her nervous.

"Nurse, give me a few minutes with Mom and Dad."

Doreen silently left the room, and Michelle and Greg sat down.

The doctor sat across from them and ran his hand over his balding head before he spoke. "I have to begin by saying that we have done everything in our power to help Natalie recover, but we just couldn't save her."

The words seemed to echo around the room a few times

before they registered in Michelle's head. "Where is she? Where is she? Take me to see her!" she shouted.

"I can take you downstairs now." He stood and silently led the way to the elevators.

Michelle didn't remember the trip to the room, but she'd never forget opening the door and seeing her baby motionless, lying flat on her back with a white sheet pulled up to her chest. She ran over to the bed and tried to scoop her baby up in her arms, but Greg pulled her back and held her tightly.

The rest of the night was a blur, a nasty nightmare that would never be forgotten. Greg stayed amazingly calm at the hospital, handling all of the paperwork and speaking with hospital staff, while Michelle stayed in the rest room trying to pull herself together. She had constant flashbacks of Natalie at different stages of her short life. She could vividly picture her baby taking her first steps in her mother's living room back in Brooklyn. She remembered how excited Natalie was when she got her first training bra and how scared she was the day she got her period. Michelle also remembered her looking like such a big girl on her first day of high school. She was standing in the kitchen reassuring her worried mother that she would be okay. It all seemed like only yesterday.

When they got home, Greg said he wanted to be alone for a while and went straight to their bedroom. Not knowing what else to do, Michelle got on the phone and started making calls. She started with her mother, who said she would be on the first flight to New York the next day. Then she called Umi and left a message on her machine, asking her to return the call immediately. Finally she called Randi and was surprised she answered.

"Hello."

"Randi, this is Michelle."

"Hi, Michelle." Randi was shocked to hear from her.

"How are you?" Michelle asked.

"Fine. And you?"

"We lost Natalie tonight."

"No, no, no, Michelle. Oh, God," Randi cried into the phone.

Michelle was wiping her own tears away. "I can't talk long, Randi. I just called to let you know."

"Do you want me to come over? Are you okay? Are you

alone?"

"No, Greg is here with me."

"I'll come over tomorrow then, okay?"

"Okay."

"Michelle, I love you, and I'll see you tomorrow." She hung up.

Michelle hung up the phone and went upstairs. She opened the door to the bedroom to find Greg on his knees by the side of the bed praying. His words were mixed with his sobs, making them difficult to understand.

She closed the door and went down the hall to Natalie's room and got in her bed. *"Earth has no sorrow that Heaven cannot heal."* The scripture fell gently from her lips. It was one she hadn't heard in quite a while. She rested her head on a pillow and fell fast asleep.

The next morning, at almost six o'clock, Greg woke her. "Michelle, the phone is for you." He handed her the cordless and stepped back out.

"Hello?" Her voice was full of sleep.

"Michelle, how are you feeling, baby?"

"Mama, I'm doing okay."

"I told Greg that I'll be arriving at two o'clock at Kennedy airport on Delta."

"One of us will be there to meet you, Mama." Her call waiting beeped. "Mama, I have a call coming in, I'll see at two."

She clicked over to the other line. "Hello?"

"Michelle, baby, how are you feeling?"

It was her mother-in-law. "I'm fine, Estelle."

"Greg called late last night and told me the news. I couldn't believe it. He said she was doing so well and would be coming home soon."

"It was a shock to us too." Her voice trembled as she fought the urge to cry.

"You stay well, Michelle, and I'll see you soon. Call me if you need anything."

"Thank you." Michelle ended the call and went down the hall to her room to put the phone back in its cradle.

"Good morning."

Greg looked up at her. "Hey." He came over and put his arms around her.

"I feel a little better today." She spoke softly into his chest. "I'm determined to get through this."

"We're going to get through it together." He rubbed her back and took a deep breath. "Now, we're going to have to have our heads on straight because in the next few days we're going to be making a lot of big decisions."

Michelle nodded. She knew this would be a long road traveled, and they would take it one step at a time.

The first step was going back to the hospital to collect Natalie's things and making arrangements with the morgue for the upkeep of Natalie's body. Then they headed to the airport for her mother, which was an emotionally draining experience for Michelle. Just seeing her mother in tears made her tough exterior crack and crumble. When they got back to the house, Michelle helped her mother get settled in the guest room, and Greg returned calls that were left on the answering machine.

"Michelle, come sit down for a minute."

She stopped what she was doing and took a seat on the bed next to her mother.

"I wanted to let you know how proud I am of you for being so strong at a time when it's easy to be weak."

"Thank you, Mama. Your being here with me means a lot." She patted her mother's hand.

"God is standing with you, and don't you ever forget it."

"I know God does all things well, Mama. But just when I thought things were looking up, he took my baby from me." Tears were traveling down her face.

"Yes, he took your baby. But before he did that, he gave you your husband back so that you wouldn't have to bear the loss alone." She took her daughter's hand in hers and gave it a reassuring squeeze.

Her mother had a point, but even with Greg being there, this was a tough pill to swallow. "You're right, Mama."

Greg tapped on the door and stuck his head in. "Sorry to interrupt. Randi is here."

They all went downstairs together. A teary-eyed Randi was

sitting at the kitchen table. She stood up when they came in.

"Michelle." She hugged her best friend. "How are you holding up?"

"As best as can be expected." She pulled away and took a long look at her friend. "I've missed you so much, girl."

"Me too."

"Hi, Randi." Grace kissed her cheek.

"How are you been, Ms. Grace?"

"I'm okay." Grace was looking through the cupboards. "Michelle, I see I'm going to have to make a run to the market."

"I'll take you," Randi offered.

She closed the cupboard and turned to face Randi. "Well let's get going so I can get back here and get something on the stove."

Grace left the kitchen. Michelle pulled Randi aside. "I didn't tell Mama about the fight we had, so don't mention anything to her about it. Okay?"

"Okay. By the way, I'm glad to see Greg here." She smiled.

"I'll tell you all about that another time. Just know we have a lot to catch up on."

"Randi, are you coming or not?" Grace huffed from the front door.

"I'm coming."

"I could have walked there by now." Grace said, annoyed.

Michelle shook her head at them and went upstairs to see what Greg was doing.

The next three days practically flew by. The word spread about Natalie's death, and the house was constantly buzzing with visitors. Michelle wasn't taking any more phone calls. She left that job for Randi who was acting as her personal assistant. There was still no word from Umi, but Michelle hardly had time to concentrate on her with everything else that was going on.

Greg handled most of the funeral arrangements and was making sure that everything was going as planned for the services the next day. Grace was keeping herself busy by cooking everything in the house, which was good because they had a lot of hungry people stopping by.

Michelle took one last long look in the mirror before leaving the bathroom and heading downstairs. Wearing a pair of beige

Donna Karan slacks and a brown print silk sweater, her outer man
was dressed and ready. It was her inner man that was unprepared.
Be strong, black woman. Be strong. She repeated the phrase to herself. Michelle could hear the chattering, laughing and sobbing even
before she got to the bottom of the stairs.

Randi's mother was the first to spot her and come running
over. "Michelle, I'm so sorry about Natalie. How are you feeling,
honey?"

"I'm hanging in there, Ms. Dollie."

Michelle decided to hit the smaller crowd in the kitchen
before addressing the larger one in the living room. Her mother
was in the kitchen, as usual, along with a few of Natalie's class-
mates, one of her teachers and two people she didn't recognize.
She accepted their hugs and condolences with her brave smile in
place and entertained a short conversation before going into the
living room to greet more visitors.

She was half listening to one of Natalie's elementary school
teachers talk about how Natalie started out as a prize student in
her class (as if Michelle wasn't there to see it for herself), when
Randi rushed over and interrupted.

"Excuse me, Michelle, I need to speak to you right away."

"It was nice speaking to you. Thank you for coming," she
managed to say before being whisked away.

Randi pulled her into a corner by the basement stairs. "I don't
want to upset you, but the media is outside."

"What?"

"Don't get angry."

"Where's Greg?"

"I saw him leave with his brother earlier."

When they heard Grace outside shouting, the two women ran
to the front door to see what was happening. After making her way
through the small crowd that had gathered behind Grace at the
door, Michelle grabbed hold of her mother's arm.

" . . . This is a private tragedy, not a public circus! Get your
asses off our property or I'll sue you for every damn dime you've
got!"

"Mama, Mama!" Michelle was trying to shut her up.

"Let's go back inside, everybody!" Randi was shouting over
Grace.

Michelle was on the verge of panic when she saw Greg's car pulling into the driveway. He got out and calmly walked to the front door as if he didn't see the horde of reporters on the lawn.

"Let's go inside, Grace." He put one arm around his wife and the other around his mother-in-law and went inside.

"It's a damn shame you can't even mourn in peace," Dollie was in the kitchen complaining.

"Michelle, Grace, why don't you go upstairs, and I'll bring up some tea," Randi offered.

Michelle went silently, confused and enraged by the scene that had just taken place. She hoped she wouldn't see her mother on the evening news cursing and carrying on.

Grace was on the stairs behind her, still grumbling. "Done upset my stomach. I'm going to the bathroom."

Michelle went in her room and watched the crowd of reporters from her window as they stood around waiting for more action.

A police car pulled up in front of the house and one of the officers spoke through the bullhorn. "This is private property. Remove yourselves immediately."

Michelle closed her eyes and prayed that this nightmare would end soon. She opened her eyes just in time to see Greg walking out to the police car. He spoke briefly to one of the officers and came back inside. The reporters were packed and gone in minutes, but the police car stayed.

She heard her bedroom door open and shut. She didn't bother turning around, she knew who it was. "So they're going to stay here and guard us now?"

"Only for a little while. I don't want the media making Natalie's death a public affair." He stepped behind her and put his arms around her waist. "Are you okay?"

She shook her head. "Where were you?"

"My brother wanted to see some of his friends over in Westbury. I was only gone a few minutes."

"I don't want you to leave me again. I need you with me." She turned to face him.

"I need you more." He kissed away the tears that began forming in her eyes.

Randi walked in. "Oops, sorry, I should have knocked. I'll

just leave your tea and come back later."
    Neither of them moved. "It's okay, Randi." Greg spoke up.
"You stay here. It's my turn to entertain." Still holding his wife in
his arms, he whispered, "I'll see you later?"
    She nodded.
    He kissed her forehead and left.
    Randi sat on the bed and patted the spot next to her. "Come
sit with me."
    Michelle sat next to her and rested her head on her best
friend's shoulder. "Did I tell you how glad I am you're here? I
really appreciate you taking time off from work and from your
wedding plans. I haven't forgotten your big day, you know."
    "Michelle, Natalie was my little girl too. I wouldn't be any-
where at this time except with you."
    "Thank you, Randi."
    "Besides, there may not be a wedding to plan."
    Michelle lifted her head and looked Randi in the eye. "Tell
me you're joking."
    "I wish I was." Randi told Michelle what happened at her
apartment with Brian and Franklin, which led to a long discussion
about love, life and everything in between. Michelle then told the
story of her breakup with Gail and the revival of her marriage.
They talked and cried well into the wee hours of the night, before
they both passed out from physical and emotional exhaustion.

                                    *

    Umi sat nervously in the precinct as she waited to see
Detective Heglock, despite LaVelle's comforting words reassuring
her that everything would be fine. LaVelle went to the small stand
outside the precinct to get her a cup of coffee, and she was anxious
for him to return. The place was busy and noisy with people complaining and arguing. One woman was in tears and speaking loudly
in Spanish to an officer. Another woman was asking everyone who
passed her for a cigarette. A few people were slouched on the
benches across from her. She guessed they had been waiting all
night since it was only nine o'clock in the morning.
    She glanced down the hall once again looking for a sign of
LaVelle. When she finally spotted him, she instantly became more

relaxed. He had been like her knight in shining armor over the past week. She had made more progress in one week with LaVelle than she had the entire time she spent with Darren. LaVelle convinced her to go alone on a short walk around the block she lived on, and on another day he helped her make a quick trip to the grocery store. It wasn't easy, but with his encouragement, she did it. He also insisted on accompanying her to see her doctor, and now he was here with her in the precinct. She was overwhelmed at his willingness to help her and make sure she was happy and safe. He didn't hesitate to agree to let her stay over at his house, when she told him she would feel safer there. Nor did he give a second thought to using his vacation days to spend time with her.

He sat on the bench next to her and handed her one of the cups. "Did the detective come out yet?"

"No." She sipped her coffee. "This is good."

"Yeah? Will you believe I asked the guy to let me make it myself?"

"Stop playing." She laughed.

"Seriously. You know I know how you like your coffee."

"That's true," she agreed.

"Ms. Grayson?" Detective Heglock was standing over her.

Umi jumped at the sound of her name. She and LaVelle both stood and she introduced them. He led them into a small private office in the back of the precinct.

Umi and LaVelle sat opposite the detective in the cramped office and listened attentively as he told them about the questioning Valerie went through, where she constantly contradicted herself and almost admitted to attacking Umi. He also told them that a court date had been set for the following week where Valerie would get the opportunity to make a plea.

"Valerie has a court-appointed attorney who will probably make a plea of guilty, then ask the court to grant her community service."

"Community service?" Umi and LaVelle said in unison.

"I'm not saying that she'll only get community service, but her attorney is there to get her the lightest means of punishment possible. Your case is not so simple. There are a lot of issues to weed through. First, your attacker has a history of petty crimes, like shoplifting and possession of marijuana, and now she has attacked you. The court may see her as someone who needs to be rehabilitated and not punished."

Umi was speechless. Since when had community service become rehabilitating? "Does the court realize that she could have killed me?"

"But she didn't kill you. If she had, then we would be looking at a murder-one case and not an assault case—two totally different things."

"So the law would be on my side if I were dead."

The detective held up his hands defensively. "It doesn't sound very fair, I know."

"Well with her running around loose on the streets, I may very well be dead the next time she snaps and wants to attack me."

LaVelle patted her leg in an effort to calm her down.

Umi complained from the time they left the precinct until they reached her house. She went there to check her messages and pick up a few things before going back to LaVelle's house to relax, but that didn't happen once she heard Michelle's message.

She went to the front door and waved for LaVelle to come in the house.

"What happened?" he asked from the doorway.

"I need to return one call. It sounds important." She had the phone in her hand.

Michelle didn't say much in her message, but after years of friendship, Umi knew when something was wrong with her friends. And after their argument, she knew only an emergency would make Michelle call her.

She was annoyed when she heard Michelle's recorded voice. "Michelle, this is Umi. I'm returning your call from a few days ago. Sorry it took me so long to get back to you. I hope everything is alright." She put the phone down, grabbed her things and left.

Umi dreaded the day she would have to come face-to-face with Valerie, and that day had finally come. LaVelle coached her all morning on staying strong and reminded her that she was in control. All of that went down the drain as soon as they stepped inside the large courtroom. Umi instantly became jittery and had to step back out for a minute to pull herself together.

"You have to either sit in the courtroom or sit out here. You can't stand in the doorway." A court officer was speaking to the small crowd gathered by the door.

The people slowly obeyed, dispersing a few at a time. Umi and LaVelle took a seat on a bench a little ways down the hall where he started in on another pep talk.

"Are you going to be okay?"

She nodded.

"We'd better get back inside so we can hear when your name is called."

Umi followed LaVelle back in the courtroom and sat down like a wooden dummy. She kept her eyes straight ahead and couldn't believe she was sitting in a roomful of people she spent her entire life trying to avoid.

"Is Umi Grayson here?" the judge asked.

She was shaking so badly, she thought she would topple over on her way to approach the bench.

The judge looked down at her strangely. "Your court date has been postponed. The defendant in this case in unable to be here today. You'll receive a date in the mail to return to court."

That was it? She met LaVelle out in the hallway half disappointed that she didn't get this over with and half delighted that she didn't have to face Valerie.

When she got back to LaVelle's apartment, she ate a quick lunch and tried to reach Michelle again. She'd left three messages in the past week, and no one had returned her call.

She waited as the phone rang and got the first of several surprises when Randi answered Michelle's phone.

"Randi?"

"Umi, where have you been?" Randi asked with an attitude.

She immediately became defensive. "Where's Michelle?"

"I don't care what you're doing. You stop this very minute and get your ass out here now!"

"What? Randi, where in the hell is Michelle?"

Randi slammed the phone in its cradle.

"She hung up on me." Umi waved the receiver at LaVelle. "That crazy bitch actually hung up on me."

"Try calling back, maybe Michelle will answer," LaVelle suggested calmly.

"Oh no, we're going out there. Right now." She slid back into her shoes, straightened her suit jacket and headed for the door where LaVelle stopped her.

"Don't you think you should call back first?"

"I've known Randi almost my entire life. She's one of those crazy types that has to be dealt with face-to-face. Get your coat, you're coming with me."

LaVelle took a deep breath and followed her out the door.

Umi was unprepared for what she was about to encounter as she parked her Mercedes at the curb in front of Michelle's house and marched up to the front door and banged on it.

"Just a minute," a voice called from inside. Seconds later an old woman wearing an apron opened the door. "Yes?"

Fueled by her anger and her unwillingness to accept any more surprises, Umi let her bad side take control. "Where's Michelle?"

The woman eyed her carefully and asked sweetly. "May I ask who you are?"

"I'm a friend of hers." Umi had her hand on her hip.

"If you're her friend then why don't you know she's at the services for her daughter?"

Umi went from being angry to being confused, then shocked in one second flat. "Natalie? Oh, God, when?"

"Last week. Why don't you come in?"

Umi took a seat on the first chair she could get to. "Where are the services? We have to get there."

"It's already after three o'clock. They're probably on their way back from the burial up in Hicksville. You should wait for them here." She patted Umi's shoulder. "I'm Michelle's aunt. Can I get y'all something to drink?"

Umi shook her head. She couldn't believe Natalie was dead and she wasn't around to support Michelle. She was ashamed of herself. Randi had every right to be mad at her. She deserved it.

The doorbell rang and Michelle's aunt went to answer it. Umi and LaVelle stood up when Randi came in the house.

"Hi, Auntie." She kissed her cheek.

"How was the service?"

"Very emotional, but it was a lovely turnout. People came

from all over."

"Where's everybody?"

"I left the cemetery early to get back here and prepare for the crowd, but they should be right behind me."

"A couple of people are already here."

Randi finally saw them in the living room and walked over, eyeing Umi nastily.

"Randi, I had no idea," she said softly.

"I should kick your ass," she hissed and walked upstairs without looking back.

Umi sat on the sofa in disbelief. LaVelle tried to comfort her, although he had no idea what was going on.

Shortly after, people started arriving, and the house filled quickly. Somehow, Umi felt very out of place and just as she was about to suggest that they leave, Michelle, Greg and Grace came through the door. Immediately everyone rushed over to greet them and have words of encouragement. Umi watched Michelle smile politely and thank everyone for their support, and felt instantly guilty. What kind of friend had she been?

"Are you okay, Michelle?" her aunt asked.

She hugged her. "I'll be fine, Auntie. I just need to get upstairs and lay down for a minute."

"You do that, and I'll bring up a plate of food for you."

"Thank you."

"I'll be right back," Umi told LaVelle and rushed over to the stairs to meet Michelle.

Michelle was speaking with Gail when she turned around and practically bumped right into her. Umi could tell she was surprised and waited to see what kind of response she would get.

"Umi, I'm glad to see you could finally make it." She gave her a half smile.

Although her voice was soft and polite, Umi could sense her disappointment. As Michelle started up the stairs, Umi tugged her arm gently. She knew this was her opportunity to make amends—it was now or never. "Michelle, do you mind if I come up with you?"

She shrugged and continued walking. Umi was right behind her.

When they got to the room, Randi was changing into a pair

of jeans and a T-shirt. She gave Umi a sharp look, before turning to Michelle. "Michelle, how are you holding up?" she asked.

"I'll be okay. I'm already okay, I just don't know it." She took off her shoes and started undressing. Umi stayed by the door and kept silent.

"I ran the iron over your jeans for you."

Michelle slid into the jeans and pulled a shirt out of a drawer and pulled it over her head. Umi finally took a seat in one of the chairs in the room.

"Be careful where you sit. You don't want to pick up any diseases, remember you're in the house of a lesbian," Randi warned.

"Shut the hell up, Randi." Umi snapped.

Michelle held her hands up to silence them. "Look, ladies, this is not the time. Randi, give it a rest for now, for my sake."

"I don't even know why you came," Randi said.

"You don't know what I've been through. I would have been here if I had known." Umi wanted to be tough, but Randi's words were cutting her like a knife, and her tears were welling up.

"Oh, poor, poor Umi," Randi said in disgust.

There was a knock at the door and Greg stuck his head in. "Is everything alright up here?" He immediately sensed the tension in the room. "Auntie said something about bringing up some food, I'll tell her to wait a while."

No one answered. Randi turned her back and stared out the window and Umi hid her face in her hands.

Michelle took a seat on the bed. "We're fine, Greg. We just need a minute to pull ourselves together."

He backed out and closed the door.

Michelle welcomed the silence that had blanketed the room, but she couldn't leave their friendship in this state, so she began talking. "This has been an emotionally trying day for all of us. Why don't we just cool out for a while, then meet up next week for lunch so we can all talk?"

"You hurt me," Randi said with her back to them. She slowly turned around to reveal her wet face. "Knowing that I didn't have your support, that you weren't standing in my corner and ready to back me up, really hurt me, Umi. I know and accept the fact that we're very different—our perspectives, our ideals and even how we conduct our lives, but in spite of those differences, I somehow thought you would always have my back."

Michelle listened silently. In all the years of their friendship, she had never seen Randi show such heartfelt emotion.

"Then, with your self-righteous, judgmental ass, you can't even pick up a phone and apologize!" Her words were mixed with sobs. "Who cares what you've been through. Michelle and Greg are going through much worse than you can ever imagine! Wake up, Umi. The world doesn't fucking revolve around you!" She turned her back and faced the window again.

Umi took her verbal beating silently. She had no smart comeback or quick-witted defense. She simply listened.

Michelle couldn't stop her own tears from falling at the outpour of emotion. She watched Randi's shoulders as they shook with her silent sobs.

Umi said a silent prayer before approaching Randi. She went over and rested her hand on her friend's shoulder. "If it means anything now, I'm sorry."

She didn't know why she expected Randi to run into her arms and say all was forgiven, when she knew that only happened in the movies. Instead, Randi continued to stare out the window giving her no indication that her apology was accepted or that she was even listening.

Umi backed away and went to the door. "Michelle, I'm so sorry I wasn't here for you when Natalie died, but I'm here for you now if you ever need me."

Michelle nodded as she left.

CHAPTER 16

The next morning, Randi was up bright and early and heading back to Brooklyn. She had been at Michelle's house all week and needed to prepare herself to go back to work and back to living her life again. She needed to drop some of the dead weight she'd been carrying around, and that included Franklin, Brian and Umi. Hector, the doorman, helped her upstairs with her luggage and all of her mail that had accumulated over the past week.

When she finished unpacking, she checked her answering machine, secretly hoping that Brian had called, but he hadn't. She knew there was no hope of repair for their relationship, but she at least wanted to remain friends with him. Her only call was from Toni, saying she hadn't heard from her and wanted to talk. That was the second message she'd left, and Randi swore she would eventually get around to calling her, but she just had too much happening at the moment.

Finally, she settled on the sofa, clicked on the television and started opening her mail. Someone sent her a small brown package without a return address, and it was stamped *Hand Delivered*. Eager to see what was inside, she ripped the brown paper off and opened the box, only to find her old wallet and a typewritten note.

NOW YOU KNOW THE HEARTACHE AND HEADACHE
OF LOSING SOMETHING THAT'S VALUABLE TO YOU.
MAKE THIS A LESSON LEARNED.

Franklin's wife had stolen her wallet? She looked through it and everything was still there, except the money, of course, and all of her credit cards and bank cards had been cut in half. It was an ironic thought, but she took having her wallet returned to her by her ex-lover's wife, as a kind gesture. Jackie held the key to ruining her financial stability, but she didn't. Instead she only dished out a big dose of inconvenience. Randi thought about her own willingness to forgive and forget. On one hand, Franklin's wife, whom she'd only seen once, had every right to ruin her, but didn't. On the other hand, she, herself, was unwilling to cut a life-long friend any slack.

The thought stayed with her all afternoon as she went about business as usual. When she could no longer tolerate her nagging conscious, she decided to call Umi, but her phone rang just as she reached for it.

"Hello?"

"Hi, is this Randi?"

"Yes," she hesitantly answered.

"You may not remember me, my name is Darren. I'm a friend of Umi's."

Why is he calling me? she thought. "Yes, Darren, I remember you. How can I help you?"

"It's not me who needs your help. It's Umi."

"What is this about? I just saw Umi yesterday."

"Oh, so then you already know. I'm probably confusing you. Let me explain. See, I haven't spoken to Umi in more than two weeks and was concerned about her because she wasn't answering her phone. When I went to her house on two different occasions, she wasn't there. I have been worrying myself sick because I didn't know what kind of state she was in after the attack and all. I feel much better knowing that she's alright."

"Darren?"

"Huh?"

"What are you talking about?"

After her conversation with Darren, Randi felt like dirt. She thought about calling Michelle, but figured she had her hands full and this was probably something she should handle on her own anyway.

She tried calling Umi's house, but got the machine. She hung up, grabbed her pocketbook and headed to Bensonhurst. Umi wasn't home when she got there, so she waited on the front steps for about fifteen minutes when she spotted Umi's big black Benz coming up the street.

When Umi pulled into her driveway, Randi could see her talking to the person in the passenger seat before getting out of the car.

"Why are you here, Randi?" Umi asked angrily from the car.

"I want to talk to you."

"Have something else you want to get off your chest?" She was now standing face-to-face with Randi on her front steps.

"Darren called me," she said softly, not sure if she should say more in front of Umi's guest, who was standing nearby.

Umi stomped past Randi and led the way inside. She spoke to LaVelle privately in the kitchen, before leading Randi to her bedroom.

Umi closed the door behind them, and Randi took a seat in her big rattan chair. "So, why are you here? As I recall, nobody cares about what happens to me."

"I didn't mean that. I let my anger get the best of me."

"You expect me to accept that from you, but when it comes from me, I'm self-righteous and judgmental?"

Randi got the point and after the way she acted, she didn't expect anything but resistance from Umi. Now it was her turn to listen.

Her tears were falling before she could even open her mouth. "You don't think I know what it's like to be alone? Not to have anyone to turn to at my weakest moment? I know, Randi, and I'm sorry I made you feel like you couldn't depend on me." She choked on her words and couldn't continue. She turned her back to Randi.

Randi totally understood what Umi meant. She went over and put her arms around her best friend tightly as they shared a good cry together.

"I've missed you so much, Randi. I'm sorry for being such an ass."

"I'm sorry, too, Umi, and I really do care about what happens to you. I want you to know that if I had known you were going through such a tough time, I would have been here for you."

"I know you would have." She was still crying.

Randi went into the bathroom and came back with a box of Kleenex to dry their faces. They both had red noses and puffy eyes.

Umi led them over to her bed, and they sat down. The tension between them was lifting more and more with each passing moment.

"Are you feeling better about the attack now?"

She nodded. "I was having a hard time at first, but every day I get a little better."

"Good for you. Is Valerie in jail now?" She wiped at her eyes and nose again.

"Heck no, she's innocent until proven guilty." Umi sighed. "We have to go to court. I should be receiving a date in the mail shortly." She toyed with her used Kleenex as she spoke.

Randi was disgusted by the thought of Valerie going free. "That's the system for you." She shook her head.

"Yeah, it seems as though the system is working against me instead of for me. It's a situation that can easily frustrate me, but I know Valerie will eventually get her just reward."

"Umi?"

"Huh?" She was blowing her nose.

"Who's that guy in the kitchen?" She was trying hard to hold back a smile.

"Damn, you're nosy, girl." She smiled. "That's my man."

Randi's eyes opened wide. "You left Darren? Oh, Lord, I must be in the twilight zone."

"No, you're right here on earth, where Darren is history and LaVelle is news."

"Your assistant, LaVelle?"

She smiled.

Now it all made sense why Darren hadn't been in touch with Umi, because she was with someone else trying to recapture her groove. "Wait, does Darren know he's history?" Randi's smiled grew as she asked the question.

Umi shrugged. "He's smart. He'll figure it out eventually."

Randi was a little confused though, it wasn't like Umi to date people like LaVelle. "So I'm guessing LaVelle doesn't make a six-figure salary and drive an expensive luxury car?"

She shook her head. She knew what Randi was thinking.

"Nor does he have a high-powered position in a Fortune 500 company and wear imported Italian shoes and suits?"

"No, he certainly doesn't." She laughed and then became

serious. "Spending time alone gave me the opportunity to learn a lot about myself, the kind of person I am and the kind of person I want to become."

"Umi, you are one of the most well-rounded and resolved people I know."

"And even with that, there's still room for improvement."

"I know what you mean, I could use a refresher course on humanitarianism myself."

"If *you* think you could use a refresher course, imagine what the people who have to deal with you must think."

"Oh, shut up." She playfully shoved her friend.

"Speaking of people, how's Brian? Getting ready for the big day?"

"There isn't going to be a big day."

"I'm afraid to ask why. Do you feel like talking about it?"

"There's not much to say except that it's my fault the wedding was canceled. In case you haven't noticed, I can be a bit selfish and inconsiderate at times."

Umi put her hand to her mouth in mock surprise.

Randi gave her a look that told her not to start.

She became serious again. "I'm sorry. Are you okay with that?"

"Not right now, but in time I know I'll feel better about it."

"Well, if you need me, I'm just a phone call away. Oh, and Randi, I'm glad to have you back in my corner."

"Girl, I'm glad to be back. It's a cold, cold world when you're all alone." She slapped Umi five.

"True that, my sister."

Randi stayed and ate dinner with Umi and LaVelle before going home. She felt much better now that she had made peace with her friend, and she actually thought Umi and LaVelle made a nice couple. Spending time with Umi had given her a couple of ideas on self-improvement techniques she could use. At dinner Umi said something about recognizing personal flaws and beginning working on the ones that seemed the simplest to improve. Right now she saw herself as a mannequin, all dressed up on the outside, but fake and hollow on the inside. So on her drive home, she made a mental list of things she wanted to improve the most

and would work hard at becoming a woman of substance, someone that both men and women would respect.

*

Michelle slid into her favorite pair of navy blue slacks and
a matching blue-and-beige blouse and went downstairs. She had
to meet Randi and Umi at one o'clock at the South Street Seaport
for lunch—their first lunch date since reconciling.

She was happy to be continuing a standing tradition, and it
was the perfect opportunity for her to get out of the house. She
didn't want to be there while Greg was cleaning out Natalie's
room. It had been a little more than a month since her death, and
Greg had declared himself emotionally ready for the chore, so
Michelle let him handle it. However, she wasn't even emotionally
ready to see him doing it.

"Hey, honey, you look nice," Greg said when she walked into
the kitchen. "You're leaving so early?"

"Thank you." She gave him a peck on the cheek. "I was
thinking I would leave a little early and stop and get a manicure."
She looked at her nails. "The salon I like to go to can get crowded
early on Saturday mornings."

"Oh, what I have to do here shouldn't take long. So if I'm
not here when you get back, I'll be at Allen's. He said he would
try to take a look at the car today. That rattling noise has me concerned."

The phone rang and Greg answered.

"Hello?" He listened for a minute. "Sure hold on." He handed
Michelle the receiver. "It's for you."

"Hello?"

"Hi, Michelle, how are you feeling?" Her voice was cheery.

"I'm fine, Gail. How are you?"

"I've never been better. I'm not going to keep you long, I
just wanted you to be among the first people to get the good word."

Michelle was smiling. "Oh yeah, what word is that?"

"At my court date yesterday I was acquitted of all the charges
against me for tax evasion."

"Thank you, Lord. Gail, I am so happy for you."

"Girl, I am so excited, I don't know what to do with myself.

I hardly slept a wink last night."

Michelle laughed. "I know you're glad to have this nightmare behind you."

"I know that's right. But Michelle, I have to thank you for helping me. You were a friend to me when I needed one the most."

"It was my pleasure. I'm glad I could help."

"One thing I've learned from this entire ordeal with my manager, going to court and our friendship is that God puts people in our lives for a reason and a season. All friendships are not supposed to last a lifetime." Her voice lost its cheerfulness.

"What do you mean?"

"I mean, when I met my manager, I was desperate for help, and she was desperate for work. My shop was fairly new, and I didn't have much money, so I was able to hire her at a reasonable salary. God put her in my life when I needed her to be there, but she wasn't meant to last. She was only meant for that time, or that season."

"Deep, but I see your point."

"Then you came into my life at a time when I needed an accountant and a friend, which was also only for a season. By the way, I haven't forgotten that I owe you for your help. I'm holding on to a check for you. You can come by and get it anytime you're ready."

"I'll do that when I get a chance." She didn't want to make any promises. She hadn't had any episodes with Gail since Greg had been back, but she still wasn't sure how Gail felt about her. "So, what's happening with the shop?"

"Well, I kept up my lease with Roosevelt Field, so whenever I'm ready to reopen, I'll be back in business."

"Good. And what about your manager?"

"The court sentenced her to a year in jail, but my lawyer said with good behavior she'll be out anywhere between three and six months."

"That's it?"

"Yeah, she gave this sob story in court about stealing my money out of need for her children. The judge bought it and get this, she doesn't even have to repay me."

Michelle huffed. "Well, the good thing is it's all behind you now. Money can be replaced. I'm just glad you avoided spending time in jail because of that kleptomaniac." She laughed. "Gail, I'm glad to hear everything is working out for you, but I have to go. I'll stop by soon for that check, okay?"

"No problem, see you then."

Michelle hung up and smiled at Greg. He was loading the breakfast dishes into the dishwasher.

"Good news, huh?"

"Yeah, Gail was acquitted on charges of tax evasion."

"Good for her." His back was to her.

"I love starting the day with good news. I'd better get a move on." She glanced at her naked wrist. "Oh, I left my watch upstairs." She ran to get it. On her way, she heard the doorbell ring and wondered who was visiting so early in the morning. On her way back downstairs, she could hear the conversation in her living room.

"Kate, you look wonderful."

She chuckled lightly. "Greg, you're too kind."

Michelle stopped in mid-step. Kate Parker? Why was she there?

"We're sorry to just drop in on you like this, but we would like to talk to you and Michelle about some issues surrounding the accident."

Michelle recognized Larry's voice. She still didn't move.

"Oh?" Greg asked.

"If this is a bad time for you, we can come back." Larry sensed Greg's hesitation.

"But I think it's something that requires your immediate attention," Kate added.

"Well, we had plans this morning. Michelle will be down in a minute. Let me see what she thinks."

Michelle came to the bottom of the stairs and stepped into view.

"What do I think about what?" She walked into the living room. "Hello, Larry, Kate." She greeted them flatly.

"Hello." They immediately picked up on her attitude.

"Michelle, the Parkers want to talk to us about the accident."

"Have you ever heard of picking up a phone?" She eyed Kate.

The room was silenced by her bluntness.

"We have plans. Next time call before you come. Nice seeing you again, Larry." She went into the kitchen, leaving them with their mouths gaping.

Michelle was standing over the sink, looking out the window when she felt another presence enter the room. She didn't bother turning around.

"Michelle, you have every right to be mad at me. I was way out of line that day I came here. I had no right saying those things about Natalie. One of the reasons I came here today was to apologize and ask you to forgive me."

Michelle listened quietly and continued staring out of the window.

"The other reason is to solve the mystery for you and put your mind at rest about what happened the night of the accident. Rachael told me what happened, and I thought you would like to know as well. Maybe it would help bring closure."

Rachael! Michelle had forgotten all about her! She held the missing pieces to the puzzle and could answer all of her questions. But did she really want to know? Let the past stay there. Her top layer had healed. Did she want to reopen the wound she had worked so hard to cover up?

"Why now, Kate?" She kept her back to her. "Why do you wait until my baby is dead to try and bring closure to this nightmare." Her words were hard and low.

"Michelle, I'm just finding out myself, honest. Rachael has been in therapy for the last few months, and it was only recently that she even mentioned the accident. She told the therapist how responsible she feels for Natalie's death.

"My child is in a living hell. She wakes up screaming from night terrors almost every other night. She's paralyzed and trapped in that damn wheelchair for the rest of her life. God forgive me, but sometimes I find myself wishing it were Rachael who had died instead." She choked out the last sentence.

Michelle turned to face Kate. She didn't feel sorry for her. In fact she thought Kate was selfish. So what? She would put with the inconvenience of a wheelchair and night terrors, if she could just have Natalie back. Night terrors could be repaired with the right therapy, but death was permanent. But one thing Kate said had her attention.

"Why does Rachael feel responsible for the accident?" she asked slowly as she prepared herself for the answer. She watched

Kate wipe her tears away with the back of her hand and noticed
Greg and Larry standing in the doorway.

"From what Rachael has told Larry and me, it seems that
Rachael asked Natalie to pick her up that night and drop her off
at some boy's house. Natalie told her she had just gotten in trouble for coming in late and didn't want to sneak out."

Michelle and Greg made eye contact. They both remembered
the night vividly.

"Anyway, Rachael persisted, Natalie gave in and that's why
they were out that night." Kate's eyes and nose were wet. Greg
handed her a paper towel. Michelle didn't move.

Kate, overwhelmed, sat at the table with her head in her
hands. Larry stood behind her and gently rubbed her shoulders.
"What bothered us most was that Rachael wasn't going to the
boy's house for reasons you're probably thinking. She was going
to deliver drugs." He dropped his head in shame.

Michelle and Greg looked at each other knowingly. Rachael
was the dealer, not Natalie.

"There were drugs involved?" Greg asked.

Larry continued. "According to Rachael, Natalie had been
romantically involved with this boy. I think his name is Perry, but
she was trying to break it off because he was pressuring her to
deliver drugs for him. As it turns out, Natalie wouldn't deliver, but
Rachael would. She negotiated for a cut of the profit and somehow convinced Natalie to hold the money for her along with a gun
Perry had given her and some of the drugs. Rachael suspects that
Natalie may have thrown those things away or you would have
found them by now."

Greg shook his head. "She probably did just that because we
haven't seen anything."

No wonder her grades were slipping, Michelle thought. *My
poor baby was being pressured from all sides to do things she did-
n't want to do.*

Kate finally composed herself enough to speak. "Michelle,
I came here that day accusing Natalie of the most horrible things,
and all along it was my own child that was doing wrong. I'm so
ashamed of myself and Rachael." She was crying again.

"What Kate is trying to say is that we expected more from
both of the girls." Larry's eyes were misty, but he managed to keep

his emotions under control.

Greg patted Larry's shoulder. "I know how you feel, man."

Michelle's heart went out to Larry and Kate and at the same time she was relieved to know that Natalie wasn't directly involved with the drugs. She was proud of Natalie for being able to resist the temptation of fast money and peer pressure. After all, she had taught her daughter well.

Michelle went over to Kate and hugged her briefly. "You're forgiven, Kate. Try not to be too disappointed in Rachael. She made a terrible mistake, one that has affected us all in different ways, but I think she's learned a valuable lesson and is mature enough and wise enough to handle the tough road ahead of her. But don't make her travel the road alone. Stand by her and be supportive."

"And we're here for you guys if you ever need us," Greg added.

"Man, I appreciate your support. It's important to us at a time like this. We don't want people finding out about Rachael's involvement with drug dealing, but it's difficult not having anyone to talk to about it," Larry said.

"I understand. Just give us a call if you ever feel like talking," Greg offered.

Kate stood. "We don't want to keep you from your plans."

"Oh, don't worry about that. Are you okay?" Michelle asked.

"I'll be fine, but we have to get back to Rachael. We left her with a home attendant."

"Oh," Greg and Michelle said in unison.

When their guests were out the door, Greg and Michelle looked at each with pride.

"You know, we should be ashamed of ourselves," she scolded jokingly.

"You're right." Greg put on a serious face. "Larry and Kate are going through a tough time."

"They're going through the same thing we went through when we thought Natalie was the drug dealer," Michelle said matter-of-factly.

He nodded.

She looked at her watch. "I'd better try Umi on her cellular and let her know I'll be late." She went into the kitchen to get the phone.

"Hello?" Umi answered.

"Hi, Umi, this is Michelle."

"Don't tell me you're canceling."

"I'll be there, but I'm going to be a little late. You ladies start without me, and I'll be there as soon as I can."

"Is everything okay?"

"I'm fine. I just had some unexpected visitors this morning. I'll tell you all about it when I see you. Bye." She went into the living room. "I'd better get a move on."

Greg faced his wife. "Drive safely, and I'll see you when you get back." He kissed her lips, and she was out the door.

*

Randi figured the train was her best bet to the South Street Seaport on this beautiful afternoon. She was dressed in a one of her nicest pantsuits, a dark beige color, maybe one shade off from being light brown and it was made of a very comfortable wash-and-wear cotton. The jacket was single breasted, and she left it open to show off a white silk camisole. She complimented her out-fit with simple gold accents and a pair of matching sling backs she had recently treated herself to when she caught a sale at Saks Fifth Avenue. Confident that her short cut was perfectly curler-ironed, she was ready to begin her day.

When she got to the restaurant, Umi was alone at the table sipping something that looked liked iced tea. She startled her as she approached the table.

Umi put her hand over her heart. "Hey, girl, are you trying to give this old lady a heart attack or what?"

Randi kissed her cheek and took a seat. "Who are you call-ing old? If you're old, that makes me old. And that just ain't so."

Umi laughed as the waiter approached the table, stopping her rebuttal.

"Would you like to start with something from the bar?" He placed a glass of water in front of her.

"No, thank you."

"I think you should have a drink. You're going to need it when I give you my news," Umi said calmly.

"Oh, God. I'll have a fruit punch, heavy on the ice, please."

She waited for the waiter to leave before she started her interrogation. "And what news is this?" She folded her arms across her chest and leaned back in her chair.

"You know I can't dish out anything without Michelle being here." She sipped her drink. "You'll just have to wait."

Randi looked at her watch. "Where is she anyway?"

She hunched her shoulders. "She called me on my cell phone saying she had some unexpected visitors this morning, which caused her to run a little late."

"Unexpected visitors, my foot. Her morning quickie turned into a long one. Don't forget Michelle has a man in her bed now."

"And Lord knows I'm glad they're back together." Umi waved her hand.

The waiter brought Randi's drink. She took a good long look at his butt as he walked away. "Those are some tight biscuits, there," she commented quietly.

"You're disgusting. He's a human being, not a piece of meat. You would be fuming if a man did that to you."

"You're damn right I would, but he is looking good. He's probably an out-of-work actor." She dismissed him with a wave of her hand.

"Nope, a starving artist."

"I'll bet anything, a musician."

"Living in his mama's basement," Umi added.

"With his phone in her name."

"And his car insurance too."

"What car?" Randi laughed.

They slapped each other five across the table.

"Good afternoon, ladies." Michelle surprised them as she took a seat at the table.

"Oh, Michelle." Randi was still laughing. "Umi is so silly. I didn't even see you."

"Hey, girl." Umi kissed her cheek.

"What's so funny?" Michelle was a little out of breath. She practically ran in from the parking lot.

"Randi is over here talking bad about people again."

Randi's mouth dropped open in shock. "Girl, you lie like a rug."

The waiter came over and set a glass of water in front of

Michelle. "Can I get you something from the bar, ma'am?"

"Sure. What are y'all drinking?" she asked.

"Long Island Iced Tea." Umi raised her glass and took a swallow.

"Plain old fruit punch." Randi tapped her glass with her fingernail. She could barely contain her giggles.

Michelle turned to the waiter. "I'll have a margarita on ice, stirred, not shaken, please."

He looked to Umi and Randi. "And would you ladies like an appetizer, or will someone else be joining you?" He indicated the empty chair.

Umi wanted to laugh, but after years of practice, she'd learned how to smother the emotion and put on her poker face. "An appetizer sounds good. We'll have the crab cakes and dip."

The waiter was barely out of earshot before Randi started laughing.

"What is wrong with her?" Michelle asked Umi.

"We were trying to guess what kind of man the waiter is, and it's not as funny as Randi is making it out to be." She swatted her hand at Randi. "Behave yourself."

Michelle didn't think it was funny at all. "Anyway, you won't believe what happened to me this morning."

This snapped Randi back to her senses and they all leaned in close together. They listened quietly as Michelle ran down the details of her visitors. She stopped when the waiter brought their appetizer, then continued. She was near tears by the end of the story.

"I'm relieved just knowing that at least Natalie was trying to do the right thing." Michelle dabbed her eyes with her napkin.

"I knew all along there had to be a reasonable explanation for her having those things in her room. Being a drug dealer was just too far from Natalie's character," Umi said.

"Not really. I would have never suspected Rachael—and didn't. Who would have known? Larry and Kate are so ashamed."

"It seems to me that Rachael is a follower. Ever since you moved to Long Island, she's been following Natalie," Randi said.

"Then she should have followed her when she told this boy she wouldn't deal drugs for him," Umi reasoned. "She may be a follower, but she's also greedy. It sounds to me like she did it for the fast money."

The waiter came and took their orders and freshened their drinks. Randi snickered every time he came to the table.

"You're going to make that man put something in your food if you don't stop giggling at him," Michelle warned.

"That girl's parents are loaded. Why would she need drug money?" Randi asked.

Umi shrugged. "I don't know. Maybe she wanted something her parents wouldn't buy for her."

"Like a car," Michelle said matter-of-factly. The full picture was slowly coming into view.

"See—"Umi pointed her finger at Michelle—"She was Natalie's friend, but at the same time she was secretly jealous of her."

"That's a best friend for you." Randi was surprised by her own words and tried to avoid her best friends' stares.

"What is that supposed to mean?" Umi asked softly.

"It doesn't mean anything." She was ready to be defensive. Instead, she put her guard down and answered honestly. "It's just that at times I've found myself being happy for both of you and a little jealous at the same time." There was a long, awkward silence.

Michelle reached over and patted her shoulder. "Then I guess it's only natural because I've had that same feeling at one time or another myself."

Randi smiled with relief.

Umi nodded. "Although, I'm ashamed to admit it, I know the feeling well myself." She held Randi's hand and gave it a tight squeeze.

"I guess even in our old age, we're still learning about friendship," Randi said jokingly.

"I guess so."

After having lunch, the waiter brought them coffee and dessert and Umi was prepared to share her secret.

She took a deep breath. "Well, I have some news I would like to share with you ladies."

"Spill it," Randi said.

"What kind of news?" Michelle asked.

"I have made a decision to make a big change in my life, and I'm going to need a lot of support in my transition."

Michelle and Randi sat wide-eyed and anxious.

"I'm going to start my own advertising agency." She casually sipped her coffee, sat back and waited for the question-and-answer session to begin.

"You're nuts." Randi turned to Michelle. "She's nuts."

"Umi, this is so sudden. Why?"

"For a lot of reasons, but the most important one is that I know I can do it. I know it's within my reach. Instead of spending my life working for people and making them rich, I can put my skills and know-how to work for me. I'm almost forty—if I'm going to make this kind of move, I have to do it soon." She could see they weren't convinced. "Come on, I need you now."

"Have you worked out all of the details? Sounds like there's a lot involved." Michelle was concerned.

"Most of them, but not all," she answered honestly.

"How are you going to live in the meantime?" Randi wanted to know.

"I have some savings. And I'm going to cash out my 401(k) for the up-front collateral."

"What brought this about? I thought you were happy where you were," Randi said. It all seemed too sudden and too overwhelming in her opinion.

"Well, it's something that I've always wanted to do."

Randi eyed her suspiciously.

"Also, at the last annual advertising banquet, one of the people on my team, Greta, was promoted to head her own team. I figured this was good, until I discovered that her team would consist of the better half of my team members. I have to give it to the executive board, it's a good strategy to promote growth and clientele, but I don't want to compete against the people that I've spent the last ten years training."

Randi nodded in agreement. She could understand that.

"Well, you have to have office space, employees—at least a receptionist—and supplies. It's a big task to take on, but if you feel up to it, I'm more than confident you can do it," Michelle said.

"So, you're willing to help me?"

"In any way I can."

"Good. You're hired." She smiled.

"To do what?" Michelle frowned.

"I need a receptionist slash bookkeeper."

"Oh, Lord," Randi moaned. "I knew Umi's project would easily turn into *our* project."

"Now, Randi, you know it's all for one and one for all. Are you willing to help your best friend make a dream come true?" Umi asked.

She hesitated before answering. "Alright. I'm in. Just shout whenever you need me."

"Good." Umi was bubbling with excitement and pulled out her planner. "Well, so far, I had a meeting with the executive board and told them I would be handing in my resignation."

Randi and Michelle looked at each other in disbelief.

"Oh, Randi I'm going to e-mail my resignation to you, so you can proof it for me." She went back to her planner. "They offered me a lot of money to stay, and it was tempting, but I'm looking at the bigger picture, here. If things go the way I plan, I will have made triple that amount in my first two years in business for myself."

"And Michelle, I want us to sit down sometime soon and go over a financial plan. We're going to need to do this before I start looking for office space." She took a sip of her coffee.

"Question," Randi spoke up. "Do you have any clients yet?"

"Not exactly. See, this is a bit complicated. If I try to solicit clients that I've worked with at this firm, I can be sued. However, I'm going to build my business solely on reputation and references. I'll let my polished career work for me and as for my current list of clientele, whenever their contracts have expired, they're free to do business with whomever they wish. Hopefully, they'll put their trust in me."

"It's easier to put your trust in someone who has a big firm backing them," Michelle said.

"The firm doesn't do the legwork, the individual does. The firm is only a name. Remember that," Umi said sharply.

"Is that bitterness I hear?" Randi asked slyly.

"I'm not going to indulge in that emotion. I have to admit, at first I was a little bent out of shape about it. The board asked me to pick my best person, the one I thought most worthy of leading a successful advertising team. Then they set that person up to compete against me, giving her an edge by giving her my best team members. But that's business, and when you're not in it for yourself, you have to play the game by other people's rules."

"How does Darren feel about this?" Michelle asked.

"Who?"

"I'm sorry, I meant LaVelle."

"All I can say is, be prepared to see a lot of him." She was smiling.

"He knew before us?" Randi asked.

"You know, it's kind of funny. When I first learned about their plan, LaVelle was with me, and I don't need to tell you I was livid. I started saying things off the top of my head like I should quit or form a protest of some sort. But as I calmed down and gave it more thought, it all seemed clear to me that I should go into business for myself. Well, of course, LaVelle and I talked about it at length, then I prayed about it, and I feel confident in my decision."

"Umi, you never cease to amaze me," Michelle said. "I'm so proud of you. What you're about to do takes a lot of guts."

"Thank you, Michelle." She looked at Randi.

"I'm proud of you too. Just don't give me an excuse to say 'I told you so.' "

"You always know how to spoil a good moment," Michelle complained.

Umi rolled her eyes. "Mark my words, I won't."

When the waiter brought over the check, Umi laid her credit card on the table and insisted on paying. "This is our first staff luncheon. Remember to include it when you do the books," she told Michelle.

The ladies stood and started toward the parking lot. "I am so full," Michelle complained. "I should have left that pie on the plate."

"I feel a little stuffed myself. I think it was all of those crab cakes I ate," Umi said. "What about you, Randi?"

No response.

"Randi?" Umi called.

"Huh? What did you say?"

"What's wrong with you? What are you looking at?" Umi asked just as she spotted Brian and a beautiful young woman walking toward them. "Oh, Lord," she mumbled, but it was too late,

Brian had already seen them.

Brian and his companion stopped directly in front of them. No one spoke for a few seconds.

"Hello, Randi." His words were polite and completely void of emotion.

"Brian." She nodded. "Hello, Toni, how nice to see you again." Randi's words were tart.

Michelle and Umi were shocked and silently communicated to each other with their eyes.

"Hello, Randi," Toni said sweetly. "I'm sure you're surprised to see me here with Brian, but—"

"No, I'm not surprised at all, in fact my girls and I were just talking about what to expect from a friend." She turned to Michelle and Umi. "She's a prime example of our conversation."

"Hold on a minute, Randi, maybe you should tell your friends how this situation came about." Although her voice was calm, Toni's words were dripping with attitude.

"No need to rehash bad memories, they already know the scoop. I'm the one who needed to take a trip to Baskin-Robins because this was one scoop I wasn't aware of."

Brian intervened. "Randi, our relationship is over. There's no need to include you in what happens in my life."

She was hurt, more hurt than she cared to admit. She put on her stern face, but her silence gave her away.

Toni softened her tone. "Look, Randi, I wasn't trying to hide this from you. In fact, I called you twice to talk to you about it, but you never called me back."

"Does my brother know?" She didn't know exactly why she asked. Women went in and out of Hugh's life like a public rest room, but she somehow thought he was serious about Toni.

Toni nodded.

Randi was jealous beyond belief because she knew Toni was a more together woman than she was, besides the fact that she and Brian actually made a handsome couple. But why did she have to see them together? It was one slap in the face after another. A couple of days ago at the office, she got word that Franklin had been promoted into the editing department—of *The Los Angeles Times*. He didn't even have enough decency to say good-bye.

Brian took Toni's hand in his. "Come on, baby, we better get going."

They went toward the restaurant leaving the trio standing in the parking lot with their mouths gaping.

"Are you okay, sweetie?" Michelle put her arm around Randi's shoulder and they continued walking.

"I'll be alright," she said softly.

"Of course you will," Umi said.

They came to Umi's car first. Randi went around to the passenger side and stood there. "Well, ladies, I had a wonderful afternoon. Now I'm going to go home and take a long hot bath—with a toaster." She gave a half grin.

"No, you're not." Michelle didn't think it was funny. "If you keep talking like that, you're going to make me pack my things and move in with you until you get your head straight."

Umi was laughing at Randi. "Girl, you are one for the books. You need your head examined."

Randi laughed too. "I'm just jealous. I'll be over it in the morning."

"Where do you know her from?" Michelle asked.

"She's Hugh's girlfriend—or ex-girlfriend. She was helping me with my wedding plans, and I guess she was also helping Brian mend his broken heart."

"Well, you knew he was going to eventually move on with his life, and Toni is who he chose to move on to. Life is too short to be bitter, just let it go." Michelle waved her hand.

"That's right," Umi chimed in. "Drop that dead weight and lighten your load. It's easier to move on when you don't have so much baggage." She held her hand up for a high five, but Randi didn't respond. "Excuse me?"

"You're talking right." She slowly agreed and gave her five.

The women got in their cars, heading to separate destinations, but they were still together and always would be.

CHAPTER 17

SIX MONTHS LATER...

Michelle spent all of the previous night and half the morning on the phone with Randi and Umi. How could she prepare herself for the wedding if she had to baby-sit those two? She was already wearing her bridesmaid dress, which wasn't as bad as she thought it would be when she first saw the pattern. It was a full-length, mint-green, satin dress with a split up one side almost to the thigh and a cluster of flowers that gathered right above her butt. The neckline was V-shaped and it was strapless, which she was glad for because the Indian summer heat was already in full effect.

She was struggling with her hairpiece, a wide-toothed comb with plastic flowers on it. Something the bride thought would look nice, but Michelle hated it. She kept her thoughts to herself because she didn't want to argue and ruin her best friend's wedding-day bliss.

Greg came into the room, handsomely dressed in his best suit and stood closely behind her. "You look beautiful," he whispered in her ear.

She smiled. "Thank you."

He kissed her bare shoulder. "Did you tell your mother yet?"

She turned to face him, still holding the floral comb to her head. "No. Why? Did she say something?"

"No."

"Good, because this morning she heard me vomiting and when I came out of the bathroom she asked if I was alright. I told her it was wedding-day jitters."

"How are you feeling now?" His voice was full of concern.

"Much better. Mama made some toast for me, and I was able to keep it down."

"When are you going to tell her?"

"Probably after the wedding. Not today, but before she leaves."

"And what about everybody else?"

"I was thinking we should hold off on that for a while. I hear it's usually a good idea to wait until you're past the third month." She knew her husband was excited about having his first baby, since Natalie wasn't his biological daughter, but she was actually very nervous. Terrified was more like it. Her doctor said it was common for women who had late-in-life babies to be fearful, but it was more than just having a baby at the age of thirty-seven that frightened her. Her fears and concerns surpassed medical-book reasoning.

There was a tap at the door.

"Come in," Greg called.

"Oooh, Greg, you are looking sharp, and Michelle you look so beautiful." Her mother came into the room, already teary-eyed.

"You look beautiful, too, Mama, but save the tears for the wedding. Right now I need you to help me with this hairpiece." She sat on the bed as her mother fiddled with the piece.

"Lord, I can't believe this girl is getting married."

"Me either. It's been a long time coming. Mama, make sure you get it straight."

"It is straight."

Michelle felt the hairpiece. "It feels crooked."

"Greg, tell her it's straight."

"It is." He eyed it closely.

"Okay, okay. We'd better get a move on. The limousine has been waiting for more than thirty minutes." She checked her hair and makeup once more and followed her mother and husband outside.

At the church, everyone was buzzing with excitement. The musician was on the organ playing something soft and mellow, the florist was arranging and rearranging flowers, and the bride's mother had the wedding coordinator cornered and was demanding that everything went as planned. Grace and Greg took a seat in the back of the church and Michelle went to the lounge where the rest of the bridal party was gathered to check on her best friends.

She made her way through the crowd of ladies and spotted Randi sitting at a vanity table touching up her makeup. She stood behind her chair. "You look beautiful."

"Oh yeah? I feel like I'm going to pass out."

"Do you want me to get you something?"

"No, I'll be alright once I get through this wedding." She turned to face Michelle and rubbed her big swollen belly.

"And how are you feeling today?" Michelle spoke directly to Randi's belly.

"Like he's tired of being trapped," she joked. "I guess he's excited about the wedding because he was moving all night. I got very little sleep, but that's nothing new."

Her unborn child's movement wasn't the only thing keeping her up at night. It was also her thousand and one fears about being a mother and how her life would be changed forever. The one thing that bothered her the most—so much so that she couldn't even bear to mention it to anyone—was the fact that Brian may not be her baby's father. According to her due date, there was a good chance she could have gotten pregnant by Franklin.

"Well, he won't be trapped for long since you're due in a couple of weeks. He's going to be a Libra." Michelle smiled.

"I know. I could strangle Umi for getting married right before I'm due to deliver."

"Where is Umi?"

"She went in the pastor's office a while ago mumbling something about needing prayer. She hasn't come back yet."

"I think we should go get her." Michelle looked at her watch. "It's getting close to show time."

"Help me up."

Michelle helped Randi to her feet and laughed. "Girl, you look like nothing I've ever seen in that dress with that belly."

"Ha, ha. You think that's funny? Michelle, I'm emotional and short-tempered, that's a bad combination on a hot day. Don't start with the jokes, okay?"

Michelle covered her mouth to muffle her giggles as they headed to the pastor's office. She wondered if she would look like that seven months from now. Just as they started down the corridor, Umi turned the corner.

She looked regal in her wedding gown, a simple fitted, full-length white dress with very expensive beading on the front. Her hair was in a bun at the very top of her head and covered with a beautiful diamond tiara and a flowing veil.

"We were just coming to get you," Randi said.

Michelle gave Umi a big hug. She could feel herself becoming emotional. "You look so beautiful. I'm so happy for you."

"Thank you." Umi bit her lip to keep from crying.

"Don't cry, don't cry. You'll ruin your makeup," Randi warned.

"We'd better get back to the lounge. It's getting late."

In the lounge, the wedding coordinator, with Umi's mother stuck to her side, was going over instructions for the bridal party.

"Here's the beautiful bride," the coordinator announced, and everyone turned in Umi's direction.

Umi's mother came over and whispered a private word of encouragement to her daughter. Then stepped back and took a good look at Umi. "You're beautiful, baby. Remember to keep your head up and keep smiling."

"Uh, before we go out, I would like to say something," Umi interrupted the wedding coordinator.

Everyone was silent.

"I just want to say that it means a lot to me having each and every one of you here today. Not only to participate in the wedding, but to have your support on my special day." Tears rolled down her cheeks as she spoke.

"Get her a tissue. She's ruining her makeup," her mother barked at the coordinator.

Umi dabbed her face with the tissue and continued. "I want to thank you for the beautiful bridal shower and all the gifts and also for the effort you guys have put forth to make this day as memorable as possible. I'm fortunate to be surrounded by such wonderful friends on a day that I thought was only going to happen in my dreams."

As hard as she tried to resist, Randi couldn't keep her tears from seeping out. But she was in good company, since there wasn't a dry eye in the room when Umi finished. Even the wedding coordinator was wiping her face.

Finally, the wedding coordinator convinced Umi's mother to take her seat in the church, the ladies freshened up their faces and lined up for the march. Michelle and Randi gave their best friend a big, tight hug and went to the front of the line, where they met up with their partners. Michelle was at the front of the line, paired with one of LaVelle's army buddies. Randi was behind her and had the pleasure of marching with Umi's fine cousin, Jerome. But she was so miserable, she could have been paired with Howdy Doody and wouldn't care.

The coordinator opened the double doors, a cue for the soloist to start, and the couples slowly marched down the aisle, taking their respective places. When the wedding march started, the congregation stood and Umi and her great-uncle started down the aisle. Michelle couldn't see Umi's face through the veil, but could feel her radiant smile.

Randi nudged Michelle with her elbow.

"What?" she whispered.

"I have to sit down. I can't stand on these swollen ankles," she complained.

"Not now, Randi. She's almost to the altar, wait one more minute."

"Oh, God. Oh, God," Randi whispered.

LaVelle's sister was standing on the other side of Randi. She leaned in closely. "Are you alright?"

Randi pointed to the puddle she was standing in.

"Oh, my Lord," she whispered loudly.

Annoyed, Michelle turned to Randi. "Then go sit down."

"Her water broke," LaVelle's sister whispered.

Michelle looked down at the puddle. "You will not have that baby now and ruin Umi's wedding," Michelle whispered.

With all the whispering back and forth, the bridesmaids were beginning to draw attention to themselves. LaVelle, who wasn't standing very far from them, was staring and began mouthing to them, wanting to know what was wrong.

His sister shook her head, indicating nothing, but Randi couldn't stand still and that was a big tip-off that something was definitely wrong.

By the time Umi made it to the front of the church, more

people were staring at the bridesmaids, than the bride. The wedding coordinator came over to them. "Is everything alright, ladies?"

"My water just broke," Randi whispered.

"Oh, my goodness. Are you in any pain?" she asked.

"Not labor pains, but my feet are killing me from standing."

"Maybe we should go in the lounge and have you lay down."

"Oh no, Randi, you are not going anywhere. You have to see Umi get married," Michelle whispered.

The pastor began speaking. Umi was so consumed with what was happening with her friends, she wasn't paying attention to a word he was saying and blurted out, "I do." When he asked, "Who gives this woman to this man?"

"I'm sorry, Pastor Lewis," she apologized, and then turned to Michelle and whispered loudly. "What is going on over there?"

Michelle closed her eyes and pointed to Randi's puddle. When she reopened them, Umi and her mother were both standing in her face.

"What in the hell is going on over here?" Her mother's whisper was enraged.

"I don't feel good enough to stand through the ceremony," Randi whined.

"Do something!" Ms. Grayson snapped at the coordinator.

"Let's go in the lounge and lay down." The coordinator had Randi by the arm and led her down the side aisle. Umi let out a disappointed sigh and went back to the altar. Her mother angrily stormed back to her seat.

The pastor resumed speaking, making light of the interruption in the ceremony. "Nature has to take its course, and man can't do a thing to stop it." He chuckled and so did a few of the guests, but Umi's mother was steaming mad.

He continued, "Children have to grow into adults, the caterpillar has to become a butterfly, and men and women inevitably will fall in love, just like LaVelle and Umi."

By the time the pastor gave permission for LaVelle to kiss his bride, Michelle was a bundle of emotion. On one hand she was overjoyed for Umi, and on the other hand, she was worried to death about Randi. At the end of the ceremony, she darted down the side aisle and into the lounge. Randi was stretched out on a chaise, barefoot, and wearing one of her maternity dresses.

"Hi, Mama. Hi, Ms. Dollie. How are you feeling, Randi?"

"I'm okay. Sorry I missed the ceremony, but it sounded beautiful."

"Shouldn't you go to the hospital?"

"I paged my doctor. He said I should wait until the contractions start before I go to the hospital. But if I don't feel anything soon, I'm going to go and let them check me out anyway." She shifted to get more comfortable.

"Good idea," Grace said.

"I think you should go right now," Dollie advised.

"Do you feel up to the reception?" Michelle asked.

"I'm fine as long as I'm sitting down." She sat up and slipped her shoes on.

LaVelle's sister came into the lounge. "How are you feeling, Rhonda?"

"That's Randi. I'm feeling fine. I'm going to use the ladies' room and I'll be right out."

LaVelle's sister was embarrassed. "Michelle, the wedding coordinator asked me to come in and get you. They're ready to take pictures."

"Okay, please tell her we'll be right out."

Umi's mother came through the door. "We're on our way to the Brooklyn Botanical Gardens to take pictures. We're leaving in ten minutes, with or without you." She spoke to no one in particular.

Randi stepped out of the ladies' room.

"What are you wearing?" she barked at Randi. "We're just going to have to leave without you."

"Ms. Grayson," Michelle started to explain, but she was already out the door.

Michelle could tell Grace was more than ready to explode with anger, but thank God she held her peace for Umi's sake.

"You'd better go without me. I'm bleeding," Randi announced calmly.

"What?" they all asked in unison. Randi nodded.

"Heavily?" Grace asked.

"It's pretty heavy."

"Oh, Lord," Dollie prayed out loud and sat down in one of the chairs.

"Come sit back down." Michelle took Randi by the hand and led her back over to the chaise. "Mama, I think we should call an ambulance."

"No. A big scene is only going to ruin Umi's day more than I already have. Ouch." She put her hand on the side of her stomach. "I'm not sure about this, but I think that was a contraction." Her eyes were filling with tears, and so were Michelle's.

"Oh no, sweetie, don't panic. You'll be fine," Grace encouraged her. "We'll wait for the crowd to thin out then we'll take you to the hospital in a taxi, okay?"

"Randi, you're going to be a mommy," Michelle sang through her tears.

"I know." She smiled nervously.

Umi burst through the lounge door with her mother right on her heels. "What is taking y'all so long?"

Michelle turned to face her. "Randi's in labor."

"What?" She came over to the chaise and knelt beside it. "Are you okay?"

Randi nodded and wiped away her tears. "I'm sorry I ruined your wedding, Umi."

"You ought to be," Ms. Grayson complained.

Dollie grumbled loudly.

"You didn't ruin anything. It was a beautiful ceremony, and I owe that to you and Michelle for working so hard to put it together for me." She leaned in and kissed Randi's cheek.

"Umi, let's go. The photographer's waiting at the garden."

"Then let him wait! He's getting paid by the hour, why in the hell should he be complaining?" Umi barked.

"Your mother's right, Umi. Go ahead and take your pictures, and I'll catch up with you later." She winced in pain.

Umi gave her a hug, stood and turned to Michelle. "You stay with Randi. I'll be alright."

Michelle could hear the disappointment in Umi's voice. "Are you sure? My mother can stay with Randi while I take the pictures."

"Umi," her mother called impatiently.

"Wait a damn minute, Mama!"

Obviously shocked, her mother quickly turned and left the lounge. That put a smile on Grace's face.

"Michelle, go," Randi insisted. "I have Ms. Grace and Mama here with me.

"Stay with Randi and later on we'll take private pictures of our own, just the four of us." She smiled through her tears.

"Four?"

"The baby." She hugged her best friends and was gone.

And what a beautiful baby indeed. After only three hours of labor, at 8:15 that evening Randi gave birth to a beautiful baby girl, weighing in at six pounds and ten ounces. Michelle, Grace and Greg were sitting in the waiting room with Dollie when the doctor came out and gave them the news.

"You'll be able to see Mom and Baby in a couple of hours. They're both resting peacefully," he said.

"Lord, my baby is a mother," Dollie said to Grace.

"It's a beautiful feeling, isn't it?"

"Maybe we should go downstairs to the cafeteria and get something to eat while we wait to see Randi and the baby," Greg suggested.

"That's a good idea. Lord knows I'm starving," Grace said.

"Y'all go ahead. I'll wait right here," Michelle said. "Greg, bring me something with chicken in it."

"Okay. Ms. Dollie, what can I get you?"

"Really, I'm too excited to eat."

"You should put a little something on your stomach, though," Grace advised.

"Alright. A salad sounds good."

Shortly after Greg and Grace left for the cafeteria, the elevator doors opened and Umi and LaVelle came rushing out, heading for the nurses' station.

"Umi! Umi!" Michelle called. She briefly admired Umi's beautiful reception dress, a cream-colored dress that stopped a little above her knee, and she was wearing a bad pair of clear sling backs.

They came over and sat down next to her.

"Congratulations, Mr. and Mrs. King," Michelle said.

Umi was blushing. "Thank you, girl."

"Let me see that ring," Dollie said. Michelle leaned in to eye it as well.

"How's Randi?" LaVelle asked.

"She's doing just fine. Her and the baby." Dollie was smiling from ear to ear.

"I'm an auntie?" Umi asked.

"Yes, you are. You have a healthy little niece."

"Oh, a girl," LaVelle said.

"A bride and an aunt all in one day. Gone, with your bad self, Umi," she said jokingly.

The elevator doors opened again, this time dropping off Grace and Greg.

"Umi. LaVelle." Grace was surprised to see them. "What are y'all doing here? I thought you'd be halfway to Hawaii by now."

"We're going to catch a flight tomorrow afternoon instead. I wanted to be here with Randi," Umi answered.

"She'll be glad you stayed," Dollie said.

"The wedding was beautiful, Umi." She patted her hand. "And LaVelle, let me be the first to counsel you. Take care of your wife, but don't let her run all over you. You may not know this yet, but Umi can be a little bossy."

"Ms. Grace, no you didn't." Umi put on her shocked face.

"Am I lying?" Grace asked Michelle.

Michelle turned her head in the opposite direction. "My name is Bess, and I ain't in this mess."

LaVelle was grinning. "Don't worry, Ms. Grace, I got her under control." He smiled politely.

After a short wait, which seemed like forever to the anxious group, they were allowed in to see Randi and the baby.

The doctor led them to the far end of the maternity ward, where Randi's private room was. He stopped in front of the closed door. "I'm only supposed to let two visitors in at a time. So, if the nurse comes around, she's going to ask some of you to step out and have a seat in the hall."

Everyone nodded gratefully.

"Why don't you go in and have a word with your baby, while we wait out here," Grace suggested to Dollie.

"I think I'll do that." She was smiling broadly. She tapped on the door and went in.

Greg kept giving Michelle knowing smiles—his excitement

about the baby in her womb was written all over his face.

Minutes later, a teary-eyed Dollie stuck her head out of the door. "She asked to see Umi and Michelle."

Overjoyed, they stepped in the room with Dollie.

"Randi," Michelle said softly. She became emotional the moment she stepped in the room and saw her best friend sitting up in bed, and her tiny baby lying peacefully in the basinet beside her.

"She's beautiful." Michelle couldn't take her eyes off her.

"Thank you. You're still wearing your bridesmaid dress." Randi was fighting back her tears.

Michelle nodded.

"How are you feeling?" Umi kissed Randi's cheek and sat on the bed next to her.

"A little tired actually."

"Well, you look beautiful and so does the baby." Umi stretched over to get a better look at her new goddaughter.

Randi covered Umi's hand with hers. "Mama told me you and LaVelle postponed your honeymoon to be here with me. I can't tell you how much I appreciate that."

"I wouldn't be anywhere but here to share this moment with you."

Michelle was still in awe of the baby. "Can I hold her?"

"Sure."

"You're going to wake her," Umi said.

"It's almost time for her feeding anyway," Randi said.

Michelle pulled a chair over to the basinet, and then went into the bathroom to wash her hands. When she came out, the rest of the gang was in the room peering into the basinet and wishing Randi well.

Michelle gently lifted the baby and took a seat in the chair. She held her little hand and examined the details of her tiny face. She remembered holding Natalie when she was first born, and her heart sank a little.

Grace and LaVelle were leaning over her shoulders admiring the baby, while Randi rattled on, giving a detailed account of the labor and delivery.

" . . .And the delivery, from beginning to end, could not have taken more than fifteen minutes."

"Randi, she's beautiful. God bless her," Grace said.

"I tell you, she looks just like Randi when she was born," Dollie said. "Too bad your daddy's not here to see her. Oooh, he would be carrying on some kind of bad." She laughed at the thought.

"He made such a big deal over the children, even when they were newborns, which is unusual for a man."

"That's true. Russell wouldn't touch Michelle until she was almost a year old. He was afraid of her, said she was too small." The memory made Grace smile.

Michelle glanced over at Greg to see how he was receiving all of this, but he was seemingly unmoved and still had on his overly happy face. She could tell his mind was racing a mile a minute with thoughts of their new baby.

"In years to come this is going to be one heck of a story. Randi going into labor at Umi's wedding," Greg said.

"It's kind of funny now that you mention it," Grace said.

"I know one person who won't be laughing," Umi said with an attitude.

"Your mother," everyone responded in unison and laughed.

"You got that right," Umi said. Her mother's behavior had upset her so much, LaVelle spent the entire limousine ride, trying to calm her down.

LaVelle put his arm around his new bride and kissed her forehead, before changing the subject. "So, uh, Randi, you didn't tell us her name."

"Well, I have a name in mind."

Everyone was silent, waiting to hear which name was chosen to compliment this new life.

"If it's okay with Greg and Michelle, I'd like to name her Chantal Natalie."

Michelle was pleasantly surprised. "Oh, Randi, we would be honored."

"That's very sweet of you, Randi." Greg went over and kissed her cheek.

"That's a beautiful name for a beautiful girl," Umi said, touched by Randi's decision to cherish Natalie's memory.

Grace was moved to tears. She lowered her head and covered her mouth with her hand.

Dollie embraced Grace and gently rubbed her back.

"What are we going to do with these girls?" Grace asked, jokingly, trying to compose herself.

"I guess we're going to have to let them be women," Dollie responded.

And women they were, among many other things: friends, wives and mothers. And each of them beginning another chapter of their lives—Umi as a wife, Randi as a mother, and Michelle as a second-time mother. Each excited, though unsure, about what lay ahead of them in these new roles, they were certain that they'd always have one another to lean on.